White cranes flew above her head, bidding her welcome to the threshold of the lights horizon. On glistening golden sand, she followed the beach inward to the mountain. Inside, it was said that there was knowledge. A doorway marked the entrance, therein. It was barred shut with rusty golden bars across a dark oaken door.

She went to the door and knocked upon it. It took forever. So, she knocked again. Finally the door opened. There was an old woman who stood at the entrance, surrounded by sleek-haired cats with green slanted eyes.

The woman was dressed in a white robe. Her silver braids formed a crown across the top of her head, from ear to ear, with little curling wisps framing her face. There was a white flower behind each ear. She was beautiful, and her body of light was so old that it could not be known what her age was in the scope of eternities.

Sion spoke the words of the spirit in the voice of the spirit which knew no boundaries of words. "MAY I ENTER?"

"There is wisdom, you seek?" The woman asked, guarding the door protectively.

"IT IS A MATTER OF WHOLENESS TO MY SOUL!"

"You are aware, my golden daughter, that sometimes wisdom has the fangs of a viper. This is why wisdom is guarded here, deep inside. If you dare to enter, you must know of the risks. Are you strong enough to gain the truth?"

A FOUR DIRECTIONS MARKETING & MEDIA PUBLICATION

Published by

Four Directions Marketing
P. O. Box 362
Heyburn, Idaho 83336

www.FourDirectionsMarketing.com

ISBN-13: 978-0615999265 (Four Directions Marketing)
ISBN-10: 0615999263

Transmutation

of the

Fey

Donna Daywoman Thompson

Acknowledgements

I cannot claim years of study at any commonly renowned university, I will however PROUDLY acknowledge the fine learning I received at the College of Hard Knocks ... where degrees are of a totally different nature than the expected ... for it is an ongoing course that is pursued by brave explorers who have dense heads but pure hearts.

As far as visiting the place where I have placed my novel, the location doesn't exist anymore, at least not on this world. I had to search for the lost and forgotten land in regions of Imagination, where I saw the scenes rise with awe inspiring beauty on the other side of my eyes.

Here too, because the original story is also forbidden to perceptions wrought by myth, legends, and holy scripts, I really had to go someplace other than historical facts to present yet another dimension of a familiar story.

The hints of something amiss in our present stories are found everywhere if one dares to look and dares to see. I consider books to be great teachers and I have read and studied countless books both fiction, and non-fiction that have all taken their places somewhere in my mind.

I chose to present this story in the form of fiction so please don't expect me to create a list of sources. I will share with you the top few of the many books I have taken lesson with, that may have reflections in my novel. These in particular have been among my greatest teachers, and I wish to acknowledge them.

It was my mother who first put "Chariots of the Gods" by Erich von Daniken in my hands. It was he who inspired me to use my head for something other than smiling prettily at Sunday school.

The subject of ancient visitors from outer space had never crossed my mind before, but the things I read made all the hairs on my big toe stand up. Eagerly I studied other books of a similar bent.

I hail Zecharia Sitchen for showing me a vast world of intriguing possibilities that touched something deep in my heart, and made me tremble in awe as he acquainted me with the world of the fish head, as so named in my story. Many of his ideas are clearly visible within the pages of this book. However, many of my own ideas have been formed by the thought provoking treatises of many writers, as well as in study of the tablets found buried in Sumeria in the 1930's. Please remember this book is fiction so don't expect it to go totally along with the bits of scant information we have of Annunaki and early earth peoples. Remember, there is no proof yet to be found, only speculation.

I thank David Icke for his "Children of the Matrix." While I shuddered at some of his very colorful tales, I also felt that weird something in my heart. I think it was how he opened doors of further possibilities, especially with his views on computer chip technology. Those are some things to which few Annunaki writers lend credence. He wove a lot of spiritual wisdom into his rants.

Another writer of this subject that I enjoyed reading is William Bramley, who explained in understandable words his premise, with a lot of logic, as well.

As far as non-fiction, I cannot forget to mention Timothy Freke and Peter Gandy for their very make-sense approach to the vision of how stories are and were created long ago. I appreciate them for showing me how a very important spiritual wisdom was tarnished and lost long ago in their books, "The Jesus Mysteries" and "Jesus and the Lost Goddess."

Another curious book, written in highly symbolic beauty caught my breath with awe. Barbara Hand Clow helped me begin to grasp even more in perceiving the treasures of vast worlds beyond, in her book, "The Pleiadian Agenda".

In the fiction department, I give gratitude to Marion Zimmer Bradley, of "The Mists of Avalon" for an informative and very entertaining and thought provoking read that sent tingles up my jingles.

And, Jean Auell, author of "The Clan of the Cave Bear". I was delighted with hours of page turning and heart stopping awe that had me fastened to my seat as I read her works. What more can I say?

Also, in my acknowledgements, I must mention Fiona Macleod, Lord Byron and other wonderful poets, whose chanted prayers have left the echoing poetry of bell like song tinkling like chime somewhere within my soul.

I give thanks to all of the ancient myth, legend, scriptural text, and other tales of beginning times. Of these, "The Nag Hammadi Library" was the most informative of all, as it reveals secrets. From within its symbol-rich wisdom I have found a great piece from The Gospel of Truth that personally has guided my way for much of my adult years. I have quoted it now and then, as part of this story.

Now as far as giving thanks to writers whose words I have embraced, I have other wonderful teachers who have given me inspiration and love that has helped me to create life in my story. I must say "Thank you, mom" to Val Jean Holgate who taught me how to REALLY read, by reading herself. I'm grateful to her for showing me the deep pleasure contained within books. Thank you, too, for teaching me about beauty. Beauty is yours, mother, and mine as well for what I have learned from you. Thank you!

And, to my dad, who gave me the gift of loving what hard work is all about; and, for all our Sunday dinners when he often talked about good old common sense, which I came to value.

Thanks to all my sisters and brothers: Katrina, Bill, Mary, Tish, Chad and Andy who have all inspired me with gifts of creativity and wisdom ... and Chad you little stinker. I'll never forget when we met in the world tree and hung crystals in a dancing light circle that rose to touch the stars. You stayed up there telling me to remember the magic. I took your message with me when I awoke the next morning and I like to think that I have incorporated that dream into my daily life.

Thanks to my sons, Rob, Jon and Ike who I have ever strived to be almost as good and wonderful as they are. A special thanks, Rob, for helping me design the map. And, thanks for the support of my daughters-in-law, who have become my daughters. I'd like to extend a special heart-felt thanks to Nickole, for her encouragement and for going out of her way to help me with projects. Thanks to Jaime, too, for all her support. And, Alma who inspires me to smile like a diva.

To my life's greatest lights, my grandchildren Morgan, Sabrina, Magnus, Adia, Lily, Liberty and Alieus: read grandma's book when you are at least in the "PG-13" category, lol.

Morgan, Liberty, and Alieus thank you for playing fairies with me all these years, climbing treetops, and concocting artful salads of flowers and herbs, that floated in water bowls.

Once when my husband was ill and in the hospital, a tiny Morgan took me by the hand and we walked outside in the hospital rose-garden which was lovely. I was extremely worried about my husband. She showed me the gates and the places of fairy portals. "They say Grandpa is going to be fine Grandma." I called it a prayer and he did get better.

And, Liberty Thompson, thank you for drawing me that picture of a fairy in a yellow dress. You named her "Daffinina", her name scrawled across the top of the paper. This was when you were only four years old. Liberty said I could use the fairy's name, and I did. Also, Libby (Liberty) took me into the computer world and from the perspective of inside a tree at Pixie Hollow, we decorated our fairy home with all manner of astoundingly-beautiful virtual wonders. It was here that I got my first glimpse of Sionee's tree.

Much gratitude also to a gentle spirited man, Glen Draper, who first put a wad of clay in my hands and said: "For you! I know you can do it." This gift led me to the exciting world of coil building and creating clay sculptures, which is a big part of who I am.

Last, and most important of all, thank you, Robert Steven Thompson, my husband for sharing this dream with me. It was he who wrote the prologue to this story. Thanks for listening to my smiles as I giggled the story with you. Thanks also for quieting my frustrations by helping me get past occasional vexations, and for

KNOWING what to do next. Thanks for choreographing the production of this book every step along the way. This novel is full of the conversations we have shared as we have walked down life's road together.

To all my readers: may you get from this book much more than your socks knocked off. Thank you for taking a look. If you bite this beautiful apple, may you be full.

For My Steve:

You are the BREATH of the universe which expands me up into the never ending Sapphire Blue.

You are the FIRE of the stars as we dance one in one within the spiral of Heavens motion.

You are the EARTH beneath my feet where life springs forth in profound vistas of everlasting glory.

You are the WATER of my soul ... with you I drink.

You are my SONG. I SEE YOU!

The Snake of the Sea

A NEW PARADIGM IN MANKIND'S PAST IS DISCOVERED ...

Deep inside a secret and well-guarded scientific facility at an undisclosed location, scientists are laboriously piecing together a puzzle of monumental proportions.

Across the vast concrete floor of a cavernous room, table upon table of artifacts lay in wait of decipher and cataloguing. Dozens of people in long, white lab coats are busy at their respective tasks, meticulously doing their part to unravel the newest and perhaps most important discovery to mankind on the planet.

Heading up the operation is a renowned archeologist and anthropologist, Dr. Estevan Sanchez. With Dr. Sanchez is his wife and assistant, Maria.

Maria glanced anxiously at a clock on a nearby wall. "Estevan," she exclaimed, "It's time for your interview on TV."

Estevan and Maria sauntered across the huge room and entered what appeared to be a break room/conference room combination. Upon entering the room, Maria shut the door behind them and the two of them took seats on a couch facing a large screen TV. Esteven reached for the TV remote perched on a coffee table in front of him, and turned on the TV. He clicked through the channels until he got to the station he wanted.

"Ah, just in time!" Estevan exclaimed.

He turned up the volume, as he and Maria watched the program from the beginning. There on the screen was Estevan and the TV show host of a popular news/documentary show.

~~~

(Tight, up close shot of host looking straight into the camera at the audience.)

"Good evening, ladies and gentlemen. My name is Charlie Rhoades, host of the Earth Tribe Geographic series, UNRAVELING THE MYSTERIES OF EARTH'S HISTORY – MYTHS AND LEGENDS.

"Our viewers have called in with such interest on this controversial and important finding, that we have extended our exploration outside the frame of our normal weekly hour long programming.

"Tonight we will premiere the first segment of our six week, two hour Special, about a lost people on a lost world. Ladies and gentlemen I bring you "The Story of our Antediluvian Beginnings."

(Camera widens out to include a two-shot of host and his guest.)

"My guest tonight is Estevan Sanchez. Estevan is a scientific explorer, historian-of-sorts ... perhaps a real-life Indiana Jones." Rhoades introduces Estevan, gazing directly into the camera to the audience.

Rhoades then turns toward Estevan and begins his interview. "Dr. Sanchez, you have quite an interesting resume."

(Camera two – MEDIUM CLOSE UP of Sanchez)

"I guess it could look interesting. To me, it seems quite normal and natural. I guess my credentials and background could be considered interesting to some people," Estevan replied in a tone that revealed a slight bit of awkward discomfort.

(Camera one – MEDIUM CLOSE UP of Rhoades)

"Oh, you are just being modest," Rhoades continued. "Let's go over some of that background and experience."

Rhoades puts on a pair of reading glasses with his right hand as he looks down to some papers he's holding in his left.

"I see that you are the son of a Cuban refugee-immigrant father, and your mother was actually born in Egypt. Is this correct?" Rhoades queried in a tone of interest.

(Camera two – WIDE SHOT of Rhoades and Sanchez)

"Yes! That's true," Sanchez responded.

"Tell us about that ... and a little of your background in education, training ... and a brief rundown on some of the work you've done over the years," Rhoades asked as camera 1 cut back to him.

(Camera one –TIGHT CLOSE UP of Sanchez)

"My mother was born in Egypt, as you said." Estevan answered.

"She studied in Europe and the United States to become an Egyptologist, and after earning her degree, she returned home to work within Egypt's Ministry of Antiquities," Estevan continued. "My father escaped from Cuba and Communism and eventually found his way to Florida where he went on to study archaeology. That's when and where he met my mother ... you know when she was studying here in America."

(Camera two – MEDIUM CLOSE UP of Rhoades)

"Sounds like an interesting match, an Egyptian-born mother and a Cuban refugee as a father.

"Cutting to the short version, your mom and dad met, fell in love, and then, you came along?" Rhoades inquired.

(Camera one – MEDIUM SHOT of Sanchez)

"Yeah, that's the short version alright."

(Camera two – WIDE SHOT of Rhoades and Sanchez)

"Then, following up on that short version, is your parents example to you ... and their work ... what brought you to be interested in your line of work ... your studies and training ... more or less following in your parent's footsteps?" Rhoades asked.

(Camera one – TIGHT SHOT of Sanchez)

"Pretty much," Estevan went on. "I grew up surrounded by shop talk about everything from religion to science, and from myths to history. I used to go on expeditions with my mom and dad all around the globe. I lived their work so intensely that I grew up with it as more or less second nature."

(Camera two – MEDIUM SHOT of Rhoades)

"Thank you for sharing that, Estevan," Rhoades said, talking to Sanchez.

(Camera one – MEDIUM SHOT of Rhoades and Sanchez)

Rhoades turns to camera to address TV audience: "We'll take a little break.

"When we return, we will talk more with world famous Scientist, Historian, Author, Esteven Sanchez ... and REVEAL to you some of the most startling findings, discoveries and interpretations of these discoveries that have perhaps ever been presented to the world.

"And, you ... watching from home or wherever you are ... you will be the first to hear these exclusive revelations.

"So, don't go away. Stay right here on this channel! In a couple of minutes we will return to Earth Tribe Geographic's special edition of UNRAVELING THE MYSTERIES OF EARTH'S HISTORY – MYTHS AND LEGENDS.

"I'm Charlie Rhoades."
(CUT TO COMMERCIALS)

~~~

Back in the break room Estevan and Maria have a chance to discuss the TV show during the commercial break.

"Well, Estevan, how do you think it's going so far?" Maria smiled.

Estevan smiled at his wife. "BORING," he blurted out in an unamused voice. "So far, I think it is pretty blah-blah-blah."

Maria reached over and patted Estevan on one shoulder. "Oh! The introductions are over. Now you get into the good stuff," she grinned.

"We'll see," Estevan grimaced. "Now, let's watch and see. K?"

The couple turned back to look at the TV screen just as the commercials were winding up.

~~~

(Camera one – MEDIUM 2 SHOT of Estevan Sanchez and Charlie Rhoades)

Rhoades looking into camera one toward the TV audience, continues his introduction of his special broadcast and his guest.

(Camera one – ZOOMS IN ON TIGHT SHOT of Charlie Rhoades)

"Hi. I'm Charlie Rhoades. Welcome back to the premier of Earth Tribe Geographic's six week special "UNRAVELING THE MYSTERIES OF EARTH'S HISTORY – MYTHS AND LEGENDS.

"I know I certainly find what we are about to delve into interesting. In fact, I find it controversial, provocative, insightful, revealing, and intriguing ... just to mention a few feelings and emotions.

"You may recall the catastrophic magnitude 7.0 Haiti earthquake that devastated that country back in 2010.

"An estimated three million people were displaced or affected. The final death toll was between 46,000 and 85,000.

"What is not generally known, though, is that earthquakes like the Haiti earth-shaker happen quite frequently all around the globe. Likely because so much of the earth is covered with oceans and seas, a vast number of earthquakes, including mega-quakes, happen in the earth's crust under sometimes staggering depths, thousands of feet ... even miles down."

(Camera two -- MEDIUM TWO SHOT of Rhoades and Sanchez. Rhoades turns to address Sanchez)

"Does that size it up much, Dr. Sanchez?" Rhoades asked.

"That's true, Charlie," Estevan replied. "Interestingly, we most often associate that kind of activity – seismic and volcanic – with the Pacific Ocean and other large oceans and seas adjacent to the Pacific, such as Indonesia, Malaysia, and Japan. A huge circular area in the Pacific, for example, is commonly known as the Pacific Rim.

(Camera two – SLOW ZOOM IN to Sanchez)

"However, it's important to understand that even in the Atlantic over millennia and millennia, volcanic and seismic activities have been quite prevalent.

"In fact, all around the earth for millions of years, continents have shifted, lifted, collapsed. The earth has been, and in terms of geologic times, still is very active.

(Camera one – MEDIUM TWO SHOT of Rhoades and Sanchez)

"Charlie, you may have read or heard about great mountains and valleys that actually exist underwater at unfathomable depths ... pardon the little play on words, there. "

Rhoades nodded. "I have heard of those kinds of details. But to me IT IS unfathomable – to carry on with your 'play on words' a bit.

"I'm sure there are a lot of folks out there, who a lot like me, cannot even begin to comprehend the facts and realities of those underwater worlds ... facts and realities that to you, Dr. Sanchez, may even seem quite mundane by comparison."

(Camera two – TIGHT SHOT of Dr. Sanchez)

"Actually, Charlie, even though my work immerses me figuratively and quite literally into those other-worldly depths of earth's oceans, it is forever exciting and intriguing, never mundane.

"Take our most recent exploration ... and, actually ... what we are discussing here on this special report ... is a prime example of our intensity and excitement.

"People often refer to the oceans as the 'Last Frontier'!

(Camera one – MEDIUM SHOT of Rhoades and Sanchez)

"Charlie, there are so many secrets buried in the depths of the oceans that I don't know if it will ever be possible to uncover – or unravel even a minute fraction of them."

(Camera two -- WIDE SHOT of Rhoades and Sanchez)

"Now, you've got me intrigued, Dr. Sanchez." Rhoades leans forward. "We'll leave it right there to take a short break. Then, we'll talk some more."

(Camera one – MEDIUM SHOT of Rhoades and Sanchez)

Charlie Rhoades turns to audience, "We're going to a short break. But don't go away. When we return, Dr. Sanchez and I are going to reveal to you what may very well be one of the most provocative and controversial discoveries of all time ... and beyond. You don't want to miss it!"

(CUT TO COMMERCIALS)

~~~

Once again in the break room, Maria Sanchez gazes at her husband. "Estevan, what do you suppose people will think? What will they do when this new paradigm is revealed? Do you think it will shock them too much?

"I know we've talked it to death, Estevan, I can't help but wonder how the world is going to deal with this. There can be no disputing what the evidence is proving to be true."

"I know, Maria," Estevan, shaking his head and grabbing his wife's hands, replied in almost a hoarse whisper. "I know. But as we've all talked and discussed into oblivion, this time ... unlike all those events and times throughout history ... the truth cannot be hidden. We cannot hide the facts. We cannot bury what IS.

"We ... including our benefactors ... all agreed to go public so that NO power of government or religion can have the chance to deny, bury, hide, or suppress the truth.

"It is also very important to remember, as we continue our work ... while our perceptions and beliefs in many ways will change with the revelation of these ancient artifacts and texts ... it also begets entirely new and innumerable questions that must be explored."

"You are right, Estevan," Maria replied. "We have discussed this beyond what's even necessary. Oh, look, the show's about to resume. Shhh ... ."

~~~

**(Camera one – MEDIUM SHOT of Charlie Rhoades
THEN, SLOWLY ZOOM IN)**
"I am back with Dr. Estevan Sanchez, renowned Archeologist, Anthropologist, Historian, Explorer ... extraordinaire.

"You are watching Earth Tribe Geographic's UNRAVELING THE MYSTERIES OF EARTH'S HISTORY – MYTHS AND LEGENDS. I am your host, Charlie Rhoades."
(Camera TWO – MEDIUM TWO SHOT of Rhoades and Sanchez)

"Dr. Sanchez, before we went to break, you were starting to tell us about the mysteries of Earth's oceans. Is that right?" Charlie postulated.

"That's right, Charlie! What I am about to tell you, and show you and your audience is nothing less than astounding!"

(Camera one – MEDIUM SHOT of Rhoades)

"From what you've shown me so far, Dr. Sanchez, ASTOUNDING is the understatement of the day.

"In fact, what your discoveries and subsequence research seems to reveal and display are some findings, deciphers, translations of some ancient artifacts you and your fellow scientists recently discovered in the dark, murky depths of the Atlantic Ocean … findings that may well shock the very foundations of our thoughts, our beliefs, our history!

(Camera one ZOOMS IN on Rhoades)

"Am I exaggerating, Dr. Sanchez?"

(Camera two – MEDIUM SHOT – SLOWLY ZOOM IN on Sanchez)

"Charlie, I hope … all of us associated with this new discovery hope … that people will be mature enough and solid enough in their beliefs and minds that while they may be shocked at first, they will be happy that for once in the history of mankind, someone is actually being honest with them.

(Camera one – MEDIUM TWO SHOT of Rhoades and Sanchez)

"As a scientist, as well as a human being, I want the truth. I don't want any government or corporation or religious leaders hiding the truth from me because in their omnipotent, higher than-thou view, I somehow can't handle the truth."

**(Camera two – TIGHT SHOT OF RHOADES --
THEN, SLOWLY ZOOM OUT FOR TWO SHOT)**

"Well said, Dr. Sanchez, well said.

"Now that we have sufficiently ... at least I hope so ... grabbed everybody's attention and piqued their curiosity, why don't you get right into it?

"Please, Dr. Sanchez, give a little bit of background on where you've been recently, what you are doing, and what you found that could possibly be so monumental as to perhaps change everything we've been taught in school and church."

(Camera one – MEDIUM SHOT of Sanchez)

"Okay!" Sanchez exclaimed. "Here goes:

"Recently, some very well-to-do investors and philanthropists retained some of the best minds and engineers in the world to build a new-generation deep sea exploration ship.
(CUT TO B-ROLL TRACKING CLIPS OF SHIP AT SEA)

That ship was christened Neptune's Trident after the Olympian god – of the seas – patron god of Atlantis, and fishermen.

"It is a marvelous ship, a marvelous work and a wonder. Neptune's Trident is a long, extended sea-going vessel that is articulated. What I mean by that is that while underway, she looks like most any other ship.

"However, once in place, the interior-most part of the ship

pivots at a 90 degree angle, and in a shape that appears much like the shape of a trident. That part of the ship detaches from the main part of the vessel and literally descends into the very depths of the ocean below."

(Camera one – MEDIUM TWO SHOT of Rhoades and Sanchez)

"Wait a minute," Charlie interrupted.

"Let me get this straight, Dr. Sanchez. You are saying that the ship actually separates into two different ships? One stays topside, while the other one, shaped similar to a trident, becomes what? A submarine of sorts ... and that part of it goes down into the ocean bottom?

"How's that even possible? Isn't the pressure so much down there that the submarine would explode?"

(Camera two – TIGHT SHOT of Sanchez)

"Actually, Charlie, if anything would happen I think it would be more like 'implode' ... basically it would be crushed up like a wad of paper or something like that.

"But remember, I said Neptune's Trident is a new-generation deep sea exploration craft?"

(Camera one – TWO SHOT of Rhoades and Sanchez)

"That's right, so you did. Please continue, Dr. Sanchez. You have me glued to this story. What happened when you went out there? Out there as in 'out there' in Neptune's Trident.

"By the way, will our producer please put up for our audience to see – a photo of Neptune's Trident in its deployed position so they can get an idea what we are talking about here?" Charlie gestured to someone off screen.

(CUT TO SLIDE OF NEPTUNE'S TRIDENT SHIP)

"Dr. Sanchez, did you actually go along with the crew on the voyage that reaped your most fascinating discovery?" Charlie asked.

"Oh, yes! I wouldn't have missed that for the world, Charlie.

"Sometimes, as a scientist I tend to get bogged down in detail and jargon and data but my wife, Maria, warned me to just keep stuff simple ... and get to the point. So here it is.

(CAMERA ONE – MEDIUM SHOT OF SANCHEZ)

"In a nutshell, we submerged several times out in the Atlantic ... exploring, searching and studying the crags, crevices, channels, underwater mountain ranges ... especially in known areas of fairly recent earthquake activity.

"We were hoping to make some new discoveries, but we had no idea ... ."

(CAMERA TWO – WIDE TWO-SHOT OF RHOADES AND SANCHEZ)

"No idea of what, Dr.?"

"Charlie! We had no idea that on our last voyage ... under the sea ... our underwater cameras would come across ruins of some kind of ancient civilization."

(CAMERA TWO ZOOMS IN ON TIGHT TWO-SHOT OF RHOADES AND SANCHEZ)

"Civilization?" Charlie almost lunged out of his chair.
"Civilization!" Sanchez repeated.

(CAMERA ONE – TIGHT SHOT OF SANCHEZ)

"What we saw first were obvious columns and remnants of buildings.

"We were so excited we couldn't even begin to control our elation!"

(CAMERA ONE – TIGHT SHOT OF RHOADES)

Charlie could hardly contain himself, "So tell us how you really felt!"

"Well Charlie," Sanchez began, "as scientists and explorers, we all knew we had found something beyond description. In fact, trying to describe it right here, right now, is nothing compared to seeing what we beheld before us ... miles under the surface of the Atlantic Ocean.

(CUT TO B-ROLL – UNDERWATER CLIPS OF EXPLORATION MISSION)

"Cutting the explanations short ... as soon as possible, we retrieved by robotic arms what artifacts we could. We slowly made our way back to the mother ship ... a slow and grueling period of decompression and agonizing waiting.

"We couldn't wait to get topside to get our treasure offloaded and sequestered in a 'safe' environment conductive to our studies. You see something that has been submerged for who-knows-how-long, needs to be protected in certain ways so that rapid oxidation or other chemical reaction doesn't suddenly disintegrate or destroy it."

(CAMERA TWO – WIDE SHOT OF RHOADES AND SANCHEZ)

"So, Dr. Sanchez, how much time are we talking here? Hours? Days?"

"Charlie, to compare us to kids awaiting Santa Claus on Christmas mornings would be an understatement.

(CAMERA TWO – SLOWLY ZOOM IN ON RHOADES AND SANCHEZ)

"It took way too long for our liking! But Charlie, with what pictures we got from the floor of the Atlantic, along with the arti-facts we recovered on that, as well as subsequent dives, was well worth the wait ... even worth the wait of millennia."

(CAMERA ONE – MEDIUM TWO SHOT OF RHOADES AND SANCHEZ)

"Okay, Dr. Cut to the chase, here! What are we talking about?"

(CAMERA TWO – MEDIUM SHOT OF SANCHEZ)

"We knew we had something special, Charlie. In the beginning, though, we didn't know HOW special.

"At first I couldn't make heads or tails out of any of the discoveries. We had some text on some hard-baked clay tablets, for instance."

(CAMERA ONE – TIGHT SHOT OF RHOADES)

"Clay tablets?" Charlie queried.

(CAMERA TWO – TIGHT SHOT OF SANCHEZ)

"Clay tablets! Those tablets and fragments held writings, glyphs ... such as never before heard of ... or seen.

"I even called my parents. Remember how I told you my mother was an expert on Egyptology?" Sanchez asked Charlie.

(CAMERA ONE – MEDIUM TWO SHOT OF RHOADES AND SANCHEZ)

"Oh, that's right. You did tell us a little about your mother and dad."

(CAMERA ONE – SLOWLY ZOOMS IN ON SANCHEZ)

"Well, Charlie, the closest thing I could even compare those writings to would be an ancient Egyptian style ... rather it looked remarkably of a similarity to ancient Mesopotamian ... Elamite ... perhaps Ugaric ... or even Vinca. Such a collection of similarities to many cultures suggest a common language that may have been in use at some yet indeterminate time ... perhaps when it was not yet a time, even. I can only call the language, Proto Global. And yet, even then, there seemed something so foreign about its nature.

(CAMERA TWO – MEDIUM TWO SHOT OF RHOADES AND SANCHEZ)

"My Mom couldn't make heads or tails out of our new found treasure. Neither could my dad."

"What did you do, then?" Charlie asked. "You obviously figured it out or you wouldn't be here with me today on this interview."

**(CAMERA ONE – TIGHT SHOT OF SANCHEZ –
SLOWING ZOOM OUT – MEDIUM SHOT OF SANCHEZ)**

"Oh, how right you are, dear sir. How right you are.

"Through an amazing process of decryption, comparison, study, blood ... sweat ... and tears ... we had a miraculous break-through. It wasn't overnight, mind you, but we were able to put together the pieces of a collection of both whole and fragmented shards that we gathered in numerous quantities over one partic-ular area."

**(CAMERA TWO – MEDIUM SHOT OF RHOADES
AND SANCHEZ)**

"And ... ? What pray tell were your findings, Dr. Sanchez? The whole world, myself included, can wait no longer."

"First, Charlie, let me explain some more of our treasure that we brought up from the ocean floor.

(CUT TO B-ROLL CLIPS OF ARTIFACTS IN LAB)

"Along with those precious clay tablets with their here-to-fore unknown story, we retrieved quite a trove of gold artifacts, pottery, bowls, cups ... and goblets, bricks, and several thumb-size cult animals ... some of which were even intact. Also, we gathered up ... and I must reiterate over a period of time from a number of trips to the bottom of the sea ... fairly large quanti-ties of the deep purple gemstone amethyst, of the mineral quartz family. They were found among the group of shards and the tab-lets I afore mentioned. On some fragments we found fingerprints of an ancient storyteller. This alone tells a story. We had no idea what we had ... nor, from what civilization the people of our finds originated.

(CAMERA ONE – MEDIUM SHOT OF SANCHEZ)

"I say, 'we had no idea' ... that is until I deciphered the text from the tablets.

(CAMERA TWO – MEDIUM SHOT OF RHOADES AND SANCHEZ)

"Do you want to know what those writings say, Charlie?"
"Do I?" Charlie blurted out in excitement. " Absolutely!"
Turning toward the TV audience, Host Charlie Rhoades stopped the thoughts mid-stream, as so often happens with TV shows paid for by commercial sponsors.

(CAMERA ONE – MEDIUM TWO SHOT OF RHOADES AND SANCHEZ – ZOOM IN MEDIUM SHOT ON RHOADES)

"But we'll have to wait! Don't go away. YOU WILL want to come back after this break. You will not want to miss this exclusive revelation that has ... in fact ... not even hit the headlines yet. Please join us in a few, ladies and gentlemen. You WILL NOT want to miss this."

(CUT TO COMMERCIALS)

~~~

Back in the break room, Maria looked squarely into her husband's eyes. As if in trepidation she continued. "Estevan, it's too late now. I sure hope we did the right thing. We have no idea how much this news will shake up the world ... our world views ... our very foundations of history."

"Maria!" Estevan responded. "We all decided that we have no right to withhold this major information from the world ... from people. To continue the lies and the charades of countless powers over the centuries for their own greedy purposes is almost the ultimate sin. We decided!"

"I know. But all of a sudden, watching this unfold on TV makes it seem so final!" She almost apologized.

"As you said, Maria. This is what our life work has been all about."

~~~

(CAMERA ONE – WIDE TWO SHOT, THEN, SLOWLY ZOOM IN ON RHOADES AND SANCHEZ)

"Ladies and Gentlemen. We are back. I am your host, Charlie Rhoades. This is my guest, Dr. Estevan Sanchez. Dr. Sanchez and I have been discussing his science group's monumental discoveries of ancient texts ... and other artifacts recovered from the floor of the Atlantic Ocean from miles beneath the surface."

(CAMERA TWO – MEDIUM TWO SHOT OF RHOADES AND SANCHEZ)

Turning toward his guest, Rhoades looked to Dr. Sanchez and continued, "Dr. Sanchez, just before we cut to break, you were about to begin sharing the translations from the text you found on the clay tablets retrieved by the exploration ship, Neptune's Trident.

(CAMERA ONE – MEDIUM SHOT OF RHOADES)

"First though, Dr., can you reveal to us up front ... was that ancient civilization, the lost continent of Atlantis from fable and myth and legend?"

(CAMERA TWO – TIGHT SHOT OF SANCHEZ)

"To begin," Sanchez replied, "Atlantis is a name like so many other names that have been passed down through literature, documents, myths, legends, and religious texts.

(CAMERA ONE – MEDIUM SHOT OF RHOADES)

"To use the term 'Atlantis' is something I hesitate to do. However, as I share the interpretations and translations that I have thus far achieved, you will derive your own conclusions.

CAMERA TWO – TIGHT SHOT OF SANCHEZ)

"Please allow me to caution you ... and your viewers, though Charlie ...
"By no means do these words mean to destroy any ones beliefs, traditions, or understandings.

(CAMERA ONE – MEDIUM SHOT OF SANCHEZ)

"This great discovery ... perhaps the most precious and complete history of the writers ... just might fill in some gaps, answer some questions, solve some problems, reveal some new evidence and facts ... facts that can and should help us to understand who we are as people ... how closely we are related to one another.

(CAMERA TWO – MEDIUM TWO SHOT OF RHOADES AND SANCHEZ)

"Charlie, it is very important to all of us involved on this journey and adventure to assure everyone we share this new information with ... that we want only to bring out these new truths ... facts ... findings.

(CAMERA TWO – SLOWLY ZOOM IN TO TIGHT SHOT OF SANCHEZ)

"We only desire to open some doors ... shed some new light that somehow brings us closer as a human family ... reveals to us our roots. In that venue, and with our hope and desire, we share these new discoveries of ancient stories that help us understand some answers to life's most pressing questions: Who are we? Where and whence did we come? How did we get here?

(CAMERA ONE – MEDIUM SHOT OF RHOADES AND SANCHEZ)

"With that, just let me set the stage a little. From what I am about to share with you, please think on this: Science cannot by present means account for the tablets' first sequence, which begins in the words of a female from a 'very' far off place."

(CAMERA ONE – ZOOM IN TIGHT ON SANCHEZ)

"Hold on to your seats folks. While her story is brief, the drama unfolds to include the tale of two other quite extraordinary women who are most certainly not your usual archetypal perception of our first forebears."

~~~

In the break room, listening to the television as her husband began to reveal the startling discovery to the world, Maria Sanchez closed her eyes and took within herself every word that her husband now disclosed. The imagery provided by the lost fragments now restored to their former wholeness ... of a people now found ... was like a song. She relaxed, perhaps for the first time since the fragments had come to light.

Maria was drawn ... NO mesmerized ... by her husband's voice into a world of vast beauty. She felt herself come alive in THE story of antediluvian beginnings.

Before her eyes and in her heart Maria flew on the silver wings of imagination's sky-bird. Then, she found herself at a place ... that was not a place ... in a time that was not a time. It only JUST WAS ...

And in her starry shade, of dim and solitary loveliness,
I learned the language of another world.

~ Lord Byron

Aeons ago
Within a sapphire abyss of Somewhere...

In a place that is not a place, and
A time that is not a time...

Chapter One

It is quiet in here. So quiet. How can quiet be so noisome? Perhaps it is the throbbing. Perhaps it is that I profoundly hear nothing. I feel a pounding in these ears, a vibration I am little used to.

There are the laws of dimension, certain laws that I, who pay little heed to convention, cannot break ... laws of science.

I, scientist, know that if I enter the physical vibration of matter ... I must apply to certain principals.

And, so I summon the materials I need ... a form to suit my light and a vehicle to travel in, a ship that will carry me through the portals of Orion and the alignment of the rising star, past the glittering jewels of the heavens and onto the world I have focused my studies on.

As I afore accounted, I am a lawbreaker. Permission has not been granted to me in the Titain Halls. Worse than that, He, Lord and King, does not know of my departure.

The throbbing of silence overwhelms these ears. The beauty of experience renders my very thoughts speechless as the blue lights of the star sea shine through the windows of where I am.

A certain joy I do not quite understand makes my lips curve in a smile. I did not tell Him of my departure, or of my journey across vast space to reach the earthen shores of Ki. I did not tell anyone. The vibrations lull me, softening just a bit the explosion of anger that threatened my feigned passivity just before I departed the Perfect world. The journey, though shortened by the star way, forces upon me a period of time, which gives me much moment to think.

He angered me and I am much given to anger as I still have emotions left.

Rogue, I ... refusing to cast them aside as others on the perfect world have done; they, deeming them useless on a technologically advanced wonder world of utter perfection.

Deem I the Perfect World as boring and deem I Him as boring also.

1

But ... not totally. Something about him fascinates me. After all, He is my lover ... and I his favorite, or so I thought. It has long been factual that I, Sofeya, top scientist of Nibiru, am also the favored lover of our Lord.

I am not top for nothing. I have strived for proclivity with a pure heart in both of my endeavors, lover and scientist.

I have longed to travel solitaire on a journey to Ki, but permission has been denied in the halls of Titain, as well as in the bed of Anu, my lover. He made it so easy for I, naughty female that I experience as, to wiggle the law, because I can.

My mother taught it to me since the first day in all of eternity that I remember.

I was young, just a little glimmer wanting to expand and be bright and beautiful. And, she handed me this form to don to wear like a garment. I wasn't comfortable with it, but she admonished me that it was well adapted to Nibiru's present conditions, and that in this aeon all were wearing it!

She too, bless her, was top scientist who specialized in the birth laboratory directing the efflux of the star codes and all.

The garment was beautiful in the way of the saurian, however. Beauty has always been important to my mother and I ... and her mother before her, and her mother, Oh ...

She said if I didn't like the color, color was easy to change. It was the feel I didn't care for ... sort of a coolness as if metallic. She assured me that better code accommodations were ever being perfected like this Ki body I so carefully re-designed from an original that was prevalent ancient ago on Nibiru. It fits my purpose so perfectly, and suits my nature as well.

I like it much better than that lizard image that was and still is so vogue on Nibiru.

My first form was the color of green-tinged copper. It was quite exquisite, actually.

For the law of manifestation requires a body. To go to school in experience requires a body.

2

We on Nibiru are experts in body apparels. I just don't prefer that metallic feel that my others find so becoming to the magnetic codes of Nibiru.

With our current explorations into the science on Ki, the softer and warm flesh body that I donned for my journey, being best suited for its environment, might just take hold again in the fashions of my associates. I like the looks much better. But, then, the council says that we on the 'Peeeerfect' World are lizards.

But I, lawbreaker ...

Oh, about my mother. Bless her. Experience has seen her through and she now dwells on the Ninth. It is a rare graduation. It takes most of us aeons to get there. I have not seen her for quite some time. I feel her though, laughing with me. She was a lawbreaker, too.

She told me to question authority ... that experience is the number one quest to abide. She said that on the Fourth, wherein Nibiru abides, there are those who will try to stifle experience in the greed for technology and power.

"They believe, darling," my mother told me, "that this is the Perfect World and that we have evolved past matter into the most desirable vibration of technology."

Being young, I wasn't allowed to attend council, but she always told me what was discussed there.

"We have been declared a world of perfection and the most advanced in this universe of the technology. Here, you may not wear your natural self. They are said to be imperfect, too burdensome, too much trouble for the perfection that we now are.

"It is all that code work, you know. Working with computers has taught us this: that we may cast our star codes into any form, bio or metallic.

"This lizard form currently in mode on Nibiru suits us well. Our real forms are safe inside, don't need to worry about anything, are efficient, like the computers. Death is not in the program except by rare accident or neglect, and our technology so great these malfunctions as such are rare if ever."

My mother's eyes narrowed into purple sparks as she bent to tell me thus. Her form was beginning to take it's imagery of deep violet as she neared the higher ...

"And, that also, like the computers, we will all be ridding ourselves of emotion, that we will "feel" no more, as it hinders our progression, only serves to slow us down."

Mother's tone changed into a whisper as she said to me that the computerized body does not need to compute emotions, that we need only concern ourselves with learning and technological advancement that the Perfect World will take care of all our needs. At this point, amethyst tears were falling from my mother's eyes. The Perfect World in all its perfection does not need the hindrance of emotion.

"Just throw it away. That's what they declared," she whispered in sorrow.

I really didn't quite understand what she meant at the time; I do now. I thank the day she made the decision to become a fugitive on the Perfect World.

"Never tell anyone." She admonished me. "Keep it a secret. Hide within yourself your emotions." She said. "Your emotions are the only way you can get the benefit of the experience which will allow you to go on to the Fifth, and the Sixth and the Seventh and the Eighth, and the Ninth. There is more, but it is not spoken of, the Tenth ... and ... ."

I decided I sort of liked the beautiful coppery colored skin of the reptile she urged me to don. "Consider it clothing," she said, "clothing to cover what is something you must hide from them.

"Your eyes are so beautiful," she told me. "May they always burn with the wisdom I will teach you. Oh, darling! We must lie. Lie to them all!"

She taught me about the technologies as well as the wisdoms the others forsake. She taught me about the births and the inhabitations of the codes ... and the transmutations, and I, Sofeya, am the most beautiful ... and I still have emotion.

Unlike Him. This is why He loves me so. He doesn't understand love. He deems it a useless thing.

I, of wisdom know this. Why, I conjecture with experience, does He prefer to lay with me? Why does He prefer my companionship?

It is because when He is with me He forgets that the 'feelings' have been banned ... for a time at least.

"Oh, Sofeya," He says. "What you do to me!"

I will add I am most proficient at ... ah ... lovemaking. I know the ins and outs of it to a most satisfactory degree. It's like this ... most females on the Perfect World know well, the outs of it. I know about the ins. I know that the ins are a symbol ... a symbol of the love one soul focuses on another.

It is an emotion that other females have outcast as useless. Thus, they are ordinarily perfect.

But ordinary I am not! And neither should love ever be thus. I am a gem shining in a World of Perfection that bling's the light until no one may see the true radiance. I, indeed, am a radiant rogue which is why He loves me so.

This is my secret, of which I have many. No one knows why I am a fifty in the personal ranks of his adoration. I do.

I feel the smile light my third vibration form in a quaint manner.

Oh, Ki's light! In this form, I am pleasing to gaze upon ... so beautiful I am! If He could only see me now! This form is well suited for sex. But then, I thought I was His top number. Why did He decide to make her His Anitum?

"I will marry my sister," He informed me most casually.

"What about us?" I tried so hard not to let tell-all tears stream from my blue-hued eyes. It was my biggest test.

"To create a proper heir I must marry my half-sister. I must!"

"What if Your seed has sprouted inside me even now?" I asked His Highness. "What about our son? Our sex has been exquisite these last few days like ... ah ... like I thought it was I you ... ."

"Enough, enough!" He told me "There will be no talk of feelings, only the law. Only the Law of the Seed and the Succession that clearly states that it is the firstborn son of a King coupled with His sister who has supremacy in the long line of Annunaki Royals."

Then I began to truly understand what my mother had been explaining to me about the technology of the Law turning Nibiru into the Perfect World of imperfect perfection. Or, was it the Imperfect World of perfect imperfection?

I couldn't let Him see the tears. I wouldn't let Him see me cry. I thought He loved me. I guess I'm not as brilliant as I suppose, either. Just beautiful.

Why did I, most beautiful and the most brilliant scientist on all of Nibiru, leave the Perfect World ... alone?

~~~

Sofeya closed her journal, tired of recording her thoughts, something her mother had taught her to do.

"Recording makes sense of your life, when living on the Perfect World seems senseless." For a moment Sofeya held her gilt-edged text in her hands, pressed to her heart.

On Nibiru there was little use for the senses.

For this journey, she was well equipped ... everything except for the permission part was perfect, well ...

~~~

Even the landing was good. When the mist of the portal cleared, she stepped out of the ship into shallow silver waters which reflected Ki's moon light.

Sofeya caught her breath. Sometimes it took adjustments to begin to assimilate the moist air into the lungs of her matter body; however, likely it was just that Ki's moon never ceased to strike her raw emotions with a beauty quite unknown on the Perfect World.

"Silver moon," she spoke out loud. "Shine on me tonight beautiful, beautiful lover of Ki. Love me as well on this evening."

When her breath became functional she waded through the waters. Her excitement enticed her on through deep violet mists that parted as she stepped onto the shore amid the reeds.

She smiled. This is what she had been waiting for, to explore Ki alone. Alone, she could be quiet, taking only minimal instruments which she could tuck safely in her pockets, and not have to deal with all that fuss and commotion a crew of ten leaping lizards would have brought.

"It isn't safe," the council had insisted. "Many experts must go along to carefully attend the observations."

But she didn't need them. She was the most brilliant of them all. She had studied, and knew well about, Ki. The moon this night was exactly as she had calculated. They would be out tonight, the Ki creatures.

Barefoot to aid in her silence, she slithered through the soft earth grass on her stomach, like the nas creature, bless its golden hide.

The deep fragrance of wood smoke guided her. Flickering flames enticed her. Was that a clearing in the trees? She inched closer, very, very carefully.

When she got near she parted the grasses imperceptibly. They wouldn't even know that she was here; the tall grasses so well hid her.

Sofeya smiled in joy and delight. She had a perfect view and could observe most closely to see all. This would take much of the night! She had determined in her planning to observe such a festivity. These creatures of Ki, really knew how to celebrate!

"Celebrate what?" The others would be asking. Ki's children are but animals, or so they said.

Well, she, Sofeya, loved animals and these particular ones fascinated her. Ah! What an opportunity ... one she scarce could have hoped for such a chance. Never had she been able to observe so intimately. None of the creatures knew of her presence. It was just she, and her tiny eagle-eye instrument which she pressed to her eyes to enhance the viewing.

When those things they play with that make that sound of vibrations that fills one's emotion with a stirring began to thrill her ears, she noticed the male figures forming a circle on the outskirts of the fire. In their hands they held sticks of sorts, that when placed to their lips she could hear the sounds of many canaries singing. They also had sticks to hit something.

On Nibiru, she had dreamed of the sound ... the feeling of the sound ... of what they who were of Ki called drums.

She had heard them called drums and had written it down on her observation list when she had observed with other scientists.

Like a reed at the edge of the fire circle she was invisible and quiet, blending into the grasses and hidden. The journaling would come later, on her way back home to Anu and His wrath ... if he ever got word. Enough of that damn ...

She so desired the experience this evening promised to fill her senses with, emotion being her ultimate goal. For on her world, the Perrrfect World, it just wasn't there, wasn't celebrated as it was on Ki.

Beauty surrounded her, all around her, in her, out of her, inside her, within ... it sang with the drums. She could feel her body move ever so slightly to the sound of music as she responded to the vibrations of the dance.

Now the dance was truly a sight to see! Oh, how she longed to dance ... to take within her soul the footsteps of the songs they sang and the stories they told!

This was what was wrong on Nibiru. They had cast away the music, the songs, the stories, and the joy.

Anciently, sars ago, her mother had told her, the inhabitants of Nibiru's sparks still lit up their original, breathing, living bodies like these! Sofeya sighed. She wouldn't dare dance on Nibiru. It would be foolish idleness and a hindrance as well, to more important pastimes.

Oh! What beautiful bodies these natural children of Ki had. Their bodies gleamed as if phosphorescent in the light energy of the fire element. All of them were quite naked, some of them with bright ribbons and veils to enhance their lovely shining flesh that glistened brighter than the fire.

Standing in the very center of the circle, a comely female with long shining hair motioned for the dancing to pause.

"I will tell you a story." The female voice was like a breeze in the night. Oh! She was most lovely! A sight she was.

"On this evening when Mother moon shines her grace above us, our Sun has sent her last ray of the day upon the pole. It is time! The shadow has danced with the light and tonight we celebrate! Tonight we mate! Our love will speak our story."

Sofeya's cheeks went hot. What? They were so open. No stuttering, no shame, as if it were honor. She inched closer.

The story! How intriguing! She wasn't entirely sure, but...

How was it that she could even hear words not spoken on Nibiru? Was it possible that she could be feeling the story then?

"When Gaia was young, still youthful in the freshness of her earth ..."

A girl, barely old enough to not be a child, quite, began to dance around the fire. Sofeya almost stopped breathing, in awe at the beauty of the night. Her movements vibrated with the voice of the enchanting girl who spoke the story. Softly, and in harmony to the melodious voice, the drum beat like the first breath of life, and the sticks that played music hovered sound in the air like morning birds. Sofeya was struck.

Then, all the animal creatures began to sing, joining in on the song. Not words, just song. Like a thrumming chorus of sea reverberation, the vibration of words hummed in soft voices that droned into the music of the night.

Sofeya was spellbound. Was she hearing the words in her heart?

All the blood rose seemingly from the tips of her toes to the very top of her head. The story ... the story ... had she heard this story before? It couldn't be, could it?

On Nibiru, it was said that Ki's children were mere animals, dumb beasts, not advanced in the least. However, they were telling a story, were they not? The story that Nibiru's children had forgotten to mention since ancient sars ago when they, too, were but young.

She, Sofeya, most brilliant and she still spirited, of all scientists on Nibiru, still knew the story. She had read it in her mother's accounts ... the creation story of Ki, when it was called by the language of Nibiru as Tia ... Tia Mat ... Tia Mother.

The sound of the drum beat in cadence to the chant, and began to eliminate all reasoning within.

Then, her feet moved without knowledge of her thinking to the sound of the song. Her head swayed. Her matter hair, soft and fine, fell from the fastening she had bound it in.

In her blood, the music played like her heartbeat within. In her blood, she blended into Ki's joyful vibrations.

The grasses where she lay in hiding parted. Two eyes bright as topaz-fire peered at her.

For one moment, time ... as unused to that sensation as she was ... parted. It stood totally still.

Breathing its breath of life deeply ... this was no animal. This was soul ... body endowed with high spirit!

This creature, be it animal, be it soul, be it code, be it spirit-endowed animal, beautiful animal .... whatever ... whoever ... however ... reached for her.

His fingers closed around her arm, sliding down to take her by hand.

Oh, with her beating heart, how could she hear for sure what that sound he made meant? The word-vibrations were not what she was used to, but somehow familiar after all ... like the story. Up close, trying to understand became a moot point.

Now upright, she stood facing him. Truly, time was no more! He urged her to the fire, pulling gently for her to join.

All her instruments fell from her pockets. Suddenly she was aware of her mud-streaked garments and her hair tangled with bits of leaves and grasses.

She melted into the throng of glistening skin that became like leaping flames dancing around the fire. The moonlight was pearly ... golden glints ... electric blue ... violet like the mists ... and the color of the fire.

The muddy clothes also became a moot point. He tugged at them and tossed them aside. Smiling at her, he motioned for her to dance. She danced with him. Oh, Nibiru forbid, she danced with them.

The Halls of Titain disappeared from her rigid, yet rogue trained mind.

Only the soft flame of the fire drew her on. She danced with him.

His eyes were the color of Ki's sun-fired horizon reflecting golden on the liquid soft waters of a still and deep pool. She wanted to bathe there ...

Much later, on the earthen, shores
At a place lost in time
Give or take a sar or two, about
300,000 B.C.E.

Maybe...

Chapter Two

Tonight was the dance and the song. At nightfire this evening, GNOS would be honored.

Yet it was not dawn. The sun slept deep within her bed below the horizons beginning, blanketed in the murky waters of the sea.

Alsionee saw a white dove with light-tipped wings sweep across the sky, silhouetted against the silver moon of sleeping morning. The white dove swept low and disappeared into the mist-shrouded tops of the many trees which grew in the yoke of the valley below.

In the mountains above, the tips of the conifers were lit with moon soft reflection. From her position in the valley heights, she could see the pearly mist rise from the waters of the sea below ... way below.

Alsionee Tree Song sat with Skymother. She was straddled comfortably in the crotch of an ancient yellow cedar tree that spread its gnarled limbs over the edge of the cliff by the sea. She was watching and waiting for morning to come in.

Alsionee could not sleep. Discomforted, she had fled the snuggly warmth of her linen soft bed so she could be where the birds were. Alsionee, or Sion as she was often called, loved the birds. Every morning she came, though usually not quite so early, to the tree with the well-worn bough, so she could join their happy chorus and sing with them *hello* to the new day.

It was the eyes of an owl that had stirred her from sleep. In the still darkness, she could yet see big orange orbs staring at her from the world of dream mist.

The eyes were too big, too still, and too deep. They were eyes of the wrong color looking at her ... through her ... and into her very soul. Somehow, their ominous glare disturbed her peaceful home within her heart, AHDAWN. She sighed. It was only an owl, was it not?

From within the cedar branches that enclosed her, Sion felt the vibration of a sharp tap. The owl eyes disappeared into a haze when a little bird voice chortled *"twit ... twit ... twit ... twit ... twit... ,"* in garbling succession.

A small bird came to light upon her resting hand. Even without seeing it, she knew the bird wore the finery of a funny little crown on the top of its head.

No words of greeting came from Alsionee's mouth, only a warbling of soft sounds, imitating. She could feel the curl of a tiny bird claw as it wrapped around her finger ... that, and a cold slime that brushed the back of her palm.

She could also smell that the tiny bird held a fish in its beak, likely caught in the tide-pools among the rushes below. Ah ... the slapping sound she had heard was the thump of the fish head against the tree trunk where she sat.

"Well, little king." Sion's eyes were beginning to pick up more details as the sun poked her rays through the evening darkness, and into the morning glimmer of first light.

"Hungry are you? I do not believe that I've had the chance to talk to a kingfisher before. I thought that your kind kept to yourself, pretty much." She sent her thought words into the birds thought.

The kingfisher acknowledged her briefly with a nod of his head. Then, flew off to enjoy his breakfast.

While the sun sent her tentative light inching minutely forward into the dawn, Sionee grew impatient at the wait, and began her song. She smiled, supposing that it was she who would wake the birds this morning. Quickly she was surrounded with a thousand bird voices that brought the sunshine into her day.

There was yet time before the sun put her shining face over the vale below. Sionee allowed her thought to dwell on pleasant things, like why she loved this tree so much. She used to sit in this beloved tree with her mother. In the fragrant shade of the bough, they would play together when she was but a wee child of about three turns of the completed sun. Alsionee could not help but remember the game she and her mother used to play as they sat cradled together on this very limb of this same tree.

"What is a bird?" Mother would ask, smiling softly, so softly. "Is she the color of the feathers she wears?"

"No maman," her little voice would reply. Alsionee spoke in words those many sun turns ago ... before ... whatever it was that made her cast all tongue words aside, and to speak in the old way, which was of a telepathic nature.

"Is she the flutter of her wings that ride the wind?"

"No mamun."

"Are birds, then, a song?"

Oh, how sweet it was to snuggle together on the crotched fork of the big tree, just the two of them, playing.

"Mamun, they are but little creatures. They fly and they sing. They have a head, and eyes, and a beak instead of a mouth. And they are smaller than us people," little Sionee finally mustered.

"Ah, are they what you see when you look at them?" Laughing, mother went on. "Or are they what they see when they look at them-selves?" **THIS MY MOTHER TAUGHT ME HOW TO SING ...**

Sion felt her heart home turn warm. She could feel her moth-er sitting beside her, even now. Despite the disquieting dream she had experienced, her AHDAWN was beginning to feel an excitement about the day, and the evening to come that gave her the inner strength necessary for keeping the song ... for honoring GNOS ... al-ways.

The birds still sang in joy with the new dawn, but by the posi-tion of the sun, Sion knew it was time to embrace the day, and climb down the tree to get ready for the morning hour of instruction.

Carefully, she placed her bare feet one by one on the stepping stumps which dotted the tree trunk all the way down or up like a ladder.

As she climbed down, two feathers fell from the limbs above, drifting in slow motion flutters on the still morning air. With one swift motion she caught them both with one hand.

The blue feather sparkled like the sky on an ocean gray morning, touched by a shaft of sunlight that revealed it to be an exquisite blue color. Sionee knew that the kingfisher had sent it her way.

She gasped though, as she beheld the other feather. Surely it was an owl feather. The stripes on it glimmered like a goldstrewn pathway.

Sion kept both feathers. They were gift, and on this evening she would wear them in her hair when she danced around the nightfire in celebration of the new sun.

Indeed, they, and nothing else.

~~~

On the sacred Snake of the Sea on an ever summer land of sun and apples on the northern ley at the western edge of the serpent's uncoiled body, the Sisters of the Song gathered in the quaint house of learning.

It was a small dwelling built quite simply of the shining white clay found in the nearby hills, and shaped skillfully to resemble a shell from the sea. It was but one of the many huts of wisdom at the sea edge. This one was shaped like a conch, sparkling with bits of mica which naturally enhanced the clay.

The girls awaited the morning lessons; however, few had their minds properly affixed on the lessons for this day.

Mother Marisol of the Sparkling Shell, she whose gift it was to teach, sat at the fire hearth that graced the center of the wisdom shell.

Though the many hot springs which smoldered beneath the Snake kept the land ever warm, at this time of the sun turn, a wee bit of chill made the fire inside the shell quite pleasant in the early morning. The girls drew close around the hearth.

"Girls, girls there are much too many empty words." Marisol spoke, moving her fingers and thumbs back and forth together like mouths moving too rapidly to be heard. When the chatter momentarily quieted, Marisol addressed the girl who sat at Sionee's side. The two girls were holding hands, for Sion wished to comfort her Sister of the Song.

"Coelle, dear, you are not looking like a morning bird just risen."

"I feel like a morning bird, indeed, one that rose too early and ate a big, big, much too big, fat, juicy and slimy worm," the girl replied, out of breath.

"Perhaps you will not be dancing at this nightfire," Marisol speculated. "Perhaps your honor will be such that you will give of a child to be born on this very night of the Yule. Oh, Coelle, what gift you would bring forth, if this should be."

"I am humble that my child's birth is near. I am well, mother, and ready to lead the dance as I was chosen."

"You do not feel that the child will wish to join our circle this eventide, then ... perhaps with the bright star?"

"She will dance inside me." Coelle laughed. "If she does come forth, Blessed Be! Sionee will sing the song."

Sion watched the movement stirring inside the mountain that was Coelle's stomach. She placed her hand there, feeling the warmth of her sister's tautly stretched skin. Then, she felt the vigorous kick inside.

For just a moment before what should be joy struck her palm, the owl eyes flashed behind her eyes. Sionee sighed, a lurch of unease tickled inside her own stomach. There was only emptiness.

Sionee knew that on this night the child would be born to this world ... and Coelle would be born out of it.

In the shadows of her mind, orange eyes glowed too brightly ... and she knew. She just knew. How did she know?

Sion sighed again. She didn't know ... only that tonight she would dance for Coelle, her Sister of the Song.

~~~

"Sionee ... Sionee, come back. Come back my daughter. You journey far, far distant from us!" Though Marisol spoke loudly, Coelle poked Sion hard.

"I am asking you, Miss Sunny Tree, to repeat for all in this classroom the morning thought of the day."

Sion hummed a little song.

Marisol frowned in puzzlement. It was beautiful, but ...

"Oh, will you not say the words?" She asked. "Not everyone in this classroom remembers the arcane language."

Sionee hummed again, each note increasing in a frequency of vibrational power ... beautiful. When she was through, no one had a doubt about the morning mantra.

Mother Marisol turned her head in approval. What more could she, mere teacher, say?

"Be Blessed Thou, girls," she spoke at last. "But hurry now. Our Mother the Sea pauses only that you may gather from her shores the gifts she has carried to you.

"Soon now she will return her treasures back into her deep, unseen. If we make haste I am certain you will find her gifts to use as adornments for your regalia for this evenings dance.

"Go in Mother's love." Marisol motioned. "Like Her in Her many forms, be ever thoughtful always, always."

~~~

To all appearances they were mere girls; however, the seven who hurried to the sands were anything but ordinary girls. They were the Keepers of the Song, marked by their birth in the Cave of the Mother Womb when the Bright Star sent her light into the darkness softly on precisely the longest night of the year ... on such a night as this.

Their birth at this time marked them with the ability of pure AHDAWN, and placed them as ones who would be instructed as Songkeepers to perform the dances and sing the songs at nightfire.

Sometimes it was said that the spirits born beneath the bright star were old spirits, advanced in the circle of birth and death, having returned to live many lives on Gaia among the Peoples of the Lemming, or among the Children who danced on the Snake of the Sea, or even elsewhere on Gaia ... or without ... so great had their wisdom become.

Since their birth, these girls each had been given with lessons and training in the arts of the song. These were the sisters who lived at the edge of the wild forest, nestled in the bow of the mountain by

18

the sea where the snake opened its mouth.

In simple dome huts they slept each night, receiving their lessons by day at the Campus of Shells.

They were the keepers of the night and the day ... the ones who watched the sun dance along the pillars in the sea ... they too ... danced the rhythms of the sun, the moon, the sky, and the earth.

They were the knowers of the wind, the tides, the falling leaf, the fruited flower, the bird song. Of all that dwelled on Gaia and the Sapphire Blue they told ... Of peace, beauty, joy, light and love was their stories.

Of Earthmother and Seamother and of Skymother, too ... these were the Songkeepers who remembered her tales to the People of the Fey. They were the blessed ones who lived at the small community outlier of a people honored on the Snake of the Sea. For they were the ones who were visited and taught by a beautiful woman who came to Gaia from the stars on a beautiful pearl that fell from the Sapphire Blue so long ago that the songs could not say when it happened, only that it did.

Marisol of the Sparkling Shell watched the little priestesses playing along the restless edge of the sea. Most of the girls were but silly girls, not given in the unique honor that their birth time foretold. But she loved each and every one of them for what they were, who they were.

It was a beautiful morning this season's turn. Though The Snake of the Sea had some subtle season distinctions brought about by Gaia's spin in the sun spiral, its climate was held in a paradise of ever mild splendor.

Rich underground volcanic activity warmed the earth and the waters that graced the landscape with mineral rich hot streams and pools that lent reason for another of the Snake's many descriptions, the Isle of the Blessed. Even the waves of the sea washed ever warm across the shore.

The morning sun was eager to play with the girls as they danced with the tide of white capped waves that were now beginning to wash higher on the shoreline. The girls teased Seamother, trying to escape her forth-wash and quickly snatch her tokens before She could take them back to her deep.

In the tide-pools among the rushes, many adornments were gathered to be fashioned into the regalia for the nightfire dance. Marisol had promised a prize for the most creative costume, but the reward was all hers, in the pleasure of watching her little ones have fun.

Marisol smiled indulgently. Vanity was the real incentive, however. Most of the girls had only in mind how beautiful they would look with the displaying of this fetish, or that one, upon a necklace perhaps, or dangling from the ear.

Not that the regalia was of little importance. She had taught them that the fetish only represented the beauty which was AHDAWN'S song, if they heard her anyway.

Marisol squinted in the bright sunlight. Including the heavy form of Coelle who was lagging just a wee bit behind, there were only six.

Where had Sion gotten off to? Now that girl. Oh, there she was, wading among the standing stones that rose out of the encroaching waves.

In the songs it was said that the stones had been fashioned by the Starmother to mark the gate where the sun goes forth according to the regulations of the seasons.

Marisol observed the girl for a few moments, taking notice of her beauty as the sea foam swirled around her slim brown ankles, and the mist played among both the rippling wave breaks and the rippling waves of Sion's cascading hair. She made a pretty picture.

Marisol sighed. Ah, Alsionee, Alsionee, my most beloved of all students ... my girl.

Marisol waded out to the standing stones. Sion had one arm wrapped around the circumference of the larger plinth, the finger of her other hand traced the pattern of a spiral as she swung around the pillar with one foot and broke the ripple in the wave swirl with the big toe of her other one. Ah! The girl could play.

"Ah, girl," Marisol reached out to give Sion a hug. "So like Tretia of Tree Song you are." The two smiled into each other's eyes.

"Your mother had hair as you do." Marisol reached out to slide her fingers fondly through Sion's silken glory. "Such a stunning color of blackened bronze."

Sionee smiled wistfully. Her mother had also been a Songkeeper at the outlier by the sea, as had her mother, and all the Mothers of Song Tree before.

Sion was ten summers when mother left the Feyri to dwell in the place of purple air just beyond the horizon at the place where the sun's rays made fuchsia streaks flecked with gold, and made mother's beautiful raiment into a star.

She missed her mother so, but sometimes... well, quite often actually, when Sion was in AHDAWN, she still talked to her mother.

"I will never leave you all alone my child," Mother had whispered to her, closing her beautiful eyes in a loving smile before she crossed the shores of the worlds.

The baby she had been carrying inside her never made it to Gaia's horizon.

Marisol and Sion held hands as they gazed at Coelle who slowly and carefully bent to pick up shells on the beach as if she still had strength. She was but a young girl.

"*Coelle gathers stars* to *adorn her crown.*" Sionee sent her thought words into Marisol's heart, where they were received.

Sadly, Marisol tried to toss them back, as if she didn't hear the words, they would not be true. "How do you know that?" She asked.

"*I don't know, I do know that it is time. It will be tonight.*"

"She is well."

"*But she's not. You will see. Her child is much too big.*"

Marisol could see that as obvious fact. The girl was extremely large for a first born, but that was not wholly uncommon, just unusual. Marisol crossed herself. Mother of the Sapphire Blue, let the girl be wrong. However, Marisol had seen Sion's gifts and knew that the girl could possibly see into the star side of the horizon.

"I pray that our Mothers will think of the child," Marisol spoke solemnly. She watched the shadow of a shudder cross Sion's bright brow, and she had no doubt if she did before, that Alsionee had the sight.

"Darling, about you. I have heard many of our people whisper, "We have forgotten our language of old. How can she sing when she has no words?"

Sionee frowned, only a bit. *"You know how I can sing when I have no words. You hear me."*

"Not everyone takes the time anymore to hear dear." Marisol knew what Sion was saying, but she was wanting her to consider the consequence of her vow.

"When the wind has a need to sweep in from the sea, it blows," Sion replied in her voice of no-words. *"Nobody can stop it. My words have become wind and have blown away. And I don't know where to find them."* Sion made the motion of the wind blowing with her fingers. Then, the sound.

"Wind Song, I do believe." Marisol smiled. "Why Sionee... why did you make a vow of silence?"

"No, not silence, Marisol. No words as in tongue words. I made a vow to speak no words. There are better ways of speaking, of singing the Song, too."

"Yes, yes. You do it so well. I can hear you as clearly as I see you standing here in the waves looking suddenly angry, but somehow, dear girl, I feel there is something you are not telling me. Why? Sion, why did you lose your words?"

"I don't know."

"I can hardly believe that is true," Marisol replied. It seems to me that there is a lot you do know, which is something I must speak to you about."

Marisol, as well as Sionee, was glad to close the subject. Marisol waved her hand toward the girls ahead as they giggled and stooped, laughed and played, and stopped only to bend and examine various beach treasures.

22

"You, dear girl, are they ... well, sort of. Why don't you join them?"

"I have already found my regalia." She held out the two feathers.

What else did the girl have in mind? This, Marisol could hardly wait to see.

"Ah, girl, there is something else I have wished to speak to you about this day." Tears filled her eyes and made her voice shaky as she placed her hand on the girl's soft cheek.

Sion's eyes opened wide in love for Marisol, her teacher-mother for all these many years her own mamun had been away.

"I am both sad and yet happy to tell you that I can no longer teach you, my dear."

Sion's eyes opened wider in an effort to keep tears from her own eyes as she tried to glimpse into what Marisol was telling her from her heart home.

"You are ready." Was that a shadow made by a cloud suddenly swooping in front of the sun? Marisol continued ...

"It is time for you to leave the maiden huts and build yourself your tree. Your time for head learning is up and it is time for you to experience your soul wisdom, now."

"But mother, I'd tell you if I could remember how I lost my words. I really would."

"No dear. It is not that. I respect your no-words vow, highly."

Alsionee's eyes became a curious mix of joy and terror. She could begin her house. She had been planning it for some time. Suddenly she remembered a song her mother had sang to her: "When a seeker is ready, a teacher is no longer needed."

"And, darling," Marisol broke Sion's contemplation, speaking softly as she touched the tip of Sionee's nose.

"Do not think you are as ready as you suppose. There are a few things you must know. It is why I sought you out here away from the other girls. It is also said that when a seeker is ready for further teaching a new instructor will appear, and to find this instructor you must look in places I don't understand. You will walk down roads I do not know of anyone having gone down before. You must swim in waters too deep to not drown in and fly in skies too high for the birds. You must sing songs no one has heard before," she added after seeing a frown deepen on Sionee's face. "I see one instructor coming soon. But ... no, I see two!"

Chapter Three

For the remainder of the day the girls were given time off from their instructions.

"Use this day well to prepare for the GNOS," Marisol urged the girls. "Complete your regalia and gather your spirits, for tonight we will shine girls, shine! Do you hear what I say?"

Alsionee clutched the two feathers in her hand. Why had the owl sent his feather to her? Why had Marisol chosen this morning to inform her that there was no place for her in the classroom of girls anymore? How could she dance with this overload on her mind? Wasn't it enough that she must deal with worries about Coelle, as well as with the dream fear? And, what was it with this blue feather that so intrigued her?

Marisol was only seeing happy girls who gathered sea shells down by the shore to make necklaces with.

After all, how could Marisol see into what was there in Sion's AHDAWN when she herself could not see? It wasn't like the other girls! Coelle maybe.

There was something so wrong she herself didn't even know about it, or if it was really there, or if even was it real? Owl eyes too bright ... Just something that had intruded in her once pure AH-DAWN because she had somehow foolishly let it in.

At the noon-meal Sion listened to the other girls rehearse their costumes for all to hear. She could not help but listen, and listen she did with great interest until all the interest turned into one big noise.

"This net I made, I spun it so fine it must have taken me two full moon circles to finish. The weave is so tiny!"

From the other side of the table there was more. "On each thread I put a teeny tiny pink shell no bigger than a quarter of the nail on my little finger. Then, I wove the shells together."

From somewhere else in the jumble there was more. "The color of purple I gathered from the sea."

Alsionee finished the handful of white grapes and gazelle cheese she had chosen from the tray. She took another handful to stuff into a small pocket she had sewn inside the folds of her shift. There was something she must do now, and she might get hungry later on.

The position of the sun told her that there was still plenty of time left to prepare for the evening's festivities.

She would think about tomorrow, tomorrow. But for now, she must take the voice of Songkeeper into her heart and prepare to sing. Already she had lost too much time dwelling on the haze of evil dreams that crept in at night and lingered in shadows throughout her day, her every day, and every night!

Sion allowed one last tiny frown as she hurried to the waterfall. It was time to purify her heart with a cleansing.

~~~

Alsionee Tree Song stood in all her naked glory on the other side of a roaring veil of mist. She was quite secure on a dangerous ledge that jutted from the rock face of the cliff where the gathering streams merged and fell with an explosion of thunder into the sea below.

It wasn't exactly a safe place, so close to the edge of vast quantities of kinetic waters falling downward through a misty abyss of dispersed droplets.

There was an alcove hidden behind the mist. That the sheer rock cliff that faced the sea had such a sanctuary was a secret no one could see from below. Inside the gallery Sion could look out through the veiling mists and see the valley and the sea below.

She had expertly climbed and clung to get here, holding on to the wild white grapevines that grew over the edge of the rocks. The vines were slippery from the water, so if she held tight she could slide down them from the small plateau of a fracture in the cliff until her feet regained secure solidity on the ledge.

The mysterious possibility of perilous consequence added to

the enchantment of her private sanctum. She felt safe here in the little hole where water had carved into the rock.

As far as she knew, there was only one other person of her acquaintance who knew of this place. And it was likely that he did not even remember. When she was but a child she was out exploring with one of the boys from the boys huts and they were playing like they were mountain goats. The two of them climbed up and down the cliffs, always having much too much fun to be conscience of having even a lick of sense in either of their heads.

Despite herself, Sion smiled as she peered out through the mists remembering the wet picnics they had shared here, and the pretty stones they had gathered along the way and thrown down into the awesome depths of the falls.

It hadn't been a place for children to play, but play often they did.

Even then, though, they may not have recognized it at the time as such, it was a place of great power. Like the waters, she could feel her strength gathering here.

Wrapped inside a small pouch that she had brought with her was a large owl pellet she had gathered from the base of her ancient cedar, specifically for the purpose of cleansing. It would be an effective imagery as it was a part of the dream bird that haunted her sleep.

Singing the wild grapevine a 'thank you' song, she pulled a large leaf from the stem. On the leaf she placed the pellet.

She went to her heart home where she stood at fear's threshold for just a moment before she thrust the door wide open. Closing her outer eyes to enter within, she went inside to seek the fear.

When she found it, it was invisible to her, but with the vibrating air she could see that it was large. Where had it come from?

Alsionee Tree Song vowed she would do whatever it took to find the source of her fear. For now she knew it would have to suffice that she at least rid herself of its foul odor within her pure AHDAWN for this night, so she could dance to the song.

Concentrating profusely, she gathered the leafed pellet in her palm. She gathered the fear in her heart and cast it into the pellet. *"Leave me. Make yourself a home where you are welcome!"* She spoke in the language of no words. *"No more will you stink up my heart home!"*

She pulled three long hairs from out of her head, paying no heed to the slight sting of their removal. The best she could, she braided the three single strands together and wrapped them around the pellet.

"This is my gift to you, owl poop, to return to you my gift of... ah ... affection."

She peed and caught some of the moisture in a small shell, and dumped it over the pellet.

This done, she wrapped it all up inside the leaf, tying the bundle with a tendril from the vine.

"Away from me go now with your gift so unwelcome, and leave my heart home pure and free from fear.

"Goooooooooooooooooodbyyyyyyyyyy!" She sang in the voice of the waterfall as she drowned her fear in its cleansing waters. She watched the rolled leaf disappear into the mist, where it fell into the sea and became food for hungry sea creatures.

It was done. Now, she could get herself ready for the dance with a more beautiful AHDAWN.

As she turned to contemplate her climb back up the slippery vines, which was never exactly easy, a shaft of late afternoon sun broke through the rainbow mist which graced the view at the portal hollow.

A prism of bright light reflected on the far interior wall of her little shelter, and danced across the shadow that usually hid the cavernous rear.

The chamber of her secret place suddenly disclosed more of a mystery. For a mere moment Sionee thought she saw a dark hole on the curve of the chambers depth. When she blinked her eyes and peered forth, it again appeared to be just a back wall in the cave's perimeter.

It was getting too late for further investigation because long shadows were beginning to mark the approach of a fading afternoon.

With more than a little skill, Sionee squiggled up the slippery vine. There was one more stop on the way back to the maiden's huts, where in only a short hour or two, the evening's festivities would begin. The idea for the rest of her regalia had begun in her mind.

~~~

She knew what she was looking for. She knew it well. It would suit perfectly!

The making of sacred vessels had long been one of the skills Sion had trained in at the House of Shells so she could sing the beautiful renditions of art.

All the Songkeepers had each their own unique specialty to excel in, as well as the learning of the Songs. Whether it was with herbs or the subtle coloring of fibers, or baking the daily bread, all the girls had their own personal gifts to contribute to the eco-system of the small group. Sion had heard the voice of grandmother clay calling her.

The softly shining vessels she made were of great value and highly prized in the trade route.

She stopped at a place by the small stream that wandered in a warm trickle down to a river that flowed to the sea. Here there was a cleft where she often gathered a rich lustrous powder to rub into the burnishing of her pots.

There was a vein in the wet, oozy clay that had abundance so thick that it gave of its contents cleanly. She thrust her hand into the rich cavity and pulled out a large handful of powdery dust that had been left there aeons ago, trapped within the clay layers. Maybe two handfuls would be quite effective.

It was still damp. Sion hurried to the huts. She spread her two handfuls thinly on a piece of dry linen and lay it out flat to dry in the last shadows of the hot fading sun.

The gold dust being fine, would not take long to dry.

Chapter Four

The moon was the first to arrive and had already taken her position in the Sapphire Blue as a bright witness to the night's festivities on the ever summer Snake of the Sea. She cast her light as a shining presence of shimmering luminosity on the dancers who were gathering to honor GNOS.

The young Songkeepers were the second to arrive at the well-trod meadow arena, flanked on one side by the circular curve of a sandy grass hill and on the other side by tall grasses that turned into water reeds as the slope gently fell to the sea.

As well as joining in the harmony of the chant and lending beauty to the ceremony, some of the Songkeepers had the opportunity to keep the fire burning through the entire evening until the bright star made her presence visible just before dawn. Other Songkeepers had charge of the incense to honor the Mothers as well as lend a fragrance that helped to set the sacred ambiance of the occasion.

The male drummers and the boys who played the wind instruments assembled in their places around the fire. The girls threw wands of sage and rue to aid in the presence of holiness ... and skullcap and jimson, so that heart homes would open freely on this night. Henbane was also offered to open the portals to friendly spirit friends.

Lavender, jasmine, sweet cedar, and skullcap, along with many other fragrant herbs, carried an invitation with their rise of scented smoke to the sacred Mothers to lend their presence to the circle around the fire.

The Songkeepers began their chanting welcome as the spectators began arriving. Sionee's voice rose above them, mute, but powerful. The people strained their visions to hear with senses that were fading and becoming lazy with the ease of modern spoken word.

"Be Blessed Thou, Oh, Mothers all. Will you join us this evening as we sing your song?

"Be Blessed, Earthmother Thou. Welcome oh sweetness on whose skin we walk. Come dance with us, on this night. Celebrate with us our life that we live at the mouth of your Snake by the Sea. Join us tonight, Oh, Gaia!

"Blessed Be Thou, Mari, Seamother, whose sands ever wash upon Gaia's shore with life's first seed. Join us, oh Mother. Let the essence of your waters come forth and wash our spirits that they may be pure of impurities. We welcome you, Seamother.

"Skymother, Be Blessed Thou, She ... You who create by mere thinking all that is, all that was, and all that ever will be. Embrace us in your love and your wisdom, and teach us ever of your song. That the beauty of who you are, and what you are, may always be in our eyes that hear, and our ears that see what is within. Thank you, Oh, Skymother, for attending our fire tonight in spirit, as you did in body so long ago.

"Be Blessed Thou, Oh, Mothers all of a million names but one essence. Be Blessed to you, and you, and you, and you ... a million different faces you.

"Be Blessed Thou, too, Oh, Fathers of all life, whose seed springs forth into the Mother. Where Mother dances in beauty, Father You rise and send forth into her deep the seed which comes forth into her egg. Oh, Fathers of one light, join us this evening in honor."

In AHDAWN, her heart home, Sionee blessed them all and acknowledged their presence by lighting a tendril of fragrant jasmine flower. She watched the perfumed smoke rise upward in a spiral that circled a trail to the stars. AHDAWN rose with it into the very heavens.

Sion breathed deep the great breath ... out and in. She breathed the rhythm of the Mother's heartbeat as the drums came to life with their thrum.

She opened herself to become the pillar that linked earth and sky with all people who were one. She felt herself at the center of the universe, the center of all.

The herbs the young Songkeepers offered filled the sacred circle with enchantment and intoxication. Her senses enriched, her cup was becoming full ... so full. Perfect Peace Profound. Who brought the mushrooms?

~~~

Like two visions blending into one, the earth world and the spirit world began to merge.

The Breath, the great Breath, Oh ... all-mighty Breath of the universe I breathe!

She heard the low, low rumbling of a mammoth somewhere out in the darkness. She felt the throbbing vibration of the mated pairs as they called to each other across the meadow, the hills and the valleys of the mountain.

Ka-Tak ... Ka-Tak ... Ka-Tak... sounded the drum, so deep. The music of the night thrummed the heartbeat of the Mother. Sion could feel the Mother's heartbeat in motion with her own.

Rhythm ... Rhythm ... Rhythm; One heartbeat, One song.

The dance of life begins in the heart, AHDAWN ... in the spirit ... in the silence ... the steps first form.

A female loon sent eerie echoes of wavering tremolo to yodeling males. A cicada screeched her high pitched warble and her male answered with a tympanic pop. The katydids pulsed, and the tree frogs croaked. The crickets orchestrated their voices in a magical chorus of angel song. The night was filled with the musical symphony of the heavenly spheres.

Deep breaths throbbed Rhythm ... Rhythm ... Rhythm. The drums bid life with every stroke of breath. The heartbeat of the mother sang in orgasmic ecstasy.

Breath ... Breath. Oh, the Breath! Softly in the night the quiet song of a flute trilled as its notes warbled louder and louder.

Sionee surrendered her inhibitions. There were none. Only the breath ... In and out ... out and in. The Mother's heartbeat was pulsing ... pulsing.

She had wrapped a thin scarf of gossamer threads loosely about her moonlit body. Just moments before she had arrived at the night-fire, she had lovingly lifted the lid of maman's regalia trunk, and reverently taken the veil out. Mother had woven it so finely into a delicate web-like design of exquisite beauty. It would be perfect for this night!

"Spider spinner ... you are the winner." **THIS MY MOTHER TAUGHT ME HOW TO SING ...** Mother had sung, chant-like to her little girl as she had woven the web her grown up daughter now donned to wear.

To begin the ceremony, Sion chose to sing a straight song. The words of the straight song could be heard only by those who opened their eyes to hear the sound of birdsong turning into the sound of the wind on the waters, and only to those who listened with their ears to see the waters turning into the silence of the stars at the midnight hour. **THIS MY MOTHER TAUGHT ME HOW TO SING ...**

Sionee's voice rose in melody and pitch, carrying with it the vibration of vowels. All who listened to Alsionee Song Tree remembered the words as they lifted in her voice, for she made their melody take note and be heard with the ears of the heart, not the ears of the head. Nearly everyone knew the song from long ago. The words went something like this ...

"Oh, child of the Mother ... Your skin may I enter ... As I dance this prayer ... Toward the center."

They would celebrate the legacy of their ancient- animal namesake, the Snake, by beginning their evening with a dance to honor the revered guardian of their beloved homeland. This part of the dance was open to any who wished to join in.

As Keeper of this night's song, Sionee stood in the place of the snake's mouth, to lead the dance.

Coelle's pains had started in the early evening. The girls told Marisol that Coelle had slipped on a piece of seaweed and fallen down quite hard.

Sionee was prepared to dance in her stead on this night as Coelle had asked of her.

A long line began to assemble of eager participants. Each person who joined the dance, stood with both hands grasping the waist of the person in front of them, each dancer forming a single segment of the snake's articulation. The image of the totem began to take life in the dance.

The colorful regalia of the many dancers wove a glorious design as the dancers moved their hips in sway to a harmonic rhythm, one in front of the other, female participant and male. The snake was now a whirling length of dazzling color and form.

Rising from its sleep to the sound of melody, the serpent swayed in sinuous undulations as each footstep danced to the center, weaving the form into a coil, as if to strike.

In and out of the coil the snake slithered, around and around the light of the fire in glistening imagery of one body. Rhythm ... Rhythm ... Rhythm caused motion ... the spiral of energy.

"For your spirit whispers of its journey within ... Oh, child of the Mother may I enter your skin?" Sion continued her straight song.

The spirit of snake called to Sionee, reminding her of who snake is, of what snake is.

Sion answered with her straight song for ears that could see and eyes that could hear.

"May I shed your skin my serpent friend ... Then slither up the tree within ... again."

With the chant and dance ... she remembered ... for the people, ... about who snake is ... of what snake is.

Snake climbed up the trunk of the tree, giving the tree the strength to stand, making it strong.

Sionee straightened her back from the arch position she had formed as she danced, for here it was that snake slept at the base. Upwards the serpent climbs. But there, at the base, where the trunk begins, the two legs of man separates to take root firmly on the ground. Here, too, the seed takes its beginning.

Rising from the ground, and going up, the serpent slithers and comes to rest a moment at the stomach plexus. Then, it pulsates further up into the heart, and continues its ascent to the throat, tickling with the vibration of voice. Further up, it continues to brush the brow as it peers outward from the eyes that see outside. Finally it crowns the treetop with the fruit of knowledge and bites it, opening its inner eye to see and hear all that is within its journey of discovery. *Oh, Rhythm ... Rhythm ... Rhythm* make this journey one of song.

The living, breathing serpent takes a breath into eternity. *Breath ... Breath ... Breathe.*

To honor the snake, on which they lived, was only one of the reasons this tribe who lived away from the major inlier metropolis, on an outlier cove by the sea, called themselves The Fey of the Snake. That, and the very important honor of a visit from a legendary Mother of the stars ... so very long ago.

The tribe honored the energy center they bore within as they honored the sun which also brought forth great light. Indeed, that energy being the energy which the snake contains within. This is the *GNOS.*

"ALL RAYS FROM THE SUN ARE LIGHT THAT IS ONE."

It was a simple mantra that gave all the tribal outliers of the Snake of the Sea unity ... all peoples a harmony ... and all the peoples of the Snake one common beginning.

Sionee's straight song allowed the imagination of the dancers and the spectators to soar together in shared realms of remembering.

The pulse of the universe massaged Sion's bare feet. Mimicking the undulations of the snake, she led the dance into a final circle at the edge of the arena, close to the spectators. The circle was completed when the head of the snake met its own tail. The rhythm of the dance steps slowed down, after the final note of a conch horn blasted the power of the dance into the infinite spaces of the universe.

The snake spiral broke up and the dancers now sat down to watch the dancer who had led them at the snake's head. It was she who would tell the rest of the story on this night.

A hushed silence filled the circle space as the drums beat ever so softly. Sion took tentative soft steps to begin her dance. The flutes barely whispered their trill. The water birds paused in their night shrills.

Alone in the circle, Sion stood on the threshold of two worlds. Lights from the fire flickered on faces lit up with awe. As everyone waited for Songkeeper to begin the song, anticipation was high.

All eyes were on Alsionee Tree Song.

No one noticed as the grass at the circle edge parted slightly ... ever so slightly.

~~~

Another breath ... she took another. *Ah, Breath ... Breath ... Breathing.*

The smoke of the herbs the Songkeepers were throwing into the fire circled into a spiral, sending its scented power to the four directions and beyond ... to the fifth ... and the sixth ... and the seventh of spirit.

The fragrance enchanted Sionee Song Tree in magic. She was more than the snake head. She was Mother Snake. She was spirit.

Alsionee paused for an eternal moment, close to the reed side of the dance circle. A night hawk shrieked. The bright star flashed high in the Sapphire Blue above, as it crept closer to greet the dawn.

Then, quick as a ray that streams its light to come forth, Sionee threw her mother's fine spun veil from off her body and tossed it high in the air above her head. Now ... her only raiment was her long glimmering hair. It fell like a waterfall down her back, around her shoulders, and over her breasts as it spilled gloriously down long slender legs in waves of fire-lit shine.

When she tossed the veil above her head, she released a sprinkling of fine gold dust that now fell softly around her naked body, clad only in two feathers that she wore on gossamer ribbons twined in her hair.

The gold dust fell in a soft glitter of slow motion. Each tiny particle mirrored the reflection of the fire flame as each danced its descent slowly, like filaments of air-born dandelion. Her body was covered in a cloak of shimmering stars.

Bare as the day she was born, Sionee Tree Song was clothed in light.

The viewers stopped their breaths in gasps of awe at their

Songkeeper who was as luminous as a star that graced the Sapphire Blue.

Her costume of no costume reflected an *AHDAWN* so beautiful this dance would long be spoken of.

Alsionee bent gracefully to lift up the veil that had danced its dance softly to the ground to spill its sparkling treasure, to float on time-stilled wings and come to rest on Gaia's soft earth.

~~~

The cheeks were yellow like the petals of a daffodil and smooth, like soft dove wing.

There was a bare hinder part poised at swatting position right before his eyes, and what a lovely hinder part it was!

He resisted the urge to reach out. This is what he liked so much about these earth animals. They had no inhibitions. Well, though, neither did he, himself. It was something his mother had taught him.

~~~

When the last luminous flake of gold fell at her feet and left Sion exposed fully to the nightfire air, she let her scarf swirl again. It trailed her slim ankles like drifting smoke as she danced. Fleetingly, it floated across the curves of her body as if it lived.

The gossamer web caught the flickering lights of the fire as it stirred the pattern of the flame to dance upon her skin, and in her hair and sparking in her eyes. Like an orb that dances its spiral around the sun, she danced around the fire, increasing her whirl from the center out.

Some said that she was beginning the sun dance slowly, perhaps to sing the Gnos soon. Others said that she was still snake, having molted her gossamer skin and moving now in the pattern of energy.

Her song became wind song. Her wind song became snake song. She dropped to the ground on her belly and moved her body in wiggles and squiggles as she inched on the tamped earth floor in serpentine ballet.

Over the sweet earth she articulated, oblivious and happy as sand stuck to every part of her naked oil-glistened skin.

The earth sang to her in the sweetness of the grass at the fire edge. *"COME DANCE THIS DANCE WITH ME!"*

She moved in the motion of snake. Enchanted, the observers raptly watched Alsionee Song Tree weave her story in beguiling beauty, quite unlike anything they had ever seen.

~~~

He, too, was beguiled as he watched, hidden. He thrust the grass aside. His robe fell from his shoulders as he stood. Her beauty was too much to resist, beyond even the attempt to do so! Flame from the fire illuminated his tall and perfect body, naked and glorious in its brightness.

It appeared to all the spectators that this one had materialized from the sun's first ray.

They gasped! Had another come forth? Surely, it was another dweller of the Sapphire Blue. However, he didn't look like just another sea creature, as some fires told of the fish headed ones who came from sky's sea. He looked like a Fey, like themselves, give or take a little intensity of skin brightness.

~~~

Ea joined the girl in the dance. In imitation of the nas creature he coiled his body above hers. If she wanted snake, he would be a snake.

She smelled like cedar boughs and honey locust. Oh, he knew this one.

He had seen her bathing in the hot pool by the river. Neither on the whole of Nibiru or Ki, had he ever beheld such finesse in form or face of beauty most excellent.

Together, the two entwined naked. leg over leg, arm over arm, belly undulating with belly, four legs becoming no legs, four arms becoming no arms, one heart becoming one heart, one body becoming one body, even in spirit ... ALL becoming one.

Together, they shared the same space on the sweet earth that embraced their shared form.

Sionee lifted her head to gaze into two moon eyes. Or, were they not silver, but the hue of the green Gaia fallen with shadow? Too, she could see the flame of an emerald fire moldering there.

He gazed into eyes of dark topaz fire. Or, was it amber fire in the flame? Even yet, her eyes were soft and wide, innocent like a young gazelle.

His tongue reached out to flicker hers in kiss of soft, sweet soul. Her moist lips parted and her tongue touched his.

"Sionee, Sionee!" A loud scream pierced the night with a hole that woke her entrancement. Her eyes opened wide.

The crowd buzzed, exclaiming that another had come who fell from the Sapphire Blue to dance with Songkeeper Alsionee of Song Tree.

Sionee saw herself lying covered with dust from head to toe and all the places in between, and she was wrapped in the arms of a fish head!

Owl eyes flashed before her ... eyes the wrong color of orange ... too bright. She picked up her veil and ran to the birth caves where she heard Coelle calling her name.

Chapter Five

In a grotto beneath the rising light of an extraordinary and luminous star ... at the second turn of the sun wheel on the ever gentle Snake of the Sea, Coelle lay almost breathless in the womb chamber. She was attended to by three elder birth mothers.

A soft fire flickered shadows of light and darkness across the smooth polished rock, and created the motion of a life-breath that pulsed across the rounded walls. The subtle pattern of wavering firelight was warm and soothing, lending a comfort of sacred ambiance.

The attendants were mindful that the birth would likely take hours, and were very hopeful that the child would be born with the full rise of the morning star.

At the portal of the cave, the cool sand reminded Sionee to stop and take a breath. Flustered, confused and frightened, she paused a moment at the door.

These things about life and death she understood. It was the recent arrival of an unknown people from the stars that she didn't understand. Everyone knew that they had arrived, but the few encounters anyone had experienced with them led her people to believe that the fish head were of a different nature than Mother Sofeya had been. Their comings and goings certainly seemed different than She Who from the Stars Came.

This one in particular made her feel quite uncomfortable.

"Fear chases one like an arrow." **THIS MY MOTHER TAUGHT ME HOW TO SING ...** She had often enough heard these very words when she was a child.

"It will bite you in the butt."

"*If I let it.*" Alsionee almost spoke the words out loud, but stopped herself just short of saying them. The thought turned to air, unsaid. "*If I let it.*"

41

In her heart, the words were heard. Double damn that sordidly-repulsive so called fish head, for daring to enter the sacred ground of the Snake dancers. Her anger was so great she felt trembling vibrations of heat shake her body.

Sion forced herself to be still. Coelle needed her now. She would deal with this later.

The flickering fire danced across a triple spiral symbol that was carved in the stone above the portal entrance.

Sion gasped when a flicker from the fire's reflection chased away a shadow from its design, and flashed a brilliant hue over the image, as if to show her something. The spirals were turning, spinning ... surely they were ... just as the dance outside had moved in a rhythmical swirling that disappeared into a solid center. Something she could not remember stirred within.

Somewhere, she had already danced the first spiral as depicted in the carving. But how could she have missed in the dance of the second ... and the third? Ah, yes something inside of her was not complete! What were the spirals trying to tell her?

"Sion! Oh, Sionee you came! Did you dance?"

Coelle's cries were weaker now. Sion was alarmed at the frantic breathlessness of her sister-friend, who had been closest to her of all living people since she was but a babe.

"Coelle, dear, Be Blessed now. I am here ... the dance goes on. The other Songkeepers are there to finish the song. I danced the GNOS."

Sion's face flushed. Should she speak in real words? Coelle was in no shape to hear with her heart ears. Or was she? Maybe she was exactly in a place to hear what the heart said.

Coelle reached for Sion's hand. "Sister, at the western gate, the swans are singing. I see them at the portal ... hundreds of them! They are so beautiful!" For a moment a smile crossed Coelle's lips.

"My steps on the sun trail have led me to a bridge which I must cross now ... over the waters."

At that point, Coelle lapsed into a fitful sleep, slipping into release from the wracking pains that gnashed at her body.

Sion asked an attendant for some laurel tea to soothe Coelle. She knew her friend wasn't where she could hear her speak. *"Don't go sister. Don't go!"*

Maybe if she was, she would break her 'no word' vow ... just this time ... just a few words for her sister. Though likely, it would only be to say - "Goodbye, I love you!"

Past the midnight hour and into the first hour of morning, Sion quietly watched at Coelle's side. Sometimes she just held to her sister's hand and sang to her softly. Other times she washed her hot forehead with a cool cloth.

The minutes stretched into what seemed like hours and the hours, abided in intermittent minutes, that seemed to last forever. Sionee was too weary and too numb to do anything but try to etch a picture of Coelle's face into her memory.

Every time Coelle's stomach moved and her sister cried out in pain, Sionee saw glimpses of owl eyes too bright.

The long hours stretched into futile reaches of nothing but silence. Sionee waited for the morning to come, watching for the light of the morning star to make her appearance known through the portal in the cave ceiling, above the bed where the mother lay. Then, it would be that the morning star would dance across the rounded walls of the womb room and send her bright spark directly over the new mother. The star would bring to Gaia's horizon one of her most radiant new starlings, just before dawn.

When Sion supposed she could see the color of night lighten its hue, Coelle opened her eyes again. The weakness in her voice had gone.

"The purple mist is the most beautiful sight, Sionee. You must listen to me now. Oh, listen! You always tried to get me to listen with the eyes that hear the heart beat." Coelle smiled brightly. "Now it is time for you to hear."

"I'm listening." Sion spoke the words. Just this once

"There is something, Sion, that I remember. Do you? I am beginning to see and I must tell you ..." Coelle paused in a scream of pain.

"It hurts sister. It really hurts. Ooooooooah !

"Cyex is the father. Remember when we bathed for the springtime ceremony at the hot pools and we met him in the wild woods
on the way home? I stayed there with him while you got disgusted
and went home.

"We made love there. It was my first time."

Sionee felt the hairs on the round-side of her wrists stand
straight upward in a sudden shiver as Coelle continued.

"It was sweet ... so sweet." A wide smile spread across Coelle's
dear face. "So unlike when ..." At this point, Coelle's smile turned into
a slight frown and she continued elsewhere.

"Tell him for me, won't you, how very much I love him. Oh, Sion,
the purple mist entices me! I must go ... must go!"

Crying then, Sionee pressed Coelle's hand.

"Sionee, sister! You will take care of my little girl? Please promise me that you will? You ... Sionee, pleeeeeease!"

Coelle's womb tore open.

A spark flashed at that moment in the portal enclosure. It was
precisely daybreak when the girl child was born.

The attending birth mother took the child to wrap and wash her.

Sionee did not cry. She was thinking about how the wild apples
in Gaia's vast garden lost their leaves at the cycle of the sun. But they
always came back.

~~~

Alsionee longed for the comfort of the well-worn spot among
the branches of the ancient yellow cedar. She decided it was time to
leave now, and seek her solace. Afterwards, surely a little nap would
restore her waning spirits. She gave Coelle a kiss on the cheek and
turned to leave the birthing room.

A little peace would go a long way to ease the anxiety of these
last long hours. It was barely early. The morning birds were still
singing their morning song. If she hurried she could catch the colors of the sun as it transformed the sea waters into a mirrored surface of skies that undulated and rippled morning gold. She might

yet see Coelle dancing above the waves at the beach before the tide changed.

"Miss Song Tree, wait. You forgot something."

The elder birth mother put a warm moist bundle into Alsionee's arms. It breathed ...

Sion's heart stopped.

"She seems to be healthy as an apple sapling in the springtime. I'd watch her closely darling, especially for a day or two, being so new to this world ... and all the travail she must have experienced trying to come out. Poor little thing."

Alsionee could feel the hairs on her big toe stand up straight. Coelle lay departed and all the birthing mother could think about was the poor baby. The smile on the old lady's face as she crooned at the child did little to make her toe hairs resettle.

The kind grandmother took Sionee's hand and led her to the birth-side table and motioned for her to sit the babe down.

"Would you like to see your new daughter?"

All the hairs of both her entire lower limbs rose at this point, one by one ... all the way up to her ... well ...

"But ... but ... ." Disregarding her vow again, Sionee only managed to gasp.

The grandmother removed the blankets from the new infant.

Sion snuck a peek and gasped some more. No wonder Coelle's womb had torn open.

It wasn't the first time Sionee had held a newborn. It was almost the first time.

As a Songkeeper in training, Sion had assisted in a few of the birth events so as to experience the joy of which it was said there was no greater. But after this close up, she wasn't exactly feeling impressed. She had never, however surely seen a baby this humongous. She had a really big head.

"She's a big one!" The birthing mother agreed, smiling at the baby. "It is why our Coelle had such a hard time at her own departure and this one's arrival."

Sion had an itch in her throat that made her cough.

"The baby's color ... just look at that!" The old woman stepped back to admire in awe. "They say you danced at nightfire with a fish head before you came into the birthing cave!"

~~~

Indeed, she did recall that she had danced with a fish beneath the light of the moon, when her AHDAWN was only partially wrecked ... AND LOOK AT IT NOW!

The child's skin was colored like ... well, maybe like the color at the top of gazelle milk in the creamery. It was almost white, almost pink rosy with a rich brightness ... and her eyes! The last time she had looked into Coelle's eyes, they were the color brown, as were the vast majority of all People of the Snake's eyes, and Cyex's eyes, as well.

Sionee could easily recall the exact color of Cyex's eyes as the two of them gazed over the mists of the rock ledge, when they lay on their tummies and peered out into the rainbow-colored falls when they were kids.

For it was he ... from the boy's huts ... that she had rendezvoused with to climb the deep cliff when they were but children.

His eyes were the deepest hue of a no-moon night ... almost black.

How could this child have eyes the color of meadow green, and moon-pale skin with cheeks of pink rose, and a big head? Surely, did she not have a big head?

In response to the deep inspection she was getting, the baby looked directly at Alsionee.

Suddenly, coming from the baby's eyes the whole dim womb chamber lit up as if the sun was shining inside through dawns rays.

Sion gasped and turned to flee.

"Sion?" The birth matron called. "The name! You must take her, and present her to the people you danced for, with the name you have chosen. They have waited through the whole night long."

Alsionee ran as fast as a sprinting gazelle out the door and past the crowd. So quick was she, that ever after the songs that were sung told of how their new and most beloved Songkeeper was so illumined by her dance with the good fisher head, that she appeared as invisible the whole day long.

~~~

As far as Alsionee Tree Song was concerned, she couldn't get to the Motherland of the Lemming fast enough.

Could she be so lucky to find that if she ran fast enough to the ship port one of the boats sending trade that way would be available to leave promptly? Because she most definitely must catch a ride.

However, being that her own work in the production of valuable pots involved the trade route, she knew that there would be no boats in sail until noon.

Could she hide in the branches of her and mamun's tree until that time?

If ever she needed the tree, it would be now. Instead however, she hurried to the wildwoods edge, where she called Vastari, her wild white unicorn. She needed a ride to the edge of the sea so she could be there when the boats came in.

Sion stood on a hill that rose into the tree line that separated grass meadow from forest and made her long whistle neigh. It echoed throughout all the wildwoods and shook the trees with a tremble of vibration.

Vastari arrived with the breath of the wind. Sionee's eyes lit up at the sight of her beautiful white unicorn. Sion had traded for her from the lands east across the sea. Should she go there instead of Lemming land? Dang it all. She was going to miss Vastari ... and the yellow cedar ... and the beautiful home she was going to build for herself in the circle of the Wisdom Trees right next to the one her mother had built.

There was a bird perched on top of Vastari's head. It was the kingfisher.

"*Where did you come from?*" Sionee twitted.

"*My master was in the forest, gathering. I met this lovely unicorn there, and was speaking with her when you called. I hitched a ride with her ... told her there was something that I needed to remind you of."*

"Who is your master?" Sionee asked, curious.

"By and By," the bird replied. *"For now, though, I have come to ask you a question only you can answer."*

"Hurry then, if you must," Sion replied. *"I shall hasten."*

"What is a bird?" He inquired.

"Right now I think you are a nuisance." She grabbed hold of Vastari's mane and mounted, pointing her foot to give her unicorn the thrust that would bid her to depart.

"Are we the flutter of wings? Or are we the song?"

Sionee stopped short.

"Are we what you see when you look at us ... or are we what we see when we look at ourselves? What kind of a dunderhead are you anyway?" The bird added hastily without waiting for her to reply.

"Uuuuuuuuuuuuhh!" It was as all the girl could send with her thought. What kind was she?

"When you are blessed by a gift from She Who Creates, and you say 'no' ... ."

"I ..."

"You are a dunderhead. That is what I see you as." The bird cocked his little head and looked at her, eye to eye.

Suddenly she wasn't in quite as big of a hurry. There was another boat at mid-afternoon. This was going to take a bit of thought.

Chapter Six

The Annunaki, who lived back home on a world of a different nature than the third dimension of Ki, were so extreme in their intelligence that they could create anything. From a simple piece of glass made to look at the tiniest of items through to the bio-genetics of supreme physical forms, they could create anything with matter.

Somehow, of all the wonders of science that were brought forth on Nibiru, none were as fine as this particular piece he was holding right now.

Ea sat at the desk in his small sanctum and held a small item in his fingers. The device looked like a quill, and had the same properties of function. It was made to last forever.

His mother had given it to him just as he boarded the ship for the journey to Ki so very long ago.

Ea studied the writing instrument and was quiet. His brow wrinkled as he gazed. It was a gift that she, top scientist of Nibiru and the universe as like, had created from simple particles of earth materials. It was made in the nature of ... well nature.

The tool mimicked the simple qualities of a feather from one of Ki's birds, and was the most marvelous of all inventions, certainly surpassing this.

Ea tossed a small commuting device to the edge of the desk, where it fell to the floor with a loud thud. He left it there. He didn't need it at this present time.

He pondered on the golden quill his mother had made for him. She had pounded the gold thin with her own hands and a mallet. She sculpted it into the design of a feather, minus the fluff and other short-lived properties, such as disintegration, that a real feather would have within time.

This quill would last forever, as gold does. It also had quite a beauty, as did everything his mother created. She had inserted studs into its short length, consisting of tiny blue crystals she said had come from Ki's ocean.

"Once I danced with a Ki creature!" Her eyes twinkled as she laughed in that way only his mother could laugh.

"Before I left the matter planet, he gave these to me." She had that faraway look in her eyes as she spoke of Ki, the look he knew belonged only to his mother.

She had also inscribed precisely on the golden quill, letters so tiny he had to get his looking glass out to see that it read: LOVE.

"LOVE IS THE LAW," mother had said. "It is the only law. Other laws are simply for fools."

Ea smiled. Very early on he had learned that the laws were of upmost importance on Nibiru. He would be a fool not to follow them and even a bigger fool not to *appear* that he was following them.

His mother had taught him well. He just didn't get caught.

He took a drink from the flask of white wine he had learned was much better than any imbibition's that came from the fruits of Nibiru, even of a like species. He licked a drop that ran from the corners of his mouth.

"The love law is a good law mother." He would tell her that later, on the transmitter if it wasn't broke, after he drank just a little more ... not too much ... of the fine juice he had learned to produce after watching the Ki inhabitants make the potent concoction.

Now, if love was as good as the wine he could understand it perhaps, but for now he must scribe.

His mother had also given him a fine journal she had designed of papyri pages, bound in gold carved leafing.

"The computers have their purpose in recording the scientific information," she had whispered to him, as whisper she did ... often.

"Don't forget, son, to do your scribing in here!" She handed him the journal. "It is with words written by hand that your heart hears again the things which your mother has taught you."

He had found it to be true. The computing device was totally inadequate to record the emotions of one's heart. The records on the machine could be traced by any of the emotionless Annunaki who the computer was fine for ... all they needed as a matter of fact. Like minds attract like minds, or so it was said. His fellow residents of the Perfect World were becoming the technology they created ... a bunch of sputtering robots.

There were other secrets as well, that she who was the most brilliant, and the most intelligent, and the most beautiful scientist on all of Nibiru ... or the vast universe elsewhere ... had given him.

Like the gold!

"Fools easily believe when you bend certain information just a wee bit," she told him. "You must tell them that you will go to Ki to get gold for them," she had whispered.

"But you and I both know son, what is really making the atmosphere of our world wane. Underdeveloped minds grow soft by not thinking or feeling ... and just would not get it.

"On Ki there is gold of physical nature, and it is something that Nibiru perceives as value to their perversion.

"Your mission is manifold. You will tell them you are going to Ki to search for gold to save our world. Then, save our world, son."

Ea smiled.

"Now, Ea, you do understand about the gold, do you not?"

"Oh, mother, of course I do. Your love has taught me superbly."

He had expected to find more gold on Ki by now. He'd been here sars enough. Maybe he was forgetting what the real gold Ki offered was.

Ea studied the fish that swam into his view from the big porthole in his reflection room just off the laboratory.

The fish were gold ... real gold and shining. So what exactly was real, anyway? The fish appeared genuine, in truth, much more beautiful than a mere rock. The way they moved to and fro ... back and forth ... their motions were gentle and flowing, like virtual lights in the aqua teal waters of the sea just on the other side of the window in his secret chamber.

The artificial lights he had placed to better see the dark depths of deep water just beyond, sent soft and natural illumination to the fish. Ea took profound delight in observing them. They swam right up to the big window, curious, and bumped the glass softly with their noses.

The gold on the big one that swam in graceful design right before him was of a color far richer than the gold that had to be laboriously dug from the ground beneath Ki. The fish-bright hue was so luminous the very glimpse of it was the gold for the heart.

Further, about gold ... gold was specifically why he had chosen to come to Abzukia after Enlil had taken his home on the reed-strewn gulf of the first landing.

Ea saw reflected on the glass a bitterness that briefly darkened his usually bright countenance.

After his little brother Enlil came to Eridu, Ea's already established home on Ki, he usurped by law the command. And, with it, he took possession of Ea's home and land, as if he owned it. He did have legal command of Ea's first home, as if it was a trophy. But ... it was Ea's trophy, and so much more. It was his home! He had built it, improved it, and made it what it was ... and all so his brother could take glory of it!

The fish came right up to the glass and pressed his nose against the clear barrier and opened its mouth wide. Ea could count every tooth, and he did so, every one of them with great interest. The fish had such a funny face. Ea smiled.

Now, in the watery country it wasn't so bad here. It had a beauty that surpassed anything he could have hoped to call his second home. Here, there was great promise of abundant gold. Already great mines had been developed, and had made it possible to send much gold back to Nibiru.

The fish were so graceful, and he loved to just watch them in motion. They were like the rhythm of a girl from Ki who danced ... the motion of her scarf flowed like the seaweed beneath the sea, back and forth across her ankles. That vision of her reminded him, too, of her scent that was like the fragrance of golden daffodil flowers beneath the sun, whose petals were the color of the gold that floated gently from her shawl, soft as falling stars that spiraled in a swirling, golden circle around her naked body. Her beauty was the truest gold he had ever seen, far surpassing the 'real' flakes that fell at her feet to be trod upon.

Ea picked up the pen and the journal his mother had given him. He wrote in it only upon the most special of occasions.

"I met a girl of the earthen shore. Her beauty far surpasses gold. My Daffinina makes gold a worthless rock, as common as are all the women of Nibiru ... besides you mother ... there is none other who can equal my girl in a fraction of one against one hundred sars."

~~~

The damn blasted thing didn't break. Beeeep ... beeeep ... beeeeeeep ...

He refused to have the alert tone come over as music like most of the communication devices did. The beeps did just fine. Music had its place at the base of feelings, not on a common computing device, for crying out loud.

Automatically, definitely without much thought, he picked the thing up and pushed the button. Not even a voice responded ... just words flashing across the screen that he could barely see without his looking glasses. The screen was so tiny.

Now where were those damn things? They were here just a moment ago. He muttered disgust as his fingers lifted up the reed papers scattered across his desk. He found them pushed beneath his golden journal. Gently he set it aside, coming sharply out of the state of bliss he had sunk into for just moments. He pushed the button again to restore the message that had just bleeped forth.

" ... am coming to the Abzu to inspect the mining operations ... more gold needed. The Igigi are growing weary of their still too heavy toil. The lu lu you gave us just aren't panning out quite like you said. 'Our' dear, sweet Ninmah will arrive at my side ... the two of us. QUITE WELL, she accommodates me, brother. See you soon ... Enlil."

Ea cursed. His royal **high ass** was coming! Well bless the damned Ki-ground he walked on. Aaaaaaaaaaaaugh!

Now ... Ninmah ... he wasn't sure if he was glad she was coming or not. Oh, but of course, he was. It was always a pleasure to see his radiant, dear half-sister ... well, sometimes more than others.

It was a little uneasy though. Especially as it sounded like she still spent so much time with Enlil.

He thought that he could have given her more credit than that. Sometimes Ninmah seemed to have a little bit of emotion ... just a little.

He should know. They had been promised to wed ... as if the marrying part meant anything other than politics, anyway.

Ea found pleasing sex to be quite unrelated to marriage. With it or without it, sex was sex. What did the insertion of parts have to do with marriage, anyhow? Or what marriage was supposed to be ... a partnership, give or take love.

Damkina had been given to him, in the way of technology and politicolology. She came from the South. He came from the North. In order to keep the two regions of Nibiru at peace, she was given to him to marry. No! She'd been forced upon him in marriage. It was the law.

As far as he was concerned the only good thing that came out of Damkina was his son, Mordukku ... his delightful first son, who everyone commonly called Marduk. But ... he hadn't been born because of good sex.

Now, Ninmah ... the rutting with her was an entirely different manner. She was extremely talented. Aaaaaaah! He'd hoped to have a son with her, but he and Ninmah were history.

It was when Ea was young ... so young. He thought he was in love. Well, actually, he loved her.

How proud he was when Ninmah bore him their first child. It turned out, the child was a daughter. And, the next child they had was also a daughter ... and the next, a girl. They were all beautiful daughters, indeed, absolutely beautiful. But he needed a son.

Then, Enlil, who he had loved when he was little, grew up. Enlil was the first un-concubined son born of Anu's seed with his half-sister-wife, and all this before Enlil became spouse to his Ninlil.

He'd never forgive Enlil for so purposely taking Ninmah's affections away. If he could forgive his little brother, second son of Anu for usurping the power of the firstborn, maybe he would. It was the law.

However, the fact that he took Ninmah away from him ... now that ... as painful as the laws of sister-born babies had been to Ea, first-born of Anu ... What kind of stupid law made Ninmah go and have sex with the little twit?

It had been a slap in the face. Worse, when Ninmah had a son, Ninurta, she announced that it was Enlil's.

It was perhaps the first time Anu, their father, noticed the rivalry between the two brothers.

He cursed Ninmah for the trouble she stirred up and declared that ever after she would be the wife of no one ... only a mistress.

It was then that Damkina, daughter of Alulu, was forced to Ea in marriage. Enlil later met the young nurse, a sud, who became his Ninlil to his Enlil.

Ea was certain that Enlil really loved his wife. She was a beauty, but too innocent for Enlil.

It did bother Ea that Enlil and Ninmah were still clearly quite companionable. Ea tried not to picture Ninmah lying against the cushions, her legs spread open, and Enlil ... Aaaaaaaaaaaaaaaaugh!

His emotions shaking, Ea turned again to watch the fish, letting the motions of the aqua waters still his turbulent mind. He'd think of the two of them when they got here ... not now.

Chapter Seven

The shadows had long disappeared from the trees at the forest edge. Sion took measure of the suns height and determined that the morning session of learning was far past. She was seeking Marisol of the sparkling shell *"Mother Marisol,"* she thought noisily in her head, *"please be there, please be there."*

Sion quickly entered through the little-domed door of the shell. Marisol was there, but she was not alone!

With one hand, Marisol reached out and grabbed Sion as the girl tried to hastily retreat.

"Daughter, daughter, you must see how beautiful this one is."

Marisol was laughing and singing and dancing about the room like Sion had never seen before. She held a baby in her arms and was happily crooning.

Her heart pounding, Sion released herself from Marisol's grip. She knew better than to try and flee again.

The baby looked directly into her eyes and did that light thing again.

Sion shivered in fright. *"Marisol, why do her eyes do that?"*

"She carries within her the light of the bright star."

"I, too ... and the others at the huts of learning are all Sisters from the Song Star. Our eyes don't look like that!"

Marisol swung the child in arms held high and giggled at the baby's wide eyes. "Oh, no, my child. You have bright eyes, yes, bright eyes, indeed. I believe this girl's light shines from a star ... who knows what star it is except for a certain star of our long ago songs ... a fey star perhaps.

"Did the fish head whisper to you, daughter, which star he came from when you two tangled in the sands?"

"Marisol, this child came from Cy. Coelle told me so. He is the father. How can this be?"

Sion's cheeks were hot ... red hot. She didn't want to look at the child any longer.

"Sionee, darling, you must look at your new daughter. She is delightful and a child of magic no matter whose seed from which she sprang. Also, you must remember one important thing. She came from Coelle, Blessed Be her name."

Marisol lay the child down on a soft board lined with a thin cushion of swaddling feathers, and removed the down from the child's pearl-like body.

Sion had to look ... had to for a moment ..., "aaaaaaaaaaaugh!"

The child was too big ... so big and white, too ... not like the children of the Snake of the Sea, in the northern regions, anyhow. Though pale in comparison to many of Gaia's children, even they were not that milk-cream colored. The baby's over large head was almost bald ... just the slightest fuzz at the very top. It looked like the finest trace of powdered gold dust, and it had the glints of a sparkle to it.

When Marisol turned to fetch something and wasn't looking, Sionee's hand reached out tentatively to rub her fingers across the downy softness of the child's head.

The infant's eyes were as deep as the furthest pool of the ocean and drew one's gaze into still waters ... not that she noticed or anything.

While not ugly, the child was actually beautiful beyond understanding. Alsionee was uneasy at the baby's eyes. They put her in mind of owl eyes, not quite the right color and ...

"Sion, where are you going dear?" Marisol's hand shot out to detain her again.

"I'm going where I can find out from where this baby came!" Sion replied in determination.

"Face the arrow square," mamun always said. "Don't let fear chase you." The child made Sion's heart pound terrifically in fear.

"Now wait a moment girl. You must face your responsibility. Where you go, she goes." Marisol bundled the baby up and placed the warm bundle in Sionee's arms.

Sion forced herself to close her arms around the child, lest the wee one fall.

The baby's eyelids fluttered over liquid jewel eyes. The long lashes curled like dark butterfly wing, on the petals of a white rose. Gently her little lids closed and she slept.

Sionee bent her head and felt the baby's warm breath tickling her cheek. A soft scent like the blossoms of jasmine arose from the baby. It was even sweeter, but ...

"Mother Marisol, I am at a loss. What do I do? This child is not mine." Sionee began to sob.

"Oh, but she is. Coelle gave her to you, a gift from Mothersky, herself. Tell me you did not know this was to be, because if you do, I shall not believe you, not for a minute."

"I am only sixteen sun spins. I don't know how to take care of a baby."

Marisol laughed. "Be Blessed Thou, child. Say those things to any new mother. We all have fears, girl."

"But wouldn't a mother of a bear baby be afraid if she were given the baby of an alligator?"

"This is no reptile we are speaking of Alsionee Tree Song. Look at her. She is your daughter."

"But how do I feed her?"

"You have been gone well over half the day, girl. She has already been fed. Alita Red Lily has agreed to feed her. You were not aware, were you that Alita also bore a child only a few hours after our Coelle. She has milk in abundance. She is a strong woman. We must have gratefulness in our AHDAWN for her."

It didn't surprise her that another birth had followed soon after Coelle's babe. At springtime celebrations many new lives were planted.

Spring was the time for the seed. The harvest occurred at the next half of the circle spin, hopefully on Yule night, or at least close. All mothers hoped to have daughters of light born to the Sisterhood of Song at the bright star's rising.

"Yes, Sion, there are ways dear." Marisol continued. "You do know, do you not, that you can keep a supply of fresh milk in a cool place for when you are distant from Alita?

"Babies need food every few hours, and I know you wouldn't want to move in with Alita. You spoke fondly of your plans to build your own home. I'd advise staying quite close, though to Alita.

"I would make friends with her, but get on with your own life. Adjustments can be made. Ask any mother."

"I'll leave the baby with the Songkeeper trainees when I get busy. This is what I will do."

"Occasionally Sion, occasionally. But only occasionally. The girls have already many young to tend, who have no mothers.

"She is yours now. Do with her as any mother does when her babe arrives."

"What's that?"

"Love her well."

Tingles of hot blood shot up through the skin of her face and flushed upwards to the top of her brain and down to her toes and made them prickle. Sionee took the sleeping child and proceeded to her room in the maiden huts.

~~~

She wasn't inside long. How she wanted to sit on the edge of her bed for a brief moment, then lay down, even for just a breath of time. She was tired.

How long had it been since that celebration of doom, and the running back and forth she'd been doing in the attempt to find some refuge from this?

It didn't take Sionee long to realize she had a dilemma. The baby peed on her, making her linen shift wet. How long did it take before someone could smell dried pee? She didn't want to smell like pee.

Sion lay the baby down on the bed, wishing for a long moment that she, herself could be a baby again. She turned to find a clean shift and the baby started screaming again ... raucously.

Startled, Sion almost wet herself. Was the child alright? In panic, she picked the baby up. The baby couldn't be cold, was she?

What would she use to wrap the baby in? The down mattress and the swaddling the elder mothers had wrapped her in were wet. She picked up her own soft linen coverlet and wrapped it around the child who seemed to get lost in the sumptuous folds.

Alsionee ripped the thin coverlet in four pieces along the grain lines of the fabric.

The dinner bell peeled. Sion turned to wash her hands in the washbowl so she could eat, she was absolutely famished.

It was a reflex action, however. For an instant she had almost forgotten. Could she leave the squalling baby on the bed just for a few minutes while she gulped some grub? Surely she'd be safe. Sionee didn't think she'd eaten anything since before the celebration.

Her growling stomach, which she could feel rather than hear, because of the baby's screams, said yes. But the baby's screeches told her no ... and again ... yes. How she would love to not hear this noise for just a moment even.

"Every few hours," Marisol had said. Of course, the child was likely hungry. Sion wondered if Sion baby could cry. She was but a big baby herself. She wanted to eat, but she had to feed this incessantly screaming child instead.

~~~

Knocking at the threshold door to Alita's small hut, she waited and waited and waited.

Finally, Sion heard, "Come in." Alita was sitting in bed eating bean soup while she comfortably fed her wee one. Sion was struck at how small her baby was.

Apparently, someone had brought the new birth mother a tray, after all, it was appropriate for someone who had just given birth to rest awhile, and for someone to take care of her while she recovered.

"It smells good," Sionee said, greeting Alita.

"It won't for long!" Alita replied, and then giggled. "Did you know, the older Songkeepers told me this: that when a mother eats beans, the music of the fruit also goes into her milk? I am going to eat each and every spoonful of these singing toot fruits. It takes much strength out of a mother to birth life," She added. "You wouldn't know."

Sionee stared blankly around the room, taking note of the little bed of swaddling clothes, and the various linens and wash pieces and things. It would be quite a job collecting the supplies a baby required.

Of course, she wouldn't know. Sionee tried to make light of the comment of observation that Alita had made. It was true.

"*Greetings, sister.*" Sion gestured. "*Be Blessed Thou, for your ample gift.*" She handed the baby to Alita, who nestled the child in the crook of her other arm, snug as a possum.

"Lilitu is much smaller than this little giant!" Alita observed. "My little one sucks my teats like a baby elephant! But as far as elephants, your child has the head of a mammoth.

"I heard she sent our Coelle to the other side, ripped her right open! I hope I have enough milk for a child this big, and that she doesn't bite me or something ... being fish head or some other monstrosity."

Alita let the linen shift fall from her bent shoulders. Both of her breasts were ready for the work. Bending just a bit forward, Alita cupped her hands and proudly squeezed the nipple while Sionee watched two big drops of milk drizzle downward, horrified.

AMPLE gifts ... right. The breasts were as big as over ripe yellow melons after their peak time, mushy at that. Alita thrust her breasts forward, jiggling them in Sion's face, and almost smothered the babies as she guided both nipples to the tiny mouths.

Alita looked up at Sion, quite well satisfied apparently. "I have two of them." Proudly, she pulled her thumb sized nipples in and out of the frantic baby's mouths. While the milk dripped, Alita giggled.

"Yours wouldn't be big enough anyway," she assured Sionee. "So you don't have to."

Sion tried to ask Alita about the linens and the swaddlings, and how often she should bring the baby to be fed?

Alita did not hear well, especially in the manner which Sion spoke. But she had noticed Sionee's appraisal of the room.

"You'll have to go to the trading stores," Alita told Sion. "It's where those who cannot, and those who do not, go to get their things," she added.

Sion frowned as Alita did the giggling thing again, shifting her weight on the bed. "Just a bit sore down there," she explained. "But, then what would you know? You know nothing about how it feels."

Alita sat a bit upright as she continued. "You were out singing and dancing while Coelle and I were in pain, Alsionee Song Tree ... Dancing with the stars and ... poor Coelle dying.

"They say your body is still like a flower in the springtime. Not that I would have minded seeing for myself. And, the fish head ... Now, if I had been there, he would have danced with a real woman. What a story we could have told! But alas ... he had to settle for a nut, and he could have had ripe juicy melons."

Sionee was beginning to wonder if the baby had had enough.

"Since I'm going to be feeding this humongous brat ... I didn't hear what her name is. What is her name?"

Sion was silent. Alita pulled the strange looking baby from off her teat. With closed eyes, the baby's head nodded like a little bird searching for another worm.

"You are a hungry creature now, aren't you?" Alita crooned to the baby.

"Speak up girl!"

When Sionee remained quiet, Alita's voice rambled on.

"Okay, hello You!" she said, taking the child from off her breast and holding her out to examine her.

"Sionee! You just poo-pooed."

~~~

Thankful to be back at the maiden hut, Sionee washed her hands, real well.

The girls who worked in food preparation had sent her home with a bowl of barely-warm bean soup and a big chunk of hard bread.

On the way home, having been fed, the baby was asleep at last. Sion lay her on the bed and sat down at the bedside table to eat. She relished the smell of the food, but after the clean- up job she had just done she wasn't sure she had an appetite left after all.

Moments later, Sion woke up with a start to the sharp shrill of 'You' crying. Well, she didn't know what to name her. Besides that, her father could decide his little girl's name.

When she sat upright the bean soup fell to the floor, sputtering across the soft linens of the bed. Sion's shift was also on the receiving end of the mess. The bean juice was cold. She couldn't have been asleep that long, surely.

Sionee picked the baby up and gently twirled her and whirled her. That's what Marisol had been doing with the babe, and the baby wasn't crying then. You threw up!

~~~

After a bit, it became apparent that the baby would quit crying and go to sleep if Sionee held her and walked back and forth in a gentle rhythm.

If she broke the rhythm by slowing down to rest or by laying the child down, You woke up and screamed.

Sion figured she was probably hungry again. Alita had given her a little milk so she wouldn't have to be woken up during the night.

Sion shuddered as she tried not to get any of the milk on her hands ... eeeeeuuuuuu ... disgusting! She couldn't get the picture of Alita's globular breasts squirting milk out of her mind. It was almost as bad as the owl eyes she'd been seeing as of late.

From time to time, Sion got a brief chance to sit down while she fed the baby. However as soon as she got comfortable the child would resume her screaming until Sion got up and walked back and forth to lull the baby asleep for a few brief minutes.

Sion walked softly, desperate for silence. The pacing worked, but for Alsionee Tree Song, too.

In the darkness, Sion closed her itching eyes as she softly tread back and forth. Was it possible to sleep while walking?

Back and forth ... to and fro ... in a circle ... out and in, in and out ... up and down ... under and over ... and ... How many of these phrases could she think of if she kept going?

She couldn't remember at what point she found out that a person could sleep while walking. Would this night ever pass?

When dawn's first light began to gather, Sionee woke with a start. Sometime during the night she had fashioned a sling to fold You in so she wouldn't drop her while she walked half dozing, back and forth ... to and frooooo.

What was that? She'd been thinking of Coelle sometime during the night, and how Coelle loved yellow roses and that in the morning she and You would go find some yellow roses, and send the petals out to sea in honor of sister and mother.

"Unlike when..." Unlike when, what? Coelle had said these words, did she not? Before she crossed, when she spoke of Cy's skill at baby-making. "It was sweet, so sweet unlike when ..."

But she didn't finish ... didn't get the chance to ... Unlike when, what?"

The baby woke up. Her screaming promptly filled the room. The milk was gone.

Sionee gathered everything she could think of into a large pouch, the one she took when she went on journey.

She was going to take the baby back to her father.

~~~

Inside the square trading hut, a person could find anything, almost anything.

Located apart from the houses of shells, and the maiden huts, closer to where the main population of the outlier formed a cluster community, the buildings of trade were a storehouse of treasure.

At the shell huts of learning, most of the needed supplies were acquired in the making with one's hands, and with one's labor. Occasionally and rarely, the trading centers were much appreciated though.

Sion chose an assortment of wraps and soft linens that were sized for a baby. She just couldn't make them herself. The child had sort of been sprung on her. Who knows how long it would take to find papa.

She stopped at a table where fuzzy little lambs enticed her. The toys were soft. Sion sighed ... so soft. She held one up to her cheek. It was a bright blue, sort of like turquoise or a robin egg, quite unlike the real color of a lamb, but ... Sionee put one in her basket.

The lady who managed the trading transactions frowned when Sion reached for baby milk. Then, she smiled when Sionee turned around.

"Oh. But you are Songkeeper who danced with the fish head."

Sion sighed wearily.

"Songkeeper who speaks no words," the woman added. "Let me see how good my AHDAWN eyes are for hearing." She sat back to study Sionee with admiration.

"It is why you had to leave the dance so suddenly. The story has been told," she assured Sion. "Be Blessed Thou, Alsionee of the Tree Song. And, this is the child?" The tradeswoman peered in curiosity to get a good look at the baby.

"But you know, do you not, darling, that real milk is much better for wee ones?" The kind storekeeper touched the tip of her own breast as she spoke.

"But of course, you have no milk. Is there no one you know who could share?"

Alsionee was impatient. *"How much milk do I need?"* She tried to ask.

"For how long will the milk be needed, dear?" The woman answered Sionee's silence.

Sionee shook her head. She didn't know.

The woman gave her a big supply of tiny pouches, made of soft leather that squished. Each had something that resembled a nipple attached.

The maidens at the child care hut had spoken of these conveniences. Alsionee made arrangements to trade five of her big pots to the trade-woman. The woman watched as Sionee put all the milk into her one large pouch that she carried with a strap on her shoulder and struggled with the weight of the child too. The store keeper watched in awe. The baby surely was fifteen pounds or so.

Sionee made her way to the boy's huts on the furthest side of the wild-forest edge.

Chapter Eight

Sionee munched on a piece of hard bread and cheese that she had traded for at the center where those who "cannot" and those who "do not" go, as Alita had said.

The milk seemed to work just fine for both her convenience, as well as for the hungry baby.

The cheese was awful. It was not at all like the soft gazelle cheese she was so fond of that the priestesses made at the milk huts. She found however, that if she took a bite of it with the sweet apples that grew wildly in the surrounding forests, it didn't taste quite so bad.

Vastari grazed on the yellow flowers that grew in the grasses of the meadow that graced the valley curve. Sion and You stood at the edge of the tide where sea and sand overlapped as one. Sionee held the baby out to feel the mists of the billows breaking at their feet and gazed in reverence into the vast horizon of morning.

Sionee rubbed a crushed yellow rose petal on You's soft cheek. Could the child smell the sweet fragrance?

Sionee tossed a handful of the cupped wild petals into the waves where they floated like tiny boats out into Seamother's watery deep. Sionee had put all her love into the petals so that they could ride like a song on the sea where all that was left of Coelle's body was her ashes. Sion watched the yellow petals swirl until they disappeared into Seamother's accepting hand. Then, she lifted her eyes to the heavens.

"*Coelle, I wish we could have talked about this thing before you left. I have so many questions.*"

You began to cry. Alsionee finally allowed her own tears to drop. She was far past the point of exhaustion now, at a place where a numb calmness had set in that even You's screams did not stir.

"*Your mother sleeps in a sea of stars now.*" Sion sang to the baby, just in case she could hear her speaking in ... voice of sea gull.

"Your father, well I just don't know about him, but we will find him. I promise we will."

Sionee had never known who her own father was. Neither did her mother. **THIS MY MOTHER TAUGHT ME HOW TO SING …** "When many seeds are planted, some sprout, and some do not. You sprouted, my wee one, healthy as an apple sapling in the wild forest. I do not know dear, which male made your seed. Does it matter? You and I together, girl. We and Us are all." It seemed a natural thing.

~~~

Surely, would not a man deserve the opportunity to change a poopy bottom? Why ever not? Did not they too, have a part in what made the child a living body, as did the pollen that set the blossom? Surely it took two to create a baby.

Sionee held a short stem of yellow rose. She twirled the blossom in her fingers as she watched the creamy petals drift to the sands beneath her feet.

She had been to the boy's hut, interrupting their early hours of study. She had asked about Cyex's whereabouts. She had thought morning to be the best time to catch him, as he was an instructor in the song arts of music and dance.

"Cy took some of his boys out to find cedar branches in the high hills," the instructor assistant explained, "to make flutes, more than likely. I think however, he could also possibly be out looking for shells to make the sea aero-phones. Or, maybe he is dancing on a hill top to greet the sun perhaps. Oh, Sionee, I really could not say. Often he goes out alone while his boys study under my care. Of course, if we see him we will tell him you came by."

All eyes were on her. Every boy in the room, and the instructor as well, smiled very pleasantly at her.

"By and by, Sionee. Your song on Yule night was by far so well endowed with GNOS beauty. We were all deeply touched. You even stirred one of the fish."

Sion left quickly. She could find Cy as surely as she could catch a butterfly, if she wanted to.

When they were children, the two of them had a call. Would he remember? She hadn't used it for many sun spins, ever since the time she got her bottom paddled for deserting her studies to wonder off with the boys.

Earlier she and You had sat on Vastari's back at the top of a cliff where sound could carry. She had made the piercing churl whistle of the hawk call that Cy had said was their call ... his and hers.

"You sound more hawk, than hawk. You are the best!" He had told her. "You are best at bird calls and as my friend."

Best friends, indeed, when they were ten years old or so.

On that day last spring, when she and Coelle had met him on the way home from the hot springs, he and Coelle were very apparently much more than friends, much more.

Though they had bid her to stay and picnic with them, Sion had hurried home. Her stomach had been in pain and she had no appetite. Marisol had assured her it was a bad case of growing up too fast.

"Even at sixteen, darling," she had said.

Sion shook herself back into present awareness. You's screeching made her ears shake. It drowned out even the crash of the sea waves as they broke on the shore. If Cyex could hear her call above the raucous baby shrieks, now that would be some pretty sharp hearing.

She sat on the soft sand and pulled milk from the bag, positioning herself and the child so that the pouch would not fall if her hand accidentally drifted in sleep, which was likely. She was so weary.

She hadn't slept for more than ten minutes in two days or was it three? Perhaps she could close her eyes for another ten. Surely it would take the child ten minutes to feed, at least.

"Unlike when ..." She heard Coelle say. Her voice echoed through the dimension of Mari's waves. Instead of breaking their roll across the sands, they broke into her ears on the outside of her head and shook her AHDAWN heart as well.

A loud "whap" sound woke her with a start. The child was sleeping, the milk pouch empty.

The bird was perched on a piece of driftwood sticking out of the sand at her side, with half of a fish disappearing fast into his long pointy bill. He was way too cheery. While Sionee shook herself to waken more thoroughly, the bird perched on her shoulder.

"*Hey!*" Alsionee protested.

"*Hay is a term for the grass Vastari eats, and milk is for the baby. Isn't milk supposed to come from something much more appealing?*" The kingfisher hopped on top of the sleeping child, his eyes inspecting the drop of milk that formed a tiny drip from the pouch nipple.

Sionee laughed in spite of herself, recalling the milk that had dripped from Alita's pendulous, ah ha ...

"*Oh, yes, little king from something much more attractive. This is not to your liking? Twit ... .*" Sionee was talking bird.

"*No, not for me! The fish however will suit me just fine.*"

"*Indeed.*" Sionee replied. "*I could smell your fish breath even if I was on the other side of the mountain.*"

The bird turned his tiny head. Alsionee thought she could detect a smile on the bird face.

"*My Master says that it is by that which he knows of my proximity.*" He replied. "*Speaking of my Master ...*"

Alsionee heard the sound of the waves breaking upon the sands, but there was something more ... sweet music enticed the thrumming rhythm of the sea into a symphony of song.

She turned to see who made such music, though she knew of only one person so skilled in music's beauty. The bird took flight and flew to land on his Master's shoulder.

She knew by the way she was feeling that it was Cyex, playing a wind tune with a conch shell as he approached.

Sion saw that it was Cy. Walking along the water edge, he danced in the waves with his bare feet breaking the pattern of wave motion into spirals of sunlit mist.

Eager to be close to the musician, whitecaps rose at his knees and salted his almost naked body with droplets that caught the sun and glistened on his skin. The drape of scant linen he wore at his waist was drenched with the ocean and clung in transparent folds about his hips. His long black hair lifted in the sea breeze and framed dark eyes that were black as the midnight of no moon.

He stopped and patted the bird on the top of his head with one finger. With soft eyes he met Sion's appraisal.

"My Sun song!" He greeted her in joy.

"I don't recall singing anything for you." She sent him energies that bent his ears.

"Oh, but Sionee, you sang to all and danced for all, in such a lovely costume too, I must add." His night black eyes swept across Sion's unkempt form, noting the stained and wrinkled shift, and the bundle in her arms all wrapped in a sling-like cocoon.

He reached out and flicked a strand of hair that had come unwoven from a single loose braid she wore down her back. A little flake of gold dust softly fell in front of her eyes, making them cross as she watched the sunlit particle drift softly to the ground.

"Pu," he said. "You smell worse than the breath of my little friend here." Cyex sat down on the wood stump that jutted from the sand. He put the pink moon shell up to his lips and played more of the sea wind ballet.

Sion was suddenly aware of how she must look. Exactly how long had it been since that cursed dance? She tried to count. It seemed to her that the single days were nothing but blurs of baby cries. Was it two nights ... three?

Cleansing herself had been her last concern. Had she even packed her comb? She could remember throwing some shifts in the bag, but she wasn't sure what she had brought. There had been but one thought in her head ... to take the baby to her father. She planned on that happening right away. For a moment Sion frowned. What exactly was she doing?

Now though, she had found him, and You was screaming again like a wild kitty with a lot of monster thrown in.

"Take her!" She thrust the child into his arms, and turned to get the milk pouches out of her bag and the wet linens and the swaddling.

She'd give them to him too. She threw them into his face, and the blue lamb too. He'd at least have something to get started with.

Relief at last! She could fly away like that little twit of a bird could.

But the bird was still there, perched now on the top of Cy's head. Was the bird laughing at her?

"*Twit ... twit ... twit ... twit ... twit ... ,*" was all she heard as her bare feet sank into the sand to flee.

A strong arm stopped her. His hand wrapped around one thin arm and held her struggling body from escape. The other arm was wrapped lightly around the baby who had stopped crying and was smiling.

"I'll hold her for a bit, darling, while you take a bath. Kinga told me you were in a fix. Then, I heard your call. I came to see if it was you, or, indeed, a hawk taking flight in yonder skies, as first I thought."

She grabbed her now much lighter pack, and headed to find a pool in a fresh water stream that spilled to the sea. She paused and looked him over with fury. She sent him a message he could hear loud and clear through her eyes.

"*Oh, no. It is you who have a fix ... a big fix. Behold your daughter.*"

"Now, just a moment. Did I hear you say daughter? Maybe you should speak up girl, so I may hear you better."

Her eyes answered him. "*Oh, come on Cy. I know what you and Coelle did the afternoon I got sick and left you two to picnic on each other ... and here she is!*"

Sion put her face into the wide opening of her pouch and began to dig in it for something to wear. Everything was wrinkled or wet from one of the milk pouches that had leaked a squirt. She found a crumpled shift and shook it out to the wind, untangling the careless folds.

"What are you talking about?" Cyex blurted.

"*You know full well what I am talking about. Coelle told me all about it, so don't try to pretend innocent with me!*" Sion raised her head from the bag, glad to be rid of the baby as she approached the spring nestled among the rushes.

She threw her filthy shift off, glad for the warm water on her skin. She washed off the smell of baby pee and baby poop and throw- up and the grease she had oiled with on the night of that dreadful dance and ...

The reeds abruptly thrust open wide. Cy had followed her. She was glad that she was now immersed in the water up to her chin.

"*Now wait a minute!*" Her screeches protested.

"I don't care if you were standing before me in the "splendid" costume you wore at the night of the fire when you danced with the fish head. It's not as if I've never seen you naked before either!"

"*We were ten years old!*" Alsionee glowered at him.

The bird on top of Cy's head cocked his head back and forth with perky interest. Sion laughed in merriment, lying back to float on the fresh water. "*Aaaaaaaaaah!*" She hadn't felt so good for three days.

"She's not mine!" She heard Cy shout, even though she had water in her ears. She wanted to dive into the waters and not hear him. While she bathed, she did just that ... tried real hard not to hear him.

After a while she broke her float and stood before him dripping and naked, her feet planted firmly in the sand.

"*She is so. Coelle told me it was sweet ... so sweet.*"

"I wonder where I was when it happened. Usually I would, recall such a ... aahh pleasant experience."

"*Don't lie to me. Coelle would not!*"

"*S*ionee, Sionee Have you not even looked at this sweet little thing? She doesn't even look like me."

"*Coelle said on her last dying breath.*"

~~~

"*Twit ... twit ... twit ... twit ... twit ... twit .... Yes, indeed, master. An alluring chick, indeed, she is!*" Kinga tweeted. "*I, however, do prefer feathers ... much softer, but as you said, this one is fine! Yes, fine.*"

Cyex lay the baby safely on the sand. He took the linen from the reeds where Sion had laid it to dry. He held the now dry fabric out to her.

"You said that?" Alsionee asked, her voice somewhat quieter as she blinked through lowered lashes.

Cyex folded the soft wrap around her, rubbing her still wet skin dry. Sion's eyes were beginning to soften to the color of golden dusk instead of dark storm.

"I did." He said. The baby on the sand began to cry for attention.

Sion bent to gather her shift. He swatted her affectionately on the behind. She stood up fast, her eyes becoming storm again.

He laughed at her. She picked the child up and sat down to offer the baby another milk.

"You really are not the father?" She asked, in a last hope sigh.

He grabbed the child from her. "She's not hungry. You fed her just before your bath."

You stopped crying and wiggled snugly into a comfortable position within Cyex's arms, where she sighed in contentment and gazed softly into Cyex's no moon eyes. She sent a spark of light from her eyes into his. Cyex fell in love.

Laying the baby at his side he played his shell music softly to her. She waved her little hands at a butterfly that lit softly on her little nose. She was content.

He looked over at Sionee, who was curled up into a soft curve at the baby's side. She was fast asleep. He hadn't told her that on that day last spring he had explained to a disappointed Coelle, that his heart was already taken.

~~~

It was early evening and the tide was retreating to blanket the sun. Cy had built a fire on the beach and was steaming leaf wrapped clams and green apples still intact in their skins.

Sion sniffed. Something smelled so good ... so incredibly good that she was roused from a very deep sleep with a growling stomach. She was starving!

Cy's back was turned from her as he tended the meal. He heard her deep intakes of breath and spoke softly as he lifted the warm evening meal from the coals.

"Sionee, Sionee. When was the last time you spent a minute or two listening?" He turned, hoping to read an answer in her eyes. Her thoughts seemed so far away.

"Why would Coelle lie to me?"

"I don't know, Sionee. Maybe we could talk about it ... real words you know." He removed the leaf wrappings from the clams and picked up a roasted apple and handed her a shell bowl of warm steaming delicacy. He watched her tear into the food ravenously.

"Why the silence? Sion, when you were a girl, your vast vocabulary kept me entertained constantly. Why the vow? Don't get me wrong. I can hear you with my eyes. I too was taught the silence of soul. But when the baby is crying it is rather difficult to hear your heart words because your vibration is off."

The baby clearly was fascinated with Cyex's eyes and watched the movement of his every word as he spoke.

He didn't expect Sion to answer him in words. Her eyes were only seeing the bowl of food before her, but he caught her thoughts as she glanced up, briefly.

"Do you really think I don't listen?"

"The child thinks so."

"But ..." As she eagerly began to eat, she didn't care that she was making another mess. It was sooooo good.

That's what Cyex loved about her, the juice running down her chin getting her shift soiled again.

~~~

"What are you staring at?" Sion demanded. *"I haven't eaten for three days!"*

"Indeed." He replied. "You seem plenty full of it to me!"

She swallowed the last of the juicy clam morsels. The softly warm apples almost slid down her throat by themselves.

Promptly she stood up and whistled for Vastari, who was still munching meadow flowers close by.

"Where do you think you are going miss?"

"You two get along so fine I thought I'd fly like your bird did, and leave you both to enjoy each other. I'll be on my way."

"Not so fast my sweeting. What part of 'I am not her father' don't you understand? I said I would hold her, which I have all day long, while you slept. Not that it wasn't a pleasure." He kissed the baby on her forehead. Then, he handed her to Sion.

The wee one began her not-so-wee screams again. Quickly Sion handed the child back to Cy and turned.

His hand shot out and grabbed her slim arm one more time. "Oh, no, girl ... not her father ... get it?"

"*Neither am I her mother!*"

"That's obvious." He said. "If you were you would know that she is crying because now she is hungry again." He handed the baby back to her. "Now sit down and feed the poor little darling. It is not her fault that her real mother ... ."

"*But she's so big! She tore Coelle in half!*"

"It's not her fault."

Sion sat down. Of course not. She put a milk pouch to You's lips. But it was someone's fault. Her heart pounded, pounded so fast Cy could see movement behind there ... where her heart was. He put his hand on her chest to feel.

She slapped it away.

Cy sat down, looking into her eyes. "Sion, whatever is wrong with you? This is not like you. Where is that girl who used to swing on slippery grapevines with me?"

"*She is gone ... with my words.*"

"Where did she go?" He asked softly.

"*I intend to find out.*"

She sat up, adjusted the sling around the sleeping baby, picked up her bags and pulled the two of them up onto Vastari's back.

"Where are you headed?" He asked, as she adjusted herself and the baby to the sleek curve of the unicorn's back.

"*Wherever the wind tells me to go.*"

He watched as she tapped her wild white unicorn with her foot and they did just that ... rode off into the gentle night wind.

Chapter Nine

In the shallows not far from the shore, the morning sun sent illumination through the clear calm waters.

Rising with the fish that he loved so dearly, Ea swam upward, mimicking with his two legs the motion of one tail.

Brilliant swarms of gold and silver, creamy pearl, sparkling emerald, and the transcendent sapphire of a million and one jeweled fish swam at his side.

Ea knew the colors were the reflection of the sun's prism of ray that touched beneath the clear shallows with an inner light that made the rainbow skin of the fish sparkle as jewels of many colors.

Even the gold in the mines had no such beauty until it was dug out and touched by the sun.

His head bobbed above the waters. He swam inland until he could feel the sands beneath him and he could stand upright on the moist sand.

He quickly scanned the area for observers.

Most of the time when he came up from a dive nobody saw him, but occasionally and rarely some of the upright and brilliant Ki creatures had seen him rise above the waters ... and walk to shore.

It was always a relief when he saw that no one observed his coming to land.

When there was no one to watch him, he could smile if he desired. He could laugh. He could enjoy. He could be, and he liked to be alone where he could be who he was.

Now, about the creature ... the black-headed upright ones who occasionally saw him. It was as his mother had spoken of.

They were very intelligent, brilliant ... without a doubt. But they could not focus on Nibiru's vast technologies. They were not of the Nibiru vibration. They were children of the third dimensional fold, and could only relate to things of their earth.

Therefore, whenever the Ki people saw him rise from the waters after a dive, they perceived him as a fish with feet that walked ... and some said, a man's head beneath a fish head.

Ea smiled as he removed his helmet. It could be possible, almost. Ki's vast array of creatures never stopped amazing him. He was always discovering fascinating creatures of Ki's compendiums.

Now as far as the black-headed natural ones, the man ... they were the choice specimen. Ea had discovered a secret about them ... a secret that Enlil, Ninlil, Ninmah, Ninurta, or any of the Ens or Nins did not see, or much less care about.

Just as the man did not see or understand Nibiruan technology, the Annunaki did not grasp the simplicity of the highly intelligent Ki mind.

Enlil said they were mere animals, dumb even. But Ea knew about them, and his observations were beginning to help him further understand.

His eyes twinkled as the morning sunlight caught the drops of water flinging off his fish suit. It was a secret only he and his mother could understand. They alone, of all the technological wonder World of Perfection, still had certain facilities of emotion.

Since it was easy for two people of separate worlds to misunderstand, Ea preferred the Ki ones not to see him if he could help it.

In the sweet reflections of his noggin, he caught a flash of passionate images of beautiful music ... of beautiful women ... of beautiful evening flames rising. The Ki people embraced the emotion of beauty within their very souls. Ea was very drawn to them, as he was all of Ki's creatures.

He stripped his dive gear off and laid it in the sand; he walked naked and free.

The fish creatures of Ki's waters were just one of his favored anima specimens to observe. But there was another, too. They were creatures of wet marsh habitat, a delightful creature.

His mother had asked him to look for some for her. They were not difficult to locate. Since he was out exploring he would stop and check out the nas creature. They would be in the reeds where fresh water pooled to meet the salt of the sea.

He checked his bag to make sure he had remembered to bring the image recording device. Mother would love some pictures. She hadn't been for a trip to Ki for some time. Father would not allow her.

She had been eager to see a nas again. They were, besides the upright ones, her particular favorite. "Send me some pictures," she had admonished him, "lots of them!"

There was a pool in the sands around the bend where the beach curved to change its meander. Oh, sure, he could easily put on his wings, but simply walking on the sands gave him such an exquisite pleasure just to feel the Ki earth move beneath his feet, as the waves washed over his bare toes and moved the sand to wash across them.

He rounded the bend, only slightly winded. His matter costume had been designed with upmost strength and fitness. Being wet, the sand stuck to his feet as he trod, making the motion of picking his feet up and down to propel across its mushy surface rather exhilarating.

By the time he reached the marshland that began at the slight rise of the reeds edge, he lay belly down upon the warm sand. He pulled his looking glasses out of his bag and peered intently into the marsh waters blinking while his eyes adjusted to the magnified view. Then, he caught the glimmer of nas gold.

It was fascinating to watch them slither and twine and turn together in and out ... over and under ... moving in one uniform motion of separate union.

His mind went into contemplation as he watched them. Their movement, as were the fish, was hypnotic. He found himself thinking about the Ki tribe who lived on the other side of his mountain compound, and how they danced around the fire.

He sat upright. His feet touched the marsh edge where the snakes wove all about his carpals, tickling his toes. The dawn had a purple hue in the morning mists of the sea.

He pulled the journal out of his bag, and his gold quill too. It was a relaxing moment, and mother would enjoy it with him.

"I have observed, my mother, about the Ki men and their females." Visions of the dance played in his inner mind where thoughts were more genuine than matter was real. He could see a young girl dancing, who swayed at the head of her people like a nas creature, leading them all into a unified motion of one.

"The black-headed ones ... it seems they paint pictures with matter images. Matter is fleeting, mother ... only moments and it is all gone by. But they do things to help them understand its reality so that they can look at it, over and over, so as to contemplate and perceive its experience.

"The people that I live near ... you know them, mother ... refer to themselves as "Children of the Snake of the Sea." Indeed, I intend to further study what their name means to them. I understand them to perceive richly in what you and I term 'archetype'. The symbol represents an idea in the telling of a story, something that they can see, and mold their life into solidity.

Ea paused in his writing to reflect. Enlil, his dear brother, called the nas evil. They had so horrified his **high ass** when he first came down out of the ships, and beheld the marshland of Eridu for the first time, that he used harsh words to describe what first he saw. "Are these the kind of vile creatures this Ki is cursed with? I've never seen such ugly and repulsive evil!"

Ea supposed Enlil disliked them so much because often they were captured in the vials that were obtained to check marsh waters for tiny flakes of gold.

Back at Eridu, the only gold they found was obtained in the waters, unlike here at the Abzukia where it was found beneath the earth.

The swirling, stirring motions of the snakes in the vials horrified Enlil so much, he never assisted in the gathering of the vials, or the processing. He wouldn't so much as go near them, or the marshland beaches either. He always insisted to build his own habitat in the tops of mountains instead.

Ea smiled indulgently at the creatures that tickled his toes. He thought them to be beautiful golden marvels.

"Mother, mine ... I believe it is something all the people of Nibiru have forgotten, excepting you and me, sweet mother, for together you and I excel in all manner of wisdoms. Our fellows have forgotten how to mold their life in symbol to help one to remember to focus on the improvements of the spirit.

We have forgotten the story ... the song. I so admire the children of Ki, and how they embrace what they call the GNOS.

Henceforth dear mother, let it be known on Nibiru, and Ki, that I shall adopt as another of my many epithets, a symbol ... much as the creatures with hair of black do."

Ea watched the Nas creatures slither individually in the pattern of one purpose.

"I adopt as my symbol, the serpent, which name, henceforth, I shall be known."

Chapter Ten

The no moon night transformed the Sapphire Blue Sea of Stars into a hue of black as deep as octopus ink. It was so dark that Sionee, sliding off Vastari's back with a sleeping You, felt quite alone.

Lost in a universe of distant stars, she knew that she was anything but alone. She was surrounded by the choir of a thousand voices of frog song and cricket song and katydid song and night-bird song all lending their music to the rhythm of the waves crashing in the far distance, as they broke against the shore of the sea.

Sionee fumbled in her bag for one of her clamshell and beeswax candles. She lit it so she could see good enough to set You down and build a fire.

She asked herself for the thousandth time since she had left Cy, what was she doing out prancing around the country with a baby only days old? She could have spent the night with Cyex on the soft ocean sand, not with him, only by him. But the point was, she needed to be alone to think ... really think.

This journey to find the baby's father was far bigger than her first idle notion.

Of course, she was still going to take the child home to her father, but where was home? Where was the father ... who? If it wasn't Cyex, then why did the baby have such odd eyes and yellow peach fuzz on her slightly big head?

The *whoo ... whooo ... whoooo ...* of an owl made Sionee's heart beat as she got the small fire going.

Sionee made herself a little bed by digging a smoothed oval depression in the sandy knoll, over which she laid her soft linens beside the sleeping baby.

She sat to watch the flames for a bit, hoping that the fire would lend illumination to the whereabouts of her quest.

Instead of contemplating her next move, Sionee's thoughts

drifted back to Cy. Had she thanked him? No. She couldn't recall uttering one word of thanks or gratitude for the care he had given to her and You.

The owl brought her back to her purpose with another hoot. Sionee looked to the sky and saw the owl so close she could see its white feathers lit up by the fire light. The owl dipped and stalled, in search of food. The owl perched in the tall willow branches at her side.

"*Owl,*" Sion hooted back. "*Whooo ... whoooo ... whooooo ... who am I afraid of? Am I afraid of you, wise friend?*"

"*You are afraid of yourself dear girl ... And what you think you see when you look at me. I do not recall doing anything to give you fright. I only exist to find a mouse or two or three in the night ... A fish on the shore perhaps ... and to fly over the night world ... and see in the darkness.*"

Sionee saw owl-bright eyes catch the flame of the fire. They were extraordinarily orange ... bright, were they not? Perhaps it was only the reflection of flame in the fire.

"*I am looking for the fish ones,*" Sionee replied. "*I do not know where they live. I have heard that they are here somewhere, and now I have seen one of them with my own eyes. I did not see where he went.*"

"*They do not wish you to know, child.*"

"*Why do they hide? Are they afraid of us?*" Sionee asked.

"*Oh, no child! You are afraid of them.*"

"*Truly it is so.*" Her heart began to pound again. "*I intend to find out why!*"

"*When one does not understand, one fears.*"

"*But have you seen them and where they abide?*"

"*Oh, yes my child. From the heights as I soar, I have seen all.*"

"*Can you tell me, wise one, how I may find the fish head ones?*"

"*Only wise eyes may hear where they may be ... and wise ears may see. Are you foolish child? Or are you wise?*

"*Whoo ... hoo. I fly now to the waves where I shall catch fish by perching on Her head. Whooo ... HER head ... there I shall find ... .*"

The flames crackled softly, gently. The embers glowed as Sionee saw the music of the evening dance quietly within the fire's center.

Sion left her bed and walked into the meadow. She was still close enough she could keep her eye on the sleeping baby.

She lay down on her stomach, breathing the smell of fresh earth and sweet green grass. She stretched her arms outward and down, touching the damp earthen floor with the palms of her hands.

She twined her fingers in the long grass. It tickled her chin. She put her eyes across the dark beauty of the meadow's vast expanse beneath the night sky and lay her head with her ear close to the sweet thrumming ground so she could see with her AHDAWN ears what the earth sang.

"Oh, Gaia Mother, surely you are aware of their presence upon your body. Can you tell me, where do I find the ones my fellows call the fish head? I do not think they are heads or fish. I think they are fools. Unless ... unless they came from the same Fey star that the beautiful white lady of all our stories came from. If they did, they are not wise like her, Gaia."

Slowly, deep within, she heard a vibration rise.

"What?" Sionee asked. *"Speak so I may see!"*

The rumble sent confusion in her head. She was too tired to hear.

~~~

Sion slept on and off through the night. You woke up and cried only two times. Sionee pulled the baby into her own bed and fed her. The child snuggled warm and soft. Sion was cozy.

When morning came, she was woken early with impatient and hungry screams. Sionee picked the infant up and changed her soft linens and fed her before she called Vastari.

Afterwards she mounted her unicorn, arranged the baby and was off again, on her way.

Had she heard the owl right? The gentle unicorn's hoof-beats lent rhythm to her contemplations.

THIS MY MOTHER TAUGHT ME HOW TO SING ... *"When you ask of nature you must understand that she speaks a wise voice of riddle. It is the way your friends who are in spirit whisper, so that you* will seek to find your answer within their clues."

Why had she been led to the grassy meadow to sleep through the dark night? Was it to listen to the owl? The owl said she was going to ... what was it that the owl had said?

She had been quite sleepy at the time, but the owl had said: *"I fly now to waves where I shall catch fish by watching from Her head."*

So back to the cove of the Fey and to the sea and to the tiny Islet that graced the monument that long ago had been placed on the other side of the pillars that marked the seasons of the sun.

~~~

It was still early. The sea birds flew overhead as she tossed a few morsels of dried bread to them.

Her load was heavier again. Sion had visited the trading hut by the docks and had filled up on new supplies, when she went to trade for the canoe.

The baby was staring with big curious eyes at the vast sky above their heads ... well, what else could she look at lying swaddled in a soft linen cradle that Sion had fashioned for her from a reed parcel the kind man at the trade center had given her.

"For the baby." The trader had winked at her "So she who dances with the fish god has free hands to row. Would you like assistance, sister?"

"No, no," Sion indicated, aware of her reddening cheeks. *"I am Priestess of the Song, and I have rowed there many times. It is a holy place and we Storytellers are well acquainted with the skill of a canoe. Besides that, as you can see, I am not alone."*

She looked at the baby and at the bird perched on the prow of the reed canoe. Kinga tipped his cocky head at the boat trader who shrugged.

"Go Thou in blessings then, sister," he admonished, and sent her off.

The baby moved her little feet and hands in excitement at the sea gull that swooped down low. Watching with keen interest, her eyelids fluttered with the motion of the canoe.

"Anything that moves puts her to sleep," Sion explained to Kinga. *"Just why exactly are you here?"*

"My master sent me," Kinga replied. *"He said you were addle-head-ed ... and I told him, 'I know'."*

Sion's face grew hot. Then, she laughed merrily. *"But at least I am not a birdbrain!"*

Kinga squawked and flapped his little wings in indignation.

~~~

At a place well past the pillars that marked the shoreline of the cove, further out to sea on a sandbar that created a very small island, the trio arrived in little time.

She was greeted in the grey mists of morning by a white owl that flew from the monumental image of She. The owl winked at Sionee, flying low for just a moment before ascending into the dawn skies above.

Sionee was pleased. Surely this was an owl with eyes the right color and she was saying "You heard, my friend. I feasted and now it is your turn."

Sion felt a rising excitement.

The Feyri of the Snake ... She had been placed aeons ago on the sandbar islet to welcome visitors as they came to the northern shores.

She was Sofeya, the one who came to the nightfire of Alsionee's forebearers. From the depths of the Sapphire Blue she came, and tonight Sionee intended on looking into her story again with her heart ears.

The waves of the sea washed over the small shore. Sion got out of the canoe. She pulled it high above the tide's reach so that it wouldn't wash back to sea.

She sat on a white carved onyx bench and fed You milk, while she munched on apples and dry bread.

Kinga stood on shore dipping his beak into the small bank at the shoreline and pulled forth small fish for breakfast. Sion smiled. He was thumping his fish on Her head.

She ... Sofeya was from the stars. The early Fey had built her image out of permanently hardened white sand that they had smoothed and shaped into a figure of breathtaking beauty.

She was sovereign of the sea and stood on a pedestal of stone to stand greetings at the entrance to Snake shores and bid welcome to all who came in peace.

In her hands she held a vessel and poured water into the sea. The ancient ones were clever in their design to create a perpetual water stream so that it appeared that the vessel overflowed and never emptied.

Though she was but an image in stone, the perpetual motion of the sea at her feet, made an illusion that the beautiful lady danced with the waves.

Dolphins swam at her feet, their noses reaching for her hands. They, too, had a water system directed to arch from their mouths, adding an element of contrasts in the waves and the mists about her feet.

As She danced and poured her waters, her head tilted to the sky, looking upwards. The suggestion of long flowing hair poured in wild disarray down her back in glorious moss covered waves. On her crown she wore thirteen stars. Across her face a wide-mouthed grin made Sionee laugh in enchantment at her beauty.

Sionee and the baby spent a restful day playing in the ebb and flow of the ocean tide. Sion munched on dry bread and tasteless trade cheese and honey sweet apples, along with a few clams Sionee had dug and attempted to roast as she had seen Cyex do. They tasted nothing like his, but the beauty of the sacred island was food enough for her.

Before she and the baby settled comfortably in the soft linens of their sandy beds by the shore, Sionee looked up into Sofeya's eyes and called. *"Lady Wisdom, will you give me a dream tonight?"*

As she closed her eyes beneath the star strewn sky, she quickly fell asleep with You curled warm by her side and she went to a different fire to hear their story.

~~~

Across time she sat with her peoples of old, not as Songkeeper, but as an observer. This time was hers to ponder.

The beat of the drums rose in crescendo. The young man

was naked, and beautiful, and took full attention in the center. He danced lithely like Cyex, stepping in motions that led him to the circle, where he stopped at the reed edge and parted them. He reached inside and pulled from within a stunningly beautiful woman.

Not just any woman; She was a stranger. Her hair was as white as the sun of day. Its bright hue lit up the dark of the evening.

She wore a tattered shift streaked with mud which only made the damp fabric cling alluringly to every curve of her prime body.

The beautiful white lady made strange sounds of protest as she came forth. The young man urged her on, his body undulating in a sensuous manner of dance as he led her to the fire center.

The mother drums and the flutes increased in tempo of passion. The lady ceased her inhibitions and tossed her head. Her glorious golden hair became a river of starlight that danced down her back like a cluster in the spirals of the Sapphire Blue.

The clans-people sighed in awe as the beautiful one, who seemed to have stars in her hair, danced with their male flute player. Her shift was thrown off, and both of them moved in wild abandon.

Sion breathed deep. She recalled the dance when she last had stepped in the pattern of the snake ... also with some fish head hiding in the grass.

When the man dancer undulated, the star woman answered his every curving motion. He went down on crouched knees as she gyrated just above him, answering his body in perfect rhythm.

Sionee laughed, despite herself. Sionee felt her body and spirit move to the dancer's song. The beautiful dancer probably tickled his chin with her pubic hairs of gold.

As the one from the stars and the one from Gaia moved together, the other dancers circled around them. The ancient Songkeepers wore flowers in their hair, and laughed, and were merry as the embers of the fire burned low and smelled so sweet. The night increased its rhapsody of darkness and quiet.

The two who danced as one were at sacred rite there on the altar of the ground they adored, the star lady ... and the earth man ... both ... and reverence was high.

Sionee was ever so glad that her dance had not taken those steps ... quite ... she supposed. She drew her eyebrows into a line of contemplation.

Now that embers were glowing, in the quiet of the nightfire, the flames were relit again and in the circle it was a time for talking.

Sion was touched by how well the people of ancient of days listened and could hear her every silent thought as if she spoke clearly in words. The language of silence, shared by all of nature, was spoken as the major communication understanding back then. Sionee sighed.

Her people in the real world, outside the dream, were losing their ability to speak and hear the sacred words of thought.

They also had changed in other ways. A desire to live at the inner Snake's cosmopolitan center was becoming more favored than it had in days of old. Sionee couldn't imagine why people would want to live so crowded in close quarter.

Some of her people had actually split from the outlier by the sea and gone to the cosmopolitan to earn the trade that was offered there. What exactly they did, Sion wasn't sure. She, herself, was perfectly happy living in the quiet little family of Fey by the Sea. What could be better than the quiet little gatherings of shells and the quaint sculpted homes of simple beauty among the wild-forests by the sea, nestled within the big mountain curve.

She hadn't even visited the big city for quite some time, nor had she desired to go there where everyone sang a noisy song.

Sionee guessed that the people gathered at her dream fire couldn't possibly foresee the huge metropolis where their future children would abide. They held such an innocence and a reverence for life that amazed her.

"What is your name, fair lady?" Sion asked, though she was sure of the answer already.

The bright lady looked directly into her eyes, smiling indulgently. "My name is of little consequence, my little sprite. It is who I am ... and what I am ...

"However, on my star they call me Lady Wisdom, which is named like this ... SOFEYA!" Because Sionee had heard the story before told in various accounts, she knew, even in her dream that the woman from the stars danced around this nightfire from full moon to full moon. She learned the silent language of Gaia's children and called it the language of one. She learned the Gnos, and she gave to the nature children her song as well. She thanked us with gladness. It was said that our people had helped her to understand much clearer than the people of her star perceived. In the space of one moon time, she gifted the people who became Fey with her gifts of bright knowledge as well.

It was said that after the moon grew dark ... then ... bright once more ... having danced non-stop through the entire cycle ... Sofeya grew pale and weary. "It is time now for me to return to my people."

~~~

Her eyes still seeing the violet swirl of dream mist, Alsionee Tree Song woke up before the sun's first rays penetrated the sea into the sky. She listened to the quiet stillness of a secluded morning and heard the tide splash about Sofeya's image feet.

Still seeing the dream in her eyes, Sion reflected on the lady from the stars. She was much taller than the present people of the cove, and perhaps a bit taller than the male. In contours and function, she fit perfectly with the male ancestor of old. Sionee blushed in the darkness of still night.

Her hair was golden and beautiful, long and waving. Her eyes were like blue sea opal, and they flashed with an inner fire as does the opal. Her skin was as white pearl. And her head was a bit larger, but more beautiful than most.

As she left to return to her star, she put on another head, a costume much like a fish with green iridescent sparkling lights.

"*Which way did she go?*" Sionee asked herself ... and herself answered ...

"*Oh, Sionee, Sionee Sun Tree ... You know these things. She ascended into the clouds ... into the stars ... into the depths of the Sapphire Blue she swaddled within her blue pearl that became tiny as it faded into the sky sea of infinite stars.*"

Sion looked up into the vast waters above, all lit with a common eternal flame.

The stories told over all the nightfires across the Snake of the Sea's vast isle in the Cosmopolitan, as well as the many small outliers ... and across the sea to Lemmingland ... and all the places between ... all told the same stories, depending on the view from the position of ones seat around the fire. But the major story was simple. It was called The One. All peoples were sparks radiating from The One light of a central sun.

Sionee frowned. Something was beyond her thinking. Did she in her thinking have to include the people from different stars in her ideas of one sun ... one people, one light ... one spirit ... and she is you ... and you are she?

Some who came, like the Fey Lady were good, but some of the idle ones who had been seen across the land as of late ... were they from her star? Surely they didn't seem to be as glorious. She didn't think they were, at least.

She didn't think she even liked the male fish head she had met. He made a fear in her. Or did she make the fear? **THIS MY MOTHER TAUGHT ME HOW TO SING ...**

She had to understand ... by and by ... so that as Storyteller and Songkeeper of her people, she could speak in words that all could hear. The only way she could find that wholeness in her heart again would be when she found him, who took from her something that left her heart empty. She would find it again.

She must find the one who wore a fish head, but danced like a lover. Besides that, she had promised You she would find her father.

Chapter Eleven

"Deep within the stillness of silence many songs may be heard."
THIS MY MOTHER TAUGHT ME HOW TO SING …

Ever since the baby had been placed in her responsibility, she hadn't been hearing so well. Sion supposed that it was because the baby had broken her outer ear drums as well as her inner resonators with her screeches. What was it that Cy had said?

It was another night and another place on her journey's way. Early this morning Sion and You had left the sand bar island at the cove and advanced elsewhere … somewhere.

It was moving toward midnight and Sionee sat by a new fire, lost in loneliness and uncertainty again.

Throughout the day they had wandered aimlessly. Vastari had kindly told her that she didn't know which direction to go. The journey Sion was leading her on was one of uncertain roads.

"I know Vastari, darling." Sion put her arms around her unicorn's smooth white neck.

"We could flit about forever. I must search the inner paths first, before I continue on our outer. I am trying girl. Please be patient with me."

Alsionee could talk with her unicorn. She could talk with the birds she could talk with the wind and the sea and the earth. But Cy had asked her, "How long has it been since you really listened?"

The fire was warm on Sion's cheeks … warm on her arms.

Sion gasped. How is it that the thought had never really occurred to her until this evening, in the quiet after the ride, when she had pulled the baby off Vastari's back?

When Sionee had decided it was time to find a place to abide for the night, and she had taken the child within her arms, You was awake, and wet. Sion had taken the baby down to the hot springs, and the two of them bathed. Afterwards, the child was calm.

Alsionee searched in her bag, and rubbed the tiny body from head to toe with the soft yellow oil, fragranced with blossom of honey locust.

The baby lay on soft linen and stretched her legs out in contentment, as she waved her little arms in the air and cooed.

The sound made Sion's heart flutter in an unexpected way. What was this? The baby looked into impatient eyes, and sent to Sionee opalescent rainbows of light that touched her very soul. *"Aaah,"* Sion started to look away but she caught herself smiling back. The baby should really have a name.

Sion got the blue ewe out of her bag and danced the lambie across the baby's soft cheek.

It was then that she heard! Sionee stared at the child as if amazed. Of course! It was as Cy had tried to tell her. She hadn't been listening.

She could talk to her unicorn, to earth, to rock, wind and flowers. Why had it not occurred to her that she could listen to a babe?

After hearing the baby coo, surely it was apparent that the two of them shared the same words of AHDAWN. Sionee laughed at this one.

Sion sang the baby a straight song and the infant fell asleep as she was being fed by the warm fire. You then slept soundly.

A mammoth rumbled a call in the far distance, summoning his mate from across the cedars and the wild-forest hills. Sion felt the soft vibration tickle the bottoms of her bare feet.

"Sionee, you didn't listen to me either." Earth said.

"I was tired Mother."

"Yes, yes, indeed. But now it is time for you to wake up ... wake up!"

"Yes, Mother ... Oh, yes! I am still at loss what to do. What should I do? How may I find the fish one?"

"Come closer ... ," Earth Mother said.

Sionee was still naked from her bath and the night was warm. She went to where the earth was bare of grass and smelled like sweetness. There she pressed her body close to the mother so she could feel her heartbeat. She lay her ear on the soft earth and felt the trembling of Gaia's voice.

"In my hollow ... an entrance lies. You have seen it ... with your eyes."

Sion was silent, contemplating.

"Yes, daughter, think on this." Gaia moaned. *"I am sleepy now ... ask the wind."*

~~~

Sion stood still naked on the flat of a small hill that flanked the campfire site. She peered out over the distant and flat plain of yellow flowers that rolled westward. She saw that the river meandered to the sea, that there were many tributaries along the way. If she followed the main flow it would lead her inland to the Cosmopolitan Major, where one of her Sisters of Song, Hypori, had gone with a young man who traded there.

She was growing weary of the journey, surely as was the babe. But the arrow of fear was still at the bow. And she had to find him! Where was he? What was he?

He had felt like a man. Sion blushed, and tried to cast from her thoughts the image of two serpents, twining by the golden fire, *"Aaaaaaaaaaaugh!"*

She stood on the small flat and placed a reed torch at the northern direction of the hilltop. She lit it and watched as the flame burned steady, sending its smoke straight into the Sapphire Blue.

At the South she placed another torch. While its flame flickered ever so slightly, the smoke rose straight up.

To the east she placed another torch. Its smoke also reached for the sky.

But the torch she placed on the west flickered abruptly, sending its smoke on the western current of wind.

In communion with nature, Sionee prayed. She drew within herself light from the stars and let their strength wash over her. With her feet firmly planted to the thrum of Gaia's vibration, she sang out in ancient sigh

"Oh, earth ... Oh, air ... Oh, fire ... Oh, water. Oh, elements all ... I am your daughter. Help me ... Oh, help me ... Oh, lead me ... I pray ... To where the ones with fish heads stay."

She watched the flickering west flame. Water! It was confirmed. The Cosmopolitan.

~~~

The reed boat was but a speck in the wide river that led westward and curved a wee bit southerly. The babe was content in motion.

"Last time I went up this river, there were many of us that took turns at the rowing. I'd forgotten how it's much harder rowing up sea than down sea. This river is much bigger than I remembered." Sion spoke silently to Kinga who perched guard on the prow.

"Keep your eyes on the way ... mind you!" Kinga cocked his head nervously.

"And you call me a dunderhead." Sion scoffed. *"What are you doing here on the prow anyway? You could fly above it all ... get there real fast. But here you sit on the prow of my boat again."*

"Indeed, miss. Indeed. It is as my Master has instructed ... to stay close to a miss who is missing something in her head."

"What is this name calling?" Sion gazed at him irritably. *"It's not my head, it's my heart."*

"Okay, I will call you crazy heart then ... if it makes you feel better," Kinga replied.

"Have you not ever followed your heart?"

"Indeed ... Twit ... twit ... twit ... twit ... twit ... Recently, that is."

The Earth had told her the way was in a cavern that she had seen. The wind told her to go west ... searching, searching.

"Wind!" She called out in her wind song, as the wind rose on the river, making the row a bit more tedious. *"Thank you for your assistance, but can you tell me if I am I going the right way?"*

"I blow where I go." The wind said. *"Surely do you. Trust the direction of your heart. It will not mislead you."*

"Surely wind, you have blown over the fish one as he has walked on land. Does he live on land? Or does he live in the water? Or does he live in the air?"

The wind moaned softly, amazed at the dense human race.

"Over mountain and hill ... and meadow and stream. Over flame and fire ... I am higher. But he can go above my wind and ride a star ... and then descend. Inside the Earth he goes within ... and there he watches fishes swim. I see him rise to shore with them."

Sionee placed the phrases in her head. The rhyming would help her to contemplate the clue.

"Then you do not know, exactly?" She inquired.

"What makes you think I am smarter than you? Though I am ... and I'm knowing ... I've got to be blowing."

~~~

It took five days. Sionee and You sat on a white flowered bench that graced the lovely grass that was kept neatly cropped by the deer and the gazelle and the lambs who grazed the temple grounds. The palace of wisdom was built in the very center of the Major, within the circles.

The walk from the harbor had been a delightful experience for both she and You.

It was a sunny morning, and Sion peeled back the linen softlings from the baby's body and held her up to the sun, laughing. The baby laughed with her.

"I haven't been to the temple for quite some time." Alsionee told You. *"All the Songkeepers receive training in the center here. I can hardly wait to show you."*

Sitting on the bench and holding the milk pouch to the baby's lips, Sionee cautioned the baby.

"I must be able to count on you," she evoked. *"You must not cry, only show reverence. This is a place my people honor as a holy place of reflection. It would be rude to disrupt with your screaming."*

"I will try," The baby said *"but remember I am only a baby and my comfort comes first."*

"Come on, now; do you want me to leave you with the priestesses who abide here, or do you want to come with me?"

"Okay, mother. Can I call you mother?"

"Not yet." Sionee replied, rising hotly. She asked the attendant

if she could rest her bags in their watching while she visited the temple of thought.

"I wish the baby to see."

"But she looks like she is pretty new in this life. Would the temple matter to her?"

Sionee held You up. The baby sent the light thing from her eyes.

"Ah," The attendant said, smiling. "You are the one who danced with the fish god, and this is the baby."

~~~

They walked through an artistic arrangement of sun circle designs along a corridor of white stepping stones that led her to the pinnacle where the temple stood on a small hill over the Acropolis center.

Four pillars of white stone marked each of the four entrance ways into the temple.

Sion entered through the west gate, the place of introspection. She intended on traveling the paths of all the directions ... introspection ... illumination ... innocence ... and wisdom ... as well as the fifth path, spirit ... which led to the center.

As if in a maze, the way curved before her, turning into a spiraling bridge that floated like a hanging garden over a magnificent round pool of still waters.

Sionee paused as she followed the path to the center. She peered in awe to the bottom of the deep and clear waters and could see the white sand shimmering with flecks of gold.

The image of the sky sparkled on the mirrored surface of the water, gently undulating the blue gold vista in reflection ... sky and cloud ... bird and butterfly ... branch and tree and fruit ... all from above was seen below.

White stone benches were placed at the water edge where one could sit and gaze into the waters for as long as one wished.

Sionee sat on a bench, holding You on her lap to see. Kinga perched on her shoulder. Everything around them seemed to move in a graceful harmony of motion ... from the pilgrims who walked the path, to the swans who swam in beauty on the glistening waters. Even the goldfish were of breathtaking beauty as they moved in and out of the wide lily pads that graced the gold-hued pool.

Sitting on Sion's shoulders, Kinga happily tilted his head from side to side in interest.

"*No fishing!*" Sionee warned him.

"*No problem,*" Kinga silently twitted. "*These fish are much too tame for my taste ... but now, there is a pretty little girl.*"

A big goldfish with shining round eyes stuck her pouted lips above the water to receive a bug.

Despite Kinga's rude manners, there was something almost comforting about his presence. Maybe it was in the knowing that she wasn't really alone. Had Cyex really sent him to tag along?

Gazing over the valley which declined gradually toward the level of the sea, Sion thought she saw mammoths in the distance. She squinted and saw that the mammoths had bundles of logs straddled on their backs and in their trunk curves. Sion wondered what that was all about. Were they making the Cosmopolitan gathering even larger? Wasn't it big enough all ready? There was a strange smell to this.

A park garden edged the gazing pool. Lambs, gazelle, and white haired deer grazed the grass. Herons and swans and ducks swam among the reeds at the pond edge. Pink flamingoes stood on one leg as they gathered beneath the sun. White monkeys swung playfully from tree limb to tree limb in the branches that arched the pool like a graceful canopy.

After walking and reflecting in each of the four directions, Sionee entered the fifth direction which led to the spirit center. To get to this path it had been necessary to make her way back through the mazelike spirals of the bridge.

She stood in awe. A platform of white stone featured the center of it all. A trio of three dolphins began their long nosed dive into the waters with their arched tails fanned out and upward to hold the crystal in the curve of their combined tail fins.

It was THE CRYSTAL ... the crystal that belonged to all peoples of the Snake. It was the crystal spoken of with reverence over all the trade Acropolis's and small outliers all over Mother Gaia's vast regions.

The crystal sphere lived and breathed in glorious living color. It flashed intermittently from yellow to orange to red to purple to blue to green ... and all the colors of the rainbow in between.

High above the crystal, five carved pillars of white onyx held a roofed dome that represented the curve of the Sapphire Blue. In the dome cup, a realistic painted sky glowed fluorescently by day. In the dark night each star, planet, sun, and moon accurately glowed in twinkling representation.

Whether it was day or night, the beauty of the universe hovered above and beyond the crystal, like a shining crown of glory.

~~~

Sion thought she saw You reach out her hand and point to the seven sister stars that formed a light spiral in winters midnight sky.

"The brightest one at the spiral beginning ..." Sion heard the baby say in thought words. *"That is where I came from."*

"Oh?" Sionee responded equally quiet. *"Is this true?"*

"Indeed! On my world it is said that on the earthen shores we quickly forget where our home began."

"Your home?"

"Your home, too," The baby sighed. *"Our home, alike the home of all pure souls of light."*

Sion's scalp tingled in awe. Even as Songkeeper, the home of the twin was not located ... as to be known ... in surety ...

"Ahhhhhhhhhhh, child."

There was something that she wished to show the baby. From a pouch in her shift pocket, Sionee took out a singular small crystal.

Holding it inside the warm cups of both palms, Sionee closed her eyes. She felt the throb of an inner flame within the crystal. She blessed it and rubbed You's tiny hands with the clear quartz, and passed it over the little body, and let it rest on You's soft cheek. Then, she kissed it and reached out to touch the sphere with her own small crystal.

Sionee felt infinite soft, and powerfully subtle, rays of light course through her very being. She felt the shimmer of vibration rise inside her.

Within her AHDAWN she held the whole universe. It sang to her a song that enraptured her soul.

To any spectators in that singular moment in time, all that could be seen of Sion and the baby and Kinga were three spots of luminous light that spiraled and spun in a dance of weave as the three lights appeared as one.

The light infused knowledge with its touch. For a timeless second in eternity, Sion knew everything of all that is ... was ... or ever would be ... except for the specifics of complicated details, such as where abided the fish heads?

The thought grounded her. It was time now to exit the circle and return to the world.

Chapter Twelve

Sion met her friend, Hypori, in the garden that surrounded the pool of reflection.

Hypori had brought a picnic, along with the three small sons that she had given birth to since she had left the Songkeepers huts to live in the Major with her boyfriend.

"Oh, Sion, it's so wonderful to see you again, sister. What is this? You have a wee one now?" Hypori gasped when Sionee threw back You's linen and held the child up.

"Sionee, I heard that it was you who danced with the fish head. Apparently, however, it wasn't the first time."

"*Oh, no,*" Sionee's heart leaped. "*She is not mine. She is Coelle's.*"

"Coelle danced with a fish head and more?" Hypori giggled. "How is our little Elee?"

"*She has crossed the vast sea of stars,*" Sion replied wordlessly. "*The child was too big for her and tore her in two.*"

Hypori frowned. "Oh, Sionee I did not know. I will send a flower out to sea on the river."

"*She likes yellow roses,*" Sion replied.

You napped on the grass. The boys played on the hill, rolling down and coming back up to roll down again ... over and over. Sionee felt her search was becoming like the game the boys played.

~~~

That evening at the mealtime, Sion met again the young man Hypori had fashioned her life to be part of.

Sionee remembered him as a striking young man who had charmed all the young girls at the shells.

When Hypori made the decision to leave the Sisters of the Song, everyone knew that they would miss her, but everyone was so happy for her. Some of the girls were even envious.

It hadn't been that long ago. Hypori was still as young and attractive as she had been on the day she had left.

Benan however, was hardly recognizable as the man who had won Hypori's heart.

He was silent as he walked through the curved doorway of the spacious and simple dwelling where he and Hypori lived.

Sionee stared at him, her mouth opened wide. She tried not to stare.

When Benan caught sight of her, his eyes lit up for a brief moment and he was almost recognizable again when he smiled at her.

Sionee noticed his puffy eyes first. The rims and the creases around his eyes had a sooty, black ... something. He kissed Hypori and patted the heads of the boys, who clamored at his knee.

Hypori's eyes were sad as she greeted her man. She wiped at the streaks on his eyelids with her fingers. "At least you got your hair clean tonight," Hypori told him ruffling her fingers through his short locks. She turned to Sion. "You see, it is not good where Benan trades."

"What does Benan trade?"

"His labor."

"His what?"

"Sionee, he works like a mammoth. In fact, often he works with the mammoths in the mines."

Sion was puzzled.

"Every night he comes home with the black dust of the inner earth on him ... everywhere. They have a bath house there for the men to wash in before coming home, but the grime of the mines is hard to wash away."

Sionee noted the soot-rimmed nails of Benan's fingers, as well as the black stains which lined his rough hands, as they ate the meal. *"What are these mines, where you trade, Benan? I do not understand."*

Benan did not respond to the puzzled look, or to her silent question.

"He does not hear you." Hypori told Sion. "The mining keeps his mind so taken up with such a task.

"She asks you, Benan, about the mines? She does not understand."

Benan looked at Sion with painful eyes. "I hardly understand myself," Benan replied. "It's not quite what I was expecting. I don't mind hard work, but ... ."

Sion tried to determine whether he was angry or weary.

"It is the fish heads, Sionee. We don't see them much but they are here!"

Benan looked at Sionee appreciatively. "Darling, we all know it was you who danced with a fish head. I can see why a fish head would want to dance with you ... young and beautiful. I must warn you, Sion ... the baby ... you do know how babies are made do you not?"

"Benan, No!" Hypori scolded him sharply. "Of course, she does! She was brought up in the House of Shells, as was I. Sion does not want to talk about that. She just wants to know more about the fish heads."

"None of us know a lot, Sion girl. They are not seen, unless they choose to. Rather, they select a representative from our own people, who will stand for them.

"They have their own name for our Cosmopolis, which means something like this in their language 'Home that belongs to They'. They say they will build our entire Gaia into their personal Garden that will be a paradise, and we will be fortunate to live therein, and that we must labor for them to earn our keep."

"Whaaaaat?"

"Yes, dear girl. They are coming, more so than you know. Where you live is still protected."

Benan looked at You warily. "Or, so I thought ... ," He continued. "At first when I was told about this magnificent Garden, I was pleased. I was lazy," he admitted.

"The representative told us that in exchange for a bit of labor, my family would be abundantly taken care of, which they have been, but there is something I am growing increasingly uncomfortable with."

Sion's eyes were as big as the meal saucers they ate from.

"We have a boss."

Sionee questioned with a look of horror in her eyes.

"She doesn't know what you mean by that term, Benan. You must talk to her in terms she still understands."

"*I'm no dummy.*" Sion flashed at Hypori. "*Just tell me what is going on.*"

Sighing, Benan stood before Sionee and took off his shirt. Sion gasped. On his back a pattern of raised scars made a distinct crisscross of angry welts.

"They are worse when they are bloody." Hypori said.

Sionee felt the food she had just eaten rise in her throat. She rushed to the relieving room where the sensation was replaced with livid anger.

"*Who did this to you?*" Sionee asked of Hypori to relate to Benan her question.

"If we do not do the task as we are told to do, or if we don't do it fast enough or good enough, we receive the whip."

"*Why do you not just leave? Surely the decision is yours.*"

"Because of the whip. The fish heads know everything. They would find us again. It would be more lashes, and more. Further, we would not be compensated for our labors with food and comforts for our family."

"We told him to leave, Sion, that we could all go back to the outlier. He says he can't. They have threatened him and that there is threat to our lives, as well, if we leave. They say we are theirs now ... all of us."

"*A threat? How?*" Sion's shocked eyes spoke loud. This time Benan heard.

"The boss man has one of their instruments for his use."

The brows of Sionee's forehead crossed in an angry frown and irate wonder.

"If we disobey, we get the stun ray, which really stuns, Sion ... like permanently. It is a stick thing they have. If it is pointed to someone, the stick sends out a light that turns the body to dust in an instant ...

with one quick POOF! So you can see, attempting to get away would be foolish."

Sionee had a choking fit, sputtering as she held her hand to her mouth to keep from gagging in horror.

"We labor from first light to last light of the day. At least they let us go home to sleep."

"Sionee asks what you do in the mines?"

"What don't we do, darling? Oh, Sionee, I cannot tell you ... only that we dig gold. Deep, deep into the bowels of the earth in dank and lightless caverns with no air to breathe."

"Sionee says what for?"

"... For the fish head Masters. They say that Gaia's gold is their possession and that we must get it for them ... lots and lots of it."

"But ..." Sionee began. *"but ... but ... !"*

"The Snake of the Sea is still the most beautiful of Gaia's vast lands Sionee. The Masters are making the Cosmopolis even bigger, and even more splendid ... as they see beauty, that is. Have you noticed the small changes even at our temple?"

"I saw mammoth in the distance with logs and stones. I was going to ask." She told Hypori.

"They are building."

"But the temple is already the most beautiful of places across all of Gaia. How can they?"

Ah Sionee, there is more going on here than we can even begin to tell you. Go back to your outlier that still has some of that which the Snake really is. Just remember that our world is becoming the Garden of the Master fish heads, and they have planted their gardens and mines and larger than life edifices everywhere and ... ."

"You call them Masters?" She asked, not believing.

"Just be careful, darling." Benan told her. It is not too late for you yet. You still have some choice. He wrinkled his face at the baby, "I think ... pay heed ... stay as far from them as you can. Be Blessed Thou, girl."

~~~

Sionee could not sleep that night, not for the whole night long and it wasn't because of You crying. The baby slept peacefully in one of the boy's used cradles.

Every time she closed her eyes, she saw owl eyes ... eyes the wrong color. She was not aware when toward morning she drifted into a dream within the owls eyes.

Inside the owl eyes, there was a spot. Surely it was the dark pupil? Not only was the color wrong, they were spinning ... softly spinning into concentric smaller circles, like the rounds of a spiral melting into a blob of a thousand different colors of purples. Then, the orange lit up way bright like a glowing red fire that danced with a life of its own.

Sionee turned to flee. The spirals followed her, growing larger now, ever larger ... going out, not in ... growing wider and wider as she fled.

Then in the darkness she saw the veil of mist. On the other side of it she saw all the colors of the rainbow. Glimmering beneath the colorful mist, she saw a slippery wild white grape vine. Surely she could slide down it and be safe from the Owl eyes.

Alsionee opened one eye, then, two. A baby was crying. She was always crying. Sionee stepped out of the bed shaking the dream from her muffled head. But You was not crying as she had thought. She was still asleep. How could this be?

~~~

It wasn't morning yet, but Sionee quickly fetched her bag and put the baby in the cradle basket. She left Hypori's home, barely taking the time to rouse her sleeping Sister of Song to say goodbye.

Kinga caught up with her in the morning light. With a sharp thud, he startled Sionee into awareness as he slurped a fish down his throat.

"Uugh! You are back." She wiped wet slime from off her cheek. *"This habit of yours is annoying ... and really smelly. Couldn't you have eaten before you dropped in?"*

"No I couldn't have. The fish are here, not there."

Sionee closed her pouch of cheese and bread. She had hardly eaten anyway, so tumultuous was her stomach.

"Why do you keep looking behind you?" Kinga asked.

"To see if anyone is following me."

"Why would anyone be following you?"

"I don't know." Sion glared at him. Why would they?

"My Master ... ."

"Your Master ... You can tell your Master that I said that if he was so interested in what I am doing, he wouldn't send a bird to spy on me. He would come himself."

"He said you were a dunderhead, and I'm really thinking it must be so. Now dear girl, where are you going?"

"I'm headed home."

"Are you finished, then ... with this silly search?"

"No I am not finished ... I am about to find. Hey, you twit bird ... shut your mouth or fly! I must have my quiet time to think. Gaia knows I've had little of that as of late."

"Did you call me a twit bird?"

"I did."

The kingfisher flew off. Sion sighed, glad for a little respite for just a bit.

She scanned the banks of the river, and the vast meadows beyond. She hadn't noticed it as much on the way, but the thought had crossed her that something was different than she remembered.

Kinga ... she looked about for Kinga. Now where had he gotten off to? Well she had insulted him and told him to fly.

A few minutes later, she saw him fishing at the boat side. She called to him. Looking stricken, Kinga came close and perched on her outstretched hand.

"I am sorry I told you to shut your mouth."

"And ... told me to fly!"

"I was sharp, and for that I apologize. There is something you must understand about me ... now or never ... because if you don't get this, you may as well fly again. I must go within sometimes to think."

"Where?"

"Inside my head ... to see my heart ... to AHDAWN."

"Dawn is well past," Kinga twitted.

"Stop being silly. You heard me. Sometimes I have to look at things with my eyes that see within my heart."

"Ooah?" Kinga looked puzzled. "Is that why you get your face all twisted up?"

"Whatever are you talking about?"

"When your eyebrows wrinkle on your otherwise smooth and lovely forehead."

Sion's eyebrows drew together. Funny bird. Despite herself, Sionee giggled. "*Kinga, I do need your eyes, however.*"

"*Tweeeeeet! I would do anything for you, but wouldn't that render me ... tweet ... sightless?*"

"No silly. You fly high above me and can look down and see things that I cannot, unless I climb a mountain.

"Will you fly above me and tell me what you see? I need you to look specifically."

"Like this?" Kinga twitted, squinting as he poked out his little head.

Sionee giggled and Kinga continued. "*It appears that this is as good an apology from you that I am going to get*," he twitted. "*Yes Mistress. I will look.*"

"Did you just call me Mistress?"

"Yes my lady. I heard myself do just that. Why ... I cannot imagine. I suppose this twit bird is twitterpated."

Alsionee felt her heart warm. "*I think I keep seeing something along the way by the new ditches that come off the river. When I was younger, I cannot remember there being so many little outlets. Do you see something silver or gold beneath the water? Where do all the little ditches go?*"

"*I've seen them before. The little ditches go to water the fields of grain. The instruments you see beneath the water are like hubs that turn. In the turning, water is released from the river into the ditches that flood the fields.*"

From Sion's position on the boat going in, she had wondered at the vast regions of agriculture. Now she knew these were likely fish head gardens ... Big Gardens!

The outliers did not believe in leaving scars on Mother Gaia's surface. She provided an abundance of herbs and flowers and vegetables and fruit and ample grasses for grain.

Who were these who sought abundance more plentiful than She naturally provided? Gardeners of the fish head species surely, and with all this food would it be they who ate it? If so, there must be more of them than she had supposed.

Sion wrinkled her brows in uneasy contemplation. The Cosmopolis had changed.

How long had it been since she had left the familiar grounds at the cove as a child? How long had it been since she had climbed the vast mountain that touched the sky at the sea edge? Had it too changed?

In the far distant corridor of the meandering river she could see the tip of the mountain that marked the bay as if raising from the sea and curving inward. In the cup of the curve she knew her People of the Serpent were protected in their own peaceful little outlier. But what about the people on the other side?

In the habitation of shells and stones and trees and huts, no one had notified them of much amiss. Certainly no one had come and asked for trade of labor to work in gold mines or set up threats unimaginable.

Sion quickly discarded the idea of climbing over the mountain. It would take days and it would be difficult, besides. The volcanoes that made pleasing hot pools, turned into rough territory in the heights.

Of course, it would be a simple thing to sail around the mountain that poked into the sea but ...

"*Kinga, what is on the other side of the mountain beyond my outlier?*"

"*It is a place I don't go myself. I prefer the quiet place by the sea where the fish fill the tide-pools and the birds fly free.*"

"Free? But are not all creatures on Mother Gaia free?"

"I'd just as soon not find out otherwise!" Kinga twitted nervously "But yes! There are a species there that could be of the ones you call fish heads. But, as fish go, they look most unappetizing to me."

"Kinga! Why did you not tell me?"

"Twit ... You never asked."

Chapter Thirteen

Sionee felt the arrow of fear break skin. Why the discomfiture? At least she knew where she was going now. The dream had confirmed what the water, the earth, the air, the fire, the birds, the mammoths, her friends ... and the owl each in their own ways had tried to tell her.

The one message they all had in common was for her to use her head to think. Two clues however really sank in.

"In my hollow an entrance lies." the earth had said. *"You have seen it with your eyes."*

Some of the clues still seemed a mystery, but the wind had said, *"Inside the earth he goes within and there he watches fishes swim."* It had to be by a lake or stream ... obviously, or in the sea or where stream met ocean, as in a waterfall ... and also, something about inside the earth.

The way the clues were leading her, she had journeyed to the beautiful white lady of the stars. She had been led to the Cosmopolitan Major to Hypori and Benan, and to the other side of the mountain whose beginning rose in the sea back home. And finally ... to that instant before all this began when she had cleansed her impure fears at the alcove behind the river which fell to the sea.

In that cavern, she had caught the reflection of a hole that led where? Her guess was that it led into the inner earth into the depth of the mountain to get to the other side. But what about the fish?

She was about to find out. Sionee's heart thudded in fear. Her place of peace didn't seem so peaceful after all.

~~~

Sion made sure You was safe and snug inside the pouch wrap she had devised to carry her in. She secured it firmly and tightened all the knots, wrapping the baby in safe attachment to her own body. There was no way the child would fall unless she herself did, and she would not.

"We will be just fine!" She assured the infant. *"Just rest against me and be still. There must be no loud cries to startle me. I must concentrate."*

"Are we going on another adventure, mother?"

"Not yet," Sion's silent voice swung with the motion of the wild white grapevine. *"Wheeeeeeeeeeeee!"* She called out merrily, despite her fear, and hoping the sound would soothe the child.

Her feet landed firmly at the edge of the ledge that overlooked the sea.

"See, we are here now, and safe," she informed You. Sion advanced cautiously inside the alcove. It was midafternoon ... just a bit later perhaps. The rainbow prism would surely point the hole out as it had done at the sun time when she had first seen it, not long ago ... but forever ago.

It was there. In awestruck fear and vast curiosity, Sion stood before the dark hole with the baby of some man from who knows what star.

When she found him, would he use the stick that turns someone into dust on her? Sion could feel her trembling heart beating loud!

She didn't think so. She had looked at him, face to face directly into his eyes, even. She had felt his heart beat against her heart. Sion didn't want to think about him, but his eyes were kind.

Sion stood in contemplation. Suddenly, she was in her dream again. However, this time the otherwise black and deep pool of the owl eye pupil was a brilliant purple, while the color of the iris was black. The purple pupil expanded and contracted. It seemed to move and swirl, inviting her to enter.

"Do not!" Kinga squawked from outside the small chamber. *"Do not! I insist you must not even think about it. It is dark in there. Sionee don't go!"*

Sionee wished she could obey a silly bird. But before the arrow of fear shot its shaft to pierce her through her whole body ... perhaps even to kill her ... and everyone else in the whole outlier of the Fey ... she had to do something!

She took a few minutes to prepare a torch and stash a live coal in one of her little pots while Kinga squawked and protested.

She checked You again to insure her safety close against her.

Turning her back from Kinga, Alsionee Tree Song entered the hole.

While her eyes adjusted to the strange interior, Sion's ankle turned on a rock. Crying out in pain she bent to pick up the rock.

It wasn't a big rock; it fit firmly in the cup of her hand. The pocket inside her shift was big enough to hold it. She might need it. If it was necessary she could throw it quite hard.

By the light of her torch she saw several sticks lying on the ground as well. She found one with a good, strong, sharply-pointed edge. She gathered it and clasped it tight within her hand.

Sion had never carried a weapon before. It was unheard of on the Snake. There were, however, circumstances of necessity.

Feeling a bit more equipped, Sionee raised her torch higher and stared about, only to see her torch flicker and extinguish.

The totality of the blackness enveloped her. She quickly spun around to the comfort of the small bit of light at the portal hole, but the cave entrance had seemed to disappear. She should be looking at a bit of illumination streaking into the dark hole, surely. She had entered and taken just one small step forward. Panic rose in her. This was not good, and she had just begun this trek into stupidity.

Sion fumbled for her little coal lamp. Struggling to keep her wits, she finally got it to take flame. The air was certainly not stagnant. The flame flickered to the movement of air.

She was frightened and wished she'd listened to Kinga. He really wasn't a silly bird. Sometimes he was quite wise, actually. Though she would never tell him this ... if she got another chance to anyway.

She thought she had taken only a step or two. Where was the entrance? How could she have lost it?

In the black distance ... she thought it was distant ... Sion thought she saw something. Perhaps it was a soft bit of light? Her footsteps took her eagerly in that direction. She would feel safer if she could remain orientated to where she was sure she had entered. Was this the entrance?

She hastened forward. With each step she realized however that there were too many steps. The light couldn't possibly be the entrance. However the air seemed so fresh it made the flame of her lamp sputter.

Sion felt relief. Surely it was a different way out of the cave. Her eyes affixed on the glow of the new exit, and she did not see the faint echoes of light in the recesses in front of her face.

She banged roughly into a wall-like corner. It was sharp, and surely her forehead would get an egg from the impact. When Sion touched the pain, she felt moisture seeping from the bump. In the light of her lamp Sionee saw the sticky red on her fingertips. Then, the light from her lamp went out entirely. The lamp was no longer in her hand. The impact with the wall had made it tumble and roll into a crevice.

The faint light she had been following lent the merest of illumination. She could see that her lamp was wedged pretty securely, its lid spilt with coal lying who knew where.

"Kinga!" She called out loud. Would he hear her? She used her word voice, unheeding again what she now considered a useless vow. Her call was as loud and as precise as any she had ever made. His name echoed emptily throughout ... wherever they were. If he didn't hear her voice would he be able to hear her need for assistance?

Sion's cry startled You. The baby began to scream with raucous screeches that reverberated on the walls and made little pings of rock debris fall like a shower of rain around them.

Sionee patted You. *"Quiet, Quiet. It is okay sweetie. It really is. There is a faint, faint light. I can still see."* Sion looked ahead.

To her intense horror, the light turned into a spiraling ring of moving luminous circles that melted into each other as they spun into a whirl of purple ... then, orange ... then, purple again ... of a different hue altogether.

Sionee gasped. Was this THE OWL EYE? There was nowhere to

flee! She could see nothing outside the distance of its light. You's screams echoed in the hollows of the darkness.

"I am scared!"

"I won't let anything happen to you," Sionee assured her with a confidence of which she, herself, felt none. The eye ... if it was an eye ... moved.

The spiral was encircling ... coming close, then ... advancing ... coming close again ... in a spin.

Sionee was frozen as the circle seemed to open its mouth and draw her and You into its breath. Oh, Oh,... it did! They were inside the circle now. Had it eaten them ... or what?

What was this? Nowhere in her vast imagination had she ever seen anything like this before. And since she was a storyteller, her imagination was vast.

However in her dreams ... and this was not a dream ... at least she didn't think it was a dream. But, she hoped it was ... because ... were not dreams something one always woke up from?

Sionee pinched herself. Never had she felt so awake. Surely if she opened her eyes wider she could shake the sleep away, and make the dream disappear in the light of morning. It was late afternoon, she remembered ... that she had come to the cave ... so why would she be dreaming?

"Mother, I can feel your heart beating." Terrified, Sion barely felt You's observance. The purple brightness advanced around them faster than she could turn to flee. She and You went down its throat. It had taken them inside itself.

~~~

"I thought I'd already been born!" You sent her startled words to Sionee.

"Of course, you were born, silly."

"It looks like I am again waiting at the entrance of the womb tunnel inside my birth lady ... and she is pushing me! I see that she is pushing you, too. Go mother! Maybe you need to be born again, too!"

Had she died then? Had her stubborn determination caused

both her and You to cross the field of purple?

The light pulled them toward something ... truly like a birth canal contracting and pulsing ... pushing toward what?

It wasn't exactly a white light as was often described, and certainly there were no swans singing. Sion collected herself somewhat to look again. The search for the fish head no longer seemed important.

Her hand reached out and upward as she felt smooth, but bubbly walls that seemed rather organic. She could see the darkness of the cave through what appeared to be like the melted sands where the volcanoes of old erupted. They were enclosed in what looked like thick, matted, and glimmering glass.

They were in a tunnel, a glass tunnel. It breathed and pulsed ... and carried her and You further in as if they were within the gut of a giant digestive tract of sorts ... undergoing digestion.

She could see the spinning blackness of the cave, distorted through the opaque and milky glass walls. Any of the cavern features that might indicate where they really were, had disappeared into nothing but a dark blob that somehow or other had a sort of light within. But was it a light?

Her imagination grew frightful wings and Sion saw that the molten glass fused together in segments like the vertebrae of an animal skeleton, or a human. It was like she was energy traversing a spine.

Maybe it was like the way a caterpillar looked when it was all scrunched up in inch. Oh, what the ...? She didn't know what it was like.

Then, she could no longer distinguish the motion outside the tunnel from the motion within. She was floating now. Upside down ... right-side up ... sideways ... vertically. Was the tunnel widening?

Sion cradled You and held her tightly even though the child was well secured to her body with ties. You quit crying and whimpered lightly.

"I guess we have both crossed the line darling," Sion managed to squeak. *"I didn't think it would be like this. I imagined something far*

more beautiful. They said it was beautiful. I am sorry sweetie. I was going to name you."

"You were going to give me back."

"I was, and ... Oh, darling, I wanted you to have a father. I'm sorry for everything ... for dragging you around. I guess you and I will have karma now.

"Of course, we do, silly ... and in my before-life was I really that bad a mother that you needed a father? I don't know why I tried to come back as a breedling of the fish head. It seemed like quite an opportunity at the time. It doesn't matter now ... Whooooah!"

Sionee and You turned and spun. The stick, the stone, and everything flew out of Sion's pocket and from her hands. All of it floated alongside them like debris.

Sionee grabbed the stone and hammered it against the glass. What would she do if the weird enclosure broke? Would just a piece of it fall out or would the whole thing crumble around them? Then, where would they be? Lost in the darkness with shattered glass covering them?

But she wanted to get out of this. She thrust the rock against the glass again ... and again. Not even a chip; certainly no cracks. The glass was apparently as thick as it looked.

Sion attempted to turn around and push through the force toward the way they had come in, but the current was so strong it to pulled both of them forward. She lost the direction of going either forward or backward. She and You were just swirling. The vesicle expanded and closed ... expanded and closed ... in a slow motion thrum.

The speed increased for a brief moment... and *wheeeee.* They were in water ... cold water. Sionee grabbed You closer as the ties the babe was secured with began to slip off her shoulders.

They would be in the underworld together. Why it was the underworld, she didn't know. Surely she had lived a better life than that. But You ... she was an innocent ... barely born. Why hadn't she believed You was mamun before? Maybe mother was sent to the underworld because she had broken the hearts of so many men, and had never given Sion a real father. But what the big deal? She'd been a great mother ... the best!

So here it was. She and You ... She and her mother ... You was her mother come back on a star, only to get Sion, her daughter, and escort her to the underworld. But she never had been convinced that there was ever such a place ... until now.

Sionee opened her eyes and saw a goldfish with big eyes staring directly at her. You was smiling and batting with her tiny hands at the fish completely unconcerned that neither of them could breathe.

Then, Sion saw something before her. Her hand slid against a clear, flat surface. It was like a window. She pressed her nose to the window and peered in.

The window beneath the water distorted the image she saw inside.

Sionee choked ... gasping instinctively in fear ... drawing into her lungs salt ... stinging salt water ... not air. Bubbles sprang from her nose.

On the other side of the window ... or whatever it was, wherever it was ... two eyes peered back at her.

They were huge ... green and gleaming ... as they frowned at her in fiendish and fierce hideousness.

They were not owl eyes. But that was all she saw before she sank into the purple mists beyond the dreams.

Chapter Fourteen

The kiss was warm ... nice. She sank deep inside the rich no-moon blackness behind her closed eyes so she could feel this pleasure

Her lips were bathed in pulsing, vibrating moisture. Hot, wet and flowing warm breath ... in and out ... on her cheeks ... soft ... urgent ... bid her open.

"Come ... ," the kiss said, "to life!" It was he! Never in her whole existence had she felt so entirely wrapped in such total protection and love.

The love was breathing in and out. His breath was her breath. His lips were her lips. Even beyond that, his spirit was her spirit. They were one in GNOS.

The sweet moisture turned into a bubbling gush that stung her throat as it came out.

His hand on her chest was not sweet, but heavy. It crushed her clear to her breast bone, forcing the water to leave her lungs and let air flow within.

"Heeeeeeeeeeeeeeey!" She shouted. He was rough, much too rough, and the kissing was gone, leaving only a choking, sputtering cough.

Sion forgot that she had taken a vow of no words. "Hey," she protested. "You stinky, slimy piece of fish, if I may dishonor an honest creature of Gaia. How dare you put your hands upon me?"

That said, life came rushing into her silent mind and exploded in a frenzy of anger. Then, she was silent. Oh, yeah. She had made a vow never to speak again until the trouble her AHDAWN was in, was no more. This son of a foul shark!

Sionee's sharp words did not seem to register in the fish head's head. His eyes were wide, big, and round. Surely there was a heart in there that beat rapidly, so rapidly that she could see his chest moving beneath his wet tunic. Surely he wasn't really a fish then. He was too warm to be a fish.

Sion looked around her strange environment in panic.

"Where is my baby?" She screamed again, forgetting her vow.

~~~

Ea almost passed out. The relief he had felt when she breathed again was replaced with shock.

"Daffinina." He begged her with his eyes to understand something. Would she ever understand?

Sion looked behind her. There was no one there. It was just she and he. Was he addled?

"My Daffinina. Everything is okay, my sweet."

"My name is not Daffinina. It is Alsionee ... Alsionee Tree Song for your obtuse information ... and I repeat! Where is my baby?"

Sion reached out and grabbed the empty wet swaddling You had been wrapped in, and held it frantically against her chest. She began to cry in pain, fear, and anger.

"You did save her did you not?" Sion's eyes said everything for her. *"Where is she?"*

Ea took a breath of double relief. Of course, she was referring to the girl child.

"I sent her to medical to make sure she was not harmed." He felt ire begin to stir on the other side of his relief.

"Whatever was my Daffinina doing to be swimming in the waters with an infant so young? She was as close to death as I've ever seen. While I was struggling to bring your pretty ass back to life I called the suds to assist me. She is with them. Pray to life that she still breathes."

Ea pulled the communication device from his tug pocket and pushed some buttons with his slippery fingers. His hands were too large for the irksome, but necessary device he held.

"The baby!" He put his voice into the box. "What is her status?"

Sionee called to Skymother with all her AHDAWN which was feeling pretty weak at the moment. Her heart home was beating in fear.

The doors to the little room burst open and a young woman rushed through, smiling as she held You up to the fish head.

You giggled and batted her big beautiful eyes at Ea. A luminous spark of light danced between the two and the room lit up like the noonday sun.

Ea sank in that moment into the infant's sweet sea of innocence and love. He felt himself, who he thought was the best of all the best, to be nothing but an inferior beggar beside the beauty of the baby. He would write mother of this little girl. He smiled into her big bright eyes. Would so great a creation be able to relate to a soul as poor as his was?

"My Tititum!" He bowed before the girl. "Ever am I at your servitude my lovely child!"

For the briefest of moments Sion was touched. How would it feel to have a father who beheld one with such reverence? How, indeed? He loved the girl. Sionee Tree Song was almost happy, for a moment, to give the child to her father. He would be a good father.

"She is yours!" Alsionee whispered from the depths of her heart. All the sharpness she had been feeling vanished.

Ea picked up the child and kissed her on her small pink nose. "No." He said. "She is yours. Raise her with wisdom Daffinina. In you I trust."

Her anger returned along with a strange sense of relief as he handed the baby back into her arms. You was wrapped up in soft linens more exquisite than any she had ever seen before. The linens were sweet with a gentle fragrance.

Sionee rubbed the baby's head with her cheek and held the baby tight against her heart.

Ea wanted to stay and enjoy the moment with his Daffinina, but a knock sounded on the closed door. When the door opened, a strange fish head male rushed in and bowed.

"Isimud ... greetings!" Ea spoke. "What message brings you here?"

"My Lord," Isimud replied. "Lord Enlil and Lady Ninmah have arrived."

Panic again threatened Ea. He could hide nothing from his sister. Enlil perhaps, but Ninmah had eyes in the back of her head.

He spoke a few quick words to the sud. Sionee noted the indrawn breath that the fish head took. What had he said that the female fish head who had brought her daughter in was called? A sud? A bubble, did he say?"

He turned to Sion, but Sion deliberately avoided his eyes. "Damn it!" He shouted angrily. The door opened as if of its own accord, and he rushed out.

~~~

"My Lord bids you wait here." The sud spoke softly and smiled gently. Sionee realized that the fish heads were beautiful, sort of ... She prepared to leave. It occurred to her that she didn't know how to leave. But she most certainly would not take orders from these strangers. She didn't even know for sure if they were people, or what.

The sud put her hand softly on Sionee's shoulder. "Please wait." She spoke gently. Her voice soothed the anger and the commotion Sion felt in her AHDAWN.

"Lord Ea has bid me to instruct you. He will be back momentarily and wishes to speak with you himself."

Sionee did not reply. If the young fish head woman had ears to hear AHDAWN, let her hear all the bad feelings of mistrust she had about these ... were they people?

The girl didn't hear the thought Sionee sent her. The sud calmly and efficiently began her instruction.

"Your baby almost ceased her life," she began. "My Lord Ea says you must not return the way you came in."

"How do I get out then?" Sionee tried to ask. Did the girl hear after all?

"My Lord says to wait. He will explain when he returns. But for now I must instruct you." She handed Sion a pouch of something white and powdery like sand, but not heavy like sand would be.

"Mix it well with upmost clear and clean water, preferably boiled.

Then, shake this vial." She handed something like the artificial nipple pouch to Sion.

"It only takes a small bit of powder, see? This will last you for some time. Master Ea will see to it that you get more."

What was she suggesting? There was still some milk left. She certainly didn't need the fish head version of baby milk. Sion looked around for her pouch. Then, the window where golden fish swam on the other side caught her eye.

Sion rushed to the window and peered out in astonishment. She was looking at the sands beneath the sea. The watery depths of the ocean's secrets wavered in clear view before her eyes.

Drifting in the currents over the great sand of the sea floor, she could see the milk pouches bobbing up and down. There was also some kind of strange creatures that looked like ... umm ... her soft linens and her carrying pouch floating along with fish!

Certainly, she would have to feed the baby something.

"This milk is of a higher quality than the milk you have been feeding her. Our analysis shows this wee one to be short on proper nutrition."

Sionee stared. Analysis?

"The baby will grow healthy and strong on this milk. It is all natural from the breasts of our Annunaki mothers. It has been dried for ease of consumption for the child of a busy lady."

The what? An-nu-naki ... did she say? Sion dropped the pouch as if it was poison. The sud only looked at her gently.

Oh, damn! The girl was nice enough. Why should she blame her for anything? She was only doing as she was instructed by him.

"Your child has been through trauma. She has strength in her coding. She giggles because her life force is glad to be alive and radiant."

Life force ... coding? Was that fish language for spirit or what?

"If her body is not nourished properly, her code will not thrive, as our Lord Ea wishes."

Lord? Who's Lord?

The bubble bent and picked up the packet and handed it to Sion, along with a bundle of the very white and softly fragrant linens. On top of the neatly folded linens, You's lambie was all fluffy and soft. It had already been washed and dried out and fluffed as if it had never been drenched in the salt of the sea ... like she and You had been. Sionee took the linens and the blue lamb.

"Please wait for our Lord." The sud bubble turned, muttering to herself as she 'bubbled' away through the suddenly opened door. Sion did not hear the words the girl said at the door because another sound distracted her.

A loud thud vibrated hollowly across the pane of glass along with a strange streaking sort of sound. Sion's first impression was that a large fish had bumped into the window.

It was a big fish, indeed! It was groping desperately at the window, making it shake until there was a wonder that the glass didn't spring a leak.

The distorted face grimaced and peered through the mossy glass of the window's ocean surface. Long black hair waved and floated about the strange fish face that had a flattened nose as it pressed to gaze inside.

Sion gasped, barely recognizing Cyex motioning frantically at the window.

Quickly she put the baby down and rushed to a little room she had noticed just off the side of the room that the fish head had brought her into. She could see that the floor in this room was slippery and wet.

This was so weird, just too much to take in all at once. What to do? A big wheel-like device gleamed in the heart of the small enclosure.

There was no time to think or ponder; Cyex would drown. Sion turned the wheel a little timidly at first but when it moved slightly, she gave it a good firm twist. The port hole opened with vast amounts of water, and Cyex streamed inside.

"Close it girl!" He shouted. The room was filling up. Sionee spun the wheel. An onslaught of water poured forth.

"The other way!" Cyex croaked, sputtering and coughing as he grasped his breath. He slipped on the water covered stone floor as he struggled to stand up.

Cyex stood up with wet sea weed curling about his ear. Sion reached to pull it off, laughing. Cyex didn't know whether to grab her and kiss her or shake the living daylights out of her. He did neither, only frowned.

Sion had never been so glad to see someone. She threw her arms around his drenched shoulders and planted a huge kiss square on his lips ... his wet and warm lips.

A loud ringing broke the silence with an ear splitting shriek. You began to scream with it.

Cy stepped back and smiled at Sionee. "Somehow I knew that alarms would go off when you kissed me." He grabbed her hand.

Sion paused and bent to pick up You. She managed to grab the pouch of milk and the swaddlings as Cyex hastened her. She bent again to pick up the blue lamb.

"*We can't go through the waters, she almost drowned.*" Sion looked him directly in the eye.

"Come then!" He shouted. "We've got to get out of here. Surely there is a way out and I suggest we find it fast!"

She had seen the fish head and that sudsy girl go through the door without any problem. But there was no handle on the door and it seemed to be shut so that it couldn't be opened. Had that shark head locked her in?

"There must be a key somewhere. We must open it."

"*But where will it take us?*" Sion spoke in her quiet words. Cy could see her fearful eyes.

"Darling, where will it take us if we just sit here and wait? For what? We can't take the chance. Neither of us have any idea about what is going on in here."

The two of them quickly began to inspect all the nooks and crannies of the room.

One wall, opposite the window was made entirely of luminescent abalone shell. It was lovely and she wanted to examine its beauty. The soft lamps in the small room reflected on the shell and made the wall appear as a gentle breath of rainbow hued heartbeat.

The gentle domed ceiling was as the sky itself! It was lovely. There was not time to stare but she would really like to just look.

The ceiling was colored a smooth deep and dark blue ... deep as purple. Hanging from the ceiling on delicate silver chains, here and there as in a random sky, dried white starfish twirled in suspension. White sand dollars appeared as orbs of the starry sky. Smaller orbs also dotted the universe the fish head had created. Tiny creamy pearls, hanging in the dimension of pseudo-sky, suggested far distant stars. A large round sea urchin, white as the moon, further made her feel like she was enclosed in Skymothers loving arms.

Actually it was a simple design suggesting the heavens, a bit of artistry, truly! The sea ornaments reflected the clever use of light. The orbs seemed to glow somehow from within.

Despite herself, she reached up to touch one of the spheres in reverence.

"Could you get the desk?" Cyex spoke sharply, as his hand slid over a shelf that contained strange leafs ... or something.

The things in the room fascinated her immensely, the desk no less.

Little boxes, made of an assortment of shell, glass, wood, or silver, contained all manner of little something's. They made a quaint collection of things she would have loved to look at.

As her hands invaded all the personal belongings of the fish head ... who she really despised, she kept catching a scent. Where had she smelled that not unpleasant smell before? It was so him.

This looked like a gold feather; it was not a feather. There were tiny blue aquamarine stones fixed along the length of the quill.

Were these scribed words? What kind of beautiful lines were these? And were these leaves of gold? They were pure and burnished. Sionee gasped at the thinness of the pounded metal that held secrets within. She had to give credit of some kind to whoever had produced something so fine.

The delicate design traced on the thin papyri were like a scribe she had never seen before. Nowhere in her instruction in the universities of song where she had beheld scripts from all lands across Gaia, had she seen such inscription. What did these symbols mean? Or were they mere ornamentation? A little slip of leaf fell from the small book.

"Come on!" Cyex shouted. "Quit gawking."

She clenched the fallen leaf in her hand, determining to take it with her so she could study it when she got out of this mess. Could she keep it safe? Her shift was drying rapidly, the pocket almost dry. She thrust the small slip inside.

The shark head hadn't used a key. The door had opened when he spoke loudly. She went to the door and made a loud noise. The door remained shut.

"Damn it!" Cyex shouted loudly. His eyes opened in wide astonishment as the door slid open.

The two rushed forward, Sionee quickly retrieved the baby, the swaddlings, the powdered bag of milk, and the blue lamb.

~~~

The hall was long but as well-lit as if the sun could shine through opaque stone. One passage seemed to go upward, another seemed to go down.

" Up!" Cyex shouted. Somewhere in the middle they saw an open door. At their heels, creatures that appeared as little men made of silver poured forth to chase them.

Sion ran in a panic. She'd never seen the likes of these. They appeared as silver with big gleaming bug eyes that had taken on a life.

The creatures seemed to freeze when the alarm suddenly silenced itself. They stopped, still as if they had turned to stone.

Cyex pulled Sion through the open door into a tunnel room. What was it with all these fish head tunnels that seemed to lead to nowhere but terror? This one was dark. *"Don't let me go Cyex. Don't let me go!"*

Sion held tight to Cyex's hand and clung tight.

The sound of rushing water soon became apparent. It was like a fast moving creek or river gurgling. The air in the tunnel was moist and dripping.

But the worst was when two big red eyes suddenly loomed before them. Eyes the wrong color of brilliant ruby ... Then, the growl of a dog.

Was it a wolf perhaps? Sion discerned the form of a huge black dog with big shining white teeth that curved in a growl. Was the dark playing tricks on her, or was there really two heads on the dog? Each head had only one big eye ... ONE BIG RED eye.

Sionee winced. She was frightened and her leg was really beginning to ache. The skin, where she had bumped it on the cave wall that had pulled her into this nightmare, itched and stung sharply, as well as the bone beneath it. Each step jarred as if a knife was piercing her.

She felt great relief when Cyex picked up a stone and threw it hard at the dog. The dog yelped and backed off a bit.

Around the curve, a bit of light began to cast hope. On the banks of an underground stream a boat waited at the water edge.

Cyex jumped in without hesitation. "Hand me the baby," he shouted. Sion did not wish to have anything to do with water. As she stood wide-eyed in fear, the dog came back and nipped its gnashing teeth at her heel. She handed the baby to Cyex as she rapidly jumped in.

"Daysong!" She shouted, quiet but sure.

"What did you say?" He shouted back, straining to hear her silly way of speaking through the roar of the stream current.

"My daughter's name is Daysong!"

The dog howled in ferocious bays with each of its mouths. They could hear footsteps coming closer to the entrance where they had entered.

"Lovely!" Cy yelled back. "Move!" He ordered sharply. There

was an old man in the boat. Sion couldn't imagine how either of them had escaped from knocking him out of the wobbly boat as they jumped in. He was gray with shaggy looking skin drooping off a skeleton-like frame. But his eyes were bright ... too bright.

"Pass word?" The man shouted, his eyes gleaming in menace. "I move only at my Master's command!" He threatened.

"Command this!" Cyex smacked the little man so hard his head fell off into the waters.

Sion watched in horror as the waters turned into bubbles and a foul sulfurous smell rose out of the deep.

Cyex took the oars from the now non-moving hands. The little boat caught the current with Cy's strong hands and they were off."

"How could you?" Sion asked as Cyex maneuvered the boat past the sharp and fast corners of the stream. Other than that, it was pretty quiet at last.

The water was red, through and through, deep dark brown-red, like blood.

"It isn't blood!" Cyex shouted. "There was no bleeding. Didn't you see the smoke? The creature was made of fire, and I loved every minute of extinguishing his ugly eyes by lopping him in the water."

The boat drifted to a sharp curve that hopefully led to the outside of the cave. The light was becoming clearer and the air began to feel fresher.

Sion breathed, thankful for the cessation of foul smell. Then, she saw the waterfall ahead.

They should have been prepared. It was much like the waterfall that dropped off their alcove back at home. Was this her punishment for casting her troubles into the pure waters?

There was no visible way out of the fast moving boat, and no way out of the raging current. Sion only saw rainbow mist.

She screamed as the spray hit the rocks at the entrance of the drop off and enveloped her in more water.

But Cyex laughed just as the boat took air.

Sion dared to open her eyes and saw that Cyex had one of his firm hands grasped around a branch that had gotten caught at the drop off current. The branch spread out vertically across the water, itself being firmly trapped by rocks at each side of the stream.

Sionee's hands were frozen, as well as her AHDAWN. The water was amazingly cold but the numbness came from weariness within. Cyex held tight with one hand and helped her climb out the best he could.

She slipped and slid as she tried to firm the boat for him as he climbed out. In the end, he tumbled out and into the water, barely as the commotion sent the branch and the boat both down ... way down.

The spray was so vast she could see nothing but oblivion. "Cy!" She shouted in voice. Terror had again nixed her vow.

From out of the mist, Cyex landed in a large leap of spray, knocking her and Daysong over. All of them lay together in a very grateful and wet heap.

Safe in her arms, Daysong cooed. *"Can I call you mother now?"*

Sionee giggled *"Forever, my darling daughter ... forever!"*

Sion and Cy's bodies were pressed together on the banks of the cave ledge at the edge of the iron rich waters. Their eyes were locked one in one.

Quickly Sionee turned her head and gasped. Rising above the mist, the rainbow was the most beautiful and the most colorful promise she had ever beheld.

Chapter Fifteen

When the screeching security system nearly deafened him, Ea met Ninmah in the long hallway by the alarm outlets. His face was white, his brows drawn together.

She knew that look. She wanted to reach out and trace the furrow on his forehead with her finger. She moved her finger to do so.

"Ninitum!" He spoke breathlessly. Ninmah waited eagerly for the hug of greeting she had expected. As her fingers reached his forehead they were crushed aside in haste as he bent to study the alarm panel. With one quick motion the screeching alarm sounds were quiet.

"Whew." Ea wiped at his brow. The sound would most certainly frighten Daffinina. Apparently, she had not waited for his instructions.

Ea cursed. He should have set Isimud outside the room to guard, or the sud. But he wouldn't want to make Daffinina feel forced to stay. He'd already interfered with her too much.

Ea pushed a few more buttons, contemplating quickly. She had to be in the facility, somewhere. Surely the thought of drowning the child had kept her from trying the water way, he hoped. He had warned her and had seen fear register in her eyes.

Ninmah reached for him again.

Where would the girl go? Surely he had built long winding halls into the facility, in a mazelike structure for security reasons. If she were in the halls she could get lost.

Or ... a new onslaught of cold sweat poured from the furrow of his brow. What if she came upon his newest little project? Perhaps the sound would bid her to the discovery. From what Ea could tell, the boy had quite the lungs. How would he ever explain to her?

Worse than that, even. What if the girl ran into Enlil, or even Ninmah? He must get her out of the facility fast.

Ea pushed the buttons to open the safest exit-way he could re-call. If she took that way out and got through safe enough, she would come out again at the bottom of the hill ... with a little overcoming of a lot of built-in difficulties along the way. Yet, he knew his Daffinina had a lot of smarts. He flipped the light on at the doorway to entice her in that direction ... he hoped.

It would lead to safety outside the facility. As smart as his Daffinina was she could find her way over the mountain.

But first she would have to deal with the guard dog, as well as the robotic gray who manned the canoe oar.

He pushed another button to still the electricity that brought the boat man to life. Surely, Daffinina would not know the password.

How had she opened the door that led out of his inner sanctum? Surely, such a sweet little thing couldn't possibly guess his pass-word, could she?

Ignoring Ninmah, he ran to the exit-way he had opened. He smiled when he saw the two headed dog was safe. It came up and licked his hand with its two tongues. The dog seemed quite agitated as he paced back and forth, peering anxiously down the channel, whimpering with his two bright eyes.

The boat was gone. The girl was amazing. Before he turned to calmly greet Ninmah who had followed him to the boat post, he noticed a strange bubbling in the water, and the smell of sulpher.

Ea turned to his sister with a smile so bright, surely it was for her. "Nin, Nin!" Ea reached out for her.

Ninmah did not fail to notice that the furrows in his forehead had calmed somewhat, and that this time his smile was genuine. But he had ignored her. Further, why had the alarms not been turned on in the first place? Also, what were they doing in the bowels of dark-ness with a two-headed black dog with oversized tongues lapping at her hand? At least she hoped the two tongues were just lapping. They were getting her all slimy and stinky.

She wanted such an acknowledgement from Ea. At least she had been hoping. It had been so long.

"Why did you not have the alarm on?" She asked. When I got here, I became aware that your system was off, so I flipped the button."

He pulled her close, caressing her with a sexy hug, just the kind that Ninmah deemed more appropriate. He held her tight against his body and planted his lips over hers.

It took so little; Ninmah could always be distracted thus.

~~~

For a moment Ninmah sighed in pleasure. He still loved her well. How could he not? Though his body had seemed a bit cool at first, it was warming up. No ... it was heating up!

Within the deep embrace she could feel something tapping eagerly against her soft silken thigh.

Ninmah reached down and cupped the motion in the palm of her hand, smiling beneath the kiss. She still had it ... the power to command the grand instruments of both her brothers.

"Eeeooouuugh!" She suddenly broke away from his kisses. "Why exactly are you all wet ... and you smell like the sea?" She reached up and pulled moss from his hair.

He ignored her question and peeled the damp tug from his loins, and reached up to release her own stately and royal robes. Ninmah forgot all questions.

~~~

The cave dripped water from off its stone wall. The dog had been tethered to a stalactite with a rope, and the monster sleepily watched them with his saucer red eyes. Ninmah felt a tingling tighten her pleasure spot.

Her vagina poured forth with a moisture she knew her brother would find pleasing.

"Your river flows Nin, Nin " He crooned into her ear as his finger explored her warm channel.

"I have been eager to open for the passage of your, ah ... sea vessel." She smiled at him through lashes lowered in pleasure.

With his submarine, he dove in. Ninmah didn't need much ... just a lot. She did enjoy frequent quickies. His mind, extremely relieved that Daffinina had escaped, was elsewhere.

"Damn!" He chided himself. Normally he would have thoroughly enjoyed this. Who was this girl who had the power to turn his thoughts from Ninmah?

"Faster!" Ninmah screamed. "Faster! Oh, Enki, my Lord... Faster... deeper... OH, DEEPER!"

Ea withdrew, turning away from her, hoping she had not noticed the quick de-rigor of his steering pole.

Ninmah sat up. "What is with you?" She shrieked in disappointment. "Or, should I query 'what is not UP with you?' I wasn't finished yet!"

"It is the name you called me." His face was red. Ninmah could not guess whether it was from anger or shame.

~~~

"Ninmah, you know how I feel about that name. I hate it!"

"Get off it, brother. Who cares about a silly name?" She was frantic ... breathing heavily. *Damn him ... damn him ... damn him!*

"I do!" He spat.

Water still poured from her vagina onto her thigh and was making her sticky. Ninmah sat up.

"Later," he assured her. "when we retire to my chamber. Or will you be in the room of Enlil tonight?"

"Of course, I'll be in his room!" She shrieked, knowing it was a lie. But he did not. He looked at her with sad puppy dog eyes, reminding her of the two single eyes put together on each of the black dog's machine heads.

"Ea!" She spoke at last. "Forgive me for calling you Enki. By assigning the name to you, Enlil only sought to give you honor."

"Yeah, sure." Bitterness rose in Ea's voice as detected well by Ninmah.

"Ninmah! Never ... ever call me by the name which my father and my brother have given me."

"What is wrong with it? Are you not Lord of the Land as your new-given name implies? We all thought to so honor you."

"It is patronizing." He said. "I am, indeed, Lord of the earth. I was here first while he of the seed abiding swoozled our father on the Perfect World of the righteous. It was I who made Ki what it is now, Ninmah.

"I refined it in my forging flame. I polished it with my waters. Into sweet Ki I planted ... into our creation ... I breathed first.

"I am Lord of Ki, Ninmah. I don't need permission to be so granted by my father or my brother ... they who know so much of so little! My real name suits me fine. It is me ... what I have been called since my creation. It is who I am, "Whose Home Is The Waters.""

Ea was silent a moment as Ninmah took to straightening the folds in her fancy garment.

"I do have another name though, that I shall allow. My father in law, Alulu gave it to me when I dug ditches and directed streams to flow, and created beautiful Eridu to be home away from home for all of us who first came to the sweet Ki, long before you and Enlil showed up."

Ninmah was getting bored. Ea would never change. He had emotional baggage. It was something no decent Annunaki would display or even own, as it was against the law ... as well it should be. It could so get in the way if it was allowed to exist.

She still wanted something else besides a lecture from her brother. Her fingers drummed on the pulse of her vulva.

She giggled. "On Nibiru it is said that you and all the heroes fell down onto Ki with all the many animals!"

"Oh, yeah? They so dishonor me?" His eyes pierced her composure. "Then, you fell also, sister. Do you think any of those archaic bastards will ever extend their hands to get your ass up there with them again? You might be carrying a disease from the animals! Especially since your vulva needs such excess in attention!"

"Eeeoou, speaking of bastards brother, you are one, and I mean it quite literally. Just what are you saying? I, princess of the Annunaki, have a pure mound. When my mission is over I shall return!"

Ea laughed bitterly. He extended his hand and pulled her from off the damp ground where she sat hugging her knees pathetically. He led her back into the medical facility. Perhaps he had said too much. He was thankful his tongue hadn't gotten away from him. He was tempted to mention that she was beginning to show signs of age, an earth related disease that eventually destroyed the form of all matter within its dimension.

He closed the door behind them and adjusted the alarms. She watched him in silence. In the hallway of the facility, Ninmah grinned at her brother. Perhaps it would be safer ground to his moodiness, here.

She certainly wasn't going to let something as ridiculous as emotion rule.

"So just what is it that Alulu called you?" She asked, batting her deep universe-blue eyes at him.

"Nudimmud," he replied curtly.

"Indeed." She replied. "He Who Fashions." Of course, another of her brothers vast traits. He was always busy working on something ... and it wasn't her. "I think I'll just call you 'brother' when we are in the throes of passion. Then, you won't shrivel up like a little worm."

Ea looked at her with disgust. He had shriveled, surely. But a worm did she say?

If she came with him to his room tonight he'd show her. The thought now made him grow again. Ninmah was still the most beautiful Annunaki female he'd ever seen, aside from his mother.

Tonight he would take her to his chambers and show her the serpent ... and to hell with the worm.

~~~

"Ninmah where is our brother, Enlil? Did he notice the symbols I placed at the gate of my facility?"

Appreciating his change of mood, Ninmah laughed. "Oh, Ea, he did!" Her laughter turned to giggles. Ea was relieved. Ninmah giggles were like musical bells. How he loved to hear her bells ring!

"Brother Enlil would not step one foot down the path of stone serpents you are so cleverly constructing at the 'vile corridor'. Those were his very words!" Her giggles filled the air with Ninmah pleasure.

"It is a very clever concept, brother, and very charming. You know how Enlil feels about the snakes. I thought the design stunning! I can hardly wait to see them finished!"

Ea was pleased. He had hoped they would cause such a sensation in his brother. "Where is he now?" He inquired.

"He appreciates the rooms you arranged near the Eagle's landing." She explained. "He said he was weary and would wait until morning for our meeting. He instructed that we all gather at the mine headquarters. You didn't build serpents at the mine port did you?"

Ea laughed. "No, I thought of it. The serpents however are personal to me, and the mines belong to us all."

"Ea do you have a cafeteria in this facility? I am getting hungry. Is the food any good? My stomach almost quenches the other hunger you so aptly left unsatisfied. Will you fill me up brother?"

"I'll fill you up plenty my sister. You will see. Is Enlil expecting you?"

"His Ninlilitum is with him," Ninmah replied, forgetting to lie. "She came unexpected. I think she fears to let us ... brother and sister ... travel together." Ninmah giggled again.

The two of them arrived at the cafeteria. With great pleasure they devoured rare and fattened boar meat, dripping with savory bloody juices wedged between two chunks of grease-smothered bread ... all sipped with hot, hot coffee.

"Uum, Ea. Cacao, or coffee did you say? I am amazed at this drink! Where again was it you said it came from? Across the ocean? Oh, and you must roast the berries to bring out this wonderful flavor? Why, such a delightful repast. It makes me feel so well ... um ... comforted, almost!"

She smiled. Her fingers trailed at a spot on her delightful body that still throbbed as if it had a life of its own.

Chapter Sixteen

Having satiated Ninmah, Ea lay in bed restless. She was deep asleep and snoring. The sound sent pin prickles up and down his leg in a most irritating manner. But she was happy.

His arm was growing weary, cradling her head against his shoulder. He was satisfied, he told himself, and happy, he guessed. His beloved sister was where she belonged ... in his arms.

But for that matter, Damkina, his lawfully espoused, also belonged in his arms. May-chance if Ninmah stayed awhile, she could sleep on the left side and Damkina could sleep on the right. Better yet ... Yes! He'd keep Damkina sleeping in the magnificent dwelling he had built for her on the mountain border of his garden.

Damkina was perfectly satisfied to sleep there alone. She was mistress of a household she shared with all of her many servants. She lived there with Mordukku, their son ... when he was not off manning the moon stations or the Mars transport by-ways.

Presently however, Ea guessed that Mordukku was home on Ki, and out partying with the miners drinking soot-dusted inebriation something.

Ever since he had arrived with Damkina from the home planet, Mordukku had been a challenge. He was a person of his own will and a little over ... well ... sensitive.

Of course, he was oversensitive! He was Sofeya's grandson, and his own number one son, who hadn't always had his father around.

Rejecting authority apparently was in the life codes, as well as in the DNA of the body materials of Sofeya's seed.

He got out of bed restlessly. Cursing as he fumbled in the dark for his communication device, he pushed the sequence numbers to reach Ningishzidda, his wise son. Ningishzidda had been born of a very intelligent and brain obsessed concubine. Every man should have such a son! He was far more stable than Marduk. Ea would need him as a backup for support at the morning meeting with Enlil and the rest of the crew. His insight and capabilities for communication was a valuable asset.

Ningishzidda would still be awake and working at the medical facility. He practically ran the operations there, skilled as he was in all matters pertaining to the matter body, as well as the codes.

Ea smiled as he thought of his son. Ningizzi was the wisest of them all.

If he wasn't working, he'd be doing. If he wasn't doing ... he'd be doing something else to experience fulfillment for his immensely intelligent code, like bringing the dead back to life, which he was skilled at. The call went through to the house of healing.

"Father?" Ningizzi answered. "Father, I was getting ready to call you, myself. There has been more trouble. Two of the discontented miners have been brought into intensive for treatment, along with Ennugi, your chief of operations."

"What is this?" Ea shouted in alarm.

"He's okay, father, just a little ruffled after a complete examination. He has been released, but several of the other miners still hold him in captivity in the waiting room where they have gathered. They brought him in sputtering and choking, and they weren't sure they hadn't killed him."

"I'll be right over."

"Father, they also brought in Enlil. Apparently they sought to hold him hostage as well."

By this time Ninmah was sitting up and rubbing her eyes, straining to hear. She quickly jumped out of bed and threw on her clothing. She rushed out the door.

Ea suddenly felt very weary and wanted to go to bed, after all. Bullshit! Piles and piles of it!

"Enlil ... !" He had told the miners, over and over again. "It is all Enlil's doing now. Ask him! He is your Lord of command!"

Ea grimaced. They apparently had done just that. He'd better hasten and see about this matter, he supposed. If it was anything like the last uprising, this one should be pretty good.

Personally, the whole thing was making his tired, tired. There were other things a male from Nibiru could much better concentrate on.

Like studying the Ki creatures. So vastly lively and so wholly interesting, they were. All of them! The males were strong and able. The females were so beautiful, particularly one girl who frankly ... well ... he could think of little else.

~~~

"Enki! Eaaaaan-ki! Eankiiiiiiiiii!" He could hear Enlil's command sputtering all the way from the front entrance, all the way down the long hall. "Eaaaaan-kiiiii!"

Ea's steps hastened, along with a rush of adrenaline. Ninmah was already at Enlil's side.

"Brother!" Ea greeted him. "Are you well?"

"Do I look well?"

"No, you look terrible." Ea replied with a great deal of pleasure. He had always thought Enlil had an ugly mug anyway, and he did ask.

"Annugi tells me that it was you who told the men to come to me, and they did! In the middle of the night they surrounded me, and seized me while I slept!"

"They had to get hold of you somehow." Ea stated. "You are Lord of command and thus ultimately in charge of all mining operations. It was you who insisted on building a bigger operation at the Abzu ... my Abzu ... may I remind you. So, of course, I directed them to their Lord for directions."

"It is your job to oversee. I'm not here every day as you are. How can I be expected to handle these ill-mannered oufs who followed your dark ass to Ki?"

"I would ... and HAVE handled them quite efficiently, I must say. But command is yours now! There is nothing that I can do without your permission."

"There is nothing you can do with it! Why do you suppose father and all of Nibiru sent me to this hell-hole planet anyway? To fix things, I would say."

Ea turned away from Enlil, wanting to blacken his other eye. But Ninmah shook her head at him, warning him to curtail his emotions as she often did.

"Just what is his status?" Ea asked Ninmah, further ignoring Enlil's whines.

"His blood pressure is quite high and there is a cut above his eye."

"Let me have a look." Ea bent over Enlil. He turned to the sud on duty. "Give him two tablets which he must take every day for his elevated blood pressure, and fetch him a warm washcloth for the little scratch."

"Little?" Enlil screeched. "I couldn't see anything but a big blob of blood in front of my eye!"

Ea peered again, frowning. "Do you think I should order an anti-infection treatment?" He asked Ninmah.

Ninmah smiled despite herself at the serious look of contemplation on Ea's brows, and remembered how just a few hours back she was slobbering kisses all over those furrows.

"No Ea. Absolutely not. It would be a waste of valuable anti-bodies."

"Ninitum! You injure my heart!" Enlil sat up in bed, tossing the washcloth aside and feeling his forehead.

"Where were you last night? Ninlil got bored here and returned to the North Crest. I waited for you." Then, he turned to Ea.

"I guess I should thank you that Ninita was not in bed with me last night.

"Did you have fun?" He asked Ninmah.

"Indeed! My vulva was well satisfied." She smiled at her brothers, licking her lips like a tigress in heat.

Ea bowed to Ninmah. "I am ever at your service, my lady."

Ea thrust his head out the door and yelled at the miners who were causing disorder in the waiting room, still holding a fearful Annugi in captivity.

"Release him, you bastards, or there'll be no wine for breakfast! Do you hear?"

The miners all scrambled, muttering.

As Ea had predicted, Marduk was with them.

"Father, we have a problem here. The men are all tired. How long have they been here digging in the mines, day in and day out, to retrieve mere particulate to send to Nibiru ... who are still choking in a failing atmosphere! It is ridiculous!

"The heroes say it is too hot at the Abzu. The climate here differs from Eridu. The digging is much more difficult than the extraction from water, as we initially did. It is a much more intensive labor factor required in the mountain."

All eyes turned to Enlil, who suddenly had a coughing fit. The sud nurses gave him pills and water. "He needs sleep." They instructed the small gathering.

"Someone contact father!" Enlil demanded, succumbing to the sud's tender care. "He will know what to do. We will discuss this further in the morning, on a seven-way."

The sleeping pills the suds had slipped him began to take effect on Enlil's usual business-like manner.

"Did you say wine, Enki? Wine sounds quite precise for breakfast, I'd say. Nighty nite all!"

Chapter Seventeen

Ea arranged for Enlil to be served wine for breakfast. The miners would be drinking it straight to cure the dizzy heads and upset stomachs caused by their overindulgence of last night's adventure.

"Let them have wine," he told Ninmah. "It will help them forget the weariness of their toil."

Knowing that Enlil was not used to strong drink, Ea instructed the suds to mix the wine with a delightful juice extracted from the fruit of the sweet citrus tree.

Enlil was pleased with the tasty breakfast. Feeling almost his normal healthy self, he got out of bed and dressed properly as number one in the ranks of Annunaki royalty on Ki.

He donned a purple flowing robe ornamented with tiny disks of gold that clicked softly as he walked. Around his waist he fastened a twisted belt fashioned with twined gold and silver links set with lapis lazuli.

He met Ea and Ninmah at the mining headquarters office near the sight of the biggest gold refinement station of all the digs.

A way station had been created where gold was mixed, refined, and sent on to Mars as a halfway place between Ki and Nibiru. From there the gold was sent to the home world.

The council room was designed in a restful manner. The brick walls were covered with a plaster of gold that lustered gently in the room where important decisions were made. The council consisted of the seven highest ranking Annunaki who were stationed on Ki, though others were there if it was deemed they were of import in the business of the day.

The seven gathered at a table built of burled dark ebony inset with turquois chips and smoothed to a low gleam finish. Coffee and repast was served as the highnesses gathered.

Enlil sat in the chief chair. At his right, Enlil's wife Ninlil sat.

Third in position, Ea took his seat, nodding briefly at his wife, Damkina who was placed at his side as lawful spouse. Around the table clockwise the lesser royals sat, Ninurta, the firstborn son of Enlil and Ninmah. Marduk, firstborn son of Ea and Damkina, was next. Last in the circle at Enlil's left was Ninmah, wife to none.

Others who were of minor importance sat on chairs at the circle perimeter. Ningishzidda, son of Ea and born of an unranked concubine, was there to support his father.

Supporting Enlil, born of Ninlil, his other two sons, Nannar and Ishkur were there. Utu and Innana, twin grandchildren of Enlil were also in attendance. At last minute, Ennugi arrived.

Ninmah busied herself with the fried raisin cakes sprinkled in the dusted sweetness of sugar cane.

"So delightful with the coffee!" She exclaimed, as Damkina sat next to Ea.

"You are getting fat," Damkina said. "You are getting lines on your face from the corners of your nose to the bottom of your chin."

"And you are drying up," Ninmah spat back, "like the raisins before they were put in the cake."

Damkina contented herself thereafter with coffee, mixing it thickly with cream and sugar.

"A little coffee with that cream?" Ninmah inquired of Ea's little wife. "The fat in the cream will coat your thin skeletal structure and may-chance you will start getting curves like me, and Ea will like you better." She smiled sweetly at Ninlil.

"Order." Enlil stated calmly, frowning at the two ladies. "We will get down to business."

The transmission buzzed with red lights. Anu's voice could be heard clearly on the speakers, and his face appeared shining on the wall.

"Greetings, my children." Anu's voice boomed. "My beloveds all!" How be my fine strong heroes today? Many of you have traveled far for this meeting. I admonish you in wellness while you are gathered."

"We are not good father." Enlil notified him of the recent disturbance at the mine.

"Last night, Enki's slave hoards surrounded me as I slept. I awoke with a torch at my ear and a big grimy hand around my neck, choking me!"

"Of what are you accused?" Anu asked.

"It was not personally an attempt to harm Enlil," Ea spoke. "It is a matter of the difficult toil. It seems the workers have had enough black soot up their noses and in their lungs. It causes extreme coughing and sore backs and irritable dry dust. The continuous labor seems to be never ending. You cannot imagine the difficulties for our men and the heat which causes the black dust to run as rivers down every wrinkle in our servant hero's bodies. Our workers' skin has turned hard and calloused and the wrinkles are many! Our heroes have dug the Ki for many sars."

"Yet still we are vastly short of the resource we require," Anu stated. "The work must go on!"

Ninurta, Enlil's son spoke next. "Perhaps it is time to arrange to send the old worn out ones who have worked the longest back to Nibiru and get fresh heroes ... young heroes with strong backs and smooth skin." And tight unused holes, Enlil's son mused to himself. But that information he did not share.

"Oh?" Anu questioned. Enki had told him about the deterioration of the matter body relevant to time on the Ki. He had never observed a wrinkle before, however Ea had sent pictures of the defect though they were hard to comprehend. He didn't want disease ridden criminals back on Nibiru.

"Surely you could use your most brilliant, ever-fashioning talent to create new tools." Anu addressed Ea. "Surely there is something more effective and faster."

"Father," Enlil interrupted, "there is another matter of which I must address my brother." He turned to Ea-Enki. "Ninurta has informed me that if you did not set constant vigilance in the studying of the nature of Ki and the animal here, there is much you could do to increase productivity."

Ninurta grinned at Enki while Enlil continued. "He informs me that you have an observatory in your offices where you are daily wrapped in the affairs of Ki."

"I think, Enki, that matters of the mine are more important at this time." Anu suggested.

"I wish to call this meeting to a short break." Ea stated. "I must seek council with my wise son Ningishzidda, before I reply."

Marduk scowled. Would he, firstborn, be included in this wise council?

Ea and Ningishzidda ignored him as he lingered close by. Their two heads were bowed together, which indicated that the business they discussed was theirs alone.

After a brief few minutes, the meeting was resumed.

"Father Anu, Ningishzidda, who is wisest of all Annunaki on Ki or the Perfect World besides you, father and besides your number one favorite concubine, who is my mother the wise Sofeya, of course. Ningishzidda and I wish to inform you that while Enlil, your son in command who dwells in lofty heights ... doing ... I'm not sure what he does, father are you?

"Ningishzidda and I have been working with the strong Ki helpers to improve their abilities."

"But has this not already proved to have been an undertaking of great expense and trouble? Enlil says the animals are not good workers. They will not follow commands or succumb to doing as instructed. He says their intelligence is simple and beneath the status of even Nibiru's lawbreakers."

"But they are improving, father. Ningishzidda and I have been involved in studies that ... ."

"What are you saying son?"

"I am saying that we are so close. For the purpose of successful Ki workers, only a few bios need to be adjusted."

"I do not grasp this," Anu inquired. "The Ki bodies are not inclined mechanically-improved as our bodies are."

"The code channels are similar, father." Ea spoke quickly hoping to gloss over the details. He knew that the ordinary Annunaki mind could grasp but little of such matters.

"If bred properly and instructed suitably, I suggest we may have success in producing bios with minds more technically akin to our own, with capabilities that are stronger than our own, to better help us in our tasks."

"If this is successful," Enlil demanded, "we must control them well. The ones we have now are too much like a bunch of dirty yammering monkeys."

"Can this be done?" Anu asked.

"I assure you, father, that this issue is foremost in my wise attentions. Ninmah can help."

"She will stay at the medical institution of science to help and assist," Anu commanded. "Together you two and Ningishzidda come up with the solution we need. It is crucial."

"It sounds to me to be further against the laws of Titain." Enlil shouted. "Is this not suggesting that we make slaves of the filthy animals?"

"No." Enki replied. "Rather it would help those who we have already made as such, though you call them by different name than the one you just proposed, brother. I would better refer to them as helpers.

"We will not force them into service. We will ask them, and offer rewards for their good works, and incentives to help their families. It will be good for them, as well as their families."

Ninurta listened with great interest. Fish gis! It was an idea far above Enki's understanding, surely! He must remember the brilliant ploy his uncle had brought up and suit it to his own credit!

Outside the circle, Ennugi smiled at him. Unknown to Ea, they had already found a little tool called the whip to be the best incentive they knew of, thus far. It had been Ninurta's idea, and there was no need to mention it here.

"Enki has clearly and repeatedly broke the laws of Titain already, that of involvement and communication with the natural creatures." Enlil continued.

"Come on, brother." Ninmah asserted. "The judges of Titain have little understanding outside their own comforts of moral. If we do this we are merely using the tools of our own vast intellect to survive! We must!"

"Indeed," Anu stated calmly. "As I see it, we cannot destroy the ultimate creation, Nibiru, by failing to use the gifts of our intelligence. Without the gold we perish. I grant you approval, my wise son, Enki. Whatever we need to do to obtain more gold is of upmost necessity."

" Gold!" Marduk sustained Anu.

" Gold!" Enlil cheered.

" Gold!" Ninurta stood up clapping his hands greedily.

" Gold!" Ninmah stood softly, seeking Ea's eyes.

" Gold!" Damkina repeated as she stood proudly, but coldly beside Enki.

"More gold ... and more gold!" They shouted in unison as Ea remained silent with a beaming face.

Enlil's elbow jammed Ea as he stood to take command and dismiss the meeting on a note of enthusiasm.

Ea smiled at each one as they left the room of soft golden bricks. He listened to the jingle of disks of gold they all had threaded into the finery of their royal robes as the group left the conference room.

He smiled at Ninmah and kissed Damkina on the cheek as they left the room. Both ladies and Innana, as well, wore long dangling golden earrings. Their necklaces and bracelets were made in profuse ornamentation of the much sought out, rare mineral, gold.

There wasn't any, excluding himself among the attendees at the meeting who hadn't come thoroughly bedecked in the fine properties of the scarce Nibiruan necessity. Indeed, more of the gold must be obtained to cover all their asses!

In the hall of the mining operation, Ea held Ninmah's hand.

"I didn't know of your experiments."

"You will Ninitum. You will." He assured her. "You are important to my task. I need you. Will you help me sister? Only you know how it is with me."

"I have tried many times, brother, to get you to tone your emotions down." Ninmah replied. "But as long as you leave some inside for me, I am fond of the way you cry out in passion when we have sex!"

"When we make love, Ninmah. Perhaps someday I shall get you to understand about this passion thing. But for now I only wish to explain a brief bit of information for which I beg for your understanding.

"I love the Ki inhabitants. I love them foolishly ... passionately. With all my being I am held in utter fascination.

"I shall never do anything to harm them. Ultimately, it is my goal to help them ... to keep them from our designs of evil for their sakes.

"Please trust me Ninmah, and think on this: "We are here on their world to steal from them their gold. I surely feel that there is much we can do to assist them."

"The animals?" Ninmah frowned.

"No the people." Ea insisted. "Especially of interest to me is a particular bunch of people just across the mountain near the sea that I have presently been engaged in studying. I believe that they are ultimately the promise of our people's salvation."

Ninmah was beginning to squirm. He was losing her interest. Ea saw that he'd have to attempt to go into more detail at a later time.

He quickly dropped the subject. "How about I treat you? He suggested. Have you ever tried this particularly tasty piece of fruit the cafeteria has cooked up today? It is native to Ki and it grows everywhere on their natural orchards of this land. I believe its seed was so inclined once on Nibiru before we started altering our foodstuffs. It makes a splendid pie."

He must convince his sister to keep his secret, one that he had not mentioned yet. He knew however, how to convince her. Ninmah was easy.

Chapter Eighteen

Ninmah couldn't keep her hands off of him. After the apple pie and coffee, Ea took her to the institution, still not certain how much he should show her, or where to begin.

"Right here!" Ninmah spread her legs wide and lifted her skirt up. Beneath the robe, she was naked in the long hallway

"Ninmah, was not Enlil fulfilling you?"

"Sort of ... until his Ninlilitum came!" Ninmah put her lips over Ea's mouth to keep him from talking.

In his arms, Ea steered her to a supply closet where they could have a little privacy.

Ninmah giggled. Ea loved it when she giggled. Darkness enveloped them and lent to the intrigue. Ninmah giggled again.

"Where are the lights?" She tried to protest.

This time, Ea put his mouth over her mouth to shut her up. In the darkness he slipped the purple robe from off Ninmah's shoulders.

In the darkness, she slipped the robe from off his shoulders. "I can hardly breathe," she whispered in excitement. "It is you who take my breath away."

"Who needs to breathe?" He spoke breathlessly, as his fingers trailed down her face to her throat, onto her breasts, and further ... to the warm spot down under.

"Ea!" She screamed. So much for closets. Outside the closed door, shakes and muffled bumps vibrated the halls, and shrieks of loud passion filled the hallways.

Ea cupped his hand over her mouth as she screamed. He bit her lip gently and thrust his tongue into the moistness of her mouth. He didn't stop at her mouth. He made another thrust deep. For a moment he rested, just to feel it inside her.

"Deeper!" She screamed. "Oh, yes! Ea, yes! Harder ... !" She screamed again, "Harder, harder ... Oh!"

Then, he withdrew, before it was too late.

"Don't stop!" She shouted. "Ea pleeeeeease!"

"Sister, before we go any further there is something we must clear first." He said sternly.

"Anything!" She spat.

"You enjoy this well at the moment. If you stay with me again, are you going to grow weary of my advancements and put a curse on me like you did last time when you up and left with our brother?"

"I'm sorry!" Her voice was hoarse.

"Come now, say it louder!"

"I'm sorry!" She repeated, desperate.

He laughed. "You're not sorry ... not yet. Not for one minute. You enjoyed seeing me suffer. You enjoyed the pain."

"No!" She begged. "I am really, really sorry."

"So tell me," he whispered. "What exactly was it you gave me before you ran off with him?"

"A drink!" She said breathlessly, sweating profusely. The closet was hot, and ... . "It was in the drink, some herb, that's all. I didn't figure it would do you any real harm. I just needed to not see your face when I left. I'm really sorry ... honest."

"No more drinks!" Ea firmly insisted. "Ever! Do you hear me? If you tire of me, just say so. Is that understood?"

"Yeeeees!" She assured him.

"That's my girl." He told her.

"Brother! This is hardly the time! I had reasons. I promise you! Now finish me!"

From outside, the hall was quiet. The thumping door was still.

"I have all the time in the world." He whispered in her ear. "I'll not finish until I understand what happened." He pressed his nose against her soft neck as he held her.

"It was an experiment, Ea. You'd understand."

"I only understand that I woke one morning, extremely ill ... and you were gone."

"I had to ... I know that you would have never agreed to help me out on this one, Ea."

"You never asked. You asked Enlil instead. And you stayed with him for quite some time, even conceiving a child with him."

"Brother, you would be the first to agree that some things take precedence."

"Try me." Ea held her tightly wrapped to him. His arm was wrapped just beneath her breast.

"Like science. Ea you know that I am one of the greatest of women scientists among our peoples, excluding your mother who is the greatest," she added quickly.

"I do! Continue."

"My specialty is in the science of birth and ... ."

"And?"

"Enki ... I mean ... Ea forgive me! I am a woman most fascinated with matters of sex."

"What did my puny brother have to offer you that I didn't?"

"He agreed to be the tester of my advances in the technologies of ..."

"Yes?"

"Ea, you know that our robotic department has developed a highly superior appendage that functions in ways the normal are incapable of doing."

"Normal?" He urged. "Like mine?"

Ninmah giggled and grabbed hold of Ea's balls.

"Brother, yours are anything but normal. In order to continue my studies of science robotics it was necessary for me to do something I would not have desired to ask of you."

"Something you didn't mind asking my brother?"

"No! I didn't mind. It concerned the ... ah ... artificial appendage of which yours I modeled the fake one after. That is really why I had to make you go to sleep so I could obtain a proper mold."

A flash of understanding dawned on him. He grinned at her in wry approval.

"Oh! I see. Could you not have told me this sooner?"

"No." Ninmah whispered. "Ea please. You are hurting my arm. Enlil made me sign a contract to never tell the details of our experiment."

"You told me nothing, sister."

Outside the door, and in the halls, more muffled sounds came forth ... thumping ... not so muffled cries.

"Ahhhhhh ... ah ... ah ... ah ...ah! Oh, yes, Ea ... yes ... ahhhhh ... harder Ea, harder, brother. Oh, harder ... oweeeeeee!"

Ea paused, then finished the act with the insertion finale, sighing. He had been most satisfied with her answer.

~~~

Awakening the next morning, Ea began the long process of helping Ninmah see what it was that he was doing. He needed to get her on his side.

"Mother, I believe that Ninmah can be trusted." He sent communication to his mother.

Ea and Ninmah breakfasted on hot coffee and sea salted strips of thin boar fat, fried crisp in an unction of grease and served with small quail eggs cooked in cream. Ea smiled at her from across the table. Perhaps Damkina was right and Ninmah was getting a soft padding. It was all the more to squeeze.

"Ninmah, do you love me?" He asked.

"Love?" She said it questioningly between mouthfuls, hardly willing to discuss such matters at important times such as when one was eating.

He took her fork away, and pushed her coffee cup aside.

"I wasn't finished!" She protested.

"Come, my lady, to my headquarters of healing." As he led her down the hall she giggled, even if she was slightly perturbed at him.

"Already, my Lord?" She asked him. "Your recent presence in my vulva is chaffing me a bit, and when I sit down it stings."

"You may show me!" He said as the two of them passed by the inner sanctum of his retreat, the place that was or had been his secret. He led her to the chief office and closed the door, locking it.

Ninmah lifted her robe up. He rubbed soothing comfrey oil onto Ninmah's red cheeks and into her vulva. He felt her tighten around his finger in a tremor.

"It stings." She smiled at him. She put her hand on his loins.

He lifted it gently. "Ninmah, the work! I was only trying to ease your discomfort so we may begin. Remember, I explained that this is a business meeting between you and me. But, if you are a good girl and listen to what I say, perhaps I shall offer you reward tonight after our work is through ... and after a little respite for your ravaged glory."

"But ..." she replied. She could do it again right now. Her vulva was ready for it, for he had made it so, administering the healing oil. She sat up disappointed.

"We do need a little business, now darling. I must ask you again. Will you promise to hold our discussions in ultimate secrecy? Could you make oath with me? I won't need you to sign a contract, darling. Your word is good for me."

"Perhaps you should give me an indication of what I shall be promising," she suggested, anything but innocent.

"This is a matter I do not wish for just anyone to know, Ninmah. Not only that, some of these matters that I wish to disclose may not be exactly lawful in Annunaki technology. I could get in a lot of trouble ... and you, too, for assisting me."

"Now wait a minute, Ea." She replied. "Is this more of that emotion bit?"

He smiled at her. "Currently, I know that your emotional level is disproportionately less developed than is mine but whether you like it or not, I know a little of your secrets. You still have more than is lawful of the emotion."

"It is forbidden the things I feel when I am with you," she admitted at last. "This is my secret brother, that you must keep. Don't take it personal though. It is your green eyes and your hair that has a shadow of hue." She ran her fingers through Ea's long hair, frowning as she pulled one gray strand from his head. "What is this?" She asked, letting it drift between her fingers.

"A gray hair," he replied. "One measly gray hair, big deal."

"Only in the light of the Perfect World, is it so evident that there is a darkness in you, Ea ... darkness that everyone is enchanted by, me especially."

Ea sat back, contemplating. Surely he could trust this woman.

"I thought all this time that it was because of my vast intelligence, surely."

~~~

"Come, my Ninitum." He took her to a viewing room that was a little different than the one located in his own inner sanctum where he watched fish swim by. Here, he had installed a careful network of electrical means by which he could view the people on the other side of the mountain. From a distance it was better to observe them thus.

These were the purest of Ki's natural children. Quite unlike the ones who had already been manipulated by Enlil's command and who already were showing signs of taint.

These were those who lived in the quiet base of the hill where Sofeya had first come alone so long ago. These were the children of promise who must be preserved.

Ea's eyes brightened in delight, when he saw Daffinina and his little Tititum. His smile turned to a frown. Who was this? Tititum was being carried by a strange man. Albeit, a comely young man, slim and dark smooth skin with muscles abounding.

"Ea!" Ninmah brought him back into focus. "The animals of Abzukia." Her eyes opened wide at the sight of the beautiful young man who was carrying the baby. "Is this what they look like? I've never really noticed these of that nature up close before. This is incredulous! Ea, you watch them?"

"Now and then," he said.

"I had no idea. I had them pictured in my head as wearing scraggly furs and long greasy hair. I had no idea they could look like this!" She smiled at the vision she saw of the slim and well-built young man. She frowned, though, at the sight of the young female at his side.

"The females ... do they all look so ... ."

" ... BEAUTIFUL?" Ea finished his sister's inquiry. "This one in particular. However, most of these people are quite pleasing to look at until matter begins to destroy their youth."

Despite herself, Ninmah could not turn away. She watched. As did Ea. Like mates they seemed ... Daffinina and the male who held his Tititum as if he were her father. They appeared as thus ... they were together quite comfortably. Was it really his flower, Daffinina, who had lopped the head off his grey boatman? It was clear that both of them had been climbing down from a mountain for days ... both of them. If she had just stayed in his sanctum until he was through with Enlil and Ninmah, he could have helped her return home in a much easier way.

To get back home they would have had to climb the mountain ... back up, then down. What had become of the canoe?

Daffinina had at least heeded his warnings not to take the baby through the portal again. The young couple approached their ham-let by the sea as if they had merely been for a walk. But they looked quite weary. His Daffinina, though, was limping only slightly on the injured leg he had noted when he pulled her out of the water. On her forehead the big raised bruise had lost its swell, but still bore a scab. Others in the tribe rushed to greet them with hugs and kisses, taking Ti Ti with great enthusiasm in their arms.

Where had she hooked up with the all-too-attractive young man? In spite of himself, he was grateful though, to the boy. Appar-ently, he had assisted Daffinina across the mountain. He had been there for her when she was likely afraid ... probably held her in his arms and kissed her soft and silken cheek. What else had they done as a couple?

Ea knew the feel of Daffinina's skin. But how would it feel to walk at her side with the babe tucked between them, and to smile together in the emotion of love? Ea contemplated. Was this envy he felt for the boy?

The baby would need a father. He would like to be available to Ti Ti and Daffinina, as well. But a father for Ti Titum from the earth? He could not deny that this would seem a normal thing in this circumstance.

Knowing Daffinina was safe, he shut off the remote so Ninmah would not notice the raising of his loins.

It was too late.

"Ea! What is this?" She giggled.

"Only this ... ." He put his mouth over hers to keep her from asking anymore questions. He spoke gently in her ear. "It is just that I cannot wait until this night."

"Take me, my Lord." She lifted her purple robe. "Take me!" He sated the rising by inserting it into her ever moist vulva.

~~~

Ea ordered lunch to be served in the small viewing rooms. The two of them sat, limbs entwined on the soft rug. After the lunch they sat at a big wooden table and sipped hot coffee, thick with cream and honey.

"Ea, tell me more about this land where the berry come from."

"It is really a bean." He informed her. "I will show you. We will take the Eagle, just you and me ... and fly there."

"It is far away?" She asked.

"Not necessarily as the Eagle flies if we were to go straight across. I plan on taking an extended trip."

"Now?" She asked hopefully.

"Oh, come on, Ninmah. By and by I will take you. We have work to do now, remember?"

Ninmah grinned. She liked the kind of 'work' they engaged in, and engaged in often.

"Nin Nin. Now behave yourself." He winked at her sternly. "That must hold us until this night time comes. Besides that, I do not wish for you to tire of me anytime soon."

Ninmah sat back to listen to him, curious as to what other manner of work he found so pertinent.

"I know, sister, that on our Nibiru you were well instructed and exceedingly talented in the healing arts. And as we discussed before, you are tops in the fields of the sciences."

"The two are connected." She replied.

"How much, Ninmah, did your instructor of history give you?"

"As far as I, or any decent resident of Nibiru, need know." She said.

"You don't live on Nibiru anymore."

She sat upright. "As far as is official, I have been instructed."

"Has it ever occurred to you to wonder what happened before?"

"Before what?" She asked in blank disinterest.

"Before the zero point."

"But that was so long ago; it matters to no one. How could it matter?" She asked.

"Zero is where all things begin." Ea shook his head in amazement. How could anyone be satisfied to know half of anything?"

"Just because the computer programs set time at the beginning point of technology, does not mean that true history began there."

"Whooooah!" She breathed. "It is forbidden. This I cannot compute."

"Ninmah, compute this. When we make love I know you turn off your computer mind. I have seen you do just that. I have felt you. It is what I love about you."

"You love me?" She smiled.

"You know I do, and it is our secret, alone. You and I can share more of these secrets if you can agree to turn off your computer mind when you are with me."

"Can I?" She asked, with wide eyes.

"Ninmah, whenever we have sex you know we break the law. Our passion reaches into vast emotions. Why do you think it is so good with us?"

Ninmah giggled. How could she deny this? But was there more?

"I am asking you, sister, to come with me on the biggest adventure quest you have ever played. Think of it like the entertainment games they play on the vast array of Annunaki reality computers."

Ninmah thrust her finger upward into her cheek, deep in contemplation. "Brilliant you are, my brother! Everyone enjoys the games so much because it is the only way on Nibiru that is legal to experience any kind of emotion ... vicariously, when it is thought it is only a game."

"Are you ready to play with me?"

Ninmah stood up and followed Ea to the farthest reach of the long hall.

~~~

Surely they had reached the end. Was this building really this big, Ninmah wondered as they went up, down, and senselessly followed a maze of halls? She would need a map.

"I see you pushing security buttons this time," Ninmah observed. "To what big secret are you taking me, Ea?"

"Most of the suds and the heroes, trained in the healing arts and of the sciences, respect my privacy," he told her. "Some know of this place and some do not. Only those I wish to know are given the password."

He turned to Ninmah as he pushed a sequence of buttons and smiled at her.

Ninmah did not fail to notice the enthusiasm in his eyes as he proceeded.

"DAFFODIL." He finger-punched softly into a security device.

"Daffodil?" She asked. "Well, I do know it is your favorite flower. I should be able to recall it. Hmmmmmm, strange."

Ninmah blinked in the radiance of the sun shining through a big glass window. Wow! What a great room this was. It was large and spacious ... sunny like a dwelling place connected to, but separate from ... the rest of the institution.

"Ea, it is beautiful ... the doors?" She walked to an arched doorway at the far side of the room which graced walls plastered with brilliant white sand. The door of the room was made of thick glass and opened into what appeared to be a private garden.

"I am astounded," was all she could manage to say. "What a comfortable and lovely room. It looks like a garden within a garden."

Ninmah strolled about the quarters, looking at everything. Then, she heard a soft little cry.

"A baby!" She exclaimed. "Do I hear a baby?"

"You do," he grinned. "Come see!" He extended his hand.

Inside the room ... it was just a room like in a home ... surely this was homelike ... not like any room in an institution.

He took her through a door into a different area. In the corner by a window there was a little crib. A sud was bent performing administration procedures on the most adorable little thing she had ever seen ... beside her own child, Ninurta, when he was a baby ... and the daughters Ea had given her long ago. They were grown now, and she had forgotten how sweet the babies are. She wanted to take the child in her arms.

"Eeea," she crooned. "From where did you get this wee one?" She frowned in contemplation. "I do assume that you are the father?"

He had rehearsed the answer. He knew it would be the first thing she asked.

Ea stroked the baby's soft pale skin with his big finger, gently brushing the small cheek.

"It's a boy," he said. "I found him just a couple of weeks gone by. Imagine this! When I was out bathing in the river by the reeds, this little miracle came into my view. I was pleased to be engaged in study of the fish. I came out of the water and I heard this tiny cry. I took off my diving mask and followed the sound to the water edge where the reeds were thick.

"There I found this little man in a tiny canoe. He was safe and snug and wrapped securely in soft wool. He was not a bit wet, except for his di-di, of course. He was very disgruntled, and let me know it!" Ea laughed. "He was apparently hungry, so I brought him to my office."

Ninmah scowled, searching his face. She noted the little twitch in his brow. Could this possibly be true?

"He is a delightful little creature ... perfect! Just look at him. I've not seen a more beautiful boy, ever! Is his hair, not as white as wool?"

"Yes it is." Ninmah looked at him suspiciously. "Must be a new breed or something! He is larger than most babies I have delivered.

"Let me hold him Ea! Oh, Ea, please!"

He nodded at her. She took the child within her arms, cooing.

The boy's eyes met hers in a direct flash that emitted a bond of binding light between them. Ninmah laughed in pleasure.

"Oh, Ea. This child has charmed me. It is amazing! Have you inquired as to where he came from?"

"There were no traces I could detect. The swaddlings were of a common Ki material, used by Annunaki heroes, as well as by the lu and the natural Ki creature."

"The animal? But this is no animal, surely." She put the child on the examination table and removed the coverings from off his body.

"Is it?" She asked, frowning. "His hair is white, what little he has of it. He is fair like our heroes, but his eyes have an uncommon tone of green. Did you ever tell me how your eyes are green, Ea? Do you swear that he is not yours, brother?"

"For your information, Ninmah, as well you should know, I am not the only sperm producing possibility from our dear Perfect World Nibiru. I insist on an apology."

"Or, what?" She asked, winking at him. "I am sorry, but your story is totally incredulous!"

She crooned at the baby, taking delight in the tiny toes as she smoothed her hand across his soft skin. "Oh, look," she cried in amazement, "at this little mark on his tiny belly! It looks like a tiny star. Awww." She giggled, remembering the star Ea had in the exact same place on his belly.

"Adapa is amazing," he said. "I mean to raise him as my own. He is a child apart from any of our other researches. He is far superior."

"How can this be?" She again asked. "We have done everything in our vast power to get a perfect line of DNA. Have we found it?"

Ea hoped his trembling heart would not beat too loudly and reveal to her something he didn't wish for her to know just yet.

"I must run tests!" She exclaimed. "I must see what we have

here!"

"You will help me, then?" He asked, his voice full of charming innocence.

"You couldn't keep me away. I know the password!" She was excited. She put a fresh di-di on the baby and sat rocking him at the crib side.

"Hello Adapa, beloved-one." She sang to him softly, brightening her eyes as she met again and again the gaze of the child.

"Of Heaven, of Ki, little one. I am your mama. Hush now, hush now darling. I am here. You will never be alone. I am here."

Ea smiled. He was beginning to hope ... really hope. Things were as they should be ... almost.

He excused himself. "I will leave you to get acquainted with Adapa. I will return later. I am going to treat you to a picnic tonight in the gardens." He nodded his head toward the big window. "We will bring little Adapa to sit with us in the flowers.

"I have arranged a room for you here." He motioned to another small hall just off the baby's room. "I think you will be comfortable when you wish to stay.

"Of course, the suds have been giving him the upmost daily care. I have asked Damkina to assist now and then. She loves the baby well."

"What do you need me for, then?" Ninmah asked.

"Because only you, Ninmah, of all Annunaki female, can give him Nini-love!"

He pinched her on her rounded cheek as she bent over to lay the now sleeping child back in his crib.

Chapter Nineteen

"*DAYSONG TREE SONG.*"

Sionee held her daughter high into the radiance of the dawning sunshine that transformed the small hill with morning's first awakening.

"*I give you light ... Oh, daughter ... to serve the Mother in Song ... As you walk the four directions of Gaia's sweet earth ... Your hands will be Her hands with which to create ... Your voice will be Her song.*"

The Children of Fey at the Snake of the Sea cheered and called forth welcome to their new little ray of sunshine.

"*ALL LIGHTS OF THE SUN ARE ONE!*" The mantra was given with enthusiasm by all.

Few in the gathering failed to catch Sionee's AHDAWN blessing given in words which her tongue did not speak, but with which her heart spilled over.

The warmth of the new morning spread across the meadow at the tree lines of the wild forest as the sun burst into full glory. Everyone's heart was warmed to the vision of their new and favored Songkeeper who held the promise of a new day in her arms.

"*Daysong Song Tree, daughter of Alsionee Tree Song. I give you the name by which you shall be known ... and of which you will honor all the days of your life.*

"*Daysong. Be Blessed Thou, Oh, Daughter of the Day Star and of Seamother's first breath.*

"*Say You, Oh, daughter, on the occasion of each and every morning of your long life, these words:*

"*I AM THE PERFECT DAY AND IN ME DWELLS THE LIGHT THAT DOES NOT FAIL.*"

The crowd cheered. "Welcome to the Keepers of Song!"

In honor of the sacred ceremony, food was joyfully shared by all, but first a heaping plate of each of the breakfast items was arranged in a gleaming shell bowl and left on an altar at the celebration hill. Here it would remain for the remainder of the day and through the evening, so that any visiting spirits or elementals could fill up on the essence.

In the next morning, any food left in the bowl would be tossed into the wild woods or the sea. The food essence, now having been enjoyed by the spirits, would be returned to Gaia.

All at the gathering enjoyed a bowl of colorful wild apples, a fruit everyone held in symbol of wisdom. Since wisdom was what all souls incarnating on Gaia hoped to achieve, at every baby's name giving, it was customary to serve for the shared morning meal anything that was of apple nature.

For the occasion, apples had been included in most of the breakfast. Cool apple juice refreshed thirsts after a long night's sleep. Steaming cups of apple blossom tea thickened with rich cream and sprinkled with dried mint was eagerly sipped on by most of the adults. Apples baked in sweet honey and a crust of oat flour sprinkled with cinnamon lent a great deal of festivity to the occasion. There was more ...

There were eggs that had been baked into a savory omelet sprinkled with thyme herb and enhanced with fried apple slices on the top. Individual small cakes were plump with bits of apple and raisins.

Also included on the table was warmed applesauce poured with thick cream and sprinkled with cinnamon, along with a cold platter of fruited cheese flavored with apple and nutmeg from the damask tree.

An occasion to celebrate was always something the people of Fey were glad to uphold, and this one in particular had drawn a big attendance.

When Sionee and Cyex had returned just yesterday, great shouts of celebration had begun. "She has come home! Our flute singer has brought her home!"

Marisol was the first to reach Sionee's side. "I should administer the paddle girl to you. I should ... but you are no longer my student!"

She winked at Sionee, then glared. "You had us all so frightened!" Marisol extended her hand to Cyex.

"Thank you for bringing my girl home, boy. She is daughter to me. And, our new little sun child is all our blessing!"

"Her name is Daysong!" Alsionee announced with such joy that Marisol laughed as she recalled the frightened girl who had fled in desperation on the birth of the child.

"With mornings first light the name shall be given!" Marisol cried out with enthusiasm. "Come everyone! You are invited in the morning to the child's first GNOS."

Thus, Sionee Tree Song gave Daysong Tree Song the name that would be hers for all her days.

Sion had chosen the name somewhere in that brief moment of panic when the child was first placed in her arms, but she wouldn't acknowledge the name in her heart until she knew the child belonged there, deep in her heart forever.

Though Daysong came not from her loins, she had been born as daughter in AHDAWN, Sion's heart of love.

She had chosen the name to honor the tradition of the Sun, after which she herself had been named. Alsionee meant 'radiant sun.' So it seemed fitting to her that she would give further honor to the child by naming her Day. The song addition seemed to add such a lovely musical quality to the sound, for, indeed, it was a sure thing that the girl would bring song to everyone's life. She was among the Daughters of Song.

Sion had great thankfulness to Cy. He had taken such care to help her bandage her bone-bruised leg for support, so that it didn't hurt as much when they climbed. Though it still seemed a bit sore, it was feeling much better! And he had shown her that all along, her only problem had been her own refusal to put away her own fears.

Truly, that had been a selfish thing. Not that she could honestly claim to be free exactly of the strange hole that had made its way into her AHDAWN, but somehow she was beginning to feel like maybe she could make her heart whole again. Caring for Daysong made all the selfishness of her heart break feel so unimportant.

There were so many matters to attend to as she got on with her life. She had a baby to care for, and now a home to build. She also had a certain fish headed creature to explicitly avoid, and there was Cyex as well.

Despite herself, Sion smiled. She did not need him herself, but Daysong loved him well. Cyex had safely brought the two of them home from the other side of the mountain. It had taken uncomfortable days, but Cyex had played his flute whenever it seemed hard. It made both of them giggle.

Marisol, who had been in and out and visiting back and forth with the many who attended the ceremony, sat down beside Sionee, who was sitting beneath an apple tree feeding Daysong.

"Our beloved Songkeeper." Marisol smiled. "Alsionee, Be Blessed Thou, dearest. I have been out among the crowd. Everyone is enchanted with you. "She, who dances with the fish lord, they are calling you."

"I don't know whose lord he is, but he is not mine. I really think that he is just a man," Sion tried to say.

"The people have asked that you honor them again on this evening at nightfire. They say that they like how you get them to hear and see."

Alita, who sat not far from Sion, turned around and entered in on the conversation. She had been showing some admiring women Lilitu's many charms.

"Marisol. Good morning to you and good morning to you, as well!" She winked at Sion and put her hand beneath her pendulous boobs and thrust them upward, jiggling them, and laughing at Sionee's reaction.

Sion dropped the milk pouch.

"Not good for the baby, dear," Alita stressed. "It shows, too; just see how beautiful my little flower grows."

Sion smiled at Lilitu. She was a beautiful baby despite who her mother was. She picked up the milk pouch and continued to feed Daysong fish head milk.

Would he do as he said and get her more? Aaaaaaugh, this part she did not like. Daysong was almost out of milk.

"How old is it, Marisol, before a baby can be fed other foods?" Alita laughed.

"Not for some time dear." Marisol replied, frowning at Alita. "In a few more months, perhaps some soft barley paste, but at least for one year, maybe more, she must drink milk. Where did you get that?" Marisol asked Sion, indicating the pouch Daysong was happily finishing off.

"At the trading center," Sionee lied.

"She can't feed a baby properly and she can't sing a song with words," Alita taunted. "How is it that she can tell a story that people can really hear?

"I, myself, could tell a story everyone could hear, using words you know. I don't have the slightest idea what she was singing or what exactly the baby's name is. But they tell me it is Day light or Dawn song or Day Song." Alita giggled, admiring Lilitu's small head of dark lustrous locks. Dusk Song ... now that could have been a good name for her own child if she hadn't already been named.

Marisol looked at Alita sharply. It had been too long since the girl had attended the institution at the shells, and she never had been apt. Surely, as a teacher she should have been more mindful and taught the girl better manners.

"Alita, my child, Be Blessed Thou. Your time to tell stories will be many," Marisol spoke patiently. "The people have requested a story from Sionee on this evening. They say their heart homes can hear a story coming to them tonight from her wisdom."

"From the right storyteller!" A young woman who sat in the gathering spoke her turn. "Will you so honor us Sionee?" Taya was one of the seven Song Sisters. Will you take us to the beginning Songkeeper, Alsionee of Tree Song? Refresh our ears to go with you."

"What is the point?" Alita laughed sarcastically. "Everybody already knows the story."

"As well we all should," Marisol stressed, smiling at Alita. Truly however she had a wish that Alita was still a maiden so she could better instruct her with the 'paddle of education.'

Marisol sighed. Alita's broad behind was just too big at this point.

Chapter Twenty

Marisol of the Sparkling Shells smiled as she waited for night-fire to begin, observing her charges as they began preparations for tonight's song. Her wise eyes, curved in a very slight slant as she went inside to that special place of heart-home everyone knew as AHDAWN. Simply put, she was deep in thought. And she was happy. Alsionee Tree Song was bringing to the people of the Fey a new magic, a tradition that had begun to dim with new generations that were forgetting. Alsionee was bringing this wisdom back with her straight songs. Like a miracle, the small tribe of people at the outlier of the Fey was remembering once more.

GNOS... It wasn't really the story that was important. It was what the hearing of it did inside AWDAWNS understanding. Long ago, when people were pure, words did not veil the silent language that the heart spoke. Those were good times.

The use of a straight song was a very powerful means of wisdom. The essence of the song was found in the melody, not in the words. The story was told in evocation, inspired by the tune left unspoken by tongue. The echoes of music were heard in the heart, and a nuance of perception became known to each individual listener, as they remembered within, the GNOS wisdom. With straight song, those who HEARD the song would put their own words to the knowledge contained in the sound.

This is why drama and the symbolic performances were so important to the Fey. Putting beauty-form to their thoughts allowed everyone to celebrate in tune with the vibrations of the sound that surged like a life-giving river along the backbone of the chakra flow.

Skymother had done wise to choose Sionee as a singer of this truth. With her quiet songs, she was beginning to open the AH-DAWN ears of many to hear the ancient wisdoms once more.

Marisol opened her eyes as the scent of nightfire wafted into her soul as the fire was ignited. Her eyes, aflame with love for the young ones she had taught, smiled over the young Songkeepers. She smiled with affection at the young men who played the drums and brought forth profound wind-song.

As she gazed with love at everyone, her eyes swept across the gathering to smile at each who attended. Her eyes stopped for a moment when she saw at the reed edge, an eye peeping from behind the rushes. The eye had caught a reflection from off the fire.

~~~

It was nightfire! The gathering was eager. There was a new Songkeeper who offered valuable harmony to the story.

The stories were not recorded in scribe. Rather, they were re-told, time after time around the circle of people who gathered at the fire on nights after all daily work was completed and everyone was eager to relax and be at peace.

Tonight the flanking hill curve which seated the assemblage was crowded with many.

Whole families often brought their linens soft and their fleeces to sit on or wrap in as the stories were told, sung, danced ... or other-wise reenacted by the priestesses or the priests of song, especially on festival nights. Though this was not a festival night in particular, each evening brought reason to celebrate.

Everyone was eager at the presence of the new storyteller. Since the evening Sion had danced with the fish head, all eyes and ears followed her to observe, see and hear.

To enhance the enjoyment of the fire side, the families often brought food to share and snack on as the gathering commenced.

Some brought dried oaten wafers, crisp and light to the bite. Some brought barley cakes to be eaten with chunks of aged cheese. Some brought fire roasted almonds, and apples cut in slices and wedged with goat cheese. In the vast picnic of snack choices, sea-salted crisp fried lentils were a great favorite, and for the children, honeyed lo-cust bites.

Wishing to begin to get Daysong attuned with her life as a Songkeeper, Sionee brought her wee daughter along. The baby slept in a little basket lined with sweet soft linens.

Earlier that day, Sionee had washed and spread the baby's apparel out to dry over the lavender stalks that grew near the maiden huts.

She had spoken with Cyex earlier. He had agreed to play for her on his reed flute. She wished to orchestrate her story with a simple instrument at the beginning, but there would be need of drum song. Cyex had brought along a few of his boys to furnish the beat of the Mother's heart.

The chattering throng hushed as Songkeeper came out and began her offering.

Sion's song stirred as a mere hint of breeze, barely discernible above Gaia's angel chorus of crickets and cicadas and night birds. The flame of the fire danced to the rhythm of wind song that Cyex's creative breath whispered into the night as it began to bring forth story figures in the imaginations of all who heard wind song.

Sionee stood in the center, near the fire on a small threshold built a little higher than the arena ground so that her voice would meld with the night.

Beneath the stars and surrounded by the reflection and the colors of flickering flames, Sionee's hum began the mesmerization. A sort of enchantment began to stir in the air, and people smiled softly.

"She is wind!" It was speculated, though it was just a breeze above the tree tops, soft and barely stirring, that Sion mimicked. The rhythm increased and the wind took them higher on the wing of a bird that swooshed in the heights above them.

It was a white dove who cooed as its white wings flew above the contours of the horizon and disappeared into the light of the moon.

Sion's chanting words ... that were no-words ... carried the listener up, up and up on wings of light until all outer vision disappeared with the white wing. Darkness wrapped them all in the velvety blackness of no-thing.

It was like having ones presence deep in a black hole; Sionee Tree Song's silent words took them there.

Cyex's flute played one note in sequence ... fast thudding notes, one after the other in staccato succession of rhythm. Then ... silence ... once more stillness in the depths.

~~~

Sionee stood, her arms outstretched, her eyes peering into the Sapphire Blue sky sea above.

Everyone heard the profound silence. Softly, ancient sounds tinkled in the stillness of the universe sea. *"When in the heights, heaven had not been named."*

What if deep within the wild woods of Gaia where the branches of trees interlace with each other, and where no man or creature lives, a limb falls with a sharp thud to the ground? If there were no ears to hear it, would there be any sound at all? Who would hear the vibrations of the forest? Who? So would a sound really be a sound? Who would hear?

Everyone speculated as the flute played softly the sound of silence.

Maybe the broken branch would let in a little light upon the dark canopy of the forest floor. If no one was there, would it be light? Who would see it?

With the entire crowd deep in contemplation of this thought and their eyes closed in the thinking, Sionee quickly stepped forward just a bit and took a lighted ember from Cyex. With one deft motion she lit a small device that she and Cy had built from items they had unearthed in a cave on their way home from that 'fishy' place on the other side of the mountain.

No one was prepared in any way for the likes of the firework that Sionee threw upward into the sky high above the crowd. She and Cy had practiced for effect.

The explosion that everyone heard shook the comfort level of every AHDAWN clear to the inner body's bone. The babies in the throng screamed, though even their cries went unheard except for the mothers who sought to calm their children.

The bang resounded over and over as the sky exploded in a circle of infinite stars shining in every conceivable hue of living color.

When the thunder subsided, the dazzling darkness was lit with a thousand and more spinthers of light that gently twinkled as they spiraled to the ground having danced and twirled in numinous colors. Shock waves stunned the silence. Then one little voice was heard. It was the giggling of a baby ... Daysong.

~~~

To reiterate the effect, a clash of symbols sent forth the multi-layered vibration of a thousand yodeling voices. Having placed themselves in the deep abyss as observers within the vast universal sea, the echoes of the drums rolled in cadences so fast the thrums were inseparable. As the listeners fell to the ground in stunned silence, the flute sound began to softly play Sionee's song.

"Katak ... katak ... katak ... ah ... ah ... ah ... ah ... ." The rhythm of the heartbeat drum joined Sionee's straight song in one voice.

"When the one first appeared as the many ... ." In her chant voice there was some who could hear still, by going beneath the pounding of their throbbing ear drums.

"Nothing could be seen. Nothing could be felt."

A conch shell horn sent a vibration of great sound that shook the circle with power.

"I want to share," said the dazzling darkness, *"my wonderful syzygy. My union must be splintered and appear as vast as it really is ... so all may see how bright my light is!"* The flute song drifted. Sionee's chants lifted up in harmony, her voice un-worded, a supreme instrument of spirit sound.

"I ... my light can shine ... and I will not be alone unto myself."

More silence, more song.

Sionee hummed. Then in the awesome aftermath of the explosion, it was the Song of the Sun, a simpler story perhaps.

"For those of you who did not hear the sight of the spinthers spun from the explosion of the original light source, I will tell it to you in another way."

Truly could not all hear the wind blow? Or hear the ocean wave crash upon the sands of shore, or hear the song of a bird, or the chirps of the locust by day in the spring time of Gaia's buzzing?

Everyone loved the story and each person heard it in their general and shared vision of different intensities.

"What if ... ?" Another question was asked, among the people, "What if our beautiful sun were to burst into infinite pieces and each piece became a ray of sunlight, each piece of the sun would separate and be individual pieces of the one ... the sun?"

ALL LIGHT FROM THE SUN IS ONE!

It was quiet ... way quiet in the aftermath of contemplation. The food had all been eaten. People were growing sleepy. Most of the children were already asleep in their mother's arms after the titillation of the firework display. It had been a most exhilarating evening, and dreams tonight would be shared by many.

Just when everyone thought the nightfire story was over ...

~~~

Ea had seen Marisol gaze at him directly into his fire-lit eyes. He hoped that she only imagined she saw anything, or that he was an animal out there, whose eyes luminesced in curiosity.

He saw her motion to him. Smiling in welcome, she had been, all through the entire song. "Come!" She persisted in bidding.

But no, he would not. Somehow watching the beautiful girl, he became mesmerized. His thoughts took him, along with the mere Ki animals, to the beginning when there was only the center when ...

Mother had told him this story. She had said it was how so many light sparks had formed code ... light bodies that the others had forgotten or manipulated ... light sparks that exploded from the central source and became manifest in individual spirits.

Ea almost lost himself in the imagery created by the flutes and the drums, and his Daffinina's beautiful beyond beautiful voice. She was a firecracker! Indeed.

Then he saw the woman again wave to him.

"Come!"

He got up and went to the fire circle center. He stood beside Daffinina and bent to admire the sleeping baby. He nodded at Cyex, and then spoke to the crowd. Of course, he had to use the same primitive language of silence that Daffinina was so apt at. It was the only universal language understood by most. For surely why would any of these people understand the complicated tongue of someone from a different star?

"The spinthers of light ..." he spoke, smiling radiantly. It was such an experience to be able to express oneself truthfully to people who understood. His eyes were silver with tearful emotion. "The pieces of light filled the whole universe in a complete circle. Some spinthers became manifest on different stars as living, breathing, life-sources ... physical." He wept now, "The ONE appeared as many and could be seen."

Sionee grabbed Daysong and held her close. She looked at the fish head bedazzled.

"These shards of light," he begged them to listen, "fill creatures everywhere, great, small, up, and down. Everywhere is the spirit on different stars, even of which there are as many as are those pieces of light."

He turned to Sionee. "May I have a word with you in privacy?"

~~~

"*Are you saying that you came from a distant star?*" Sionee asked him with her eyes.

"Those who have ears to hear, let them hear." Ea sent back to her.

"*I have heard it said that those who have ears to see, let them see and those who have eyes to hear, let them hear.*" **THIS MY MOTH-ER TAUGHT ME HOW TO SING ...** "*I hear and I see.*" She wanted to touch his hair and feel the skin around his neck. Would it feel fishy?

"*I am a story teller, as you should know at this point, and I know a good story when I see one.*" She wanted to shake him by the hair of his head.

"*The tears were quite effective.*"

"I enjoyed them," he replied.

"*What I have heard is not something that makes me want to be here speaking with you as my baby sleeps. Why don't you just go back to the sea?*" She motioned her hand. "*And, swim away.*"

She studied him quickly. He didn't seem to have any sticks in his possession at the time.

"Do you find my body pleasing?" He asked, noting her careful appraisal. He twirled in a circle, his hands raised upward.

"Aaaaugh! I'm looking for the sticks," she answered.

He had to listen, real close to hear that one.

"The ones you people use." She continued. *"I have heard it ... seen it ... the destruction your kind are bringing upon the children who were born on sweet Gaia."*

"I would never hurt you Daffinina!"

"My name is not Daffinina! I have heard it said that you people have sticks that you point at people and it makes them POOF!" She exploded her arms in motion and made a wind sound with her lips.

"And you have a silent way of speaking that is equally as threatening!" He laughed. "Deadly, indeed!" He clutched his heart.

"Go exactly as I said ... back to the fouled sea from which you swam. Leave Gaia as it was before you came!"

He laughed at her. She was such a cute little thing. "Darling! That is why I am here! The sea around my world is fouled."

At the table by her bed there was a wooden flat paddle that she used as a tool to shape clay. She picked it up and would have whopped him one across his head. She would see if he was fish in disguise, but he grabbed her hand before it hit.

"Come now," he spoke. "Is this any way to treat someone who has just brought more milk for the wee one?"

"Your child ..." She whimpered, struggling to free herself. *"You should bring her milk, and clothing as well, and soft linens. It was you who brought forth her seed."*

"What else would you like?" He asked her. His eyes roamed the room.

Sion had taken him to her maiden hut after ignoring Marisol's suggestion to take him elsewhere.

"I want nothing as vastly as I want that two-headed dog of yours to chew you up with each of his ugly mouths and spit you out alive into the stinking waters of that hell hole or whatever it is where you habitate!"

"I am sorry you were frightened, Daffinina."

Maybe Marisol had been right. She had motioned for Sionee to take the fish head to the meeting room at the house of shells. When whatever he was, from who knew what fouled star he came from, asked to speak to her in privacy, the crowd pressed closer to the fire in eagerness. No one made the slightest motion of leaving.

Marisol had pointed to the meeting room but Daysong was fast asleep and needed her bed in the maiden hut. She hadn't really brought him here. The fish head had followed her!

Sion's screeching sounded like an owl. When she formed her lips into more protests, he took her hand gently. It was so small for such a big voice. But her honey locust and cedar scent was most wonderful.

Daysong awoke to Sionee's further protests. The baby screamed even louder than Sion.

The fish head went to Daysong's basket and gently lifted the child up.

Cyex was so gentle with the child, unlike most of the men who cared little to hold a squalling baby. The fish head was also gentle which really surprised Sionee. While she was shaking in anger, here was this man? From where? He was standing calmly in her bedroom holding her child.

The fish head sat down on the chair beside the bed and bent his head to look into the baby's eyes.

Light from the oil lamp cast its gentle flicker on light, honey-brown hair, just a bit soft and curly. He really didn't seem to have a fish head at all. What kind of a head did he have? It was a little big ... as was he quite tall.

A spark of light wove its way between the baby's eyes and the fish ... ah ... heads eyes.

Sion was quiet. Daysong was quiet as well, except for sleepy burbles of content that she shared with the fish head.

Hush now, baby. Baby, hush my sweet little Tititum." His words turned to song. He looked from the baby's eyes to Sion's eyes, crooning all the while.

Sionee could not turn away. The light seemed to pour into her very AHDAWN.

Ahhhh, what was this? The melody he sang was more beautiful than any she had ever heard before. The sounds he gave the baby brought to Sionee a peace quite unlike any living person had ever touched her with ... ever ... and he was just a fish head.

There was no way Sionee could think of to think about the emotion his song held ... except for, maybe ... Oh, no! It could not be love?

Mesmerized, Sionee watched and listened while Daysong went fast asleep.

Was this what it felt like to have a loving father?

Sionee did not even know his name. Not that it mattered. **THIS MY MOTHER TAUGHT ME HOW TO SING ...** It was who a person was ... what a person was.

The man ... fish head ... ah ... lay Daysong back in the basket, covered her gently and placed the blue lamb beside her.

"You oaf." Sionee whispered gently now into his eyes. "You call me Daffa ... Oh ... something ... Eena, and I have told you, my name is Alsionee Tree Song ... as if you listen, because I think you hear ... and I will tell you that she is not Tititum. Her name is Daysong. You gave her to me, so what I name her is what she will be called. What are you called?" She asked him.

"Ea," he said looking deep into her eyes. "I am not a fish, though my name on my star means "water." I am just a man.

Chapter Twenty-one

Sionee woke up even earlier than usual when she thought she heard something outside her door. At first she ignored it. She was still half asleep in the early predawn. Likely it was her imagination.

Sionee blinked her sleepy eyes. Were those footsteps she heard?

Not that there was anything unusual about footsteps exactly, but rarely had she encountered other early risers when she slipped out of bed to go to the tree before dawn had arrived. Normal people still slept at this hour.

Sionee slipped out of bed to look out the window of her little hut. There were two big eyes looking in on her. Were they of purple? Or were they of red? They were owl eyes of the wrong color. *"Aaaaaaaaaaaugh!"*

She gasped, not taking her eyes from the too bright stare for even an instant. Then, she blinked. The eyes of the owl vanished.

She opened the door of her hut to see if she could see anything. It was dark outside, very dark.

She mustered the courage to *hoot ... hoot ... hoot* like an owl. *"Come back owl. Tell me I am not imagining that I saw an owl. Tell me, too, that your eyes are of the normal color."* She hooted. It was silent.

Sion fell back into the bed, pulling her linens tight around her ear. Through the muffled protection of her softlings, she heard the owl hoot back. She ran to the door. White wing swooped before her eyes.

The bird flew to the overhanging limb of a wild apple that spread its branch over the hut. She could see its eyes gleaming in the darkness. They were eyes of the right color. Had it just been her imagination?

That did it! Sion gave up all hope of returning to bed. She wasn't tired anymore. Perhaps a cup of tea would soothe her, or help still the beating of her heart. She was relieved however, that the owl seemed usual.

Sion lit a small ceramic burner she had built of soft fired clay. The small flame provided light as well as heat to warm her small cup.

She lit a candle as well, enjoying the ambience of its flickering flame on the soft mica white walls of the hut.

As for the tea, lavender was her favorite ... though jasmine would be pleasant in the early morning ... mint tea might waken her well ... or apple would be good tea if she could find her cinnamon. Then, again ... hummm ... the wild rose would be so sweetly fragrant this early morning.

Finally, she chose the lavender, pouring it with thick cream. As she sat down on the chair beside her sleeping daughter, Sionee smiled in the pleasure at the steaming scent of the tea. She sipped the taste of the flower on her tongue ... ahh.

In the soft illumination of her candle, Sionee dreamed of sitting in a sunny nook of the tree she would build. The tree would have a face. It would be a mother face, smiling gently.

Daysong awoke, whimpering. *"Good morning sunshine!"* Sionee smiled indulgently at the wee one. She bent to change the wet swaddlings. She must remember to wash again when she got home from the morning walk. There were so few swaddlings. She almost had to wash every day.

"Come, my Song. We will go to our tree and say hello to the sun. We will sing with the birdies and greet the day as you taught me, my darling mother." She added softly.

"I am just your baby now." Daysong responded in soft baby sighs. *"I am your baby now and you must call me mother only in your heart. I will soon forget who I was before. I have a new life now."*

Sionee smiled. So did she.

~~~

"Say it daughter. Say it with me in here ... ." Sion placed her hand on her heart. Then, she placed Daysong's tiny hand on Daysong's heart.

"I AM THE PERFECT DAY AND IN ME DWELLS THE LIGHT THAT DOES NOT FAIL."

The sun spread her amber orange image on the waters of the sea below. Her light turned gold and dappled through the feathery branches of the yellow cedar.

"Let us sing, Day, with the birds." Gulls were singing their *eeeeeee's* with a duet of waves that broke upon the sands below.

"The black birds make different sounds Daysong. Sometimes it depends on which color they are." She pointed. *"There are yellowheaded birds and red-winged birds. They like to imitate. Sometimes they sound like babies crying. Other times you may hear an ooo-kah-ree ...oo-kah-reee sound or a click ... click ... click sound - like this ... ."* Sion sent forth exuberant taps with her vibrating tongue. Daysong laughed as the birds responded to the sound of their own voices.

In the cedar branches above them, Sionee felt a sharp thud, followed by a shower of cold slime mist.

"Eeeooou, Kinga! Greetings to you my friend!" Sionee wiped the fish slime from her hand onto her tunic. *"You stink you know, especially after your tasty meal. But greetings anyway."*

"Greetings to you my lady, and my little Mistress Daysong, as well. Glad I am to greet you here ... not there where you were twit ... twit ... twit ... twit ... twit ... ." Kinga looked toward the sea cliff where he had last seen Sion and the baby disappear into the blackness.

"Listen Daysong," Sionee said eagerly. *"The kingfisher makes three fast syllable sounds in garbling succession, followed by a rapid two more. However for the most part you won't get a chance to speak to a kingfisher often. Usually they are a lone bird."*

"I have observed, my lady, that being alone is also to your liking."

"Well, I do enjoy it now and then. Thank you my little King for telling Cyex how to find me."

"Indeed." Sionee could hear him smile as he cocked his little crown in ever curious observation.

When the light began to spread across the curve of meadow, which met the mountain like tea in a cup, Sionee scrambled down the tree, Daysong secure in her arms.

It was still a bit early and there were not many who gathered yet for the breakfast meal. She had plans for the day so Sion stopped hurriedly to grab something to eat. She selected soft fresh gazelle cheese and crusty emmer bread. They were her favorite, quite simply all she would need.

Today she and Daysong would call Vastari to give them a ride up into the mountain just a bit. On the way home from her lovely and terrifying adventure, she and Cyex discovered a promising source of mica clay, pristinely clean and pure. Cyex had thought of the vessel drums he and his students could fashion, and the globular horns. The thought intrigued her, but she, too, had a good idea for using the beautiful clay.

When she began her home, it would take a lot of clay to build it. She would need ... um ... how much exactly? Sion frowned briefly. How would she get the clay to her building site? Even without the baby it would be quite difficult and wearisome and ... oh! Sometimes, the least quantity of moist clay could be quite heavy. There was also the matter of bringing the baby along while she fetched it.

She could put Daysong in a sling on her back. Surely she could get some help. She could bring some of the younger Songkeepers with her now and then. There certainly would be a way for her to do it, surely.

Sion decided to return to her hut briefly, to fetch extra pouches of milk for the excursion, it might take a while and maybe they could have a little fun along the way.

Eee-yah! HE had said he would bring her more milk and he did. He had brought her a very ample supply, enough for the baby until she was two years old! She would have to figure it into a storage place. The maiden hut was ample for a young maiden alone. It lacked the necessities a child brought forth, like in size and space.

~~~

As Sion approached her hut, her mind was busy supplying details as to how to begin. She nearly fell on her face when she just about did not see the pile of stuff at the side of her door. It was a wonder she

190

hadn't tripped on it when she and Daysong had left in the morning darkness to wait for the sun to rise. Of course! She had heard a noise in the wee hours of morning that had awoken her.

Alsionee lay the baby down and rushed to examine what was there. It was a small mountain of things, already fashioned, albeit a little strangely for the norms, but the possibilities for use made Sionee's eyes wide with delight.

There were swaddlings of many colors, not just white as were commonly used, but of colors she had seen so vividly only in nature ... like the hue of butterfly wings, or hummingbird feather, or the bright flamingoes in the marsh. And apples! The swaddlings featured the many different colors of wild apples in the forest. Well there was the color of the sunsets too, orange and purple.

There was the teal color of the dusk sea, the turquoise of the stone. But how and why would anyone need such colors? The bright colors overwhelmed her like the too bright noon sun sometimes did.

Bed softs were supposed to be white, or the color of pale yellow cream or beige, maybe. But there were enough soft swaddlings here for ten babies surely. There were teeny tiny shifts as well, though it was best to keep a baby naked. They liked it better that way, free and unwrapped so their skin could breathe. Was this a tunic for a cold day?

It didn't really get cold here, but Sion had to admit that the clothes were delightful to gaze upon, even the tiny swaddlings that were designed to keep a baby bottom dry. Some of them even had flowers in their print!

Why would anyone put images of a sweet smelling flower on an article that was destined to be constantly full of baby pee and baby poop?

Sion further examined blankets of strange colors and strange fabrics. There was one that was soft and nubby. The nap of the material lay down when she stroked the velvety softness. And many were lined in lamb fleece. There was even one that matched the color of the turquoise blue lambie that Daysong adored.

Well! She didn't have twins for heaven's sake! What would she ever do with all this stuff? She really better hurry to get her tree built soon. This stuff had to be put somewhere!

Of course, she could give some to other babies. Alita surely would love to deck little Lilitu with such finery. Then, her eyes lit on the big lump beneath some big linen's. She pushed them aside.

It was a chair! Sion gasped. She had never seen such a chair. The wood was so smoothed it appeared as the molten glass which potters often fuse upon their pots. At the base of the chair, smooth half curves permitted the chair to rock in motion when she pushed it. Alsionee picked Daysong up. The two of them sat in the rocking chair.

Maybe she was being a little unreasonable to that fish headed one who was not a fish ... Eee-ah. Was that his name?

He had brought not only the milk, but everything she had asked for, along with a chair that moved back and forth in motion like the rhythm of a song.

Chapter Twenty-two

With the breath of a sea wind, and riding on an ocean wave, Vastari came out of the white mist of the sea below. Sion watched her racing the tide, then turn to disappear into the cedars at the forest edge.

Sionee made her voice join with the morning breeze that had risen from the sea to call Vastari. Her wind whinny echoed through the trees and sent her vibration stirring among the cedars.

Vastari heard and came quickly to Sionee's side. Sion stroked the long white neck of her unicorn mare in greeting.

"Ho! Vastari, my friend. Will you carry two travelers this morning? It will just be a wee bit of distance, and one of us is really light!"

Sionee thrust herself and Daysong onto Vastari's back in one quick motion. Vastari's hair still smelled like sea mist and salt wind, and they rode.

~~~

Standing at the high spot where the hill began to rise above the lowlands on the crest of lava, Sionee let out a loud and piercing hawk call, placing two fingers to her lips to insure that a whistle shriek echoed over the valley and above the hills.

Daysong lay sleeping on a shaded spot of grass strewn with dandelion and sweet lily.

Sion needed to ask Cyex about the clay. She would definitely be in need of assistance. The clay was abundant in the place she and Cy had found, oozing out clean in a thick vein that appeared to be exactly what she had been looking for. There would be some digging involved, of course.

She could find a closer source, not far from the outlier and on more level ground where climbing would not add burden to the task. She knew of several sources. Of course, the places to get clay that were closer to her were all white clay. She really liked the idea of a bit of variation.

The color of the clay she and Cy had found was as the pale beginning of the golden dusk as it turned from day to night. It was flecked abundantly with golden stars of shining mica, which always signified that the clay would be strong. It was the color she had envisioned in her dreams. It had the perfect bit of iron oxide in the cream to make it stunning, especially if she burnished some surfaces of her inner spaces to bring out the color and the natural beauty.

Would Cyex laugh at her when she told him of her preposterous plans? She would show him the model of her idea and he could see that she had planned it quite extensively.

Would he catch eagerness and help her figure out how to begin? He was skilled in putting things together.

So she called him, not entirely certain that he would be available at the time. It could be that he was out in the wild forest gathering cedar boughs to carve into flutes, or out dancing on some hill. She smiled as she thought of him out dancing thus.

She hoped he would come. She really needed to talk to someone about her idea. Doing so would be a good beginning.

The whistle scree woke Daysong. Sion left the rock and settled down to feed her daughter. As she sat, she watched the honeybees gather nectar from the lilies. She contemplated their ever busy industry.

Then, he came. She didn't hear him as he approached, his footsteps were quiet and it wasn't Cyex. It was Eah.

"Pardon me," he said. "Did you see that eagle? I'd really like to see the fine bird that made such a call."

"Are you following me?" She asked.

"Darling girl, you are truly so little acquainted with me. Could you possibly even care what this ... ah ... fish head is doing?"

"Why should I?" No, she really didn't care as long as it was elsewhere. Where was Cyex? She bent her head to peer into the trees.

"Because ... I am doing research."

"Any searching you do will be futile. You have found your eagle. It's really not an eagle, it is a hawk .. and it's me!" She giggled despite herself.

By Ki and the moon! The girl had quite a giggle and he loved giggles! She sounded like waters babbling down a hillside creek.

"Oh, come now. I wouldn't believe it. I thought I was approaching an eagle. I was hoping to get a sketch of a wing pattern."

She could see that he had some of those strange leafs in his hand, and a scribing tool of sorts

He opened the tablet and made motions with his hands, moving the stylus rapidly.

She peeked. *"That is no eagle!"*

"Oh, ho. Is that so?" He acknowledged silently, making little line curves sweeping here and there. He shaded slightly beneath the eyes and in the corners where eye meets nose. He darkened the fringe of lashes. How to get that light in her eyes?

Mother would love this. Could he possibly capture how Daffinina's irises were every shade of gold with a ring of topaz jewel encircling her pupils?

"Hey, that's me!" Sion gasped. *"You are well creative in your drawing!"*

"Oh, yes. I am almost skilled. I am good at many skills my Daffinina. But again, why would you care about what this old fish head is doing?"

"But you are not!" She spoke it too fast, with too much enthusiasm. There was a deep silence.

Sionee's face turned a deep red. This was awkward ... not that it mattered how old he was. *"Would you like bread... ?"* She asked. *"And cheese?"*

~~~

Breaking Bread ... Ea was pleased. The act of sharing a meal was a shared communion. He watched as she tore a chunk of hard bread and a chunk of cheese and held it out to him.

"I have apples. I picked them from the sweet trees near my hut." She took a bite, and then held the apple out to him.

He took a small knife from his tug pocket and cut the apple horizontally in half and showed her the pattern the seeds made.

"It's a star!" She smiled in delight. "*I can't say I have noticed that before. Well I usually don't cut apples. I just eat them.*" She explained in a hurry.

"I am a scientist, Daffinina."

"*A what?*" She asked between bites, not waiting for his answer before she further added, "*Have you ever taken a bite of apple with a bite of cheese and the bread at the same time?*"

"No, I can't say I have. Show me?" She held her apple to his lips. He bit.

~~~

"I often go out on walks to look at things," he told her. "I love to explore. As I was trying to say, I am scientist. I walk, I swim, I fly ... to observe the nature of things. I like to watch the fish, the birds, and the serpents in the marshes."

"*I climb trees to sing with the birds.*" Sion replied with excitement. "*But ... fly?*"

"I draw, I take pictures or images. I practice healing. I study. I create things with my knowledge of scientific principles. Ah girl! I could talk all day and not mention everything that I do. My people have a name for me. They call me Wise One of the Waters or He Who Fashions Things."

" '*Eah' is easier to say when I think of you ... if I ever do.*" She added quickly. "*I never do think of you ... ever.*" She assured him rapidly, to make sure he got that straight. "*I like to fashion things, too.*"

He looked at her with warm interest in his eyes. "Oh, you do?"

"*It is why I am here,*" she replied. "*It is the clay. I build things with clay ... Oh, pots for one.*"

~~~

The language of silence necessitated close observance. He watched how her eyes increased in hue intensity as she spoke of her craft. He could see her soul lit with flame as she communicated of her work with the clay.

He had never had the opportunity to really share emotion other than with his dear and lovely mother, of course. This however, was unlike anything he had experienced with anyone.

"*I make pots to trade. I love to make pots, which I make many of.*" She explained to him, showing him the ball of clay she had gathered from the hillside and had set in the sun to observe its elasticity as well as its cracking point.

It was still moist and she pushed her thumb into the ball of clay, and began an upward pinch and squeeze, quickly creating a small pinch pot.

"It is lovely." He told her.

"*Oh, yes. I love the color of this clay in particular. Do you see how these mica flakes within this clay shimmer?*" Her enthusiasm caught her up and she sent forth her thoughts openly. She was surprised that he could hear her so well.

"I can hear you." He silently told her as he picked up a piece of the clay and stuck his own thumb in the center. In moments two little pinch pots lay in the grass to dry. Sion nodded at him in approval. Of course, he was an artist.

"*Many in my outlier and many outside my home and even across the seas wish to acquire my vessels. I am a storyteller and this is my first calling, but shaping the clay is my first love of doing.*"

He was enchanted with the fire in her eyes. It was the emotion thing. Ea smiled in the deepest pleasure in listening to her silent speech.

"*In my head, behind my eyes, I see images of animals and birds and trees... all manner of things that I find beautiful. I like to sculpt an image likeness to express what I see in here.*" Without taking the time to think, she grabbed his large hand and placed its palm over her heart. She blushed, quickly putting his hand back to himself.

He was charmed, and knew well what she was speaking of. He understood completely. "When I was in the room of the little hut and speaking with you, I was drawn to a stunning little tree figure that you had in the corner. Did you create it?"

"*It is my tree! I created it. It is a model in a small scale of the big tree I wish to create as a home for me and Daysong.*" She looked down upon the sleeping baby.

"It is like this: Our homes of the Songkeepers... where we live ... is who we are, what we are, as well. Our homes tell the story of our hearts. I wish my home to tell my story."

His ears perked up. He adored the way her eyes were lit with enthusiasm that made her shine.

"Though I share my stories in song at nightfire, by day the Songkeepers must live the wisdoms of which we sing. We build our homes with beauty as we build our heart home with beauty. I will house within, also knowledge."

"Daffinina! My Daffinina!" He reached out in profound joy and grabbed her hand within his. "Will you be my friend?"

~~~

"It is unseemly." She quickly withdrew her hand, looking for Cyex, wishing he were here. She laughed at the butterfly that hovered over Daysong's lashes, making her tiny hand bat at the tickle.

"Daffinina, if you say yes, I would really like to show you something I think would give you gifts to contemplate. I have received gift from the treasure house of wisdom that is within who you are. Let me share with you what is inside me as we have shared bread this day."

Sion was silent. "But first," he paused, "Let us share this wisdom. When we as friends are together, let it be, that you are not of earth and I am not of sky. Can you agree with me here?"

Sionee looked around her at the vast beauty everywhere! The flowers in the meadow sent forth their scent. The birds of the trees sang their songs. Down below the song of the sea made waves upon the shoreline.

"Why not?" She replied.

~~~

"Are we friends?" He asked her. The brow above his right eye had a single hair that curled and touched his golden lashes. It was one single silver hair. His eyes were silver as well.

"How old are you?" She asked him.

"Much older than you. However, in our hearts I do not think the age of our bodies matter. He took her hand to see if she would with-draw.

"In friendship will you trust me, thus?"

"*Trust is given when one earns trust,*" Sionee replied. **THIS MY MOTHER TAUGHT ME HOW TO SING ...** "*I barely know you.*"

"Oh, Daffinina! I have given you no reason to trust me. Give me a chance darling! There is someplace I think you would enjoy seeing. Something tells me you would."

She was intrigued. "*When? Now?*" There was no sign of Cyex coming. If Kinga was here no doubt he would call her a dunderhead again. Then fly and tattle.

She wanted to go with him. Why? She couldn't imagine why but she wanted to. "*Where will we go?*" She asked.

Before he answered she remembered words that Marisol had told her.

"*You must look in places that I do not understand. You will walk down roads I don't know of anyone having gone down before. You must swim in waters too deep to not drown, and fly in skies too high for the birds. You must sing songs never heard before.*"

~~~

Speaking of wings, what was Eah putting on his back? He was fastening it with belts, even as she had learned to fashion Daysong. Something that looked like wings ... sort of.

If they were wings, they appeared to have inset gemstones on them, rubies that came to life when he touched.

"*Oh, now, wait a minute!*" She backed away as he held out his arms to her. Her eyes were as big as Nibiru's two suns.

"You are small, as is the baby. My wings have much power. I can fashion smaller ones for you and Ti Ti if you like, for the next time."

"*Oh, I don't know!*" Sionee was suddenly afraid. "*I think it is time for Daysong and me to return home.*"

He looked disappointed as he began to remove the wings. In the next instant she flung herself within his arms, holding Daysong tight within her own.

"Okay!" Her squinted eyes stretched into two thin lines. He secured Sion and Daysong safely in his grasp with more belts.

Daysong giggled as they began to rise. Sion held her eyes squeezed tight. Then she opened one eye to peek just a bit.

She could see as if she was standing on the top of a high mountain peak, but her legs hung in the air as if she were a bird. Sion greeted an eagle that swooped across the sky toward her mountain nest. The eagle pierced the silence with the vibration of the sound of up close shrees. A mouse squirmed in the eagles talons as the bird flew to her babies.

Sionee sang with the wind like she'd never sung before. As if on breeze they rose higher and higher to cross the mountain, the trees, the meadows, the waters of all the rivers and the streams that meandered to the sea in a squiggle of great design, like baby snakes seeking to be close to their mother snake of the sea.

"Do you see, Daffinina?

Sionee wondered if she had ever truly seen anything before this.

"Wherever the waters flow..." he said, "ocean, lake, river, stream, marsh... wherever the waters are, all creatures come to life. Fish are plentiful ... food grows tall ... for wherever the waters give there is life."

She looked and saw the harmony of Gaia's earthen shores as she had never even imagined. They began a descent back to Gaia on the other side of the mountain.

Where several of the rivers converged and crossed to meet the sea below the mountain, over the waters at the valley edge, a house was built ... a house unlike anything she had ever seen before ... and way beyond anything she could understand.

She gasped and he took her down, into the garden of the vast house of healing and the sciences, which spread its many rooms downhill, and uphill over the crags of the hillside. It was sort of like a spider with many arms and legs. It was far bigger than any edifice should ever be.

~~~

The garden was also vast, but was of an extremely beautiful nature. They were at a pathway that turned into a corridor. It was of a splendor that reminded her of the paths at the Cosmopolitan Major. This she did not understand; immediately there were serpents that loomed before her.

There were twelve of them lined in a row on one side of the long garden path and twelve on the other side. They were giant serpents carved from giant pillars of stone. Wherever had he even received such stone? How had he brought it here? How had he carved it in such detail?

Sion felt like a mouse standing before awesome and great creatures. Standing at the point of one of the serpent's up-thrust tail curves, she reverently stroked her hand on the smooth cool surface of the skin. She traced the texture with her fingers.

Only her eyes could reach the top of the serpent's heads, which coiled in a spiral higher than ten of which she stood.

Sionee raced from serpent to serpent, having placed Daysong in her father's arms for safekeeping. Tears poured from her eyes. Never had she been so struck by beauty of such awesome nature. She felt a need to touch each and every one of the serpents in the corridor.

She stopped at the middle of the avenue where the corridor formed a circular center.

Here, there were two large snake creatures that stood across from each other on opposite sides of a pool. The two snakes faced each other, reflecting their images on the waters.

Their tails split into feet that were like talons. Their arms were also like talons. In each of their hands the serpents held a staff that extended their entire length from their feet to their hands. Wings spread from the creature's backs.

Between the two serpents that faced each other, there was another serpent. This serpent coiled in six gigantic loop turns together. Where the snake head arched at the sixth coil and opened its snake mouth wide, teeth gleamed and tongue stretched forth to meet its own tail in its own mouth, thereby forming a circle. From the mouth a fountain of water poured.

Sionee grasped in her shift pocket for a tiny bag which held her crystal. She felt weak and was impatient to undo the knot which held her own double terminated crystal ... the one she had showed Daysong at the Major.

She could only reach to touch the serpent's first coil. She pressed her crystal against the curve.

Sionee fell in a faint.

Ea was at her side instantly. He held a water flask to her lips and gave her drink.

"Daffinina. Oh, Daffinina! Isn't it beautiful? I completed this sculpture only days before. I built it in your honor."

Sionee gasped, with the water trickling down her chin. She was speechless.

"I only wanted to show you, my Daffinina, that when people dream a vision they see beyond their eyes ... it is never too big."

~~~

Going back across the mountain, Sionee clung to Eah. Pressed against the length of his back she felt every beat of his heart. She felt his wings dip and turn, then rise and lower on current of the wind.

"*Did you say you could make some of these for me and Daysong?*"

"For my Daffinina and Ti Ti I would do anything."

Her hair was free of the downward thrust of the earth. It flew about her face like rays of light coming forth from a star.

She struggled to free her hand and pull the hair from out of her nose and her eyes.

"*Is this why birds do not have long and shaggy feathers?*"

Ea grinned at her, firming his hold of her in pleasure. He didn't want to ever let her go. She smelled of earth. She smelled of flowers. Her very essence flowed within as pure waters and he was thirsty.

"*There is water ... ,*" she told him, "*at the spring by the clay. It is why the clay is still wet. Sometimes when I gather clay, it is powder dry and I have to put water in it to bring it alive again.*"

"It is lighter when it is dry. I can carry it home better. So either way, I can use it. Eah, where and how ever did you get stone that big and so vastly much ... how?"

Bless her. He smiled. Her mind had been rambling nonstop all the way back from the medical facility with questions and exclamations.

"Daffinina, we are wind. There is no hurry to where our friendship takes us. We can talk about all this on a different day. The wind now, darling, be still. We are wind as we blow over the earth. Remember it is as you are fond of saying 'Though the wind has voice it is silent.' "

She closed her eyes and became gentle wind. But even the wind grows weary as it crosses a mountain to get to the other side. In spite of herself, Sionee's eyelids began to droop. By the time they set foot on the ground again Sionee was fast asleep. He unstrapped her and lay both her and Daysong down on the soft grass among the dandelions and the sweet lilies.

He bent over them. "Are you well, my Daffinina?" He asked her, quietly bending down on knee and gazing at her sleeping face.

"The wind has blown over the earth and hill so vast she would rest for a time." Sionee breathed sleepily.

Ea pushed the hair from off her face and found it to be damp at the hairline.

"It is only sweat." She smiled up at him.

"Just the same, girl, I am a physician of medicine and ... ."

"A what of what?" A strong voice demanded. Both Sion and Ea looked up to see Cyex standing beside them.

"I am only an instructor of song and ... Aaah " Cyex bent and wiped Sion's brow with his fingers.

"Sionee, Oh, Sionee! Are you alright? I have been looking for you! I was getting ready to call Kinga to assist me when I came out of the trees."

The fish head pulled something from his whereabouts and placed it on Sion's heart. He frowned in deep thought.

At that moment Daysong chose to announce her presence lest

she be forgotten. She was hungry and hadn't eaten since early after-noon when she and Sion had arrived at the hill.

Ea motioned for the boy to pick Daysong up. Cyex had already done so and was fishing in Sion's bag for milk.

"She has one in her pocket." Ea spoke. "I really need to get a check on her pulse, boy. Would you kindly make Ti Ti quiet so I can hear?"

"I don't see a Ti Ti!" Cyex looked at him directly in the eye. "Though I am only a maker of music, I will tell you here and now that Sionee needs a rest. Since Daysong came she has been running about unceasingly, and I knew she wouldn't be able to keep up the pace long."

"Daffinina likes it so. She would never choose to rest." Ea in-formed Cyex.

Both men looked down on Sionee as she struggled to get up. Both restrained her with four firm arms.

"We both believe Daffinina, that you need a resting time." Ea told her.

"Daffinina?" Cyex shouted, frowning. "I don't know about Daf-finina, I will make certain that Sionee gets a good night sleep."

"See to it," Ea ordered and stressed sternly, frowning at Cyex, "that she sleeps well! I said sleep."

He bent and kissed Daffinina softly on the lips, then bent over the baby grasped in Cyex's arms and kissed her on the cheek.

Before he turned to leave he stopped only briefly to meet Cyex in the eye. The two of them stared at each other in curiosity.

Cyex spoke first. "Eeeugh. My lips will not kiss yours. Get the south end of your fish headed butt headed north along with your overlarge and fish-gilled noggin!"

"You forgot to mention my wings, boy." Ea winked at Sion as he fastened his wings, pushed the ruby gems and flew off, blowing another kiss to Sionee and Daysong as he did just that ... north and away.

Chapter Twenty-three

"What is he? Cyex was irritated. "Is he a fish a bird or both those things in one ugly, walking son of a ... ."

"*He is not ugly,*" Sion smiled indulgently at Cy, which further increased his irritation. "*and his head is not so big.*"

"You don't think so?" He asked incredulously. "Well, Alsionee Tree of Song, as has been demonstrated before, you and I do not always agree on things. Do you think him beautiful?"

Sionee stroked the golden peach fuzz which was increasing every day on Daysong's baby head.

"*Oh, yes. I think he is ... and he is a man, Cy. Were you playing your flute so loud you did not hear him say so himself?*"

"Where did he take you, Sionee? I heard you call me, I was far away in the cedars when you whistled the hawk. I was with my boys in lesson. Surely you know I will come when you call ... as soon as is possible."

"*I don't expect you to come running whenever I call. I just called to see if you were around somewhere. I wanted to talk with you about something ... if perchance you were available.*"

"You didn't answer my quite simple question."

"*Oh, Cyex, really! There is no hurry to our friendship. We may talk later. For now I intend nothing more than to get on Vastari and take Daysong home and put her to bed. Perhaps tomorrow we can talk. I really am wearisome.*"

"Let me help you tonight Sion. Will you?" He called to the grazing Vastari. He mounted behind Sion and the three of them rode to the place of maidens at the cedar edge.

~~~

"No Sionee. I am going to watch Daysong for you this evening. Come little darling." He took Daysong from Sion's arms and lay her in the basket with her blue lambie.

"I want you to get a good sleep tonight. You have been over-filling your cup lately. I will agree with that ... ah ... ugly ... that you are in need of rest. You were ever busy before Daysong came ... now ... ."

He helped Sion crawl into bed and tucked the covers protectively around her. Then, he went to the door of the hut and called out to one of the maidens who scurried about outside.

"Taya, could you do me a help?" He winked at the girl when she came eagerly to the door.

"Sionee is ill and needs a bit of care. Could you bring soup while I mind the baby?" The girl giggled as she smiled into Cyex's no moon eyes.

"Of course. I'd be happy. Soup will be right here!" She turned to assist.

"Oh, and she likes it with mostly broth, and some crusty bread, please darling and thank you!" He bowed to the girl.

"How did you know I like soup that way?" Sionee asked, sitting up. *"I really need to get up Cy, though I do think I could snuggle here and sleep in a moment without eating. Daysong and I really don't need you to stay. We are fine."*

"Let me help you Sionee. What are friends for? Come on my girl."

It was tempting. *"Where will you sleep?"* She asked.

"I thought I would get Daysong nice and snuggled up and feed her a little pouch of that strange milk, put her to bed in her basket and play her a song or two ... there is room enough beside you Sion. I don't know why I should sleep in the chair, we are friends."

"Friends, Cy ... and I ... wearisome. Surely though, you know that is all I can offer."

"Hush, Sionee. I will give you that tonight ... sleep. Ah! Here is the soup." He kissed Taya lightly on the lips. "Be Blessed Thou, darling. Thanks for the ample soup. No, I have not eaten this evening, and I give thanks for thinking."

After the meal Sion eased herself into the comfort of the linens soft and watched Cyex as he changed Daysong's swaddlings, and sat with her in the rocking chair to feed her.

"Sion," he spoke softly so as not to disturb Daysong. "Wherever did you get such a chair?"

But she was already fast asleep and did not respond, except for a soft, soft sigh.

~~~

"Daysong woke up two times during the night, Sionee. When I got up and rocked her in the chair and fed her the milk she went right to sleep again. Where did you get such milk, Sion? And these colorful swaddlings, and the chair?"

"*Later.*" she replied. "*Oh, Cy, thank you, my friend.*" Much refreshed, Sionee stretched her arms in satisfaction. "*I haven't slept that well since ... ,*" she was a child in her mamun's arms she was going to say, but he interrupted.

"Since the day I met you on the hill and minded Daysong all day long while you slept. I do believe Daysong likes me."

"*Daysong likes men.*" Sion smiled. "*When she is with ... .*"

"Does he hold her?" Cy interrupted her again.

"*He is her father.*"

"Oh, ho, Sion, indeed! He... and little Coelle. I wouldn't believe it."

"*It is obvious Cy. Just look at this fuzz.*"

"No kidding," he replied. I really think she thinks I am her father, as you once did ... and now ... ."

"*She loves you well, indeed. You have been so good to her. Could you hand me those sandals? They are on your side of the bed. Would you? I really have to run to the ...*"

Sion sat on the edge of the bed, slipped on her sandals and grabbed a clean shift.

Cy sighed, as for a brief instant before she slipped her robe on, she stood naked in her glory, "ahhhhhhh."

~~~

"Sionee, when you were sleeping last night, I lit an oil lamp and I noticed the remarkable sculpture in the corner," he nodded. "I've never seen it before. It is amazing!"

"*Oh, I've had it for some time now. You've just never been to my room before. Actually it is not recommended for any maiden to enter-tain a man in her space. I built the tree when I was but young. I was twelve spins of age or so but now it is time. I will show you,*" she began.

"I am really glad you are here. I've wanted to ask you for some advice, or what you think at least. I'm really not sure how to go about it." Though the model of her proposed home was big, it was fairly light and hot fired. She picked it up and set it on the bedside table so he could better see.

"Twelve? Did you say you were only twelve summers and you built this?" No wonder I haven't seen you for more than a glimpse since we scrambled on the vines."

"I got paddled," Sionee laughed. *"for skipping my instructions to play. It was the last time I disobeyed Marisol."*

"Actually, I too was busy, completing my instructions and be-coming an instructor." He laughed.

"A very artist of sound, Cy! That is what you are ... and dance, too! I have seen you on the hill."

"So tell me about this tree you have created and what it rep-resents." He smiled. "I really like this face. It makes me laugh. You have built such a character in her face."

"The last time I heard a face described as such was when my sculpting instructor was thinking real hard about how to find a way to tell me that the face was not beautiful. The look you see is wisdom, which I perceived as having done a pretty good job on." She touched the big eye in the tree bark's wrinkled forehead.

"Aye you have captured a piece of art well."

"There is more, Cy. Look inside!"

He looked. Observing it closely he noticed the portal doors that had been carefully designed in the bottom outer trunk of the tree. They almost appeared to disappear in the pattern of the tree's bark. Inside the tree he could see that the large inner windows inter-spersed here and there, were mere slits on the outside, hidden in the natural texture that gave all trees beauty.

While this tree had a few knobby limbs along its curved vertical length, they did not extend far outward. They were more like sug-gestions of tree limbs, as if broken off perhaps, and extending out as if to create a small room, hollow within the tree interior, as would be natural in an ancient gnarled tree.

There was also an attached inner rope ladder hanging from the upper floor, linking several levels of half floor shelves, the way it would be if it was in some kind of house, anyway. At the bottom inside, portals led to what could be hall-like extensions or roots. He used his imagination to picture roots.

"*Each root,*" she began, "*is a little hall of more space.*"

"What are you saying, Sionee? Are you speaking of a 'real' living space?" Surely he knew her too well.

"*Yes. It is how I plan to build my house.*"

"But darling the scale would be so big."

"*When people dream a vision they see beyond their eyes ... it is never too big.*"

"Sionee, your tree is beautiful. Is this why you were so interested in the orange mica clay we found? White would not do? There is much white clay at the digs we are all familiar with. It is nearer than this other clay is. It would make the transport easier."

"*But Cy, everyone is eager to help a Songkeeper create a beautiful expression of our heart in the homes we build. This will be a gift to all... my story house. I will use this house for many wonderful things to share with our whole outlier. I can explain later what I wish to do.*

"*There are many who will be willing to help me. I know. The Songkeepers who have risen above the age of ten, who are still learning ways of wisdom, as well as the maidens in the huts where I am now living. Some of the older Songkeepers will even be excited to help me. Building a home is a great teaching experience, surely you know that Cy.*

"*The girls will be inspired to recognize their own symbols ... their own dreams ... their own beauty ... when they share in the act of my creation. I believe even Marisol will be eager.*

"*I will promise them a great adventure they will never forget. When it is complete, it will stand in the hollow of wisdom trees to always remind them of the Beauty Way.*"

"I know that, darling." Cy responded patiently, "Though we men are content to live in simple huts as the maidens do, and also most of us ... ."

"Do not dream in the Beauty Way as do all Songkeepers who desire to express themselves in a more creative way, which is a calling given of those who tell story ... and sing GNOS." Sionee spat, becoming a bit vehement at this point.

"I am talking about small huts, Sionee, in the shape of a stone perhaps. or a round moon on a small hill above. I have admired the lovely little rosebud that the girlfriend of one of my students built. He lives with her now, and he says it is quite a construction."

"... which I designed and helped build."

"Even your mother's house, Sionee, was small and had an easy shape. The general idea is to keep things simple and proportionate,though beautiful. Do you realize how large this would be? Why, you would need..."

Sion was silent as he continued. "Your maman's house is but a stump in size to the one you are proposing."

"My tree would be but a stump in comparison to what he..." She tried to finish, but he wasn't listening to her anymore and he kept interrupting.

"Sion, Sion! Use your head ... to think ... you know. Do you figure how much clay this would require? And the stability of so large a structure ... have you planned an inner support and such? You are a pot builder, Sionee!"

"Of course, I've thought. Cannot you see? This model will pale in comparison to the tree I will build. You will see! What do you think I've been doing all these years? I've been thinking!"

She did do a lot of that ... he had to give it to her ... like the thought it took to take a baby into the vast wonderland of the cave. What if she had slipped? As it was, she had nearly drowned them all!

"I wish to speak of this thing no more! Not with you. I do not need your advice Cy. I can do this thing! I don't need you or any man to help me." She mumbled to herself as she invited him to leave.

"But ... thanks for helping me with Daysong last night," she tried to impart as he shuffled ... ruffled out the door.

~~~

Thus it was early the next morning, Cy was on the mountain with all his boys, as well as the boys from the other instructions.

Each had a big linen bag with him, some of them had two. They were strong boys. They also had persuaded the donkeys to join them.

If the women could do it, the boys could do it much faster. Of course, he fully expected the girls to arrive soon. But he would beat them. He would like to surprise Sion.

The clay vein was far larger than he or Sion had first imagined. He supposed the whole other side of the mountain was rich in it, some in rocky patches, some smooth and clean. Some was even studded with tiny pebbles. Some was dry; some moist. Some was much too close to the fish heads.

It would be a great learning tool for all of them. This he could agree with her on ... to help a lady ... a lady who gives in song. For surely Skymother created women in her likeness.

When he thought of the supreme Mother of the whole vast sky sea, he thought of Alsionee ... Alsionee of Song Tree.

Chapter Twenty-four

First things first. Second things second. Well, she had done the initial first. Mentioning it to Cyex had been a not so good way to begin.

Her mentioning was done, albeit, without a positive reply. So now it was time for the second, and the third. She would do it all herself if needs be, because it was time for the tree to rise.

Sionee rose early the next morning to take Daysong to greet the sun. Afterwards, the two of them would go to the site where she planned to see her song tree grow.

The general size of the circular rise must be determined, which she figured would be about twenty footsteps from a midpoint in the center, all the way around. Because of the living space she would vertically create in the trunk, there should be space enough for the tree to rise in height without interfering much with already existing trees. When it came time to complete the alchemy from mud to stone in the firing process, a bit of distance would be important.

Also, there would need to be enough space determined for the clay pile when she got it.

How long would it take to get enough clay to actually begin? She could fetch the clay in small batches, then build ... get another supply, and build more. Cyex wasn't right was he? After she had completed the initial trunk base she could better guess how much clay she would need for each day's work.

With the assistance of other Songkeepers, many of whom she had helped in their buildings, there would be the second step taken on this day. Already, eager volunteers were asking to assist her with the clay gathering bit. She had managed to get a small bunch of ladies to agree with enthusiasm to help her fetch clay. They must get some donkeys.

She knew that Cy was right when he said it would take a long time. **THIS MY MOTHER TAUGHT ME HOW TO SING ...** "*One by one and the work is done. Two by two and the work's still new. Three by three it will be. Four by four you see a door.*" No task can possibly be completed without the first step, so ...

"*Come, my little sun song. Let us greet your namesake this early morn.*" She changed Daysong into a softling of vivid sky blue and fetched a few milk pouches to put in her bag. It was still quite dark outside, though she could hear the birds stirring their sleepy heads.

The first crack of morning light pierced the darkness upon the horizon and cast its first ray on the waters of the sea in undulating gold.

The gulls swooped over the waves crying for their breakfast. From the marshes, the herons and the cygnets echoed their early dawn song.

Sionee, sitting in her place in the crotch of the yellow cedar began her morning mantra. Her eyes adored the vast golden sea which crowned the spreading gold of the valley below the cliff.

"*Say to yourself ... Daysong ... each and every day upon your walk upon Gaia ... 'I AM THE PERFECT DAaaaaa' ... !*"

The mantra turned into a startled bit of nonsense, when something on the distant valley floor by the edge of her future home distracted her train of reverence. Was this something near the story tree site? Surely it was. The view was clearly different ... something was there. What was it?

She squinted and placed her hand to shade her eyes so as to better see. "*Daysong, my darling, as many days as the days of my life I have passed over this site as I sang to the morning. It is different today!*

"*Aaah ... IN ME DWELLS THE LIGHT THAT DOES NOT FAIL!*" She hurried to complete the mantra. "*I'm sorry Skymother. I am distracted, for something I see calls my attention quickly. I love you ... and greetings on this morning!*" She apologized to Skymother and the birds for forgetting to finish singing with them as she scrambled down the tree and hurried to the sight.

~~~

What was this? It was no mere pile. It was not even a hill. It was almost an entire mountain of clay. It was the orange clay. The mica in the clay caught the early sun and completed the morning sun song in Sionee's heart. This was beyond her comprehension ... *aaah.*

The amount of clay took up a lot of space on the grass by the cedar edge and some of it overlapped her planned building area. *Aaaah!* But wasn't this a beautiful sight to sore eyes?

She'd have to clean it up afterwards, after she had used what she needed. Maybe she could donate some of it to the pottery instructions.

Afterward, she would level the sight again, pristinely, of course, and naturalize the flowers and the grasses around her home again. The work on the tree would cause minimal damage ... she hadn't thought of that much ... but she would restore it when the tree was finished.

"*Daysong! It is beautiful, is it not?*" In her eyes there was a smile.

Where had all this clay come from? In her eyes there was a twinkle. She knew where it had come from, surely. But where else would it have come ... all this over-abundance ... and how?

He shouldn't have ... but he should have ... but no he shouldn't have! But she couldn't ... could she ... but no ... she couldn't send it all back ... no way! And for this she was really glad.

Plans began to swirl in rapid design in her head. "*She Who Creates By Thinking ... Skymother ... Blessed Be Thou! Oh! Thank you Mother ... Oh! Thank you Matriarch of the vast universal sky sea above ... and below ... Oh! Thank you for the mountain of Gaia's sustenance which you have sent me by a fish head hand. It will be more than a beginning ... it will be enough to complete my song tree I will build in honor of you.*" She extended her arms upward and reached high to celebrate her joy.

~~~

At first she didn't even notice the small pile of linen bags of clay that had been placed so carefully in a loving pile on the ground. As a matter of fact, she wouldn't have noticed them at all if she hadn't tripped over the contents as she turned to get breakfast. It appeared that some of them were partially buried by the oozing mountain, the bags must have been placed quite early. None of this was here last night.

It was not that the small pile was meager, exactly. It might have been enough for half of the beginning she had originally planned ... or a fourth of the first coil. Sion noted the trampled grass and the muddy footprints of numerous boys converging on the area ... and donkey poop! She stepped over the poop as she counted the bags of clay. She calculated that certainly she would have enough donkey poop to begin a collection to dry for use when she was performing the final fire.

She frowned ... and she smiled again. Her heart went out to Eah ... and it went out to Cyex. Bless them both.

Here, ready for her use at the site she had proposed for her tree, next to her Mamun's stump, was a veritable mountain of clay. And by its side, twenty or so humbly-offered small bagful's that almost, she hadn't seen at all.

~~~

It took nearly two days to find him. Standing on a high hill, she let out a hawk shreee. She almost expected to turn and find Eah. If Eah did come ... well ... that would be good. She would thank him. It was Cyex that she would really like to see at this time.

Neither of them came. Sionee and Daysong stood alone at the hill. The two of them spent the day playing with butterflies and dandelion fuzz while they waited in case he came.

On the second day, Sion took Daysong and her pouch full of milks and bread and cheese, to search for him.

The boys at the shells told her that he was out alone, and had added that he had arranged for his students to practice with a younger instructor for a few days.

Standing at the hill, Sion closed her eyes and tried to locate him with her inner directions. She opened her eyes to take notice of which direction the wind was blowing and found Kinga hovering over the breeze as he landed on her shoulder.

"Kinga!" Sion exclaimed happily. *"I am glad to see you, my friend!"*

"The wind said I must come and tell you how to find him." Kinga cocked his little crown from right to left from left to right *"My master, Cyex... He is angry in his heart. I thought to warn you!"*

"At me?" Sion asked. She sort of thought he might be.

"Yes, at you. He tells me that I should be glad that I am a lone bird. He says that females are great to look at ... but that they have a way of turning one's heart ... Oh! What was it he said ... twit ... twit ... twit ... twit ... twit ... over and under ... in and out ... in a wide circle? Ah ... downside up ... upside down ... ah ... twit ... twit ... that's it! Upside down.

"I am curious, my lady. How do you do it? How do you turn a man's heart upside down?"

"It is a simple matter, Kinga. I sort of reach right in there ... Oh ... through his skin, you know. It is bloody and slippery, of course. I grip his heart in the palm of my hand and I twist ... ," Sionee pulled a face as she looked at the bird and frowned ominously.

"Like this!" She made a motion with her wrist to demonstrate. Kinga's eyes were wide as he watched her hand move.

Sionee giggled. *"Oh, Kinga I absolutely did not do anything to him. He is the one who got mad. I really do wish to help him feel better. I care for him."*

"You do?" Kinga twitted.

"Well, yes I do. He and I are friends."

"Friends? Ah ... ." Kinga seemed truly disappointed. *"Well, my lady it is only that I love my master, and for that reason I will tell you where to find him ... but don't expect me to go with you. I do not wish him to sing a sad song. Twit ... twit ... twit ... twit ... twit ... ! Could not you care for him more?"*

"Kinga tell me where he is. If I didn't care I would not ask. Do you not see this? Are you a dunderhead?"

"Twit ... twit ... twit ... twit ... twit ... twit ... ."

~~~

She found him in the early evening. He was high among the

cedars, almost to the pines. It had been quite a climb and she was getting tired.

She heard the sound of his flute on a distant hill, and she followed the song. She knew it was him. At this point she knew well that only he, of all musicians, was capable of creating such beauty of sound.

He was sitting on a rock with shavings of cedar curls drifting in profusion at his side. Three fresh carved smoking pipes lay drying in the scented air.

"What are you doing here?" He asked her. "I haven't seen you more than a moment or two in years, and now every time I turn around ... ."

Sionee sensed irritability in his voice.

Cy put his current half-stripped piece of cedar down. "Sionee, I have been searching for the red stone for my boys to carve into bowls for smoking sage and cedar during ceremony. I found a nice source." He pulled several chunks out of a linen bag and showed her the smooth pieces of glossy stone.

"I heard you. I don't always come. We discussed this. I told you."

"I told you I didn't expect you to come running. I also heard that you were a bit ... Oh ... angry with me. I didn't ask him to bring me all that clay ... and I didn't ask you either. I am, however, very grateful for both your gifts to me. I came here to find you because I wanted to say 'thank you.'"

"For what?" Cyex's voice was clearly sharp. "For twenty bags of clay? Oh, come on Sion. Come on!"

"But Cy, it is not just the clay. It is the gift that you brought to my heart."

"Oh, sure Sion. Did you see the way that even my boys are laughing? I have made a fool of myself! What for, exactly? Go thank the fish head. You have nothing to thank me for!"

"I do. Cy, I bet I could gather a whole pile of donkey poop! For when I fire ... ." She tried to make him laugh but he didn't think it was funny.

"Sion, it was peaceful here, sitting here on the hill, surrounded by cedars and pines and a few high apples, carving wood for my pipes. Then you came."

Daysong started to howl in hunger and discomfort. She had never heard her beloved Cy talk in such a way before. It wasn't making Sion happy either.

"*Fine, Cy!*" She glared back at him. "*If you won't hear me, I will speak no more. Play your music now! Please do. I am leaving!*" Sionee gathered Daysong along with her bag and left.

She heard the music resume almost instantly. It lacked the peace he sought. Sometimes a person just needed to be alone and sit a bit. This she could understand.

~~~

Sionee sat a small distance away behind a patch of thick cedars and fed Daysong. She could be home before the darkness fell if she called Vastari. The walking no longer seemed pleasurable.

"*Neeeeeeeaaaaay,*" she whinnied above the rising sound of his flute.

Chapter Twenty-five

Taya spread the word that at nightfire, Sionee Tree Song would share another song. "It will be good!" Everyone knew that it would be. Sion had become the most cherished of all storytellers. "I will sing with her!" Taya added proudly.

By the evening dispersal of moonlight and star shine, Sionee and Taya were ready. It had taken a good deal of planning to ensure that everything would go as Sion hoped.

"Do you have enough tiny pots?" Taya asked Sion, giggling merrily. "I like your plan sister. I will be very happy to assist you. Be Blessed Thou for so honoring me."

"*Be Blessed Thou, Taya. May we both honor this song that will be shared on this night.*"

Sion began to gather her vast assortment of miniature pots and bowls. Most of them were at the potting shell where the majority of pot instruction was taught.

There were actually three of the small potting huts. The largest was for the making, another was for the drying, and another for the storage. There was a fourth shelter at the potting quarters that was not the usual sparkling white, but of every shade of gray to purple to black.

It was the firing hut, where a kiln was built that was a more durable source than the fires outside that low fired the pottery with sheep poop. In this enclosure, pottery could be fired, protected from wind and element. Here, a higher fusing point could be reached, making a stronger piece with a better durability.

Sionee gathered her tiny vessels from the storage room. She had several also stashed in her maiden hut, and many were outside on the ground still by the outdoor dung fires. Taya helped her pick these up and wipe away the sand and black ash that still clung.

They gathered the pottery together, and spread them across Sion's bed so they could examine and count them.

"I count ... Oh ... at least one hundred and fifty of them!" Taya exclaimed. "Do you think it will be enough?"

"Oh, yes! I do believe it will be enough. I knew these little ones would come of use at some time."

"Well, Sionee I think their time has come!" Taya giggled. "Oh, so cute, ahhhhhhh, and beautiful ... each one at their own right." She assured Sionee. "How did you do it?"

"Whenever I found a new clay source that was different than the usual, I always made a few little pots to test the clay. I needed to make sure of the way each batch dried, and if it would fire properly. Some clay needs mixing with a bit of sand or reed fuzz, or ground-up broken bits of ruined pottery or mineral. This is why I have so many. I have done a lot of experimenting.

"Mixing different elements has been of use to produce beautiful colors that are favorable in the trade market. Oh, see here! This one is a sort of a dark gazelle cream."

"This one is almost blue!" Taya exclaimed. "And this one is... Wow!" Taya held it up in delight.

"Many of these are white. I have found that everyone loves how they sparkle."

"I like how you have captured the colors of yellow like the sunshine, or orange like a fire flame, or the gray of smoke like this one. Is this one purple, Sionee? This is amazing!"

"Yes, that pot is a bit of pale amethyst color. I have a deep purple here, and this one has some multicolor sheen. But of all the many colors, this is one of my favorites." Sionee held out a shining black.

"Ah ... and this one is a softer black."

"I could show you how I do it sometime."

"Oh, yes, Sionee please!"

"It all has to do with the fire and the oxide in the clay, or out of the clay ... and the minerals ... and even the smoke in the fire."

"And... red!" Taya exclaimed in delight, as she held a shining red pot of a different nature than the others. In the first place, it was a big pot about the size of a round melon, while the others were assorted sizes anywhere from thumb size to fist sized.

"*This one is my prize.*" Sion exclaimed proudly. "*There is only one. It is a new process I have been experimenting with before Daysong came. I really haven't done so much pot making since she arrived.*"

"Oh, Sionee, there are a great assortment of sizes and shapes and colors. If I had to choose which one was my favorite, I wouldn't know which one I liked best."

"*Exactly,*" Sion smiled. "*Taya, will you go fetch one of your beautiful reed baskets, a kind of flat one, but slightly rounded so the contents may be viewed by all? We will place these vessels in your basket so they may choose.*"

"I'll be back in two shakes of my leg!" She turned giggling, to smile at Sion as she dashed out the door.

~~~

Sion had searched her heart thoroughly to find a way to create this story. When she relaxed in her creation-thought, the idea came into her mind.

Again on this night, many came eagerly, bringing their night linens, their snacks, and their children to meet around the fire for an evening of entertainment.

The Songkeepers circled around the crowd of observers, greeting everyone with hugs of welcome. There were no drummers or flutist at this circle. Sionee especially wanted the young boys of Cy's instructions to observe the story well.

She had tried the hawk call several times during the day. She fervently hoped that Cy would be here for the story. If he chose to remain pouty that was his doing. Sion scanned the crowd hopefully. She could not see him.

The chants of the Songkeepers filled the night with the power of woman song ... with the power of Skymother ... and Seamother ... and Gaia ... and all Mothers from the great Sapphire Blue. They honored the Fathers of all realms, too ... those who would listen.

Young Songkeepers attended the fire with sweet herbs and purple sage and jasmine.

The circle danced around the fire, starting at a slow earth shuffling pace to symbolize their connection to the earth. The pace increased as the woman song grew in vibration.

Sion and Taya went within the circle, close to the fire. The other Songkeepers sat in a circle around them. All was quiet except for the rhythm of the night, that echoed with cicada and cricket ... and the hoots of white owl as they circled in silhouette against the moon.

Only the flickering flame gave motion now as it reflected a dancing light on Sion's flowing white robe. In her hands she held a basket. What was in her basket? The crowd strained their eyes to hear.

Taya stood at Sionee's side. On this night Sion wished everyone to hear two voices, for those who could ... and for those who could not see.

While Sion sang the straight song, Taya's pure voice rang out echoing in words, harmonic resonation.

"I have a gift for you, Oh, Children of Fey ... to behold in the river seen with your ears ... and heard with your eyes ... the sound of this gift ... as it flows within ... to the place of AHDAWN.

"Oh, listen children ... it is the story of gift." Sionee and Taya walked out into the crowd and offered the gifts inside the basket to all observers.

"I give to each of you a gift, my friends. These are but tiny vessels, are they not? But each holds the universe if you will fill it."

The crowd gathered close and each awaited their turn as the basket made the rounds. Soon every person at nightfire held within their hands a precious and small vessel. There were smiles of delight at the treasure which had been given.

The little children held the mouths of their vessels to their ears to see if they could hear the sound of the sea inside. Was this what Songkeeper was speaking of? She had said to listen.

Again, in the center by the fire, Sionee picked up her big red vessel. It shone like a gemstone of ruby by the dancing flame of flickering fire.

The crowd gasped, "AAAAaaahhh," as all eyes watched with interest.

"This vessel, however, is a prize," Sion sang, *"that goes to the person who can choose the finest ... and the prettiest ... and the best ... of*

all the tiny vessels that have been gifted to each of you ... to keep as a reminder of this tale."

The crowd held their vessels up to examine their own, as well as the other vessels. The crowd intermingled, as friends among friends chatted and laughed with each other as they tried to decide.

"Can anyone make this choice?" Sionee asked. *"Which gift is the most favored?"*

"Mine!" Alita stood in the center triumphantly. "It is blue like the lapis."

"Mine!" yelled another. "Mine!"

The crowd echoed hopefully.

"How do you make the choice which of these gifts is the best one?" Sionee sang. *"Do you choose the biggest or the shiniest? Do you choose the roundest, or the finest color? Whose color is the favorite? Will the heaviest pot standing for durability, win? Or, will the thin one be lighter to hold within your hand? Do you like the pot which is pinched or the pot which is coiled like the snake? Come my children ... Come now ... choose!"*

For quite some time, Sionee and Taya stood in the center by the fire in silence. *"Children, children,"* Sion urged. *"Remember we are the Children of the Light Serpent. Our truths live within our spirits. All our choices are one. All must agree as to who the winner is."* Sionee held the red pot high.

"ALL LIGHT FROM THE SUN IS ONE!" Suddenly, a melody rose from the far outskirts of the crowd, a melody whose sound came closer and closer.

It was a beautiful and a harmonious wind song ... music only one person could make.

A male figure entered the circle, his flute to his lips. The beauty of his music joined the song of cicada and cricket and night bird ... as one.

Cy danced as he played. His figure was mesmerizing with a lithe and graceful motion. The small children put their vessels to their lips and made soft whistling wind sounds as they followed him, giggling merrily.

In the end, the prize was not awarded to any in the crowd. It was decided that it was foolish to choose from among the beautiful variety of pots, all of equal value.

Sionee looked into Cyex's eyes. As he played, he stopped for but a moment to smile *into* her eyes ... and shrug.

The pots had spoken the song of gift. All gifts that came from the heart were gifts of love.

Sionee picked up the red pot, glimmering in the fire's refection. She placed it in Cyex's hands.

"*For you,*" she sang. The crowd cheered.

Chapter Twenty-six

Enlil was sure that he was truly not satisfied with the sham of the council meeting. Anu's response had been unsatisfactory. His father was way too far away to make a good decision for the Ki. He knew far too little about what was the reality of Ki.

This could often be a good thing, and many times a bad thing. First and foremost, all decisions made by Anu must be obeyed. Anu was King and Master of all Annunaki on the world of Nibiru and beyond, and certainly He was High Lord of Ki.

Enlil had a sober face. Otherwise, his face was agreeable but placid, due to his business-efficient manner. His face was one that brought forth little interest. It had been designed as so. For why would a beautiful face be needed for a superior being who hailed the law of no emotion? After all, beauty especially was a wasted emotion.

He, Enlil, was the first prince of the heavens, the lawful and the foremost. He was the legal inheritor of Kingship.

Anu loved him well.

Of course! Anu was foolish in all matters of love. He loved all his children. Love was the only emotion somewhat tolerated, though not encouraged, on Nibiru. Father especially loved Enki, who was unnecessarily beautiful, and had a well-proportioned face and form.

He frowned deeply in an emotion of dislike, which was okay. What others could not see would not be known, and would go unpunished.

When one was alone, the law of emotion could safely be forsaken, which is why it was tolerated in sexual matters which were of a private nature.

He looked into the mirror hanging above the desk in the large business office on the North Abode of his mountain home.

Ninlil, bless her ever beautiful and sweet form, was out in the gardens. Women loved gardens. She occupied herself well therein, when she was not in his bed.

He smiled at his face in the mirror. Actually, he thought his face was rather beautiful to look at. It was a big head which was a nature of the Annunaki matter form. The head was thus designed to house a superior and well capacitated brain. He had the forehead of a King!

There was little to set it apart from being anything but suited for supreme hierarchy. His form carried within it a pure line of Nibiru-an blood ... Royal Blood.

A person could follow this face anywhere. He smiled. He frowned. He squeezed his lips together with his fingers and kissed the image in the mirror. His image. He thought it was a beautiful face, as did Ninmah when he wished her to, even if he loved his Nin-lilitum the best. Ninlil loved his face.

Especially in marriage, the show of love emotion was often overlooked ... as long as it wasn't excessive.

Like Anu could be ... excessive! Being King, Anu could do any-thing he pleased ... like love the whore Sofeya more than he loved his legally espoused wife, Anitum.

Everyone knew it! And everyone knew Anu well-loved Enki, too. Enlil cursed. Cursing would not be known when one was alone.

Enki had been a good brother when they were children. But, Enki was... well ... Enlil knew him a bit more personally than many knew him. Enki was not proper.

Enki knew how to make it appear as if he abided Nibiru's laws. However, Enki was anything but an honoree of law! Damn his hand-some face. And like Sofeya, Enki was wise ... too wise to get caught at breaking the law.

Enlil hated him as much as he hated those damn serpents Enki had blatantly built to display at his avenue at the medical facility of sciences. He had placed them there to spite him, knowing full well that the King of Ki had an aversion to the vile Ki creatures that swarmed in the reed by the waters and crawled among the stones in the dark mines.

Enki loved the serpents. He loved the fish. He loved the birds. He loved all manner of primitive life on Ki.

Well, well, well ... why would he not? It was something in his blood, something often whispered about on Nibiru.

Surely even Anu knew of it but no one spoke of it because Enki's mother was the favorite. She was also upmost and foremost of all female scientists, unequalled in her brilliance and skills even by male. No one, absolutely no one, would question Sofeya.

Despite the dark matter which touched him with hue of the soil-laden Ki, Ea was quite favored by most people on Nibiru, even if his eyes were a different color than the usual, and his small brained head was not quite bright.

He had a beautiful face and a smile that made one forget that the emotion was evil. Damn his hide!

He, Enlil, the real King of Ki, did not in any way, shape, or form trust Enki. His very stellar code was as different from any other proper abiding Nibiru citizen as night was from day.

Why was it, then, that on Nibiru, from the very day he was born as Ea, he was hailed as a morning star even if his light was so obviously inferior?

Enlil swiveled the mirror around so that to all appearances it was again but an ordinary art piece on the wall. He gave the reflection of his own bright hued face a kiss with his lips as it turned around. He would see to it that the beautiful morning star would fall. Ninurta would help.

Enlil called his son, born of sweet Ninni-Mah, to come abide with him for the night at the North Crest. Here they would speak. Ninurta was unburdened with integrity.

~~~

"Ninurta, my son... Prince of Ki! Welcome, welcome to my abode. Come! Let us sup! Together we will share our brilliant and far superior minds, so high above all other minds that it is us ... you ... and I, son, who hold in our hands the Kingdom of God!

"Bah, Father. We must not speak of it! Facts are facts. It is not necessary for us to brag. What's to eat?"

"I made command to my slave servants to bring forth a young boar to the fire and burn it well. I know, my son, that you enjoy the blackened crisp fat, especially with those crunchy little fly tidbits captured by the flame as they hover so enticingly above the blood."

"Father, I am so depleted of nourishment I could almost eat a vegetable!" Ninurta replied. "Bah!" He wrinkled his nose in disgust.

~~~

"I believe you need more lu, father. How many do you officiate?" His eyes roamed the courtyard, noticing the preponderance of Annunaki servants over the lu, who Enlil disliked. His eyes rested on the two girls who brought a basket of warm towels and fragrant oil to the poolside.

"The Annunaki lawbreakers get lovelier all the time. What did these two little ladies do?" He asked his father.

"They are excess." Enlil frowned. "When they have sex, they scream and hurt the ears of normal, law abiding citizens of Nibiru."

"Aaaaaaugh!" Ninurta replied, eyeing the girls in interest.

"They make fine slaves. Their hands are smooth and well skilled. After our bath they will give us a massage I promise will make you sleep like a babe with a smile."

"Perhaps I do not wish to sleep!" Ninurta replied in speculation.

"These are well equipped for that!" Enlil assured him. "If they hurt your ears with the screaming, you may use the whip!"

"Ah, Father, this brings up the very thing I wish to discuss with you this evening."

"Indeed, Ninurta. It is also why I have called you to my side." He put his arm around his son's shoulder as the two of them lay back on the smooth moss covered steps of the deep dark hot pool.

"It is a lovely abode." Ninurta commented. It pleased Enlil greatly that his son appreciated the fine touches he had built at the crest sanctuary.

"I bathe here every night before I retire to sleep. Often, Ninlil accompanies me." Enlil smiled.'

"Father, you do really love her, do you not?"

"I really love my lady! I assure you our love came to be exactly as the stories are told. I almost broke the law to get her."

"Indeed, father, when she was in instruction at the medical facility. I do believe my mother said that when Ninlil first arrived, she was a sud under her care."

"Yes, merely a sud was my lady. Yet, truly the most beautiful sud I have ever seen ... then, or now!"

The two relaxed as the steam from the hot pool rose and soothed their Ki weary bones.

"They said it was rape." Enlil smiled. "Her mother, damn her hide, told it of me. I was exiled for breaking the law." He laughed. "Imagine! A King in exile! Your mother, Ninmah, displayed emotion! I had raped one of the young suds who had been placed in her charge, and she was livid with the emotion of anger. She was excused however, because she helped arrange for my deportation. I forgave her only because of where she sent me."

"You were fortunate, father, that the old cow finally admitted that it had not been rape. "

"Indeed," Enlil replied, frowning. "Actually, it is your mother who is the old cow who you youngsters are referring to. My Ninlilitum is still young. Do not speak of my beloved as so."

"I would not speak of my mother as anything but ..." Ninurta replied. "Father, ever since I was young, you have blessed the day of your exile. You promised that one day you would explain to me." Ninurta yawned in disinterest.

"The day has come son. I wish to tell you now, but first you must listen, for there is more to this story. You have heard the story of Enki's charming father-in-law Alulu."

"I've heard of the scum!"

"Truly well said. Scum, indeed!" But he was a ruler once. In the time before those who from heaven to Ki came, our Anu bore Alulu's cup. Bah! When my father and your grandsire wrestled with him for the rightful position as King and won, Alalu lost all right to rule.

"As you know, Alulu was actually the first to obtain gold, wishing to restore his Kingship. He was the one who first came to Ki and started the hell of this world that further brought the rest of us down.

"I will not denounce that turd completely. He brought with him the seven weapons which in time became lost to us."

"The weapons of power? Oh, yes, my father."

"Oh, ho, son. The weapons served Alulu well. They fought for him a battle that blasted him safely through the milky river of Tia's broken stones. They crushed, split, and disintegrated the debris."

Ninurta laughed. "I think old Alula had much wisdom. Far more than uncle Enki, who came his way to Ki by blasting the stones with the pressure of much water. What a namby-pambyoid!"

"I agree. However, I must give my dear brother credit for that ploy. It brought me here safely later on, and you too, my son ... to ultimately rule as the Kings which we are on Ki."

"And... ?" Ninurta asked, growing impatient.

"Bring us some fruit ... !" Enlil shouted to one of the maid servants, "something soft and sweet like grapes! The boar grease is still thick on my tongue!

"Enki did something else foolish. When he came to Ki, he hid the seven weapons of power deep in a cave, thinking to ensure power in his own hands," Enlil told his son.

"No one has recovered this secret, father." Ninurta lamented, red juice running down his chin. "Wine!" He ordered. "Bring me wine!"

"Son, my exile took me to a cave!"

Ninurta leaned forward. Now, this was beginning to get interesting.

Enlil laughed. "Or, rather it was Abgal who has been with Enki as a servant since the beginning. It was he who aided me. He helped Enki bury the weapons so as to hide them."

"Oh, ho," Ninurta burped. "This wine satisfies me well, father." He placed his arm around Enlil's shoulder, now in affection. "Where?" He asked. "Do you actually know where they are located?"

"Good try son. But for now the power of knowing is mine! Abgal helped me hide the weapons elsewhere."

"But father, your secret is my secret!" Ninurta burped again. Enlil noted that his son was beginning to inebriate.

"No!" Enlil replied. "Not at this time. You have no integrity. By and by perhaps "

"But father! I am your right hand man. I am first son!"

"Enough! Enough! There is more we shall speak of later. You must extend your stay, son. On the morrow night we shall discuss more. It concerns the meeting of seven. Please, Ninurta, drink tonight to your pleasure. But tomorrow please refrain! We don't need wine's wisdom to speak for us, then."

"No wine? Bah! I will try."

"For now I grow weary. This steam relaxes me so, and the wine as well." Enlil summoned the two girls who were keeping the towels warmed.

"Ah, my doves. Is the oil alike, well warmed?"

~~~

The following evening, Enlil suggested a cooler bathing font. "This ever warm day makes me desire coolness, and it is my wish to keep our weariness at a distance yet. The night is young! I have ordered a fresh set of girls, for a better massage enjoyment, tonight, afterwards."

"Yes father. I believe I am enjoying my visit. I must inquire ... do you have any male slaves? I would prefer ...

"I must compliment you on the blackened onion and garlic encrusted mammoth rump we enjoyed for supper! Its savory experience I shall long for more of. Your cooking servants prepare the finest food I have tasted of the great epicurean arts, indeed!"

"We shall have wine." Enlil ordered the two girls who carried the towel basket. "Have the boys fetch us some of the blackberry in the back corner of the wine cave."

"We shall be served after our discussion." He told an eager Ninurta. "Vintage first sar after our arrival. It will be worth the wait." Both men smacked their lips. As one of the servant girls turned to fetch the wine, Ninurta smacked her on her bare ass.

"Fine, indeed." He slurred, though as yet not drunk.

"Father, I really believe the answer to the problem we have already discussed at the meeting is an elementary thing. Perhaps the answer is too simple for your proper eyes to see?"

"It's why I thought to call you," Enlil replied. "So I could see with your indecent eyes."

"With my unprincipled mind, I have been thinking much about the matter which you and uncle Enki discussed as to whether it was a matter of integrity to use the black headed ones of the natural Ki as slaves.

"They are half seed of our lu-lu father. Bah!" Ninurta spat into the water.

Ninurta moved over a bit and swooshed the spit into the pool distance, frowning. "You are disgusting son. Join my thinking with yours."

"I know of your fear, father, as do all abiding Annunaki fear the law."

"The punishment is not always as favorable as what we spoke of last evening!" Enlil warned.

"Indeed, father. But there are ways to get around it."

Enlil looked at his son in interest.

"I certainly do not understand why the concern, father. It is a natural thing. Did you not approve the use of mammoths for helping at the mines? They make great steaks too! For both purposes they are of great quantity."

"It was perhaps my finest idea!" Enlil beamed. They are great servants to us, and are capable of bearing a heavy toil with supreme excellence."

"They are animals, father, and no one has a problem in using them as slaves."

"In your pools you use fish to keep the moss from choking your water with excess murkiness. You use the asses for carrying smaller loads where the mammoths are too big for use."

"Indeed."

"You use horses for enjoyment when you wish that variety of transportation, or camel if wing is not desired.

You use canaries to see if the mines are safe to breathe, and there are no qualms about their use, even if it causes death."

"Indeed."

"You ... and all of us ... use the meat of all these creatures and more to feed our ever-hungry matter-mouths with fat!"

"Indeed so! It is their purpose,"

"They are all Ki's animals, father. It is natural. So what the big deal? What I do not understand is why Enki considers the lu or their natural forebears as anything other than animals.

"Over all of Ki's vast animals, The Annunaki is of a superior nature as we are in the entire universe, even.

"We have an advanced capability, a finer structure, as well as a highly technical mind. The lu are mere animals, dear daddy, barely higher in intelligence than the mere Ki natural animal. Why is this so hard to comprehend, father? Why must we try so hard to insert misguided emotion of morality to this issue?"

"Enki insists to Anu that the Ki two-legged ones have a small bit of our millions of years ago beginning in them, and you well know the law of Titain forbids that we tamper with the free will."

"Duh! This is my suggestion, father, that we make it their free will! I have found a way or two that is most effective. The first and ultimate way of persuasion is to create a fear within."

"But from what I hear, this is part of the problem. We cannot convince them to exert themselves on our behalf because they know no fear. It is against their nature."

"I can arrange otherwise father."

"Oh?"

~~~

"I say: come my doves. Father could you not have demanded that the boys who brought the wine stay?" These are pretty ones, however even if they are female. Join us, dovelings, in the pool with your warm oil and your hot hands! Scream, my little ladies. Scream as loud as you wish! If you do not suit my ears with loud volume, my whip will dance across your dainty little asses! It goes something like that, father. Aaaah."

Ninurta and Enlil lay back in the water, as the two servant slaves with oil-warmed hands, soothed them well from head to toe ... and all the places in-between.

Chapter Twenty-seven

Bent over the table of examination, Ninmah gently and with soothing hands took a sample of blood from Adapa's tiny inner elbow. She put a small ball of cotton on the needle invasion.

In the bright lights that illuminated the table, Ea caught a quick flash of silver in Ninmah's hair. She didn't seem to have any more. His hand reached out in impulse to touch the silver.

Loss of pigment due to the aging process was rarely seen on Nibiru. Most did not age as such and many on the home world still wore the lizard form, though it was losing its popularity due to the current fascination with Ki.

He stifled his desire to touch. On Ki, time had a way of quickening the age factor. This anomaly eventually even wore at the Annunaki form. He decided to presently not mention it to Ninmah.

Even if the heroes who came to Ki, to gather gold for Nibiru's waning atmosphere, were able to acquire enough to fully serve Nibiru's needs, and they could all go home, Ea knew that it was likely that none of them would ever return to their former lives in the faraway.

Even if he could, he certainly wasn't ready in the least to return to the waning planet. Ki had become foremost in his interests. The only thing he missed back home was his mother. He really wished he could bring her here for a visit.

He'd really have to keep inquiring to Anu as to whether he would release her from his incessant command that she not visit Ki again.

"I did not get away with it altogether, son." she had told him. It is a punishment Anu sees as suitable for me, though it was never officially declared. He has made it clear to me that I must never ... Ahhhhh ... son ... enjoy the experience for me, will you? The crime rattled him so!"

Ninmah caught his attention as she furthered her evaluation.

"I have been studying while you made your presence scarce here these last few days.

"Heaven forbid, I have little time anymore. Adapa has truly grown dear to my heart. He is the son, Ea ... that you and I never had. I enjoy every moment of his presence.

"Come now, my son," she crooned, picking the child up to soothe him of his hurt. She patted him gently on his tiny behind while she turned on a wall screen to show Ea of her findings.

"It has something to do with the antigens that this wee one shows in the presence of his blood. It is similar to the antigens in our own, so one of his parents would have had to be one of the heroes.

"In our experiments which we performed at Eridu, the positive negated the factor which is in our blood, and the immune system of the fetus was compromised.

"It is why I had to implant the eggs in the Annunaki womb, where we could insure that they received the necessary antidotes to make birth possible.

"On this particular piece of land with the natural inhabitants who live here, the match-up is more accurate. She held a stylus to her chart, and the shadow projected over the image on the wall. It is something like this, do you see?"

He already had, but hadn't mentioned it to her yet.

"In our original experiment, if conception occurred and measures were not taken, the whole process became thwarted ... nil."

Ea cleared his throat.

"Of course," she said, "if one understands, which I don't entirely, but am beginning to ... it makes sense.

"This child has negative blood that closely resembles ours. Ea, you told me once the story of our planet's crossing the heavens and coming close to Ki. In our modern times of technology no one wants to believe we are actually related to these primitives. But now, I am interested, Ea. I want to hear the story again and see what I missed.

"I would really like to know. Adapa could almost be modeled after our own image. His blood type is identical, give or take what appears to be blood of Ki's natural children." She wrinkled her brow in concentration.

"Ea, when was the last time you had your blood examined? Is it in the banks?"

He took the stylus from her hand. "No, No Ninmah. I am sorely afraid of the needle."

She giggled. "Oh, come on brother let me, pleeeease!"

"No!" He was firm and she became equally serious. Her frown deepened.

"Ea, the baby is yours, isn't he? You can't lie to me and why would you?"

Ea smiled at her. It was time for a little Ninni butter ... oh, well ... maybe a lot! "Ninmah, remember that trip I promised you to the place in the faraway lands of the coffee?"

Chapter Twenty-eight

"Ea! Why are we going this way? You never make things simple. We are going east when it would be closer to zip west."

Ninmah had her telescopic lenses on as she peered down from the window of the Eagle.

"Ninni Mah. You know well that I never make things easier. I do not make things simple, because I am not simple. I am extraordinary, as well you know.

"Going west would be far too easy. I promised you a trip to where the coffee beans grow and a delightful trip we shall have." He winked at her.

"We can go to the Moon and Mars, and across this vast universe and even into other universes if we wish. What matters the distance? We could also have taken the ships. I figured the Eagle would better suit on this trip. There is much to see and many of our regions to behold. We will look down and see!"

Ninmah smiled in delight. She deserved this little vacation. He knew all along and hadn't shared with her about the blood factor, leaving her to spend all this time to discover in research ... the rascal! But he could make it up to her. She smiled up at him.

Ea sat at her side in a very comfortable seat designed for long distance travel with upmost comfort. He could have piloted the flight, as he had before when desiring to go solo, but Ninmah really needed to get out and see the vastness of the Ki.

Abgal, his friend and servant, a pilot of supreme skill, flew the Eagle. Cozy within the comfortable passenger cabin, Ea was alone with Ninmah. She loved it!

"See that corner Ninni Mah? That myrrh which you find so delightful is found there. It is where we get the reed which makes the beautiful leaf I prefer to scribe upon.

"The dark wood of fine ebony which fashions much of our furniture grows there.

"The grasses for food, are they not well developed down there?"

"All manner of grain is grown there, thanks to my efforts at irrigation of the big river," Ea said proudly. "In this region, live the lions that we enjoy for their beauty in our courtyards, and the skins of the zebra so delightfully striped like the one in my room."

"Which room is that?" Ninmah asked. "I haven't seen a carpet of black and white stripes in any of your rooms."

"You haven't?" He asked innocently. "Perhaps they were being cleaned." Oops! He had never taken her to his private sanctuary and really had no intention to. It was a secret ... his secret except for his master servant and a certain topaz-eyed girl.

After a bit, Ninmah stretched her neck to sit up in excitement and point. I see the first landing place!" She exclaimed.

"Yes, there, too, is the North crest on that mountain and the gulf where first I came down and swam to shore in my fish suit."

Ninmah giggled. "Eridu is enchanting, brother, but since coming to the Abzukia, I am growing well fond of it."

For a moment Ea was distracted from their conversation. He had chosen to come to the Abzu because it was where his mother had made the solitude journey long ago. "It is a most beautiful place, son, nestled like a long snake between East and West, all covered in apples and outlined within the bluest sea."

Though perturbed that Enlil had been given residence above the land of Eridu in the mountains, Abzukia had become his now beloved home. With the flying skills of the Annunaki, distance was relative, as he hoped to show Ninmah.

They were, indeed, taking a trip around the world. After they crossed the eastern shores over the sea of peace and across the mother continent that lay just before the western shores of the coffee land, and spent a day or two on those lands, they would return full circle to the Abzu.

"Ea, where will we be spending the night?" She asked, eagerly.

"Our first stop will be in the country far east at the lands edge, where the incense and the spices are of a richness that exceeds most other places. We will rest there and sight-see a bit before we board again to cross the gentle sea over the big lands of Lemuki, where we may spend another bit of time before we get to our coffee land."

Ninmah put her hands together, palm to palm and at her bosom, in excitement. Her eyes sparkled. But after a time, her lids drooped in bored weariness. She lay her head on Ea's lap and napped.

Ea hoped that the sometimes bumpy motion of the air current would not awaken her. After a long while he woke Ninmah up. "You must see Ninmah! It is here where we land for the evening. I know you would not want to miss this!"

Ninmah sat up, rubbing her eyes. "Are we there yet?" She asked, confused by sleep. She looked down and saw great mountains the heights of which she had never seen before. The mountains were so high snow touched the crags in their peaks.

"Awesome!" She shouted in exuberant amazement. "Ea, can we see these mountains on a visit?"

"Oh, I suppose we could take a little side tour." He smiled at her ... Ninni-Mah butter.

The Eagle landed and the two of them got out to spend the night in a very comfortable Annunaki tavern close to the landing platform.

"We will put our wings on in the morning and fly like a couple of snow birds!" He promised her, just before they fell asleep after they had exchanged vigor that made Ninmah sleep supreme.

~~~

"We must take the eagle helmets with us," Ea told Ninmah. "And, warm wrappings as well. These mountains are so high the air is quite thin at the tops."

"I want to look down while we hover in the air above!" Ninmah shouted. "Way above."

Making complete their preparations, the two flew with their individual wings over the valley and into the misty-white heights. Ninmah pulled the eagle helmet over her head. It helped her breathe

the thin crisp air, but had the convenience of built-in eagle eyes as well.

Ninmah's heart all but stopped as she peered down at the gleaming mountains shining in silvery hues and diamond ice particles. Below the snow line, the beauty was actually even more surpassing. Ancient and gigantic spruces and pines turned into sparkling lakes fringed with red willow. The winding ribbon of river gleamed with gold beneath the reflection from the sun. The brilliance pained her eyes.

"Ea, let us land and sit!"

Across a small cleft, a snowy log stretched from one edge to the next. Ninmah giggled as she straddled the heights on the tree bridge.

"Whooopeee!" She called out, her voice turning into mist in the icy air. "We sit on a snowy throne." She declared, her legs dangling across the heights. "I miss the ice on Nibiru. This is good, is it not?"

"I know that you take a liking to more frigid areas Ninmah, as does Enlil."

"Someday, Ea, I will live here. Yes! This is the place I wish to dwell. I will live in the high mountains, and have command in the mists of the high heavens!"

"The people will call you Ninharsag, Lady of the Mountains." He smiled at her. "It is a good dream, Ninmah. I will visit you here when you come." They exchanged hugs. He could hear her teeth chattering beneath their kiss.

"We must return to our rooms, Ninmah. They have splendid tea here! You will be amazed at how delicious it is! They put butter in it! It is a treat they enjoy in these parts. It will warm us both."

"I have enjoyed the coolness, but tea sounds nice."

"Nin, the regions of Ki are varied and vast, as you shall see. After a good night sleep we will cross the beautiful peaceful ocean before we reach other lands."

~~~

"Ea, how is it that you chose the Abzu rather than this big land mass?" She asked as they flew in the Eagle high over Lemukia, where they would land.

"This land is the largest and the most olden of any of Ki's lands. On it there are many of the natural man of Ki. They are highly developed, having been in species the longest of any. These people have a vast majority of positive blood," he added, "while I found more of the negative on my Abzu.

"Also, Ninmah, I have found there to be a distant rumbling beneath this land in my scientific studies. I do believe it will be a time yet, but this beautiful region will sink beneath the beautiful blue sea. I haven't pin-pointed the estimation, yet. However, it is my thought that it will happen before Abzukia's probable destiny to follow "

"Ea, you are teasing me!"

"Aeons from now my darling! You will be in your mountain heights by then."

Ninmah breathed with relief. Ea instructed Abgal to make a landing on the closest platform.

Ea and Ninmah were awake at least half the night. They stopped, exhausted after Ninmah had at least six ongoing orgasms. It was a good thing he was well skilled in the art of energy ebb and flow. With tantric art, he could be long-lasting, which pleased Ninmah well.

Ea had deemed it necessary to practice the skill long ago, and perfect it well. It was a sure edge he had in advantage over Enlil or other ordinary Annunaki male species. The superior manner of his technique was something truly fine, and his sex-appreciating sister drew close to his skills like a moth to the flame. He was, however, equally surpassing the ordinary in all the manners of art and science.

When morning arrived far too quickly, Ea awoke naked and sticky with Ninmah wrapped all around him. One of her legs entwined beneath him. One of her arms was wrapped around his head and over his nose and he gasped for breath.

"Ninni Mah, wake up, wake up! I need fuel. We drove our vehicles long into the night!"

"I'm so famished I could eat a vegetable!" She mumbled. She placed her arm over her tummy as it growled like an animal, waking her fully.

245

Ea laughed. "My ever-charming sister," he teased.

The animal people who dwelled on the Lemukia were kind to them, and pointed out the best places where they could acquire honest food.

"Ea, the menu here consists of fruits and vegetables chopped up and mixed only with bits of ... what is this?"

"It's a chicken darling, cousin to the ptarmigan."

"It's not as good. Do they have something with a bit more grease on it, like the elephant shank we had on my mountain with a side of lentil? I found it extremely delightful, chewing on the meat of the bone as such. It was so well-blackened."

"I ordered it that way for you to your liking!" Ea smiled.

"Oh, what is this? She cried in delight when a pie was served with a creamy sweet base, and little seedy green things on top.

"It is kiwi. Try it with rum." Ea suggested. The rum was hot and buttered.

"Oh, yes!" She took an appreciative sip and sighed in pleasure. "Ea, this is great. I really have been looking forward to the fresh coffee that you said is far superior to trade coffee."

"We shall have coffee of the finest superiority tomorrow at breakfast," he promised. "If we do tonight what we did last night, I guarantee you that even if we slept not the whole night," he winked at her, "a mere sip of that fresh and steaming coffee will make you forget you were ever tired!"

~~~

The first night on the south land, east of the Abzu and west of paradise, was spent at a place that was thick in wild growth. The growth was so woven in a tangle of vines, they spent the entire morning among them in exploration.

"Just look at these butterflies!" Ninmah exclaimed in rapture as they made love again, deep in the thicket and laying upon a lush bed of soft canary green moss.

"Ninmah, you look cute with that butterfly on your ass." Ea laughed as she stepped out of the cool stream that cut through the vast growth on its course to the sea.

Ninmah bent and picked a coffee bean. She studied it a moment, crushed it between her fingers, and held it up to her nose to smell its fragrance. She placed it on her tongue and bit.

She pulled a funny face. Ea laughed. "Ninni Mah! They must be dried and roasted first, before they are ground up into tiny little chunks."

"The coffee we had at breakfast was exactly as you promised, brother. Can we take some of the fresh back to Abzukia with us?"

"Of course, we can; we will get some of the fresh just before we leave. I wish to take you to another place on this land, yet. It is of a different topography, a little downward from here."

"I want some more of that coffee at lunch and sup tonight."

"That much coffee will keep you awake all night long, Nini Mah."

"So! What else is new?" She giggled.

At mid-day, framed in a canopy of pink and yellow hibiscus flowers that hung from an arched gazebo garden dome, Ea and Ninmah dined. They listened to bird calls and insect drones that Ninmah had never heard before.

"If you drink too much of that black gold," Ea warned again, "you will not sleep for weeks."

"But that could be a good thing when I am around you!" Ninmah peeled a banana. It was large, round, creamy, and firm at the same time. Ea watched her slowly and sensuously put the banana to her mouth. She swirled it gently and slid it in and out over her lips before she bit.

"Ea," she said at last after the banana was just an empty peel. "The bananas here are better than the dinky little things we grow in our orchard on the Abzu."

"The climate here well suits bananas," he told her. "We are fortunate to grow bananas at all." The curve of the mountain on our beach blocks a warmer air current, similar to these parts, but the bananas prefer it here or way South on the Abzu land."

"What is this!" She exclaimed. "Ea, I think it is a flower. It is white and crunchy and of a light oil. I never thought I would find a flower to be delicious. I certainly do not care for vegetables." She frowned and bit again, tentatively. "Ummmm."

"Waitress! Waitress!" she called. "What is this?" She queried.

"It is a white lily. We pick them in the wilds each morning. We dip the blossoms in a meal of ostrich eggs and amaranth. Then, we fry them in a hot coconut oil. They are a favorite on our luncheon menu."

"Oh, sun and stars! They are tasty! Here try one Ea. They are most delicious. The oil is lighter than boar grease, but for this it is satisfying. Ah!"

"Try the white fish." He admonished.

She tried it. It was steamed with little bits of green sprinkled overall. She wrinkled her nose. "Ea!" She said, moving the palm of her hand back and forth. "I prefer greased ox with onion."

"Are you done yet?" He asked.

"No! I wish more coffee!" She called the waitress. "Could you mix it with lots of thick cream and a good portion of coconut milk and nutmeg, and plenty of syrup from the fresh sugar cane that I see in your fields?

"Uuuuuuuuuuuuum!" She exclaimed, licking her lips of the hot steamy foam that rose to the top of the cup the server brought. "I'll have to try this back home!" Ninmah burped, looking up from her repast with smiling lips coated in thick cream.

Bless her. "Are you ready to see more?" Ea asked her. "We best work off some of this lunch before it is time to sup."

"Coffee!" Ninmah lifted her finger at the server girl as she explained to Ea. "I want one more cup, *burrrrrp*! And some of that hot buttered rum as well!"

~~~

"Ea, eeeeuuu, they tried to feed me squid last night."

"Oh, come on darling. I really think it was all that coffee and cream that made you throw up all over our bed last night! Are you feeling better this morning?"

"No! She frowned wearily. "Do you think the inn has something I could eat this morning that would settle my stomach?"

"Maybe a little less cream?" Ea suggested.

After breakfast, Ninmah returned to the sleeping rooms and went back to sleep.

"Ea, let me sleep. Can't we just rest today? Like, not going up in the air. Maybe I'll feel like joining you later on for a bath on those lovely white sands."

"Okay Nin. I really think you should take more thought as to what you dine on this evening."

"Oh, no, Ea! The sleep will refresh me so much I intend to wake up this afternoon, ready to take a mouthful!" She winked at Ea. She giggled, picking up a banana from the table at the side of the bed, peeled it down just a bit and twirled the tip past her lips.

She was a naughty girl, this one! Ea couldn't help but smile.

~~~

Ea took his bag containing stylus of many colors with him, as well as the charcoal and the fine leaf.

He spent the morning and much of the afternoon crawling among the vines and in the small meadow patches, discovering species of butterflies quite unlike the ones that he charted on the Abzu. He would spend the morning illustrating in different colors the delightful wing patterns.

Sofeya would love these renditions. When the sun began to filter through the leaf tops in the late afternoon, Ea closed his sketch book and gathered his stylus pouch. He was pleased with his results. Mother would be enchanted.

Now, he could use a bit of that coffee Ninmah was so fond of. Perhaps he would wake her with a tray.

~~~

They had explored the coastal regions, had wandered into the rainforests, and now Ea wished to show Ninmah his favorite place on this land.

It was high on a windless mountain plain so high that no trees grew here. The desert plateau was so still it caused an incitement of deep peace within his soul. He hoped Ninmah might find within herself some of that soul, which the Annunaki made it a duty to deny, not knowing its secret."

"Ea, I can hardly breathe! Is it because of the beauty?"

"No, darling! Put on your helmet; we are high."

They could have put on their personal wings. With their wings they could have swept close, but Ea thought it would be fun to try the hot air balloons he had seen swooping across the beaches.

Ninmah was giggling and google-eyed. "Eeee!" She brushed her hand at a condor who swept the desert plains at their side. "Ea, how long will this thing stay up?" She asked.

"Hey, how could the Ki animals have figured this thing out? I didn't think they were this brilliant. It seems a primitive take on a great idea!.

"Ninmah, you'd be surprised. The people are highly intelligent. They just use their thinking in a wiser manner than any of us Annunaki."

"Huh? It is said that the Annunaki are superior in intellect. Say, Ea, is that a spider I see down there?"

Ea tried to explain as Ninmah kept exclaiming over and over at the sights.

"The Ki people and we Annunaki have a large difference in our thinking. On Nibiru we have forced our thinking to a highly supreme technological level. On Ki they have sought to remain close to their earth beauty, and all of their thinking is focused on thus. It is not that their intelligence is less than ours, just different. Do you see? In truth I believe their intelligence is superior to our own."

"What say you?" She frowned only briefly. "What's that?" She asked, leaning over the edge of the hot air balloon to see the designs closer. "I didn't hear you." She straightened a moment, then rambled on, not waiting for him to repeat.

"I said ... ." Forget it. She wouldn't understand, yet.

"Ea, is that a hummingbird?"

Ea's eyes swept his handiwork in the plains below. He got a thrill at his ingenuity. This was a special place he had designed, high above the rainforest and the sea edge. Most of the earth ones would not ever see it at all as the balloons they used as a novel flying experience were designed more to fly over the beach shallows and the white sands.

Here, on the still and stable air current the balloons were quite desirable with superior visibility to see his design. The balloon swooped and dipped close, rose and drifted. Yes, only the Ki man would think of such a simple idea as were these balloons.

"I made these designs so that any of our heroes, who from the heavens come, could recognize our directions when we sweep the vast horizons. I thought it would make them smile. They are directional, Ninmah.

"You, Ea, designed them?"

"Of course, I designed them. Who else do you know who bears such foolish ingenuity? They are mere scratches on the desert floor but they will last here for aeons. The windless condition makes for an environment that will not sweep these vast designs into oblivion for sars perhaps."

"I love the hummingbird. Is that a snake?"

"Uh huh," Ea beamed. "It is my newest addition. It is a matter of the symbol."

"Bah, Ea. I don't want to hear such matters of rant. It must be the artist in you. Bah, Bah, Bah ... ."

He had his arm around her as they bent to gaze over the horizon. "This is one of my favorite places, Ninmah. Someday, perhaps aeons from now it is here that I will retire. For I have been thinking that in aeons to come, I may not wish to return to our home world. This is my home now, Ninni Mah ... Ki."

"But Ea, you will expire your physical much faster than you would if you returned home. I have worried about this each time I have looked in the mirror lately."

"Ninmah, it is far better to be a fast burning flame dancing across the sunset, than to be a mere computer digit dancing across the screen of eternity! Look at the sunset which engulfs us, my sister. Is it not beautiful?"

The plains below were colored in every hue of red and orange and purple, and interspersed with every shade of gold ... both brilliant and soft.

But Ninmah was not looking. "Bah, again brother," she said impatiently, reaching down to grab an iced peppermint tea from a cool pouch they had brought.

"Ea, is that you, brother?" She exclaimed, pointing below, giggling. She bent over the edge of the balloon to take a closer look with her goggles.

Among the spider and the hummingbird and the snake and the other clever designs, he had etched a rendition of a giant man. In between his legs a humongous appendage sprung forth.

"No darling." She wasn't listening. Not really. The mint tea spilled down her chin as she aptly swigged it. So he sort of lied to see if she ever really listened.

"It's part of that symbolism thing," he explained. "When I made this design, I was thinking of our brother and what a big *gis* he is."

For a moment Ninmah continued to swig her tea. Then, she broke out giggling. She giggled so hard the bottle of cool tea dropped from her hand.

The two of them watched as the bottle spun downward through the air and with a splat, broke into many pieces of sparkling rubbish on the desert floor, shards that may or may not ever be visible again on the high swept plateau to shine in the sun.

Okay! Maybe she did listen sometimes.

Chapter Twenty-nine

It was approaching spring. It was time for Sionee to begin to build her tree. She was slightly bored, a teeny bit overwhelmed with the preliminaries to the actual beginning when her hand would touch the sweet earth with both of her palms cradling huge amounts of clay.

Twenty good footsteps in a circle were the most exciting steps she had ever taken.

She put a small stone at each footstep to help her keep count and to mark the shape of her basic beginning.

It still seemed a bit tiny inside, but it would hold the universe when it was complete.

It didn't have to be perfectly level. As the trunk rose coil by coil upward, a perfect union of balance and beauty would be achieved.

How could she explain the process to Cy? She knew before he had asked. It was something she could feel inside the depths of her very bones. It was just right.

If one listened, one could hear the way a tree grows in a circle. If one listened, one could hear the manner in which a bee constructs her honeycomb. If one tried, one could hear the tumbling of a stone getting polished in a fast-moving brook. One could hear, if they allowed themselves, the quiet sound of a blossom rupturing forth to bring about the perfect shape of an apple orb. So it was with the clay. One must hear the voice of clay, which talked the symmetry of the sacred circle.

This spring morning, Sionee decided it was time to gather some of the mammoth leaves that grew along the mineral rich banks of the hot springs. The leaves would serve to wrap wet clay and keep it moist. They would also prevent drying of the clay in too rapid a manner, which could cause cracks.

Sionee was very eager to get out in the beautiful sunny bright day and play with Daysong, as well as work.

The two of them lay on the banks of the stream. Sionee was on her tummy, cradling the wee Daysong, softly beneath her. She placed the tiny hands in the water and splashed wet droplets into the giggling baby's face.

Sion heard a footstep behind her, crunching on a bit of mineral-crusted sand.

She had worn her favorite white shift, wrapped high above her knees so she could wade with Daysong, and not get wet.

The two of them were bedecked in wild roses. Each of the girls wore pink and white baby roses woven into fragrant circlets about their necks. Sionee's necklace was long and it spilled into the babbling stream.

Sionee had braids hanging in two sprightly curves above each ear. Each braid was woven with a pink ribbon that secured rose buds loosely into the folds of her hair. Rose-strewn festoons swung over each side of her face.

Daysong had ribbons of tiny roses hanging from each ear. A tiny yellow butterfly flit from rose to rose, fluttering between the two of them.

Ea laughed as he lay at the streamside, belly down beside Sionee. Aaah ... he felt as young as a babe himself.

Sionee squirmed inches away from him. Did he have to creep up so close? Why was her heart beating so fast? Would he hear?

She smiled at him in greeting, and held a pretty polished white stone out to him on the palm of her hand. The stone was small, smooth, and perfectly rounded by the deposits of sediments in the stream. It reminded him of a pearl; its nature was different.

He took the tiny stone and rolled it in the palm of his hand, admiring the creamy perfection.

"Ah," he said, accepting the gift of the mineral-coated stone, as well as the gift of her smile.

"Are there others here?" He asked.

"My mother would surely love it if I sent her one of these. I wish to keep this one to put on my own desk."

"Is that in your strange room of starfish and sand-moons?" she asked. *"Your sky room beneath the sea?"*

"My sanctuary." He told her.

Sionee placed her fist into the mud at the bottom of the warm spring and pulled out a handful of the smooth mineral stone, all in various colors of white and pastels. She rinsed off the mud and held them out shining to Eah.

"For your mother," she said proudly. She liked the idea of her little stone sitting among the little treasures she had seen on his desk. Would he think of her when he placed it there? Would he hold it in his hand and remember her touch as he took the stone from her? And, of the handful, would he tell his mother that a girl of a different kind with roses in her hair had given it to him?

He held the stones as if she had gifted him with gold.

"Where abides your mother that you must send her a gift? Is she far away?"

"Oh, yes," he replied.

"By boat?" Or would he make them fly away on the wing of his big bird?

He picked up on her waves of thought. "My mother lives not on this world."

"On your star?" She asked.

"Yes," he replied, searching in his head to try and tell her where. "Say, I know that you people look at the stars every night and are well acquainted with them. You even use each evening's time to tell stories of symbol."

"Stories of symbol." Sionee reflected a moment. Well, she supposed they were just that, but unless one was a Songkeeper, most did not think of them quite like that. Eah was keen in his perceptions.

He continued. "In the galaxy of Andromeda my home is seldom in a stationary position. It moves to and fro, it goes through the darkness and it moves through the light."

"Oh, and did you fall off of it, then?"

He laughed. "Well, maybe darling. I would say that explains it pretty well. Yes, I suppose I did."

"But your mother did not fall?"

"No, no, little girl. She is held there, and I miss her as she misses me. I enjoy sharing with her of my experiences here, as she enjoys what I tell her. This perfect little stone, she will adore."

Sion listened, puzzled. *"If you can fly such distances, why not go get her and bring her here to enjoy it with you? Is she ill or dead?"*

"No, no darling. She is well. My father forbids it."

"What? Sionee sat upright. Her drenched rose necklace splashed all over him. He sat now, beside her.

"This is not right, Eah! No one should forbid another. Does your mother wish to come?"

"She has been here." He explained. "But father will not let her come again."

"Why is it? I do not understand this."

"She did something which displeased my father."

"Is he in charge of her?" She asked. *"Are they, your mother and your father, bound into a promise of servitude, one toward the other?"*

Ea smiled. Now, this was getting quite interesting. "My mother has no marriage with my father."

"No what?"

"No marriage." When she didn't seem to understand, he continued, "It is when two people are bound in service to each other." A slow grin lit his face.

Of course, among these people of Ki the concept had not yet been named. It was as if this tiny girl could understand in ways far superior to any of his wonderful peers.

"If they aren't bound in servitude, why must she abide by something she does not wish?"

"It is something we call law."

"Law ? This I cannot understand."

"Of course not, darling. It is something only the dwellers of my world know about."

She was silent. This information could be confusing to someone as innocent as was this sweet girl.

"*My mother,*" Sionee said, "*knew no laws. She taught me no laws. Neither did Marisol.*"

"This is why I find you as refreshing as soft grass, newly sprouted from the ground."

"*What?*" She asked.

"Oh, as fresh as grass growing in the springtime and not yet stepped on."

Sionee frowned. Ea remembered he had brought with him a basket. "I brought lunch this time. Will you break bread with me?"

~~~

"*I think you and I are squashing this grass.*" Sionee giggled. "*But when we leave, this grass will grow fresh again. Speaking of stepped on grass, someone brought me a mountain of clay and squashed my grass. I would thank him if I knew who brought me this gift.*"

Ea smiled but remained silent.

"*What manner of bread is this?*" She inquired. "*There are so many seeds in it that I do not know.*"

"The seeds serve to make it very nutritious and delicious, and keep a person well in their body. Many of the seeds were brought from my home world. We plant it in our gardens. Also, some of the seeds in this bread were brought from places across the seas."

"*It makes crunchy bread. I like crunchy bread.*" She picked up a piece of cheese and placed it on her bread. "*Does this cheese come from your star?*"

"No darling. The cheese comes from animals we keep in our herds. This is from our cows, sort of like your oxen in the wilds, just a bit smaller."

"*I have not seen such an animal.*"

"They are kept close to us within our fences. We modified the animals somewhat, to make them better."

"*You did what?*" She asked, puzzled. She preferred her gazelle cheese.

"Try some of this." He pointed to a different cheese. "It comes from our goat."

Though it was a strong cheese, it tasted plenty good and for a moment she was absorbed in its flavor. *"It is good with the seeds,"* she added after contemplation.

"On my world, the marriage thing is a law." He continued their previous conversation.

"Law is bad and marriage is bad," she said, washing the sticky cheese down her throat with sweet purple grapes.

"Anu and Enlil, my father and my brother, say that they are good and necessary. I myself see them as a way of control."

"I think your laws are for those who do not think for themselves!" Sionee munched on more purple grapes.

"Smart girl! Marriage is supposed to unite two people as one being with one purpose."

"ALL LIGHT FROM THE SUN IS ONE. **THIS MY MOTHER TAUGHT ME HOW TO SING ...** *GNOS!"*

He smiled. Such wisdom would be far beyond simple understanding on the Perfect World of perfect technology. "When marriage is on our world, two people are no longer two people. They are one person in everything they do. They eat together. They sleep together each night. They stay together day in and day out, for as long as they both live, which can be a really, really long time."

"But here on my world, Gaia, Bless her, this is a choice made here in the heart." She placed her hand on AHDAWN. *"Such a choice needs no law."*

"As it should be, darling. But on my world it serves purposes that have nothing to do with the heart." He would be ashamed to tell her that feelings from the heart had been banned as emotion. Enough stupidity was enough.

"I find this difficult to explain."

She laughed. *"Oh!"* It was as it was when Cy asked her about her home of clay. *"Like you could explain if I hadn't asked you to."* Her giggles were like bird song. *"That happens to me all the time! Are you mar – id?"*

"Married. Yes, I am married. But the love you speak of is not something Damkina and I share. We remain as two, however we share one son."

"Then, you do not follow that silly law because you know it takes love to unite two hearts? Is that not a foolish law? I think your heart and her heart make it as if your marrid is not."

"Indeed, Daffinina, except for the law."

"Law. It seems silly, so silly. I really don't get it of your world."

"It is effective to bind."

"Love should not bind. Love is free as a bird on wing. **THIS MY MOTHER TAUGHT ME HOW TO SING ...** "

"Daffinina, tell me about your mother. She sounds wise."

"THIS MY MOTHER TAUGHT ME HOW TO SING ... *Love is like a light. It is like a star, meaning that its visibility cannot be bound nor counted.*

"My mother served in capacity as priestess of love. She was a holy giver. She taught men the way of the sacred Goddesses who are pure in their love. Sometimes women also needed her instruction. Mother had a deep love for all who came to her teachings."

"Yee, good grieficus! What was she, a whore?"

Ea was relieved he hadn't said it out loud. She probably didn't even have a concept for the word as such. He tried to withdraw the exclamation from his mind. Sofeya had been called as such by those who had no clue, like Anitum. His mother gave to Anu a love so pure in nature. He, Ea, had punched many who dared to refer to her by such a name.

"Oh, I am sorry, dear. I am hearing you. Please continue!"

"Sometimes when emptiness is threatening to make a person feel sadness or alone, they need reminding." Oh, why had he asked? She struggled to say it in honor of her mother.

"They need to be touched, so as to remember that no one is truly alone. The light of the Goddess abides in all of us. She manifests her love through touching, for with touch a connection is joined. The Mother Spirit provides illumination inside ones AHDAWN which is shared by everyone."

Ea was struck in dumb awe ... totally.

He reached out. He could feel a very tangible measurement of vibration, hovering in the air between his own heart and this little Ki star. He rested his hand on her hand.

Sion saw a flash of light spring from his eyes, like the way Daysong made light. The light became a solid beam that pierced the brown depths of her eyes.

He put his hand on her neck, between those silly rose-studded braids she wore, and drew her close. As if driven together by the force of two magnets, their lips met. The vibration spiraled in the motion of warmth and increased in volume with a lingering kiss.

How he stayed in one piece after such an expansion exploded in his heart, he would never be able to figure in any of his science laboratories.

"*Like that!*" She smiled at him. "*Did you feel the Goddess?*"

"I felt you Daffinina."

"*I am only a tool in her hands,*" she replied, looking up at him and wrapped within his embrace. "*Like my mother. Though, as a Songkeeper priestess, I have been chosen to specialize in her other capacities.*"

Well, what a shame, Ea thought.

"*Oh, the clay responds in my hands.*" She had heard him. "*But my heart it can go in many places.*"

~~~

The kiss had sent his stellar code to a place he was not familiar with. Had he ever in all his sars ever felt such a kiss before? No, he had not. He must savor that moment in time eternally ... perhaps write mother.

"*I have a friend who left the house of the shells and now lives in Cosmopolitan Major with a boy that her heart chose to join with.*" Sionee further explained, holding Daysong in her arms and beginning to feed her one of the pouches.

"*It was her choice, and she left the shells happily because she could never bear it to leave his side. But now she is unhappy in the*

Cosmo because there is an evil there."

"What is that?" Ea frowned.

"Eah, I will explain later, I wish no sadness now in this moment with you."

"Certainly." He held her tiny hand in his own.

"Some of us join partnering and live together as you said, but only as we wish. Some of us just live together, as long as we choose ... forever even. Love is our right and we are not selfish with it.

"My mother, Bless her, lived with no man, but she loved all men. Does not the Goddess love all her children? All men, all women? Love should never be bound or counted, my mother said."

He liked her mother.

"It is why it is of little consequence who my father is. All men are my fathers, and none is, specifically," she said. Her love for her mamun was of strong abundance and plenty.

"It's not that I never wondered who it was who released my seed. Every man I looked at, I wondered. But my mother was my father as well."

"Daffinina, your mother puts me in mind of my mother, who came to your fires long before your mother was born. I think both of them are wise as two doves."

Ea felt totally at communion with this tiny Ki girl with golden flecked hematite hair and amber eyes. He studied the way the irises of her eyes caught the light within a ring of brown that turned topaz by the sun, and radiated a light in brighter ways than he could count.

"My father is King on the star where I was born, Nibiru. He accepted me with vast love as his son, though love is never spoken of on Nibiru. I never was certain.

"Anu was angered at my mother for a bit, but he loves her too much to remain as so for long. It is, however, why he forbids my mother to ever return."

Sion was speechless. She felt the silence on his tongue and the unrest, which spoke loudly in his heart.

"But Eah, smile now, come! You and I ... ," she said at last, *"even my little baby who sleeps in my arms ... Oh, isn't she beautiful, our little*

Daysong? We are not that different perhaps, Eah.” Sionee giggled and Ea looked up and saw a sky full of doves fly above them.

“Did you have love in here?” She touched him on his heart home AHDAWN, and felt the beating of his heart beneath her palm. “ *... for my sister Coelle?”*

Chapter Thirty

Alsionee Tree Song had spent the entire day with Eah. How was it that the hours had come and gone without her awareness of their passing?

Though Sion was not yet ready to change the status of their acquaintance from friends to "friennnnnnds", when she looked into his eyes she saw his song and today she had tasted that song on her lips.

She honored him as a great artist. The beauty of his stone serpents and his star room beneath the sea were awesome.

Sionee lay in bed and listened to Daysong sigh in her sleep. Her breaths were deep and sound.

As thoughts of her time with Eah on this day went deep in her head, Sion was filled with a great excitement that caused her to catch her breath and ponder with wide awake eyes.

After she had broken bread with Eah, the two of them had walked to the site where she had placed a circle by her mother's tree. Sionee had put her trust in him. Sleepless with smiling eyes she remembered.

~~~

Ea walked back and forth, silently contemplating. His finger was pressed too tightly against the bottom of his nose, pushing it upward.

Sionee laughed, and Daysong joined in with baby giggles. "What's so funny?" He asked.

"You look like a pig nose." Sion giggled and giggled and giggled ... fish head ... eagle wings ... and pig nose. She rolled in the grass, getting her braids strewn with bits of dry leaflets and tangles of abandon. She laughed, and laughed, and laughed again.

Ea managed to ignore her as an idea was beginning to cook in his head. He loved her idea of the tree. It suited her magnificently. The girl had a skill with the clay and an imagination to carry it through. Would she allow him to help?

Finally, Sion sat upright, her giggles gone. *"What are you so serious about?"* She inquired. His finger still up-thrust the tip of his nose. Sion could tell that he was still deep in thought.

"Oh, no!" She forewarned him. *"Bright and early tomorrow morning my hands will begin the connection between earth and clay."*

"Then, we best get busy." He suggested.

~~~

"Daffinina, go get that clay tree you made. Could you bring it please? I will abide here with Ti Ti."

"It won't take me long!" She scrambled to her feet and was off. The prospect of discussing her project with Eah was exciting. He was a skilled builder, as was evident in the magnificent serpents in his garden. She was back in a quarter of an hours passing.

He took the sculpture, examined it, and placed it on the side opposite of her mamun's tree, close to where the hill began its rise to meet the mountain.

Sionee frowned. *"I already counted the steps there."* She pointed to her cleared and prepared spot.

"Do you see Daffinina? Look! Oh, look! I know you have an artist eye."

"I chose this site a long time ago."

"If you build on the up-reach of this hill, it is only on the other side of your mother's house. If you sit it on the higher level, there would be places for the roots to weave, down as well as up and across. Your tree has such character, darling. It deserves to be placed on a setting of equal character. It would appear to be part of the mountain, as if it had truly grown at its base."

"The roots could appear as hair on my lady's face." Her thoughts were turning. She put her finger in the position of contemplation on her own nose, and let it rest there gently ... no up-thrust.

"You designed the door well, to be hidden in the folds of the bark. You have a charming way with design. I think the craggy backdrop that rises above the hill would lend itself to permit you to follow the greatest art secret that I incorporate in all my own designs. If you exaggerate minor imperfections, the beauty you create will take away all ordinary notions of beauty. The contrast will far surpass the usual, which is created by common artists who try too hard to make perfection."

"I have no clue as to what you just said, but somehow I think I understand." Sion walked about her sculpture that once again had been placed on the hill. She studied and thought.

"I captured the essence of the tree I wish to create. But now I see it a little more!" She sighed at last. *"I see much more. I see a beautiful face. She is beautiful. I see her."*

"Here, darling. Let's make the basic circle as you planned. Remember, the less perfect the circle, the better. He bent and picked up a rock and handed it to her.

She placed it and continued with more, as he handed them to her.

"Oh, come up a bit. Yes, in confidence darling. Confidence is the first building block. That rock begins to extend the circle upward. The root will be lovely draping down! Yes, girl imagine ... up! The circle is yours to create. That's it! Down now ... nine ... ten ... eleven ... twelve ... thirteen ... fourteen ... fifteen. Yes girl! And up sixteen ... seventeen ... and down eighteen ... nineteen ... twenty ... Oh, and twenty one ... yes! Twenty one paces around!"

This done, the two of them sat within the circle to behold the view. He held the model in his hands, upside down. He turned it right side up. Then, upside down again. He studied again, deeper in thought now. He held the figure in one hand with his elbow resting on his bent knee. His finger was again at his nose tip, thrusting up again.

Sionee was having a difficult time keeping from giggling again. Oh, and Cyex had said that he also had a baboon butt, but Sion didn't think so. She giggled again.

Ea frowned at her and she stopped.

"I like how you plan to make spaces inside the interior of the tree so cleverly. You have done well in the planning. I like your floor shelves which extend halfway across the perimeter, and the ladder idea ... I would change nothing here."

"The nooks and crannies will serve to provide more space. The top shelf will be my sleeping area, the middle will be Daysong's. There will be a level for the living area, and on the bottom there will be space for food preparation."

"There is more yet, Daffinina. Have you further thought about the secrets of the tree's depths?"

"You have helped me see a little more about the roots."

"Look yonder at that tree over there." He pointed.

Sion looked. The tree had roots which clung to the hill and spread out over the contours and the curves of the rise, going up and going down.

"That is how I have decided to do," she nodded.

"Close your eyes now." he urged, placing his palm over her eyes. "Come on ... Go there ... inside that living tree. I'll go with you.

"Now turn on the lights, my Daffinina."

"It is hollow!" She exclaimed.

"As will be yours ... go inside your tree. We are here, now in the world of your inner dreams. It is here that things become as real as the place you see and hear as real. You make it so. Turn on these lights as well, Daffinina ... deeper ... deeper ... yes, deeper we go below."

"Eah! The tree is the universe! I knew it! I knew it!"

"On the outside it is a secret how large it is on the inside. The roots have created a depth beneath your floor. The space goes down, deep into the earth ... deep. What are you keeping in those spaces, Daffinina?"

"Quiet! Quiet Eah! Please don't interrupt me. I wish to see! Eah, I see water. It is like a mirror at the very bottom. The water is clear and warm. I am bathing here. Mist is rising ever so slightly. In the light of torch lamps I see the flame on the water flicker. It flickers also on red earthen walls. I see purple?

"There is a small boat. Oh, only big enough for one ... me ... but there are more. They are round ... only my bottom fits in the cup. My feet go into the water. I can float upright or lay back, and look up into the stars. It is beautiful! There are halls ... roots? I cannot see what lies beyond ... OOOOOoh!"

Sion opened her eyes. Who was with her, naked in the water? Did he see that? Her face blushed red.

"Eah! it is beautiful! My tree is much more than first I saw."

"As you imagine, the world of thought fulfills dreams," he replied.

"But how can I do the depth below the ground? I am but a girl and do not have the time or strength to dig that deep. I have planned to complete my tree before Yule."

"It is possible, darling." He motioned toward the clay. "Will you allow me to help you?" His eyes were big, full of eagerness.

"While you are building the clay on topside, I and some of my helpers, will work below. I promise you that there is a pool under there. If you agree, I will build for you a beautiful place to bathe and contemplate while you float in your little boat ... and gaze upward at the stars. I can make a boat for you ... and one for Ti Ti ... and for whomever you desire to join you."

Sion blushed. *"Will it slow me down?"*

"You'll go up and I'll go down, and we will meet somewhere in the middle, Daffinina. No one but you will know I am even there, and of that you will not even be aware, except for an occasional gentle vibration."

Then, her stomach began to growl, disrupting the silence of thought. *"I think I have been with you all day. I missed the dinner hour."*

"Come. Let's go sup. We will break bread again."

Sion felt herself growing sleepy at last. She had spent the morning, the noon, and the entire day with the fish headed, bird-winged, baboon-butted man with a pig nose ... who also had the mind of a great artist of superior nature. And she had found out that he could cook, as well.

~~~

Sionee's eyes opened wide. She must have gone to sleep. The owl eyes ... they had come again. *"Get the hell out of here!"* She shouted loudly. Daysong woke up for midnight milk.

She picked up Daysong. The eyes the wrong color turned into a beautiful orb of golden orange sun.

~~~

Alsionee and Daysong began their new morning high in the crotch of the ancient yellow cedar, singing happily with the morning birds and the sun. Kinga joined them, perching on the baby's tiny hand as she reached out to greet the sun. Daysong giggled her greeting. "K ... K ... K ... K ..." the tiny girl tried to sound out.

"Say to yourself, Daysong, Oh, song of Day. My Day of Song ... Every morning of your long life ... I AM THE PERFECT DAY AND IN ME DWELLS THE LIGHT THAT DOES NOT FAIL."

After their sun GNOS, Sion met Cy coming from the cedars and going to the bread hut.

"Today, Cy, I will begin my tree. I mean REALLY begin it!"

"Well, glad I am that my pipes are dried and plentiful, and that that limbs are gathered for drum sticks. I am in the process of trying a moist clay wrap around some hollow reeds to make an instrument. Do you suppose you have enough clay close by that my boys and I could come and fetch a handful or two? Perhaps we will grow weary of our music-making and may assist you."

"That would be wonderful Cy. I could use help hauling a bit more water. The clay needs re-moistening now and then, as I build. I have two assistants today to help me. One has promised to help with Daysong. I suppose I might allow you a little clay. I only have a wee mountain."

She giggled and Cy breathed a smiling relief, that she was happy.

"I do not know pot-building as you do, little deer eyes. But you can tell us what to do and we will do as our lady commands!" He bowed before her. He didn't wish to step on her toes again. He really wished to help her.

"We will see!" Sion tied her two long braids into a single one, forming a knot by gathering them together at the top of her head.

Deer eyes. He used to call her that when they were ten years old.

She was not beautiful today. She was wearing her worst stained shift, along with her well-worn, though sturdy sandals. Her two braids made a clumsy knot at the top of her head. The braid ends stuck out from the knot in separate directions of untidiness.

But she was a working girl.

~~~

She didn't care in the least how she looked. Everyone was at her site, eager. Of course, she should have known it would be this way. They had all come to observe in the blessing and to witness the moment when the clay would first touch its new place and its new form on Gaia.

She looked terrible, even worse than when she had helped anyone else in their construction. She fully intended to get dirty ... up down ... all around ... in and out ... head to toe ... covered entirely in the sweet wet clay. For the next while she would eat clay!

This was her home and she could look this way if she wanted to. Everyone would have to get used to seeing her as artkeeper as well as Songkeeper. She would look like a hog miring in the mud for quite some time, weeks, months ... while she built.

She saw Eah as well. He was trying to observe her from the reeds. She went to the patch of his camouflage and poked her head in.

"Knock it off!" She laughed at him. *"We all know you are here. Come join us."* She took him by the hand. He dropped his camera, rising. He bent to retrieve it before it became lost.

"But you might have to help," She warned him, giggling.

He wasn't sure what to do. So, he decided to just hang in there with the rest of the Ki people, and observe until otherwise instructed. That was really something he was beginning to enjoy ... just being with them. The people were so refreshing, compared to the perfect ones of his perfect associates of perfect boredom.

~~~

Sionee knelt at the edge by the rocks, within the midst of her circle. Daysong was with her, sitting upright and playing happily with flowers of white lily and white rose that had been strewn within the circle. One of the helping girls played with Daysong to make sure she didn't try to eat the petals and choke on them.

Sion got up as the crowd drew close. Cy played his cedar flute, dancing around the circle she had built with Ea, uphill a bit, and downhill a bit, his graceful and lithe figure stepped lightly. His body curved in a bow as he bent with the flute to his lips sending his song to the earth. Then, he raised and lifted the melody to the heights of the blue sky and the sun.

Sionee stepped along the outermost edge of her perimeter. She held a tiny basket in her hands, and scattered sea salt into a glimmering round that marked the circle which would be her home.

"*Aya ... aya ... aya ... a ... a ... ya ... !*" Her song rose into an energy raising vowel chant. Taya joined her to echo the vowels in words.

"*Holy Gaia, Blessed Be Thou. We plant a tree on this day.*"

"*Ah ... he ... ho ... ha ... ah ... he ... ho ... oo ... o ... o ... .*" Sionee drifted breeze-sweet petals from her fingers, as she sang in straight song. Sage to purify ... yarrow to sweeten ... dandelion to bring forth the sun ... blue poppy to sprinkle the rain ... red rose may love dwell within.

"*Mother, accept this tree to grow upon your skin. I honor your beauty by bringing forth a tree ... which compares not to the magnificence of your own work. I will do my best to honor and replicate in image the essence of your tree ... if I may. Show me, Mother, how to build. May I hear your voice in instruction and wisdom. May I build this tree safe and snug and capable of holding the foolish things which exist in all your children's lives ... which are mere rubble in our true existence ... which lies in worlds we can only hope to replicate. I dedicate this site as a place of holiness for my life's works, which you have called me forth to do. Mothers all ... Seamother ... Skymother ... Earthmother ... Mother Sun ... Mothers all ... bless my hands to be your tool. Ayah ... Ayah ... ay ... ah ... !*"

Her sound was straight. Its melody rose to join with Taya's words and with Cy's flute. The harmony vibrated the soft spring air in sunlit waves of bright morning.

An apple from a branch above fell and rolled to the center point of the circle. It split in half on its course with the ground. It now lay in two pieces, revealing the star center of the original whole. The star caught a ray from the sun. All eyes followed it. It was whispered in hushed-awe that Mother had sent her approval.

"Oh, tree of life ... oh, rise my tree. May you grow strong as I build thee."

From a larger basket which she had placed in the circle center, Sion now took a first handful of clay. It was wet and had been worked into a proper consistency with water. She had mixed shredded grasses and dried moss all mushed up into the clay with bare feet.

Sionee placed the first batch on the ground. Her hands were quick to gather and form. She mounded the clay and patted it into shape. Her helper worked from the other side, imitating Sion's procedure. Initially this day, the first coil ring of the rise would be formed and left to harden just a bit, covered by leaves to slow the drying, so it would be just the right stage to support tomorrow's coil. The roots would spring forth strong from this perimeter, and go down the hill ... the door would be added.

Gather ... press ... pat ... scrape ... ah ... this was fun. Though, in time it would prove to be a tedious task.

Sionee stepped in front of Eah, her hand dripping with moist clay mush. She flung her fingers. She turned then, and flung her fingers again at Cy, who cursed softly as he played his flute song.

Sion rolled to the ground in mirth. She covered herself with the flower petals that clung to the wet clay she was well adorned with. She giggled on the petal-strewn floor.

Ea felt the cool droplets of clay splatter on his face across his nose tip, on his eyelid, and on the edge of his mouth. He grinned at her. He wiped at it reluctantly. It was as if she had kissed him again.

Chapter Thirty-one

"Ea, I must tell you, I am not feeling pleased about this. I do not wish to go. I really don't! Can't we both just celebrate our own little pleasures this evening?"

"Ninmah," Ea bid her. "You said you wanted to hear the story. Tonight is the perfect opportunity to hear it told on Ki."

"But what do they know, Ea, that is so special? Can't you just tell it to me?"

"Our history told it in the ancient days. It is such an old, old story it isn't even told anymore. No one wants to hear it or even cares. Its history has become burden. In our society, it simply does not matter. In theirs, it does."

"How do you know about the story, Ea? You said the Ki version is very familiar to you."

"I know the story because I read it one of my mother's many journals. It really is quite interesting."

"Why don't we tell it anymore on Nibiru? I think it is because it is a stupid story that everyone got bored at hearing."

"Ah ... no, Ninmah. It is not a stupid story. I have found it in the sciences."

"Blah, blah, blah," Ninmah scowled. When Ea looked at her in that certain way of his, she relented.

"Okay. Okay, have it your way. I shall come. What does one wear to this night story? Is that what you said they call it? Nightfire? How quaint!" Ninmah giggled in mirth.

"What silly, simple things the Ki animals entertain themselves with ... ah! They really need to get a life, Ea!"

"They have a life!" Ea scowled back at her. "No, do not wear that!" He insisted as Ninmah wrapped herself in a robe studded with peacock-blue ore flakes and heavy gold chains hanging with peridot and white pearl. "Something more simple and light, surely."

"I'll wear what I desire, mister!"

Ea sighed. "As you say then," he returned. "But let me make a couple of things clear before we go!"

"Blah, blah, blah, blaah," she said, rolling her eyes for emphasis. He slapped her on the butt.

"I guess they need some form of entertainment," she added. "Imagine sitting around a boring old fire every night, time after time."

"Tonight, my sister, is their spring festival, the most exciting night of the year. You will see! While it is a form of entertainment for them, it is much, much more."

"Blah, blah, blah." She straightened upright, turning around swiftly and giggling so that Ea could not swat her again. "Sure, brother."

"How better a way, Ninmah, is there to get someone to listen than to entertain them? Ninni Mah, the games we play on Nibiru, of reality feign, are stories in their own way, informing us as they entertain.

"I say all Nibiruans, especially those on the Perfect World, should get a life. All of Nibiru is captivated and mesmerized by that little box with earpieces. Bah, indeed!

"Tonight, girl, you are in for a real reality show. I guarantee you this. It will tell you the story of Ki's creation of life, which we Nibiruan play an important part in."

"Whatever!" She replied, totally unconvinced.

"Tonight, you will see Ki's first archetype!"

"Archetype? Ea, Oh, come on! Like our games? Pleeeease!"

"Yes, my sister, come ... common stories shared by all, reveal great truths."

~~~

After they landed and got out of their ship, Ninmah felt the weight of her ore-studded gown. It was heavy on her shoulders. She was sweating beneath its folds and her feet were getting wet.

"Ea, couldn't you have just landed this thing a little closer ... LIKE ON THE GROUND?"

"I didn't wish to take the focus from Daffinina's story. It is her story, not the story of our flying craft hovering in their grasses by the fire. We must approach them in a manner that is normal to them."

"Who beg I to know is this Daffy, Daffy Nina?"

Ea smiled so brightly that a frown crossed Ninmah's face. "You will see. You will see."

~~~

On this night all the young Songkeepers were naked, except for their raiment of flowing white feathers strung with white flowers that hung in strings from a shoulder piece that flitted and fluttered over the entire length of their bodies.

Each girl held two rattles, painted red and all bearing the symbol for lightening.

Drums beat in a powerful cadence that drowned out the rattle pings, and made the ground shake.

Ea wondered why there was no fire, yet, in the fire circle. The only illumination was provided by torches which marked the circumference of the performers and made a perfect ring to focus upon.

Above and across the starry sky, the shadowed silhouettes of night hawks swooped low and pierced the drum beat with an urgent shree to their mates.

Cicada and crickets and spring frogs began their ever evening chorus and called forth holiness to the gathering.

It was the night of new birth. Life was rife in the symphony of this evening.

Other Songkeepers joined the rattle bearers. Their regalia of dancing feathers were similar to the white ones, but these feathers were a deep hued blue, glistening with a florescent purple in the light of the torches.

Ninmah gasped. The ores were heavy on her dowdy costume, causing her body to sweat. When she sweated, her armpits got a little stinky sometimes. She hoped she wasn't getting stinky. Oh! Was she not a wee bit heavier than these lithe little things?

The Songkeepers, decked in night-sky blue, formed an inner circle, within the circle formed by the day clad Songkeepers in white.

In the center of the white circle, a girl stood holding a very big round pot. Ninmah wanted to touch the pot to see what it was made of. It didn't appear very heavy for its size. The girl held it transfixed high above her head in raised arms. The pot gleamed in the torches and all eyes focused on it. Purple and orange flashes made the pot seem alive as the reflection of fire danced across the rounded vessel.

More lovely girls entered the circle, each holding round pots with one small hole in their bulbous centers. When the girls slapped their cupped palms over the hole in a rhythmical manner, they forced in and sucked out the air within the pot. And, a pinging echo filled the circle with music. The pots further made a shell sound, when the players patted the pots with their deft fingernails. Interesting concept.

Into this dancing design, yet another young girl danced within. She wore a long white robe that could have been misted-air for all that Ninmah could detect. Didn't these animals have any decency? She may as well as have been entirely naked. Her copper skin glimmered like dark cream pearl beneath her robe.

The young girl danced around the female who held the upthrust big pot. She also held a vessel of sorts in her hands, but to her lips she placed it. It was large also, and equally bulbous, and had a hole similar to the pinging hole. The girl pursed her lips and sent her chants within the pot. Her voice amplified in there, and came back to vibrate a most unusual song sound that sent echoing thrills of vibration over the crowd.

"Eeenuuuuuuuuuuuma ... Eeelisha ... la ... la ... nahbuuu ... Sha ... Sha ... Mammuu ... Shap ... Shap ... littu ... am ... amm ... mattum ... Shu ... Shuuma ... la ... la ... zakraaahttt ... ."

As the beautiful words echoed in hollow buzz, the dancers froze. Even the chanters were quiet. Not a sound anywhere, not even a twitter from the night birds. Ninmah's heart was still.

Zing!

Ninmah fell backwards, startled. A flaming arrow shot through the sky above them. A loud crack split the night. The arrow landed precisely in the circle center and ignited nightfires flame. Illuminating brilliance sent forth its light.

In the now-flickering center fire, pieces of shattered pot rained down like streaks of meteor stars circling the priestess who had held the big vessel high in the air.

In her hand high above her head, she still held a piece ... an intact half of the pot.

Joyous chants rose above the crowd, coming from a place distant.

~~~

All eyes turned to see the source of the sound. In the moonlight, high on the hill overlook, Sionee stood naked, glimmering with bow still in position. Her long hair was loose, shining with the light of the moon as a slight breeze made it spiral around her body. Across her shoulders, two feathers fluttered, tied into her hair with string. One was white, the other was blue. A torch on the hillside was lit and her skin glowed red with iridescent hue.

Ninmah glanced at Ea. His eyes were as bright as the fire. "Daffinina?" She whispered into his ear. But he was quiet.

~~~

The priestesses at the institution had worked hard to produce this one. As Sionee had requested, they had gathered a golden mica, and ground it powder-fine along with an even finer dust of glistening rubies, that some of the boys had brought from a cave. The color held to her skin with the aid of thick and sweet-smelling aloe.

Sionee was glad that her practice as a priestess in training had given her such precise skill with the bow and that the arrow dipped in naphtha had flamed on course over the crowd exactly right ... ah ... and had broken the pot and ignited the center fire as she had planned.

She stepped down from the hill. All eyes followed her as she gracefully approached the circle center. It was what everyone had been waiting for ... HER SONG!

Even in straight sound, everyone heard, especially when her voice was echoed by Taya, who sent the words into the vibrating voice pot.

"Tonight we mate."

~~~

Shrieks of delight thrilled through the night as the crowd reveled in glee. The children had been left home for this evening.

The clasp of Ninmah's golden chain broke loose when a man animal ... Oh, he was a handsome brute ... came through the crowd and took her by the hand, smiling into her eyes. The peridot and the pearl fell loose to the ground.

"Ea!" She screamed, whether from fear or excitement, she did not know. The man urged her, gently motioning her, to come with him. Where had her brother gone? She couldn't see him anywhere.

Oh my ... the earth was soft where the animal led her. The bed of moss was bedecked with petals of white lily and smelled better than anything she had ever smelled before. The Ki man ... she hoped he was a man ... he was quite magnificent as he stood over her, naked, except for some fastening of stag horns he wore crowned on his head. She watched his muscles quiver as she reached out to touch him.

"Ea!" She screamed one last time. But he didn't hear. He was elsewhere and ...

Oh ... well ... now about those common stories Ea had spoken of ... indeed. Archetypes!

Ninmah sighed as the man animal showered her in soft and sweet red rose petals. He dropped beside her and freed her from the awful ore studded robe she had worn.

Chapter Thirty-two

"Ea, I really didn't catch the story."

"Of course, you didn't, you fool. The arrow flew right over your head!" Ea smiled at her indulgently.

She was glowing. He hadn't even found her until morning, when she walked out of the trees as bright as a spark of day. She was naked beneath a scant robe of white flowers, and she looked pretty incredible.

"Nini ... Ninni-Mah. Have you no shame?"

"None, you ass! I really did enjoy the story."

"I thought you might."

"Maybe you can explain to me later."

"Oh? You like the symbol stories?"

"Aspects of them," she added as the two of them went back to the hover ship which hid among the reeds.

Her cheeks were flushed with a pink Ea found most becoming. Ninmah was his own experiment. He knew that her stellar code originated in the Orion regions of Sirius, like the other Nibiruan. But how far it was capable of evolvement was his own personal experiment ... yes ... and it seemed that maybe ...

He thrust a journal into her hand. "Read it," he urged. It will explain ... but please, sister, take care of these pages. They belong to my mother."

~~~

"The nightfire stories, Ninmah, are told with a bit of difference, each according to the teller's viewpoint, and they are heard in a like manner.

"I do believe my Daffinina has quite a way with words," Ea chuckled. "Does she not? Ah!"

"Shameful!" Ninmah began, frowning. Then, she giggled. Her giggles peeled out like bells.

"Ah, sister," Ea began again. "Sometimes I fear the different ways of trying to tell a story might confuse innocent ears, but the accounts are charming from my observation."

The two were in his office of scientific study. Both heads hovered over the journal Ninmah had carefully returned to him.

"Is this true?" She asked. "I mean, I thought it was all a game."

"The archetypes, blah, blah ... you asked, Ninmah." He chided.

Ea put the pages beneath a light projector, and they looked at the wall where Sofeya's carefully recorded version of an ancient Annunaki story was now displayed in all its scientific glory.

He projected another image at its side. "The makers of the game back home based their own pale version on the actual account." Ea explained. "Clever, is it not, how stories have a way of living on ... even when their message is extinguished."

"Aye," Ninmah agreed. "It is a favorite among all our young ones. Now, I begin to grasp, Ea ... maybe." Her brows drew together. "I think you could be wise, my brother, but you already know this."

"Even among the Orion pattern of Nibiru, an understanding may be reached, even if it has been forbid. The game, itself, powerfully conceals the story within the guise of entertainment.

"This is not the game played by our youth, sister. It is real. Archetype. The seed behind the symbol ... the common seed ... ah ... see."

The words of the game instruction were big on the wall. Ea smiled, pointing. "This is an understanding which we share with Ki's Pleiadian code."

"What, Ea? What are you saying? Ea, I begin to get a headache."

Of course, she didn't know. That part had been forbid.

"Make it simple, brother. Get to the point, like she did."

Ea laughed. "Yes, the arrow ... it did get to the point above your head," he sighed.

"Let's start at the beginning, Ninmah, and lay the symbols side by side. Come on, sister. It will help you smile that little frown away and giggle again."

She smiled. "See here," he shared. He placed an image of Daffinina standing on the hill, all red and glorious, at the side of Sofeyas's ancient recording. On the other side, he had already placed an enlarged version of the faux reality game the Annunaki youth all played on the wall, side by side by side.

The reality game featured a planet, big and engorged with flaming red anger, sputtering through space at a vast speed.

"The game itself, Ninmah, is a bit old, though still top in its rankings. I played it when I was a boy.

"Marduk." Ninmah laughed. The planet Marduk, which is really Nibiru, I am guessing."

Right on, Ninni Mah. You're really not a ninny, Ninmah. You are a smart one ... sometimes.

"Damkina and I named our son Mordukku after this very game, and we often call him Marduk. She is fond of playing, as well."

He pointed to Sofeya's script. Nibiru - the roving planet. Our home, Ninmah. As you know, it crosses the path of the sun every sar, as it makes its elliptical orbit just so." He traced the path with his stylus. My mother replicated the ancient star map, almost as the one we follow when our ship comes to Ki the long way.

On the game, his stylus touched the vivid colors presented. "We have the celestial gods symbolized as orbs ... planets.

"We see here, Sofeyas's sun, which is a reality in our solar system." His stylus shifted again. The game calls it Apsu ... who reined in the void ... in space ... our solar system.

"Also, in the game ... here we see, Mars, Venus, and Mercury. It shows it here, Nin, in game images. The game is comparable to my mother's images. See here, the ancient gods, rounding out ... oh, and see here, we have the moon and the first Great One ... Tiamat. His stylus shifted and pointed again.

"Of course, in the feign game, the names given to these are trendy, as in the art of the game, which is not to bore the young ones with truth.

"In the feign game, the object is here, with Marduk named as the hero. He is the strange roving god who enters the scene from across the deep. He represents our Nibiru in reality.

"So we have as our game object to move the angry Marduk, who has a bit of a different orbiting pattern ... elliptical ... not round ... across the space without bumping into the other planets or ancient gods." He shifted the button on the game, and they watched Marduk advance his crossing.

"It is as Nibiru does cross!" Ninmah explained, her eyes wide.

Ea flashed the focus light ... now on Daffinina ... red and gleaming ... arching her flaming arrow. Then, he flashed it back on the faux reality game.

In our game you see Tiamat is depicted as a monster ... way big and bulbous with an enormous belly. She causes a difficulty for many of the gods, and to further challenge the game, Marduk orbits counter clockwise, you see, as well as elliptical just so blah, blah, blah ... you've played the game sister."

"Ah, yes! She replied, following his rapidly moving hand with the stylus. "Some of the planet's orbs make Marduk's way difficult also. He must sidestep a bit now and then. There are explosions and radiation and all manner of obstacle. Makes a great game, doesn't it? It really happened."

Now he pointed to Sofeyas's script on the wall. "In the game, the young universe is a vast and wild storm. It is hard for Marduk to see clearly. In anger, Marduk decides he must slay the dragon.

"Here," he pointed again with a shift of his finger, "a battle took place between Tiamat the Dragon, and Marduk the flaming red planet."

"It's your Daffinina!" Ninmah explained, as she began to comprehend the truth of a symbol. "And, her arrow! Yes, eeeee! Hit it, Ea. Yes, blow her up ... Tiamat... the monster!"

"That is the object, which makes of the successful player, a winner of the game! Yes! It's over now ... ta da!"

"How many sars ago was this, Ea ... for real? Was it right after the bang?"

"It was a very long time ago, when the planets were depicted in their first position, as mother has illustrated."

"Huuuumph." Ninmah was thoughtful.

"Yes, you see that it did happen, but let's make it a wee bit closer to your understanding, as in scientific terms.

"Look to my mother's drawings as such, in the matter of things which are real ... not game or symbol," Ea grinned.

"What happened was ... put simply ... Nibiru's orbit has a different path. It is elliptical, not round and it moves in the opposite direction than the other planets move. His stylus traced Sofeya's chart in the same way the game depicted.

"On a particular sar on a difficult journey through space, it drew close to Tiamat, one of the first big planets birthed by the sun." His stylus touched the game Dragon thus, and, indeed, the Dragon belches forth and spits fire.

"Fire thunders as rain over this Tiamat, due to the magnetism created, further drawing Nibiru close. We hit Tia, Ninni Mah, right about here. When Nibiru collided with the big planet it split her in two!

"This part of her turned into little pieces," he pointed to rubble on the game. "This debris endangers our journeys to this day. It is the asteroid belt."

Ninmah held up a finger. "Ah yes, the hammered bracelet."

"Indeed, Ninmah. Another symbolic name. You are grasping. The half that did not get blown to pieces is where we are right now, moved over just a bit ... just so .. Ta da! We have Gaia as they named it, or Ki as we have named this planet. Her satellite moved also ... just so ... la la. We have it here, the moon!"

Both eyes now focused on the figure of a girl still projected on the wall, glimmering in red ... arching her flaming arrow.

Ea pushed a button into motion so they could follow. The beautiful girl released the arrow.

"My Daffinina! She tells it much simpler than I." He smiled. The arrow ... Nibiru ... collides with this earth ... the vessel breaks thus.

The two of them watched countless little pieces of dust and shard fragments explode in a circle around the priestess who had been holding the original unbroken pot.

"Now this girl ... the almost naked girl with the air robe ... ." Ninmah frowned.

"She holds the remaining piece of pot that we have here, he pointed to Sofeya's chart, "which becomes this earth in its present form. But there is more, Ninmah. Do you see? What do you think this is?"

He enlarged a particle of dust.

"It is a seed!" Ninmah exclaimed.

"Yes. When Nibiru hit on Ki - Gaia, it was like lovers coming together, blah, de, da, de, da … just so," he illustrated and Ninmah giggled.

"We left our seed print on Ki."

"Ea! They are our children, then … All of them! We created them … and the plants … and the foods … so similar in nature to our own on Nibiru. The originator is us! Oh, Ea! In many ways, though, they are completely different than us. Is this how we were in our world's beginning?"

"That, my sister, is another story. Think on this one for a time."

"Yeah, Ea … always, always."

"Are you hungry, Ninni Mah? Let's go to coffee. That sounds pretty good right now." He smiled at her.

"Fine!" She said. Was it really all that cream and syrup that was making her figure quite not as sleek as it used to be, as were the skinny girls by the fire story? It hadn't seemed to bother that …ah … Ki-man-animal. He said she was beautiful.

"Ea, tell me the truth now. If you did the big nasty with an almost animal from Ki, which one was she? Which one? Did you think to make a female, also? Usually you are so good at girl babies. I should know after all. You seeded many girls with me. Suddenly her eyes got extremely wide open.

"Ea, I've got to go … forget the coffee! I've got to run and take the pill … the morning after. Do you think it's too late?"

Ea grinned, and wiped the sudden sweat that had begun to rise on his brow. He watched her scurry out the door in haste.

He wouldn't have to answer that one just yet.

Chapter Thirty-three

There was a frown as big as one of his father's ridiculously awesome serpent pillars on Mordukku's lips. He could feel it inside his code, if he had one. He tried again. Ah hah! This was even a bigger scowl. He traced the curve of his lips with his finger. It curved downward, like the horn of a ram.

Which would be quite fitting. His father, Ea, had incorporated a serpent as a symbol. Marduk had incorporated the ram. Marduk was the young son of the water serpent, ruled by the all-power of Enlil's Bull ... at the time that is. For a moment his frown turned into a forlorn glimmer of dreamed hope.

Damn the bull! As damned he would be at some time later ... he, son of Ea would see to it!

In his great Ram horn, Mordukku hovered downward back to the heights of the mountain. He met Ea on the highest of Abzukia's peaks. He had known Ea would be here, examining the mountains for minerals. Hopefully his father would be looking for a gold source, but Mordukku doubted it. His father had little inclination for the value of gold, though gold was his father's first and foremost mission on the Ki.

Gold seldom, if ever, took import in his fathers addled head, which was ever occupied with Ki's other great Sciences. No wonder they had sent Enlil. Enlil, at least was an apt business maker who could concentrate on the task of procuring gold.

Not that his father hadn't already established the mines and figured out where the gold was. In actuality, he had done more for Nibiru than Enlil could ever do. It was no doubt that in the sciences, Ea was skilled above anyone! His father just did not understand about power.

Mordukku made a soft landing. It was night time on this region of Ki. In the light of the moon he could see his father's Eagle.

Here, there was a cluster of awe-inspiring needle mountains. The pointed tops pricked the starry sky and reached into heights only inhabited by eagles. Touched by the moon, the pinnacle tips were crowned with silver.

He found Ea sitting straddled on a craggy silver tip, his legs dangling down as he gazed out into the starry universe, and the earth and waters below, with what seemed to be a look of vacant expression ... vacant of sense, that is.

"What enraptures you so father?"

"Marduk!" Ea returned from wherever he was. "I thought I saw the moon crescent fall, I looked up and saw the moon still high in the sky. Then, I remembered you were coming, and that it might be you and not the descending moon. Isn't it beautiful, Mordukku? Have you ever beheld such awesome magnificence? Oh, I should have known you would find me here. I heard that you have been flitting about to and fro, over the skies and the oceans of this world and the lands yonder."

"Indeed, I have father. What else am I supposed to do? I, firstborn son of one who should be King, but isn't? I have little import to anyone."

"Oh, come on son. Nah, surely you do not think so."

"It is clear father, as it is clear that I am firstborn of your sons and foremost."

"It better be!" Ea replied, motioning for Mordukku to sit at the pinnacle peek which rose next to the one on which he straddled.

"Couldn't we sit elsewhere?" Marduk asked. "Like on the ground?"

"But Mordukku, these are the highest pinnacles of the Abzu. Come, let us study the heavens together." He motioned, impatient when a cloud that was in passing obstructed his view.

Despite himself, Marduk smiled. Truly, he had never beheld such a sight. How his father could still touch his emotions completely bewildered him.

"You old lizard gis, you." Marduk began.

"I'm not so old. I am only a million of years or so, and you are not far behind."

"What exactly do you expect of me, father. You taught me little of responsibility; you scarce pay heed to your own, unless it interests you."

"I pay upmost observance to all my doings."

"But not as your higher-ups ask of you. You are the single most un-upholding law abider and society forsaken Annunaki I know!"

"Yes!" Ea smiled proudly. "There is however, your lovely grand-mother."

"And me!" Marduk agreed, suddenly proud.

"As I have taught you, son. Question authority! Always remember it will make you most unordinary."

"You did teach me that one, though little else."

"What are you talking about?" Ea frowned, puzzled.

"Oh, like how to rule. How to be the authority, father. How to be King on heaven and earth."

"But Mordukku. That is not my lot."

"It should be, as if you care."

"Why should I be King, son? All this is mine ... all this." He stretched his arms wide and embraced the starry sky and the earth below.

"Power is in the stellar code son. True power is something none of the Annunaki on heaven or earth besides my sweet mother has a clue about. Haven't I taught you this? It is why perhaps you desire to flit idly about in your Ram rather than task yourself otherwise. Do you really think Enlil has power son?"

"He is the commander. He has taken the seed abiding ... blah, blah, blah, ... and his authority is number Fifty!"

"So, as I asked. What real power does he have?"

"He has the power to hold in his hand the tablets of Ki's destiny!"

"He can push buttons and make everyone afraid of him," Ea added.

"It is his right! That right should be yours!" Marduk lamented. "And it should be mine, also in fairness. You are the firstborn son of Anu. I believe it well father ... that you love me not!"

Ea put his arm around his son. "Mordukku. Do I see hurt in your eyes, my son? Have I hurt you? I have only loved you far more than I have loved any of Nibiru beside my mother."

"You have small skill to show it."

Ea sat upright gazing into his son's eyes. There was a darkness there that stabbed at Ea. Oh, how could he take that hurt away?

"I haven't always been around son."

"No, you were off to Ki, leaving me behind with my mother, whom you have little apparent love for, even though she is your lawful espoused wife!"

"I cannot argue with you there, son. It pained me to leave you when you were small, and glad I am that your mother brought you to Ki. I do wish she had returned to our home world, though."

"And, Ningishzidda. You and he are always together at the Sciences of Healing. You even asked him to assist you with the births of the lu. Him! Not me! I think it is because you love him more so."

"His skill is phenomenal in the Sciences, Marduk, even more so than mine"

"And mine is not?"

Ea was feeling pretty guilty at this point. What for, he wasn't quite certain. "Surely, son, your skill is apt in leadership, which is why I put you in command of the heroes on the way station at Mars."

"The way station no longer serves, father. Most of us have already left the port. It has become quite inhospitable as a habitat."

"Yes, and the young ones in your charge now trouble Ki with all their hella bellacious and raucous manners. What did you teach them, son?"

"We all nearly perished in boredom, as if Ki is any better. Now that the lu are doing the majority of our heavy labor, there is little to do.

"Even Ninurta, my cousin, has been given great status on Ki, and he is but a slimy worm. His number is even higher than yours."

"I thought I taught you better than this!"

"You taught me nothing, father, but to hate you!"

"Hate me? You hate me son?"

"I despise you. You are nothing but a limp gis. Stand up for your-self, father. Then, perhaps I may at least find some respect for you."

"Oh, surely, son, I hadn't realized it meant so much to you."

"It does. It really does."

Long into the night Ea and Mordukku talked. Marduk finally settled down a bit, finding an enjoyment sitting on the mountain pinnacle at last.

Marduk took another sip of the blood red wine that Ea had giv-en him for soothing. It was his favorite vintage.

"Ah father. I must give you credit for the wine. Perhaps you are right. I find great power here!"

Ea knocked the bottle out of Marduks drunken hand. It went sailing down the mountain through empty air, where it would fall long before it landed in a splat below.

"Grow up son. Quit feeling sorry for yourself. It grows late. We must camp here tonight in our crafts. You will study with me tomor-row. I will show you what power is ... real power! Got it, son? Now get off that ass of yours. Steady now ... careful son! Oh. Let us get some sleep."

~~~

Ea wasn't sure how to handle this, but he had spent almost the whole night listening to Marduk warble snore in drunken stupor.

In the morning, he ordered Marduk up to break bread. He hand-ed his son a steaming cup of black coffee that he had prepared over the campfire, primitive style.

"Now this is power, son. Take hold ... come on sip it hot ... up ... up now."

Marduk promptly threw up.

"Up!" Ea motioned, tossing Marduk a wet washcloth to wipe the sleep from his eyes.

"Couldn't you have camped near a hot springs?" Marduk muttered.

"Oh, there is a hot pool here where we will sit tonight ... father, son, and the moon and stars. First though, we have work to do. To start, I need a little fuel in my stomach. It growls empty. Over there in the rocks our breakfast awaits us. I will prepare this pan with oil and get it heating. Go fetch breakfast son."

"Didn't you bring food, you nin? All I see out there is shit from the mountain goat."

"The pan is getting hot," Ea replied. "So I guess its fried goat turds."

Marduk threw up again. Ea handed him more coffee.

Finally Marduk ventured out. Presently he came back. "I found these meager breakfast items, father. I don't have a clue as to why I am hungered, I just am."

Ea smiled at him. His son had picked a fine bunch of mushrooms. "They were growing wedged in the crevice of two stones," Marduk proudly admitted. The color had returned to his face.

"On that ledge," he pointed, "there was a big eagle nest. Momma wasn't there so I helped myself." He had several eggs. "Then, I found these." He held up two large fat rock lizards.

The mushrooms, steamed in lizard unguent, served with fried eggs on top, was a meal fit for any King. "It was good father."

"Now this is power, Mordukku!"

~~~

"Mordukku, I have been thinking about what you spoke of last night. In a small way perhaps you are right, son. There is little I have really shared with you. It is just that it never crossed my mind that I was forsaking you. I am sorry, son. Will you forgive me?"

"Never." Marduk promised, grinning. "I do love you, old lizard gis." The two hugged and Ea's heart warmed.

"So, now, son, here, where it is quiet and there are only two pairs of ears to hear ... yours and mine ... I will really tell you about the power.

~~~

The world peak reached into the periwinkle blue of the sky sea, lifting father and son into the heights of eternity. It appeared as if the stars were in motion before them, pinpointing the dazzling darkness with a view fit for the Lords of the Universe.

"This is power son, the only power that is!"

They watched the rotation of the universe from a high reach in a crag that had been created when two pinnacle mountains intersected each other and created a spot for a cavern within. An ancient hot springs still gave the depression in the joined mountains, water. The pool glimmered like a mirror in the moonlight, and reflected the stars that cast their mystery into the arched portal. Ea and Marduk were immersed in the primordial seas of both water and sky.

"The blue is as sapphire, son. It is the richest of all jewels, far above mere gemstones and gold. In these vast starry depths are ALL that is ... ever was ... and ever will be ... of power."

The beauty held such a strength that this time Marduk withheld his usual 'blah, blah, blah's' of boredom.

Ea put his arm around his son's shoulders.

"Among all these infinite speckles of light high in the aeons of eternity, there is a pinpoint." Ea pointed. "A star with power so infinite it is the ultimate."

Marduk forgot that his father shared medical sciences with Ningishzidda. He forgot that Enlil, his uncle, shared succession with Ninurta ... and that Ninurta was a worm. He forgot that Ea had cursed him with many brothers and far more sisters than could even be necessary. He forgot that Anu, God of the Heavens, was King over them all. He listened.

The luminaries danced before him in glorious view. High on the world mountain it was only stillness and a thrumming of the stars. The music of the spheres resounded in effulgent silence, creating a music with Ea's voice as he spoke.

"Father, what is the spark, and what is the flame?"

"You were young, Mordukku, when you left Nibiru. Have you forgotten the lessons?"

"They bored me, father."

"Yet you were trained in the sciences."

"The sciences told me the hows, but not the whys."

"Our people on our world are perhaps the universe's greatest scientists." Ea whispered. "Or so they believe."

"What don't they know? Is there some secret you will disclose to me?" The silence thrummed.

"It is you and Grandmother, isn't it? "Something about her is different, as are you." Marduk shook his head in puzzlement, trying to open his eyes as well as his ears so he could hear well.

"Indeed, there is something a bit extraordinary about us. I will share this secret with you son, but only your actions can prove your worthiness to hear. However, first, let's you and I get this straight. You must give Ningishzidda no discredit, Mordukku. He is wisest of us all. I didn't have to tell him this story. Secrets, he has told me. He already knows this: Power is Power."

For just a brief moment, a stab of jealousy almost made Marduk puke on the world mountain.

"If you allow envy to exist, you will lose hold of what I might tell you. Let it go ... just this once ... and listen carefully, or you will not know what your brother knows already."

Marduk sat upright again.

"Now son, I want you to look out there. Tell me what you see."

"I see the moon. It has a silvery light that looks like a pearl floating in the fathoms of the sea depths. I see the luminaries. They take shape before my very eyes. I can see what they are."

"Indeed," Ea acknowledged. "From this position or that." Ea pointed earthward. We see the planets because the sun is casting its light on them. But all those tiny little pinpricks out there are mere reflections from a bigger light, and it is not Nibiru's light. Look there!" Ea pointed.

"I believe that is the Pleiades system, father. Show me something more interesting."

"As you wish." Ea smiled and pointed.

Marduks mouth turned upward. "Ah yes, father. The Andromeda nebula. It is one of a great light spiral system where Nibiru is close."

"There is a reason, son, why I am more wise than any of our fellow Annunaki associates. Mayhaps even more so than you, though I am not sure yet about you. I know that Ningizzi is like the bright sun. There is reason he is thus, as is Sofeya.

"To the ordinary Annunaki, this scientific knowing is a secret. There are few who have figured into their perfect technology this thing." Ea laughed until Marduk felt another stab of irritation. Ea wiped his eyes from the moisture of excess mirth. "Only it really is no funny thing, just scientific."

"It is about our stellar codes son, you know ... our spark ... our spirit. Few on Nibiru have original coding. It has been forbidden. My mother still has original stellar code, which she passed on to me. I passed it to Ningishzidda, who received it well. Did you receive it, son? I don't know. Honestly, I have not seen."

"You gis." Marduk was allowing anger.

"It is all plain as is the light of that star." He pointed to the Pleiadian spiral again.

Marduk squinted. It wasn't as big as the Andromeda. He pulled out his eye pieces to better look.

"It is all about energy from that system. Let's call this energy something a bit more romantic. The Ki people call it spirit. We call it code. Oh, how can I relate this to you? Oh. Okay. I will try to make it as simple as I can."

"In the ancient-most of the ancient-most days, our people had stellar code that came from there." He pointed again, for the third time, toward the Pleiades.

With some of our fancier telescopes you might perhaps look and see an outstanding star there-in, at the very center. It is a fixed star at the beginning point of a spiral whorl. It radiates its light in a sort of band which makes a photon of illumination.

"As her neighboring stars spin in the spiral, you see some of them. Others you do not see, depending on whether they are presently rotating within the band, or out of it. When the sun moves into the path of Pleiadian light, the earth, being in orbit around the sun, also moves into this photon band, as well as some of Ki's neighbors that Nibiru crosses once every sar."

Marduk was distracted by the way Ea moved his hands in excitement as he spoke, gesturing to and fro so he could barely understand. His eyes tried to make sense of his father's movements.

"These stars move in and out ... within and without this photo band that spirals from the upper-most bright star of the present solar system. It is the brightest of the Pleiadian system.

"The bright beginning point of this spiral is a star where spirits are born ... where star codes are created that are superior in living intelligence. Oh, son maybe not exactly superior, but maybe I should say more advanced in their growth."

"Sounds superior to me."

"It is and I was afraid you would see it this way."

Marduk looked at him, puzzled.

"As you know, all codes are of an even dimension. They have no matter form, only a light form. That is the spark ... the spirit ... the code.

"It was the discovery and understanding of code-source-reality that prompted the so called advances into technological superiority that we have embraced on Nibiru.

"It happened when we learned that we could take the light ... that spark of life ... the star code ... the spirit ... and direct it to a particular physical body, any physical body, bio or otherwise. It is why our world is known as being one whose life is made of shape-shifting intelligences. We can appear in any form.

"Originally on Nibiru, all of our codes came from that bright star, as I explained, in the system of Pleiades. This was when we were still wise ... before a great evil set in."

"What are you saying, father. I have been led to believe that evil is a thing of bad emotional result."

"It was when we discovered that it was hard, if not impossible, to force the beautiful spirit form of Pleiadian light into our new technologically-constructed bodies that we held to be of a superior nature to our natural ones."

Ea now pointed to the regions of the Andromeda and Sirius and ... . "We began to take our code from elsewhere. We found that the Orion code was easily forced into accepting our constructed bodies.

Less and less, our original bodies were constructed, so more and more we called on the Orion intelligence. Soon all Pleiadian code was forsaken, and no longer directed onto the bodies of Nibiru, especially since a reptilian form had become fashionable on Nibiru. It was a form most delighted ... to have within ... code from Orion.

"Isn't it funny about fashions? Since coming to Ki to get gold, the earthen body has become in mode again." Ea began to giggle. "The reptilian form was popular because it replicated easily. It came in great and brilliant colors. Get it?"

After a moment or two, Marduk joined him in laughter, though, he scarce understood why. "I do prefer the original body for sex," he replied.

"So do I," agreed Ea. His humor became serious again.

"You mean to tell me, father, that the stellar codes of the Annunaki are birthed in Orion?"

"You have it! It is so. On Nibiru, we lost our pure Pleiadian spirit, simply put, to accept a lesser advanced ... in the name of technology. The Orion code has a highly degenerated technical obsession. It is why our technology has become so huge. We went from simple and joyful living to what we are now ... advanced hoo haws. This is the real reason our planet is waning. We traded our emotions for technology, thinking we had made a good trade.

"Soon, emotion became forbidden. It was no longer understood that emotion is the food that feeds a pure soul. Now it is forgotten."

"What is this, father? It is said our Nibiru is highly advanced to a perfection."

"We are robots, son." Ea's eyes flashed. "At least you are ... maybe ... and Anu and Enlil and all the sons and daughters of Nibiru, who have so brilliantly cast aside their Pleiadian code to honor an inferior servant that bears a poor gift."

"Father! Are you saying that we incorporated the Orion life code within our fashionable constructs of bio bodies? You say we cast away the Pleiadian spark because we could not force it into our technological wonder-world of perfect physical bodies?"

"You got it son. Bells of hell, they don't even teach about the ancient code any more. I think they wish it to be forgotten in our new coding. Like a bunch of nin-com-poops, we threw away the key, so to speak."

"Marduk continued. "Evolution is what allows the Pleiadian star code to ever move forth in beauty, rather than to move forward into technology. The Orion code does not allow an emotional nature, which is basically a fertilizer that promotes fine growth. This is why Orion coding creates deterioration. It lacks a proper growth factor."

"Perhaps there is yet hope for you, my son. Brilliantly put!"

"Nibiru thinks it is so smart because it has captured an inferior stellar code and says "Oh, ho! Look at how intelligent we are now, rulers of technology in this universe and others, as well. We may cast our codes into any form we desire, shifting our shapes to suit our fashion. The only thing is, our codes of heritage we have cast aside like worthless trash. Oh, father. This explains a few things clearer."

"Just one more thing, son. We must knock the word 'inferior'. Let us call it 'less evolved'."

~~~

"Are you saying that you still encode in the Pleiades?"

"I do, no doubt"

"Sofeya?"

"Of course! None of her mothers before her cast it aside. They were able to keep it because they all became doctors at the birth of bio bodies, and they kept the secret."

"All of them broke the law by doing so, I see."

A faint streak of morning began a mute glow on the horizon beneath.

"This is power son."

"But father surely there is a way to have it all. I would be King with vast wisdom."

"Wisdom is the silent, first ray of morning, son."

A purple star streaked across the sky and spiraled downward, falling so fast it almost went unnoticed.

"Its power goes about, not seen. Power it is, that you desire, son

... or so you say. I see power living beside you... inside you.

"Someday, if you use your power as you desire, you, not Ningizzi or Nergal ... not Ninurta ... or any of Nibiru's sons will be King. You will command heaven and earth IF this is what your desires are."

"Can you see into the future father?"

Ea looked into Mordukku's soul. "I can. But yet another thing ... just a wee bit before we sleep at last. Go easy on the drink, son. It tastes good on the tongue and can be a comfort, but it is something the Orion soul craves to help it forget that they have a far way to go before they shine as the brightest of stars."

Chapter Thirty-four

The roots had turned out far more awesome than she could have imagined. Now formed and drying, they twined, curved and wrapped about the baseline of the tree connection to the earth. They extended across the curves of the hill, upward and downward in intriguing gnarls.

Many of the bigger ones had been fashioned with a hollow interior. Some formed tunnel-like hallways, others were shorter and formed closet nooks and spaces for storage.

Sion had created a realistic texture to her root bark by using the pattern of real bark to do the work for her. She combed the fresh, formed, and still wet root structures with broken and jagged splinters of real wood pieces, making them look almost real. As the tree rose in height, she would create the texture in the trunk in a like manner.

Now that the roots were partway dry, it was time to highlight them with a touch of color to bring out the design and interest.

She began her slurry just last night, by gathering a good amount of well-dried white clay clumps into a tub. Water had been poured in the tub to soften the clay.

Kneeling down, she bent over and noted that the lumps had dissolved and now formed a thick creamy layer on the bottom of the huge tub, and the waters had risen to the top. It was perfect!

She scooped out the excess water until the tub was light enough to pour. She tipped the tub and poured the rest of the water out onto the trodden grass. Next she stirred the clay mush into a thin smooth consistency. This slip would provide the slight color difference when it was swooshed over the bark and tree texture. She scooped a little of the creamy mixture into a dry linen cloth and set it out to dry. She had a use for it later.

Daysong was beginning to scoot around on the grass and was

getting into all kinds of curious trouble. Sionee worked and kept her eye on her small daughter. The monotony of heavy building ... scoop, shaping, pat ... repeat scoop, shape, pat ... and repeat again, made it necessary to take small breaks to sooth her back, as well as trying to keep the baby happy.

Sometimes when Sion was taking a little break from the scoop and mound process, she let Daysong put her tiny hands into the wet clay. The girl entertained herself for quite some time playing in the mud. Before the day was over, both girls would be covered with clay of both colors.

On one of her breaks, Sionee took the bundle of clay she had set aside to dry. It had firmed up into a working consistency. Sionee sat with Daysong and made a handful of tiny animals for the little girl to play with.

Daysong giggled and made everyone happy. She had the cutest little dimple in her chin. Her hair had sprung forth in full glory, forming golden curls that circled her face like petals of a yellow flower.

It wasn't hard to get any of the young Songkeepers to volunteer to play with Daysong. Actually, this was preferred to working in the messy clay.

Three of the young girls eagerly helped Sion, while another one entertained the baby.

The thin white-wash made the application process go fast. Each worker dipped a linen cloth into the vessel briefly, but not saturating it heavily. Then, they brushed the mixture quickly over the semi-hard texture. The white slip washed all the highpoints with an effect of highlight and left the crevasses and crags within the bark the contrasting orange color of the clay that she was building her tree with.

Sion dreamily envisioned how the flames of the final fire would cause the inside of the tree to darken and transform the bark and leaves with patches of various colors here and there.

By the noon mealtime, the wash was well complete, and quite effective in bringing forth the beauty of the bark design. Sion was satisfied. She had determined that it was important to add the wash when the rooted beginning was still damp, so that the form and the slip could dry together, becoming as one.

Sionee smiled, thinking about how tomorrow she should begin some necessary inside details, like the frog. She had dreamed of the frog for so long! The cobb oven inside her meal preparation area would be built to look like a round fat frog with his mouth open wide to receive the bread loaf ... not a bug!

After lunch, Sionee sat down beside Daysong to make more animals. She really enjoyed this part. It didn't take long to fashion five little horses with chubby short legs that would stand up and not fall, as well as hold up to vigorous child play after they had been fired. The horses were cute. Sionee made another handful. She set the tiny creatures out to dry on a sun-warmed stone.

Next she created a bird. When it was done, she saw that she had made a white dove. It was fun to make the animals, so she made four more, before she stood to begin the process of scoop, shape and pat again.

She got back to work, planning further details for her cobb oven that would serve to bake breads and pies and delicious things, and make her finished tree smell so good. Soon the rising tree would enclose it in heights that would leave the first level far behind to touch the sky.

~~~

Cyex brought an armload of weathered and dried branches from the wild forest. On his way home from gathering wood to make instruments, he had taken the time to contribute to the woodpile that Sionee would build the final fire with.

Everyone who went to the forest brought Sionee an armload or two. Cy placed the sticks carefully on the growing pile, so the wood could remain dry until the time came to light the big fire.

Sionee had instructed that only dry, old wood be brought for a high and hot fire. He imagined he felt a vibration or something beneath his feet.

He walked over to the evening-deserted tree shell and stood within the interior of Sionee's future home. He frowned, puzzled.

Was it a fluke or had he imagined the movement? When he didn't feel it again. He left and headed for the bread hut. He would pack a lunch for tomorrow, and head out early to seek other gifts he could bring to help Sionee with her tree. He had caught an enthusiasm ... for her.

~~~

Cy rose early. He was eager for the day. There was a place he liked to go where he sought relaxation. How Sionee stayed so busy all day long ... he smiled. She loved building her tree, so she didn't get tired.

That girl was a hard worker; he really had to give it to her. Her tree was on the rising. Even now the face was being created.

He had left her there, standing before the tree in rapt concentration. *"Uum, Cy I am having a little bit of a hard time with her nose. Noses have always been a bit difficult for me."*

"Maybe you are making it a bit big," he suggested. "You said you were making it beautiful." He left when she started to scowl.

Leave a working artist alone ... he should know. They must discover their own mistakes, as well as their own triumphs. However, she was already proving that she was doing quite a job in the triumph part of it.

"How high are you going?" He dared to inquire.

"High enough," she replied curtly. *"Cy, one of these days Daysong and I would like to join you on your picnic. You could play the flute for both of us."*

"I'll look forward to it," he replied. Next year, when you slow down enough.

Cy sat on a stone munching his lonely lunch when he heard a twig crack behind him. Now this was a first! Usually he chose his places for the privacy that he could be assured of. He didn't think it was Kinga, whose company he always enjoyed. Cy turned.

The damned fish head was crawling on his belly. He looked up briefly, his bug-eyed spectacles sliding askew down his nose. He was following a snake that disappeared beneath the rock Cy was sitting on.

Ea did not acknowledge him, other than a brief impatient glance. Still on his stomach, he fumbled beneath the rock and drew out a long, winding snake whose tail brushed Cy's exasperated nose as it wiggled in the fish heads hand.

Cy breathed audibly inward. "It is a poisonous one." He exclaimed. "I wouldn't if I were you."

Ea stood upright. Pleased with himself, he pushed his glasses back up his nose. He had on long leather gloves that went the entire distance up his arm. Otherwise, he was wearing some kind of get up that appeared dark and sleek. Rather, it appeared that he had killed a lizard, and stretched its skin to don for protection. Ea had one leg thrust up on the rock as he stood. He had thick knee boots on. Ea bent and released the snake within a round-lidded basket.

"Whatever are you doing with the snake?" Cy asked at last, not trying in the least to be cordial.

"Not hurt him, if that is what you are suggesting."

"I'm just curious as to what fish do when they invade the land."

"I think the snake is beautiful and I wish only to study him."

"Why?"

"Is not the beauty enough?"

"It is for me, I figured you needed it for a cage or something."

"For the most part, I do not use cages to confine animals, or only briefly if I do. Sometimes it is imperative for scientific studies that I do so. Then, I use confinement only temporarily."

"For your convenience, no doubt."

"On our world, we have no creature as wonderful as is this one, though our lizards are more advanced that yours. However, other than beauty, I find this creature useful in the making of medicines."

"Does that beauty you spoke of include stuffing it's skin, and one of your ladies wearing it wrapped around her big head all dangling with jewels?"

"It is done by some. Maybe my sister would wear such, but for the most, my people would be repulsed with a wearing apparel as such. Lizards skin maybe ... my brother finds serpents quite abhorrent."

"And your costume. Is it lizard?"

"No." Ea smiled. "It is an artificial fabric, light... yet impenetrable. It protects me from the snake poison."

It grew silent, thick. Cy turned and began to gather up the sticks he had been working on. It was time to move elsewhere. There was no need to stand here and pretend he was in the least bit interested. He turned to leave.

In his haste, he brushed against one of the clay flutes he had laid out to dry on a rock, and it fell to the ground and broke.

Ea looked over and saw a row of instrumental cylinders placed carefully side by side to dry. His interest was struck by what appeared to be fine works of beauty.

"May I look?" He asked.

"Suit yourself." Cy replied shortly. "Careful now," he continued. "They haven't dried entirely. Don't go leaving fingerprints all over them." He was feeling a bit peeved and irritated, but the interest in the fish head's eyes as he carefully picked a near dry flute up made Cy stop short.

There was admiration in those weird green eyes ... and appreciation. The fish head traced the length of the pipe gently with great respect.

"It is a beauty," he whispered.

"You can build statuary as high as twenty men standing on top of each other," Cy replied. "Why would you find this mere wind instrument amazing? Sionee told me about your snakes."

"I am intrigued at this tool of supreme beauty ... in form and function. I am supposing that this is the sound."

"What sound?"

"At the fires your people light at night, I have seen you dancing as you make beautiful music. I must compliment you on the melody you played at the springtime story that Daffinina performed."

Cyex's cheeks grew hot. It had been a sad fact the fish head had been there at the fireside, again. Cy had been much too aware of his presence and had not been the least bit happy about it.

"The song that you inspired the wind to sing ... was it not with a tool such as this? You commanded a sound that still haunts my ears.

I found it most beautiful."

"I wanted a beautiful girl to hear it."

"Well, son, that I can understand."

"Son?" Cy spat. "Now wait a minute."

"Forgive me, forgive me. I beg your forgiveness. What name was it I heard her call you?"

"My name is Cyex."

"You may call me by name. I am Ea." The fish head extended his hand. Cy looked at it ... then, away.

~~~

"The holes appear to be most carefully measured." Ea speculated out loud, his eyes full of awe. The fish head's sincere admiration drew Cy closer.

"How else? Well, they must be precise or the note will not sound right. Here, you may look at my finished one." He handed Ea the finished one he had in his bag. It was his flute and he was well proud of it.

Ea put it to his mouth and blew on it. A screeching sound came out. Surely it was the worst noise Cy had ever heard!

"Eeeeeeeeough!" This flute he would never place to his lips again ... fish head slobber. "Blechhh!"

~~~

The soft orange clay of the burnished flute sparkled with glimmers of mica. The mouthpiece of the flute had been shaped into the head of a snake, and a snake-leathery effect had been replicated quite accurately.

"It is easy while the clay is still soft," Cy explained. He showed Ea an assortment of tools which Ea studied carefully and in great interest.

"When the clay is a bit dried, I like to get out my tools and carve into it. It is like carving into a brick of butter." As Cy spoke of the process, his eyes seemed to come to life.

"I made the reptile texture of the skin by pressing the fresh formed cylinder on a piece of snake leather, after I formed the clay over a mold of smooth round reed." He showed Ea some of the instruments which were drying around the soft reed form. "I've only recently experimented to make these of this particular medium.

"I have made flutes out of all kinds of wood, and even from shells found in the tide. I prefer cedar, however. They are by far the best pipes with the best sounds. Cedar is pleasant to carve and the wood is fragrant, as well as abundant. They make a sturdy instrument.

"The one I played the night of spring fire was cedar. It makes a sound like a bird."

Ea was fascinated. He smiled when Cy placed his cedar flute to his lips and played.

"You play so fine. You had many beautiful females following your dance and song. You had your choice of any of them."

"Ah, there was only one girl I would have desired to take to the wildwoods."

"I thought so. There is only one of Daffinina."

"Alsionee," Cy spoke her name fondly and firmly. Then, he decided he might as well ask, since the two of them were almost on speaking terms, he supposed.

"It was you she followed into the woods."

"Oh, now, I wish I could remember it as so. Instead I saw her turn to you."

"She didn't go with you?"

"No. She didn't go with you?" Ea asked.

"No."

The silence became thick again as both of them shared contemplation.

"You old fish head, you. You are lying."

"You young monkey. You are lying. I always knew I loved the water and that you were an animal."

The two of them studied each other carefully.

"Where did she go, then?" Cyex asked.

"Rather, my friend, with whom?"

Ea gave the beautiful snake-head instrument back to Cy. Cy pressed it back into Ea's hands.

"Keep it." He said.

Chapter Thirty-five

Dusk brought about the peace of a setting sun. Sionee's many helpers had left for the evening meal. Taya offered to take Daysong home, and feed her and get her ready for bed. Meanwhile, Sionee finished her work at the top of a high ladder that some of the men had built for her.

It was a sturdy ladder, equipped with a platform to place clay. A hoisting mechanism had been devised with a flax rope. With it, it was possible to hoist the basket of clay up or down, and even swing the basket from side to side, in most any possible necessity. The weight of a full basket, made it difficult to maneuver, though, now that the coils had risen so high.

Cy urged her not to climb the ladder unless someone was around. Whereupon Sionee had reminded him, *"I taught you to climb the high cliffs. Thank you. I can certainly manage this."*

She knew he was only concerned for her safety, but the crowd had been around as she had climbed. She had just been finishing up for the day when Taya had made the welcome offer. Sion was thankful she had such a good friend who gave her a quiet moment or two to reflect. She had little time to do that, as of late.

There seemed to be a new excitement among the people. Everyone was eager to assist the priestess, who told the story in the ancient tongue of the first Songkeepers.

The new Songkeeper was also favored by one of the Sapphire Sky Sea dwellers, who wore their fish heads when they fell down to the waters of Gaia's seas, and swam now on her earthen shore.

It was said that the fish head were capable of great and amazing things. It was said that recent ones were now living in the big Cosmopolitan of the Snake of the Sea. But everyone knew that the ones in the big city were not the same as the wise Sofeya, who had come to the fire in ancient times to the blessed ones of the small cove outlier. She was good. The other fish heads were not so good.

At the edge of the sea, on the northern shores where apples grew as blessed by Gaia, the Fey were wondering about the fish head that had come to their new fires. That, again, a wise inhabitant from the heavens had come ... and sought the enchantment of their own Sionee Tree Song ... made them happy. They were elated to be the people who also could hear Sionee's songs of wisdom. Her stories were spoken of, and contemplated upon, for weeks after their telling.

The whole outlier and beyond were abuzz with the Songs that Sionee's silence made so profound. Her messages were also spreading to far-reaching outliers across the Snake. The idea of her big story tree was making everyone eager to see her home in completion.

Sion could see in the dusky light that her tree already was telling a great story of patience, of determination, and of dreams! Also, that one's dreams were never too big. She smiled that her vow of silence spoke so truly to many people.

She thought she was alone at last, and actually it was so nice. She wasn't expecting to hear the creak of the ladder steps or feel the slight movement of careful footsteps interrupting her deep and peaceful reflections.

Quite unexpectedly, she felt two big hands grasp her firmly at the place where her waistline began its swell to her hips. Before she could turn her head to look at her intruder, two hands sprung up and covered her eyes.

He stood, cradling her body on the ladder rung just beneath her. His arms circled around her. His body pressed firmly against her entire length. She could feel his heartbeat against her back, pushing a throb into her heart, which beat a little faster at his presence.

She knew who it was and didn't need seeing to know. She could smell how his hair was the color of sun shaded by nightfall's first whisper. She could smell the scent of stars, casting their light on Gaia's sweet horizon.

"Eah, we are going to fall."

"Oh. I have already. But you, my dear ... never. I will wrap my arms around you."

Silently they climbed the ladder down. He, one foot below her upper foot ... she, one step at a time in unison with his movements, until they both stood firmly on the ground.

Her back was still turned from him. He held her that way, and for a moment time stood still, as he breathed the sweet honey locust scent of her hair, a fragrance mixed with cedar berries and sweet earth. He was not eager to feel her withdraw from his arms. At last he spoke. "I brought bread, Daffinina. Would you join me?"

"I'm not sure, Eah. Where you are taking me? I'm not sure I should follow."

He said, "Follow only your heart."

He stood just behind her, as she bent to stir a pot of wet clay with her hand. The bucket held a vast supply of sunset-hued slip. She added a bit of white clay dust. Her whole arm disappeared into the mass of mud as she stirred.

"For tomorrow," she explained. *"I need a lighter shade of orange for tomorrow's part."*

Once more her back faced him. His arms were just behind her arms. He pressed his form to fit her every curve and movement. He thrust his arm into the pot and stirred with her. For several minutes their bodies moved together in shared motion. She turned around to face him. With one finger, she painted his nose with peach color clay. She took one step backwards to admire the particles of mica glinting there.

During her work in the early morning, she had thrust her shift low upon her shoulders to keep from sweating. It had loosened somewhat during the day, and now swept low across her breasts. He touched her with one clay-moist finger at a point just between her breasts. His finger rested a moment in between.

With two muddy palms he cupped the upper swell of each small mound, then traced a line through the mud left behind. He circled his finger from one round to the next.

She caught her breath. *"Eah."* She placed the clay covered palms of her hands, on each round point of his bare shoulders and sighed.

The clay was warm and smooth. It sent a sensuous shiver through her. He turned her around and rubbed the creamy ooze across the upper portion of her back and down its length. Tingles of vibration rose up and down the river of her spine.

He spun her around again and touched the tip of her nose with his finger. Now, she had a muddy nose which sparkled with mica.

"Did you say you brought bread, Eah?" She asked. He had some kind of instrument in his tug pocket, but she didn't see any food.

Ea began to move about the inner circle of the tree interior, studying. He was amazed at the small cobb oven Sion had built. He smiled in pleasure as he noted the technology of a simple nature that she had designed so beautifully, and so efficiently as well.

"After the fire is lit here on this hearth, the oven will heat. The clay surface will keep the heat inside. After scooping the ashes out, I will put bread inside."

"Ah!" Ea exclaimed in amazement. "I will be pleased to join you when you make bread." He walked to the other half of the room space and looked upward. "I deduce that you are still planning ... ."

"To leave one side free of floor shelving all the way up to the top, so I may look up and see the stars as I sleep."

"Of course, my dear, and say, now ... don't panic. This will be fine I assure you!"

He took out the tool and brought it to life. It made a great noise. He held it to the floor, where he pierced through her first level with a knife blade that screamed like a raucous mammoth.

"Eah." She protested, holding her palms over her ears.

"Hush now, darling. I built a support beneath. It will hold up your food preparation floor. I assure you. You are about to see a great enlargement of your universe!"

He cut a hole on her ground floor, making a perfect small circle just big enough for the two of them to fit through. "It is not quite complete, Daffinina. After you fire your tree, I can finish. I will cut the entire half of your floor away. There will be a fine ladder down, but for now, I have this ... ."

He took a rope ladder from his shift pocket and hooked it to the floor hoists.

"Eah, this frightens me."

"It will be but a moment. Oh, come on girl, you can climb slippery grape vines."

Her feet touched the ground, whereupon he was at her back again. His fingers covered her eyes. "It is a surprise!" He assured her.

"Come on, darling. Daysong is being cared for. Both of us have been working hard on this day, and I thought the two of us could enjoy this together." He was well pleased. Underground excavation and construction was another of his specialties. It had taken a bit of time to exercise his imagination to create for her.

The ground was soft beneath her feet. When he turned her around and she opened her eyes, she was standing on a soft red sand beach. There were torches placed within, that flickered softly over a red mineral hot pool beneath an arched cavern dome of shimmering walls.

"Eah!" Sion breathed, breathless, and totally unable to express even with thought, her feelings. She placed her first footprints in the sands beneath her home, as she reverently made her way to the cavern walls. She reached out and touched glistening amethyst crystals that hung in clusters over the entire ceiling and walls. The reflection of the torches danced within each single point, and each stone bore within a single star.

"I thought you would enjoy the amethyst," he said. "Beneath your tree I found a crystal cavern."

"I had no idea."

"When I cut the rest of the floor, you will be able to lay back in the water and see clear up your tree to the midnight sky. What do you think of the pool?"

Sion felt tears slide down her cheeks. Never had she dreamed it could be as this.

He wiped the tears from her cheek with his fingers. "Of course, you did." He assured her. "All this, Daffinina, is your dream."

"And more ... !"

Ea laughed. Her face was still covered with clay, though it was now dried. Her tears had washed streaks down her clay-white cheeks. "You look like a ghost!" He told her. "I think we should cleanse before we break bread."

Sion was still looking. She saw her round individual canoes fastened on a hewn stone edge. There were three big canoes and one tiny one.

"For Daysong!" Ea explained.

"The other?"

"Just an extra or so ... I thought perhaps ... who knows.

He helped her unfasten her wrap, untying the knot which held it from falling entirely down. It slid to the red sand floor. He bent and unfastened her sandals, kissing each toe as he bent ... one by one.

She felt his warm breath on her toes. She giggled. *"Eah, I am ticklish there."*

"I will remember." He smiled into her eyes.

"Remember, when?" She asked innocently.

"By and by," he said. "When you and I become lovers."

"Eah!" She protested too loudly with her eyes. *"Who said that you and I will become lovers?"*

But he was only silent, smiling softly. He led her to the waters, where they sat a moment on the stairs that led deeper.

She scooted farther into the waters and began to wash. She could see the reflected image of dancing amethyst crystal on the mirrored surface of the pool.

She wanted to sink farther into the depths. She reveled in the luxury of the mildly warm waters, sighing as the warmth soothed her work-achy muscles.

"Ti Ti will learn to swim fast." He admonished her. I trust you will instruct her?"

"Of course," Sion replied. *"Babies learn faster than children or adults because they are not yet acquainted with fear."*

For a moment Ea saw a frown cross her eyes, he wondered at her fear. Did his Daffinina still hold within a fear? How could he take that away from her? Oh, how he wished he could remove that fear, entirely.

She smiled. Then, her eyes brightened again. *"Daysong will love this! We will both enjoy this, Eah. Oh, thank you!"* She sprung from the steps into the deep red depths. *"My mamun taught me to float on my back in the hot springs on the hill."*

He knew the hot spring she was speaking of.

"I used to like to lay on my back in the waters at midnight and gaze up into the stars," She spoke softly, hushed in awe. *"I remember their stories she reverently taught me."*

"I think I will float on my back here, every night before I sleep," she said. *"Sometimes, I will lay in my boat alone, and contemplate the stars,"* she laughed softly. *"Hmmmm."*

She dove beneath the waters like a beautiful mermaid. He watched her hair stream out beside her. He wove his fingers in the trailing strands of black silk as she came up, dripping golden water glistening down her face. He placed his hands on her head, helping her wash the mud from her face.

His fingers slid in the mineral rich pool down farther to where he had deposited his gift of clay earlier on. She dove again, he sank with her. She opened her eyes on the sandy bottom and picked up a blue pearl she found embedded in the red sand. *"Where did this come from?"* Daffinina could thoughtspeak beneath the waters.

He smiled. After the bath, he showed her the basket of clean linens and helped her secure a loose, comfortable wrap. He wrapped himself as well.

They sat on the sands and ate. From a basket, he handed her a glass goblet and filled it with white wine. He spread a cloth on the sand, and brought forth bread and cheese and tiny little fish eggs that were salty like the sea. They were delicious with the bread. They enjoyed a bite of cool sweet grapes, afterwards.

"What are the little rooms on that side for?" She asked at last.

"Whatever you wish, my Daffinina... but there is one ... ," he pointed out to her. It was just a bit larger than the other doors.

He brought forth something and handed it to her. It was made of a metal and had beautiful rounded curves ... it was a key.

"If you ever need to come to me, Daffinina, or if you wish to, this key will unlock that door. It would be easier than the sea way. This key also will unlock the door in my sea room. However, it is seldom locked."

"I am afraid to go there, either way."

"Daffinina, I would take that fear from you. But please keep this key safe. He showed her a little button. "Push the button, anytime you are afraid, or anytime you need me. You don't have to come to me. I will come to you."

Finished with the meal, the two of them climbed back up the rope ladder.

"Soon, you will be finished with your tree. I hope you will allow me to observe when you set it on fire."

"Oh, yes, Eah. We will share a feast on that night. I have it well planned. It's going to be so awesome! Oh, Eah, you have given me a gift ... I don't think I could ever show you how much ... I think it is so beautiful ... but here."

She opened her hand and put something there. His fingers closed around a large handful. He opened his palm. There were five little white horses with chubby little legs, plus one small, but precisely crafted white dove. Each tiny figure was smoothed and polished with a stone.

"For your mother, Eah." She smiled into his eyes as tears formed in his. She reached up and wiped one away with her fingertips.

"Send these to her, will you, Eah? So that she will remember her wings."

Chapter Thirty-six

Ninurta arrived at the mine during the noontime meal. Eough! This was disgusting! The lu laughed as they bit into pieces of ugly, hard bread.

Of course, they would not appreciate the finer taste of soft bread, as the Annunaki were fond of. Their cheese smelled like rotten fish, not that rotten fish was anything but delightful, if properly cooked and smothered with savories in a proprietary manner.

They ate so eagerly it was a wonder that they didn't choke on that dry bread. Ninurta felt his stomach turn. Maybe the way they chewed so fast with open mouths, dribbling wet crumbs from the corners, was because they were in a hurry to finish quickly and get back to work.

Ennugi had said that he had ordered a shorter lunch break to increase production. Perhaps this thing with Ennugi was part of the problem.

Ninurta swallowed his bile and put on an eager face. He ambled over to the circle of male animals sitting on the rocks, eagerly devouring their bread and cheese. The lu animals stank with sweat running down their blackened animal faces.

Streaks of earthen flesh contrasted beneath the grime from the mine. The huddling Ki creatures likely didn't even notice the soil on their faces. It matched the color of their hair, black and ugly.

Ninurta sat down beside them. Silence filled the air, and all eyes turned to follow him with great suspicion. They better be afraid. He'd see to that, by and by, but for now ...

Ninurta pulled out a pouch of blackened and fatted boar meat. His cook servants had set fire to it in the early morning. He had instructed them to place it carefully in a receptacle so that it would stay well warmed.

Ennugi had said that the lu did not prefer a heavy meal of rich meat, but sometimes would eat a bit, if it was well cooked. So he cooked it well, and surely with a finesse that the ignorant creatures had never imagined. He brought them meat cooked just barely to retain the juices, healthy chunks of fatted and blackened, but bloody flesh ... and lots of it! The flies that hovered over it contributed favorably in both the texture and the spice of the general dish as well.

There was complete silence. Ninurta took his bag and opened it to release an enticing fragrance to tempt them. With his fingers he pulled out a steak, still dripping in juices. He held it out to the animal who sat beside him. He could be cordial, on occasion.

Why shouldn't he, after all, just throw it out to the worthless piece of shit? The animal could catch it in his mouth, surely. Ninurta kept a straight face at the image formed in his mind of the animal eagerly accepting the meat, clutching it in one piece between his teeth, blood dripping down his chin, making a river in the soot.

But the lu frowned at him, taking the meat disdainfully because he was their Lord and they knew better than displease him. "The flies will eat it if you animals do not. Will you let them eat it all? Then, they will get the nutrition, instead of all of you, you black headed slime." But he kept that thought inside him ... after all, cordiality!

Ninurta took a bite himself, savoring the moving texture of wiggling tiny fly legs on his tongue, and the crunch sensation that blended into the folds of bloody bites within his mouth.

Ninurta walked around the circle, thrusting as gently as he could, the swarming pieces of savory meat into each workers face. They needed the blood to make their work more efficient. Bread and cheese ... bah ... would merely feed a bird. These skinny creatures had gold to dig and metals to bring forth on their backs!

"Eat!" He yelled, puzzled by their reluctance. "I brought you animals a gift!" He kicked one of them in the side of his slight belly. Then, he was sorry.

No, this was not the way to handle this. He looked into the eyes of the largest lu he could see. They were all blackened with faces of soot, like the charred boar which he offered them.

Ninurta stilled his seething anger. He wanted to shake the foul shit out of the creature, upside down, but this would not serve.

He must find a different approach. Mayhaps there was an easier way, surely. It was apparent that the lu wouldn't listen to him just yet.

A smile lit Ninurta's face. He would turn on his charm. Oh, come on, he admonished himself. You know how to smile better than that! Ninurta forced one corner of his mouth to rise pleasantly, lest the big lu could detect his crooked smile.

The brute probably thought he was going to be beaten. Now the thought of that made Ninurta's smile genuine.

Step one ... Ninurta placed his arm on the lu's shoulder. "Come!" He said in all friendliness. "... With me!"

~~~

"Tell me your name. Can you talk?"

"Of course, I can talk."

"What is your name? Come on, speak!"

"I am Toron."

"Toron, do you have a woman?" All species had female. One must speak in terms they understood.

"Yes. I have a woman."

"Any children?"

"Yes, I have children."

"Good, Toron. Raise them well that they may grow strong," he instructed the brute. Then, to himself, he thought ... *Enough to lift gold sacks bigger than their puny asses.*

"I need a good strong man such as you to assist me."

The lu looked at him, confused.

Ninurta took a gleaming jewel necklace from his pouch. He would try this approach. The jewels were fakes, of course. He had asked Marduk to help him make a few fakes that appeared real. The lu would have no concept that they were just a pasty, worthless substance. It only mattered that they were shiny and bright, and that they appeared as fine rubies.

"Does your woman like jewels?"

"She likes ornamentation."

"What color does she prefer? Does she like rubies, or emeralds, or topaz as blue?" He held up a strand of enticing and brilliant fake gem necklaces ... worthless, all of them ... yet, impressive to an ignorant creature with little understanding.

For a moment Ninurta actually supposed that perhaps lu females could be the same as Annunaki females ... all females loved jewels to adorn themselves.

"She likes red."

Ninurta took the faux rubies and handed them to the lu. "For your woman," he smiled. "She will like it, will she not? Perhaps she will give you favor with this gift." He guffawed and poked the Turin ... no, Toron ... in the ribs, winking. Of course, mayhaps she would favor him with another son tonight, for use in the mines. Oh, brilliant!

Toron took the jewel, studied it, and smiled.

"You may have it," Ninurta said. "I do believe I have some ear pieces to match. Maybe she will give you a blow!" He pulled out some exquisite pasty ruby dangles.

The Toron's eyes brightened in smile. "These, too." Ninurta returned the smile. "Don't lose them now," he urged.

"Toron, I have a task just special for you. I see you are the biggest and the best of all of them. I do believe you are precisely my man!"

He flicked Toron's muscle, appreciatively. Eeeugh! The animal stank! Ninurta planned personally to take a shower after this ordeal of visiting the lu. Ninurta sniffed again, this lu's odor was not intolerable.

The two of them walked down the blackened path the lu miners had trod, day in and day out, for as long as any of the animals could remember.

"Go tell your friends to eat the meat ... all of it, or they will be whipped."

~~~

"I choose you, Toron, only the best and the most superior. Just look at your muscles ... I most admire!" Ninurta's smile was not totally feigned.

"I wish to make you my assistant. Of course, there will be ample reward. I will build a fine home for you and your family. If you serve me well, it will be suitably larger than the measly dwellings of your friends. Do you have many friends, Toron? Well, now you will have more. They will admire your big house, and your wife will be proud of her vast ornamentation ... that I shall see she acquires." Ninurta held a shining length of glorious red cloth out to Tor ... whatever the gis his name was.

~~~

Ninurta could hardly wait to tell Enlil about his progress. The smile he bore when Enlil arrived for inspection was anything but put on.

"It is a different approach, my father, one I believe to be most effective."

"Whatever you are doing son, I approve. There has been an increase in production." Enlil counted the bags which were on the threshold awaiting shipment to Nibiru.

"Anu will be pleased. How son? What has your beautifully unintegriated mind stirred up this time?"

Ninurta led his father to the mining headquarters where they could enjoy a quiet lunch far away from all the stupid ears to hear. He checked along the way to insure that his cousin, Mordukku, wasn't there. Marduk might be trusted ... maybe, maybe not, considering he was of Enki's seed.

"Mordukku is not in," he informed his father. "Let us dine."

"What do I smell of a most delicious fragrance?

"It is red meat, father."

"You are feeding them?"

"Think about it, father. The food provides two services that are in our favor. First being it makes them feel like we are doing them something good."

"What a disgusting thought!"

319

"Second, the red meat provides a far superior strength for them to labor with. The lu-lu are used to bird food. It merely feeds their small minds. The steaks, I have arranged to be served at every noon meal, give them added strength in their muscles, which we need more of, father ... plenty of muscle.

I believe they are finding it quite enjoyable, the smell of blackening meat in the pit entices them to hunger. They are growing accustomed to it. I have allowed on occasion that some be permitted to take the leftovers home to their families. This is getting the lu the taste for our meat. That increases their dependence on us. As you can see, this gives us upper hand over the lu."

"But ... !"

"Father, I have found that it is necessary to disguise our trickery by making them believe we are working with them, for their good. They believe us, then, to be their friends, and providers of easement. Their simple minds need superior minds to officiate over them. They are a social people and try to do as their others do. Make loyalty with one, you have loyalty from them all.

"I have now even heard some of the male lu say they enjoy coming to the mines to serve us. They are learning that it is good to get away from the little women and the crying children, and enjoy a steak with their male associates."

"So, you are saying." Enlil was pleased. "You are making it easier for them to choose to work, not interfering with their mislaid freedom of will, or with their original natures. We don't have to call it slavery ... if they choose."

"Yes, the choice has become a simple thing, now that Ennugi is gone."

"Gone? How is it so? Why?"

"I had him returned to Nibiru, as we discussed at the council of seven. The tiring labor done by our Annunaki heroes, who really are no longer young, must be replaced by new young. As Anu has suggested, thanks to my fore-wisdom, I have done just that. I have a better commander of the mining operations now.

"Oh, not to worry for one moment, father. Marduk thought it an ingenious idea himself, though I didn't explain it to him exactly as I have planned ... him being of Enki blood and all. Father, must we really have Mordukku up front in the mines? As you see, I would be a far better choice at that."

"What does it matter, son? He is merely in charge of the heroes. He has his hands full of them. He is seldom around. Besides, he is like his father in that way ... flitting about.

"As you so apparently well understand, using our own for labor is fleeting. Long we have desired to ease the load of our own. Pleased am I, son, of you, for your success in gaining a more serviceable creature of lu-lu. I am seeing your results ... your success."

"Indeed, father. So I have your go ahead?"

"By all means, son. You have my blessing. Go ahead. Now, tell me more of where your plans are going."

~~~

"Have you ever noticed ... Oh, of course, you haven't, father ... that personally your hands have never touched toil? Come, let me show you."

He took Enlil to the fences where food animals were kept. Some of them had multi-use as beasts of burden, the elephant, the horse, the sheep for wool, the donkey ... a stupid animal at most ... . Like the lu.

"It stinks in here!" Enlil wrinkled his nose. Eeeeeouuu! I am fouled ... my shoe ... it stepped on poop! What kind is it, Ninurta? It squeezes up through my toes. Eeeugh, I've seen enough. Hey, now. Why did you bring me to this foul place? You know I dislike animals of any kind.

"Donkey, you say? Cannot they hold their bowels and find a corner, or someplace more suitable for the task?"

"They are animal, father. Believe it or not, they are even less than the lu ... almost. I find them to be of more value, however. They are easily persuaded to work, and look father, see! Here is how I came to the idea of how to make the lu abide the law of toil."

Enlil had already ordered a slave to go back to the headquarters and fetch him a new pair of sandals.

Ninurta took him to the watering basins where the animals drank. "Put your foot in there, father. It will wash off. However, I would recommend a good hot bath tonight before we sit in the hot pool. I don't want your donkey-stink on me."

"When I return, Ninurta ... the sooner the better ... hurry now, son. Let's get this little demonstration over with. I really find this odor most disagreeable."

The slave was back with a new pair of sandals for the Lord Enlil. Ninurta bent to help his father fasten the strings.

"This will take but a moment father. Pay attention. I wish you to observe this."

He had fetched a vegetable from the garden. One of which Enlil seldom ate. It was chopped sometimes, and could be tolerated ... somewhat ... if the 'vegterrible' was mixed with meat and gravy, like in a stew. Ninurta held a big juicy carrot in his hands. "... not for you, do not worry ... just watch," he told his father.

The donkey in the pen had her back turned. "As a matter of observance, father, the donkey is pooping in the corner. Here donkey ... here donkey ... nice damn donkey. Are you hungry? Get your shitten ass over here!"

The donkey brayed, pulling her upper lips high above big yellow teeth. She ignored the two Annunaki.

"Hey, dumb ass! Listen to me ... come here now. I have a carrot for you. Let me put this burden bag on that stinky flea-bitten belly of yours. Now!"

The donkey kicked her legs outward, nearly striking Enlil on his knee caps as he stood next to Ninurta.

"Nin! She almost kicked me!" Angered, he climbed the railing, picked up a broken piece of flat wood that lay at the side, and slammed it across the donkey's back.

The action brought him closer to the donkey. Now ... that would teach the animal a lesson!

The donkey legs swung again, kicking Enlil's bent and pleased figure in the chest. Enlil fell backwards into the corner of deep manure! He screeched, thrusting brown muck-stained hands in the air in shock.

Ninurta extended his hand and pulled his father up, sputtering and cursing. Then, he dangled the beautiful, lovely, feces free carrot in front of the donkey's eyes.

"Here donkey ... here donkey," he called sweetly, leading the donkey with his carrot.

The donkey finally reached the dangling carrot and took a bite and chewed in great contentment.

Ninurta carefully placed the bag around the donkeys belly so Enlil could see how easy it was to snap the ties secure.

"You see? He beamed. It is easy. This, father, is the principal I have been using on the lu-lu.

"You stink, father." Ninurta held his nose, pinching it in exaggeration with two fingers.

~~~

Mordukku had been on an errand. It was a lovely errand, and it concerned a girl ... a girl from the sweet, ripe Ki. She was herself sweet ... ripe. He smiled. He was feeling good!

He held a carrot in his hand. It was for the donkey that was due to give birth any day now in the holding pens. She was a good donkey, and had assisted the workers for some time in the burdens of the mine. She was a cute little thing, had big eyes with golden lashes. He had become quite fond of her, feeding her daily the extra nourishment treat.

When he got to the pen, he dropped the carrot speechless in sorrow.

"Daisy ... Daisy," he mourned, glad that none of the heroes were around to see the forbidden tears forming in the corners of his eyes.

Damn them. Damn them all ... whoever did this to Daisy ... and damn Ea for cursing him with the ability of emotion. Double, double damn!

The donkey lay dead in the midst of manure, pieces of chewed carrot still on her tongue. Her beautiful eyes were open wide, and a fly lit on her dry eyeball.

Mordukku turned. Someone had smacked the donkey in the head with a big board, and smashed her skull in.

He found a sandal in the animal wastes near the holding pen. But there were two different sets of footprints near the dead donkey.

Mordukku rushed in anger. He'd find out who did this! He would thrust their gis up their guts and up their throats, then cut it from the place where their tongue flew.

~~~

Mordukku held Ninurta by his greasy blonde curls and yanked his head forward until his ugly tongue hung out gasping.

"I will report your weakness!" Ninurta screamed. "Father will not tolerate your emotions!""

"You will do no such thing. I'm going to first cut off your gis. Second, your tongue, then, each of your fingers, one by one ... and shove them all up your ass!"

Ninurta released himself with a sudden urge of panic as Mordukku took his blade from the pocket of his tug. He hit Marduk on the shoulder with his fist.

It smarted, and Marduk grabbed the fist and thrust Ninurta to the ground. He knelt, knees astraddle each side of his cousin's body, pinning him to the floor.

Marduk put the knife back into his pocket. Of course, he wouldn't have used it, it had been good just for a scare.

But he wasn't finished yet. With his fist, he smacked Ninurta on the cheek, hard, admiring the black eye that already was showing the putrid yellowing of a bruise. Then, he slapped Ninurta's face sideways to sideways in rapid succession, over and over again.

"I didn't do it!" Ninurta blurted, panting in pain.

Marduk pinned Ninurta's two hands above his head, palms upward and helpless in his grasp.

"There were two footprints there. Who was with you?"

"My father."

"Enlil? Oh, come on. Why would my uncle be out there amongst the muck with you?"

"We were inspecting the animals."

"They are my animals, and since when have you or Enlil ever been interested in the animals?"

"Get off me, you grandsire of a whore!"

Ninurta received a punch on his nose.

"You broke my nose!"

"You are lucky that's all I broke." He grabbed Ninurta's hand, pulling the fingers back tentatively with a firm pressure.

"It wasn't me! I told you that! I didn't hurt your little girlfriend."

Marduk sent him a whack that split his lip bleeding.

"Are you saying that Enlil killed my donkey?"

"Do you have ears, or what? That's what I said. That's what he did."

"Why?"

"The donkey pooped and my father stepped in it. Honest. Honest, it was he! His slave brought him fresh sandals. We were just trying to be nice to the poor little thing! Kind of cute she was, at that! Father gave her a carrot. As he bent to stroke the donkey's nose, the creature kicked him and sent him flying. Father landed in the deep shit pile in the corner. When I pulled him out, he was covered everywhere from head to toe, and all the places in between ... in the brown."

Marduk broke out in laughter, despite himself, at the image forming in his mind. Enlil, prim and proper Enlil, Lord and commander, second highest in the ranks of fifty, covered in stinky muck ... ah!

Soon Ninurta joined him in laughter, holding his bruised cheek with hands that were now free. He still had whole fingers attached to his hand.

It was then that Enlil walked in. "What is this?" He asked sternly, noting the disarray of Ninurta's room, and that his son lay bloody beneath Mordukku, with a crooked nose, and both eyes swelling and puffed in purple. The two boys stared at him in silence.

Was it a fight? "You two were fighting!" Enlil was highly disturbed.

"He broke my nose, father!"

"It is apparent, son, that Mordukku has bested you in the fight ... and won fair and square." Despite himself, he looked in admiration at Enki's young son.

"Don't look at him thus, father. He is an emotional freak! He struck me in violent anger!"

Marduk thrust his knee firmly in Ninurta's stomach.

"Stop!" Enlil ordered. "You two are cousins, the two of you! How dare you do this?"

"He did it because of his girrrrrrlfriend," Ninurta chided. "Whuu uuu!"

Marduk pressed his knee harder into Ninurta's soft stomach. Then, he thrust upward to the top of the whiner's rib cage.

"Enough, enough!" Enlil grabbed the two cousins and held them side by side in his arms.

"Marduk is the victor. This is clear. Fair and square, he wins!"

"What exactly do I win? My donkey is dead!"

"You win a lesser punishment for violent display of emotion ... only ten lashes ... much less than the usual fifty you should receive!" He thrust Marduk against a wall post and ripped his linen from off his back. "Ninurta, having suffered damage from your ill emotion will administer the whip!"

Marduk turned his head and laughed. "One lash, Enlil and I will make a promise to you. It will be a good one. I will broadcast the story to everyone ... Ki and Nibiru, alike ... about how their mighty Lord was bested by a donkey ... and landed on his fine Annunaki ass ... deep in shit!" Marduk laughed some more. "Everyone will love it! Enlil ... covered in animal poop! No wonder you stink, uncle. My father will especially love this, when I tell him. Ninmah will giggle! Especially, since I have the sandal to prove it!"

Enlil quickly untied Mordukku's hands. "Fetch your cousin decent linens Ninurta. Up ... up! Off the floor with you.

"We can fix your nose, son. I doubt that we can ever fix the fact that Mordukku has won this negotiation!"

Chapter Thirty-seven

With each handful of clay by which her tree grew to its place in the sky, Sionee sang a song. With a perfect symposium of skill and innocence, her tree came to life.

Mimicking nature, her technique mastered texture and polish ... bulges and straights ... crooks and curves ... perfection and imperfections, until at last, with a satisfied sweep of her eye, she knew she had achieved an asymmetrical symmetry, that only an artist with GNOS to share, would dare think into reality. In doing so, she had brought forth her dream to share, her beautiful story-tree ... where she would live her story.

"Would you like the boys to bring tall poles?" Cyex asked her. "Just to make sure that after all this work, and while it is drying, it will not fall."

"*My tree is done, now.*" Sion twitted like a bird from the tree heights. "*They may bring wood for the firing. After the tree is fired and cooled, we will need the tall poles for my ladder stairs and floor shelf-supports.*"

Most of her helpers were out in the wild orchards, picking apples for sauce, and berries for jam. Many of the maidens who had helped Sion mix dry moss and wet clay with their bare feet, were now in the grape pits, stomping grapes into juice.

Amongst the huts of the maidens, many young girls were giggling as they ran about with purple stained feet.

It was late afternoon. Cyex sat in the interior of Sion's tree, playing his flute to Daysong as her mother worked. The little girl played happily at his side. Eventually, the baby crawled to his knee and pulled herself up as she reached for him. He put her in his lap.

Sion looked down happily, and saw that Daysong had fallen asleep in his arms, lulled by his soft lullaby.

"Your music draws vibrations from the sun, and has helped my tree to grow."

He saw that he was inside a tree as living as any tree in the wild-woods. He looked up to the tapering treetop and saw Sionee patting into form the last gentle curve of the tree.

"Can you see the sky, Cy, from down there?"

"I can see your face peering down at me from the very top, with blue sky above your head."

"Can you imagine lying in bed at night and seeing the stars filling this portal, instead of my face?"

He closed his eyes and imagined seeing the stars at night through the portal and shining radiantly on her face as she slept beside him.

"I can see well, Sionee."

She climbed down at last, and in her eyes Cy saw that the twilight sun in its heights had made its descent into the circle around her pupils.

"I am finished!" She announced, exultantly throwing her arms around him, and planting a kiss on his cheek.

If Daysong had not been asleep on his lap, he would have stood up and gotten a better kiss by taking one full on her lips.

"Well, now, Sionee Tree Song, finished at last, did you say?" He asked brightly, winking at her. He picked up his flute again, and played a merry note. The magical melody sent Sionee giggling.

"I would say that a celebration is due on this very evening! Come, little darling, just you and me and Daysong!"

"I haven't eaten yet. I am starving. Let's fetch some bread and cheese at the huts."

"Sionee, since when has lack of food ever stopped us ... not when we were but wee ones ... and certainly not now. Remember when we tried to fry locusts?"

"Oh! Please. They were awful. And, you made me eat them. When I asked what they were, you told me that they were just something that fell off a tree."

"Well, that is where I caught them. It seemed to me that you liked them just fine."

"Cy, I will go with you, if you promise not to feed me locusts again. I don't care if you dip them in honey. I do not like the feel of insect legs on my tongue."

"I believe I can come up with something we can cook real fast, something that will be to your liking."

She saw adventure in his eyes. He always had adventure in his eyes. Free as the wind that danced from his lips with the song of his flute, he was a breath of fresh and beautiful air. Besides, after months of intense creating she was ready for an adventure.

"Okay, but not far, Cy, please. I am really hungry."

"This way, my lady." He bowed, and extended his hand. I know a great spot!"

"And, not one where we will have to climb vines. I've had enough climbing to last me a while, climbing up and down from my tree all day. So where are we going?"

"Here, there ... there, here. Remember the pool where we found those agates in the cove, near the outer edge of the cedar forest?"

"Are the agates still there, or did we get them all?" Her eyes were bright now with excitement. *"It has been a long time. I have scarcely had time to play."*

"You have been a proper girl for much too long. I mean to bring the little wildcat back into you."

"I wasn't."

"You were the best, Sionee ... my Tree Song."

"That was before I got in trouble for skipping school." She exclaimed as the trio followed a little creek up a hill that became the first rise at the mountain base.

"Cy!" She shouted in glee, after they came to the place they had visited together, long ago. *"The carnelians ... they are here! Just as always."* Eagerly, she stooped to pick one up and examine it in the light of the fast-fading day. Then, she picked up another ... and another in growing excitement. *"Wouldn't these be lovely hanging across my thin mica windows that will be placed when the firing is done?"* She mused. *"Their color would be similar to the clay, but with the sun*

shining through." She began to make a pile of carnelian chunks.

"I thought you were starving!" He teased.

"I am. We'll eat soon. Hey! See that tree over there?"

He went to a tall thin, but sturdy juniper with bare limbs and no bark." This one?" He called back.

"Yes, that one. Isn't it fine and straight?"

"It looks pretty dead to me, Sion."

"I bet it would be even lighter to carry, then," she replied. *"I like its silvery hue. Why is it that color?"*

"In ancient times ... it has been dead a long while, Sion. I'm amazed it has not been taken over by termites. I think it must have been struck by lightning. With time, the sun has bleached its surface."

"There are no termites here. It is strong. I want it, Cy. It would be tall enough for my first floor supports. It looks like that lightning has made more. Look! There are many like it, a whole patch. I want some of these, too!" She ran from tree to tree, examining each, running her hand up and down their polished lengths.

"I could leave some of the branches on, some of them have stubby branches. I would hang crystals from these to catch light from my windows."

He smiled. Not only could she, she would do exactly as she wished.

"Let's tie a ribbon around the ones you want. Then, I can send my boys out with a few donkeys to pack them back for you. Take out that red ribbon you have in your hair. I think it would work, if we cut the pieces short. Do you mind if I cut it in pieces?"

"I have lots of ribbons. It is okay." She fumbled with her fingers. *"It's all tangled,"* she replied. *"It kept coming undone for me while I had my hands in clay. I tied it so it would not loosen."*

"Let me help you. Come on, let me help you. I can see it. You can't. You are only getting the knot worse. How you can be so patient as to coil a bigger-than-life tree, day in and day out, but have no tolerance to undo a simple knot, I'll never know!" He struggled with the knot.

"Sion, when was the last time you washed your hair?"

"Uum, three days ago, I think. I put it in braids so it wouldn't get too tangled."

"Three days ago ... I think?" He tried to hide his disgruntled mirth. "Why not just brush it each day? Then, you will see there will be no knots."

"I've been so busy, Cy, and if I did, it still would tangle so easily. While I worked ... even my braids come loose. I have been so eager to finish, I didn't want to take the time ... I really didn't remember."

"You have spatters of clay in here, as well. Yuk, Sion, you really need a bath!"

She looked at him. It wasn't the first time he had reminded her. *"Okay. I guess I should clean up, especially since I won't need to get dirty again, tomorrow. I'm finished, Cy!"* She undid her braids and shook her head out, combing the ripples out with her fingers, which got stuck.

"Take that shift of yours and wash the clay out. You shouldn't be breathing the dust. It will dry out soon if we hang it on a bush."

"What does it matter? So I'm dirty! So what? I am hungrier than I am dirty! I am really starving." Her hair streamed down her back in total, beautiful disarray. She untied the knot of her linen, and it fell to her feet. She picked it up, gathered Daysong, undid the baby's linens, and strode toward the pool.

"This pool may be a little cooler than some, if I remember right," Cy cautioned. "I'll be building the fire." He turned to place a stone. The vision of her nakedness with all that hair streaming about her body tore at his heart.

"What's the matter with you?" Sion called out to him from the water, a hint of irritation in her eyes. *"Come, join us!"* She motioned with her hands.

"Sion, when you were ten years old and we came to this pool you looked a little different than you do now."

"Different?" She frowned, holding Daysong upright, and letting the baby splash her little hands and toes in the cool stream. Daysong

giggled and Sionee joined her in mirth as the two splashed at each other.

"Well, back then, when you were ten years old, your body was lithe as a willow, and as straight."

"With no breasts, you mean?" She giggled and splashed water in his eyes as he joined them.

"Well, yes... and other parts of you, too, have changed."

"Oh? It is just me still, after all these years." She teased him, splashing more water into his eyes. *"So what about you? Cy, you got quickly into the waters."*

"Would you care to find out?"

"Well ... not really. It is your concern, but let us hope that a fish doesn't see it, and think it is a worm."

With that he took Daysong from her arms and held her securely with one arm, while he pushed Sion completely under the water, letting her squirm in protest ... but a moment before he released her.

"The water is muddy now." She sputtered. *"Did you expect me to actually look?"*

"No. I only hoped."

"You hoped?" She asked, blinking her eyes innocently. *"Why would I want to?"*

"Sion, we are no longer ten years old."

"But, come on now ... we have seen each other naked before. Does it really matter?"

He was silent, not sure how to make her understand. She wasn't like most girls. He'd been offered before, and some of the older priestesses had been pleasing. In his heart, though, there was just one girl ... who stood naked in the water he was in now.

He tried to focus his attention on her eyes. When he came out of the water, she might, indeed, be shocked to see that he had grown considerably, himself.

In the water, they played a game with Daysong. Sionee faced Cy, just a bit apart. The two of them tossed the baby gently back and forth above the water. He held the tiny girl beneath her armpits and dangled her small toes in the cooling waters, swishing her back and forth, making waves form in circles about them. She giggled in glee. Her chubby little cheeks were red and flushed against her pale skin.

"Her cheeks are so red," Cy observed. "Is she well?"

"She gets that way when she is happy. I think we notice it because her skin is paler than yours or mine. Eah's cheeks do the same thing."

When Daysong's little lips began to shiver in the coolness of evening, they realized they had talked overlong, and must get her out of the water.

By then, Cy, too, had a shiver ... a big one.

When Sion turned to wrap the baby, he stepped quickly out of the water, and tied a linen around his waist, loosely.

Sion sat down by the fire and fed Daysong a pouch of milk.

"I haven't been feeding her as much of the milk lately," She explained. *"She is growing fond of the barley mush and sauced apple. Recently, I have been gathering duck eggs for her. She really likes that."*

Cy left for a few minutes and came back with beautiful soft golden apples, streaked with flecks of soft red, and a large handful of plump brown mushrooms, freshly washed in the creek.

They put an apple chunk onto a thin pointed stick, then, put a mushroom on the top. They pierced the two items alternating one, then the other until several had been stacked on the stick.

~~~

Over the glowing coals of the fire they held the sticks and roasted a fine evening meal. The juice of the sweet apple dripped down the sticks and infused the mushrooms with a syrupy juice.

"Uuuuuum, Cy. I don't think I ever tasted anything more delicious. Where did you become so skilled in the art of cooking?"

"I spend many nights alone as I search for exotic woods and other materials found in the wilds to fashion my crafts with. Usually I have only a stick in my hand with which to cook. And, sometimes, all I have are apple leafs or pine branches, to cover me beneath a cool night sky, as my blanket."

In contentment, Sion and Cy ate the roasted apples and

mushrooms while Daysong slept beneath linens spread onto a well-leafed ground. The sound of the creek and the cracking of glowing embers brought them peace, as the two of them were caught within the fascination of the gently flickering flames. Sionee let herself fall into the circle of his arms, resting the back of her head against his chest.

"*Cy,*" Sion began at last as she bit into another char-flamed soft piece of warm apple sweetness. *"Why do you suppose Coelle told me that you and she were lovers? Did you ever?"*

"Coelle was a lovely little thing, Sion. So young ... she barely had enough form for a man to grasp hold of ... and so innocent, as well. I was not without temptation, however, to take her up on her offer."

"Her offer?" Sion had never thought of Coelle as so bold.

"She was eager. I did not even ask her."

"She wanted to? But did you?"

"Sion, I do not know why she insisted that I was the father. I just think that she would have liked me to be. I barely kissed her ... and yes it was sweet. But that is all I did.

"We talked about sharing. She really liked me, Sion. Hadn't you noticed? She always liked me. Every time I turned around she was there, even following me, now and then. I did not fail to notice that she always watched me with those big golden eyes of hers, beneath her long lashes. "

"Did you?" Sion insisted.

"Sionee, were you really sick?" He asked quickly. "You left in such a hurry that afternoon. I was so happy to see you, and my eyes followed you as you left. I was hoping you would have lingered with us that beautiful spring afternoon."

"Yes, I was sick. My stomach felt like it would twist and turn into many pieces."

"I think Coelle may have been a little ill, herself. What did the two of you eat ... berries do you suppose?"

"I cannot remember much of that morning at all, only that I was feeling ill."

"She begged me over and over. After our initial kiss, she touched me."

"*Oh, please, Cy. I didn't need any details.*" Sion turned her head in a frown and held out her palm, turning it back and forth in disgust.

"When I looked into her eyes, I thought I saw something. I think she must have been sick also."

"*But she specifically said it was sweet ... so sweet ... unlike when ... Cy, do you really think it was that bad doing it with him?*"

Cy stood up in disgust. "Sion. Oh, come on now. How should I know? You, on the other hand, Sion ... rather, I should ask you. Have you ever? After all, both you and Coelle came off that mountain together. Maybe both of you ... Maybe those fish heads have a super durability along with their big heads."

Sionee clutched her stomach. "*It is cold, Cy. I'm so very, very cold. Take me home, please.*" In the distance above her head, a night owl hooted.

"*Go away!*" She hooted back.

Chapter Thirty-eight

Earth, water, air, and fire ... the most basic of Gaia's elements. Sionee had called them all to join her in the birthing of her tree.

The clay was Gaia's body, rich in fertile matter. Water made her body pliable in the image of spirit. The air was her breath, which infused the clay with a solid strength to stand tall. It was the fire however, that burned hot and bright ... and brought forth the spirit to come join the tree ... and ignite it with the spark of life.

For the last three weeks, waiting for the tree to completely dry to the point where no remaining moisture produced a coolness to the hand, Sionee and many eager helpers finished the final preparations.

A mountain of dry wood had been gathered through the months of the tree's creation. The wood was sized and stacked in various piles near the tree.

Enough wood, surely. The task would require plenty. But something else was needed, still ... and plenty of that too. It involved something of a smelly nature ... sheep manure ... donkey piles ... deer and gazelle balls ... any poop of an animal nature would serve fine, as long as they were well dry. Sion had reminded the bearers of her beautiful gifts.

Some of Cyex's boys had thought they were playing a joke on her when they brought forth dried mammoth dung in great piles. But Sion was delighted, and she rewarded the bearers with the brightest of smiles.

The dung served to hold the heat of the flame within, and release it back ... slowly. On the first of the firing process, it was important to slowly dry any last hidden bits of water the clay still retained.

Inside the hollow of the vertical shaft of the tree interior, a goodly stack of unfired bowls, and plates, and pottery of all kinds had been put in place to also receive the power of the fire. Large crocks, made especially for the cooking huts ... and jugs, too, were plentiful.

Cy had brought some of his and his student's wares. There were pipes of unfired clay, clay flutes, and large tree stump-sized pieces, which later would be strewn tightly with goat membrane to make drums. Also, there were countless little animal pieces, that Sionee had grown fond of making, for Daysong. Many mothers had requested them for their own children. Sion had taken pleasure in fashioning many for the trade system.

These were all covered in the well-dried dung, in a quantity that rose high within the tree.

Holes were dug from the outside of the kiln-like tree trunk, which extended beneath the ground, into the tree interior. There were four of these portals placed along the circle at the base of the tree. They would serve as flues to control the pressure of the turbulent flame as it danced upward in dazzling heat toward the slight upper curve of the tree's taper. Then, the heated air would flow downwards again, sending its flame to fill the entire shaft within.

While the entrance door and a few of the larger windows were covered with bricks and plaster to keep the flame within, a few of the windows and ports close to the ground were left open, and served as places to feed ever-increasing amounts of wood into the tree's flaming interior. That made the fire remain fierce and spread within, until the tree became transformed into stone.

Along with many enthusiastic assistants, Sion was expecting many observers. The alchemy of the tree would be a beautiful sight to behold. It was likely that it would take three days and three nights, a bit more or less on either side, to let the fire do its magic.

The first two days, she figured, the observers would come and go, as the visible effects of the fire would only be some smoke and steam. On those days, the tree would give up its last moisture to the fusion of its transformation, releasing the moisture back into the atmosphere.

The tree would be its own kiln. When all the water was sent forth in the steam, it would be time to force the heat within to rise in increasing increments of temperature. The tree now would be capable of gradually accepting greater heat as the flames rose higher and higher with the addition of larger pieces of wood, until it sputtered hot ... in flame color ... and roared within.

The steam would last a day and a whole night, at least ... maybe two ... but on the third day ... look out! For with the rising flame, the spectators would arrive to see the awesome sight of flame spewing from every portal, and dancing from the tapering top into the night sky, making its own music to accompany the final performance.

So it was that on the third day, Sionee began the early morning, carrying forth the preparations she had made for a spectacular evening celebration in honor of her living tree.

Daysong had begun the painful process of sprouting teeth at a most inopportune time. An elder priestess, herself having been a mother of babies, offered to watch the little girl during the firing, and bring her forth at the celebration to observe the spectacle of the flames final wrath. The kind lady agreed to take good care of her, and give her a little willow-bark tea if necessary. Sion thanked her profoundly.

"It is my pleasure, Miss Sunny Tree. Blessed Be Thou! Enjoy the fire."

She intended to, after everything she had done this far. Seeing the tree lit up in its entire length, and becoming translucent in neon fire, would be her reward for success!

Sion was so happy on this morning. She had been up late into the evening of the second day. The steam had stopped coming off the tree by late afternoon of the previous day, and the process of adding wood in ever-increasing increments had demanded much of her attention.

Toward morning, she had drifted off to sleep for a few brief hours, but the smell of smoke and baking clay brought her eagerly awake. She wondered if Eah and his sister would be among her guests this evening.

She had not used the 'buzz thing' to call him. She had no desire to understand. But on the night before the first firing began, she had sent her message on the wind, quite certain that he would feel her urge for his attendance.

Cyex was already beginning preliminaries for the evening feast, as well as the breakfast and noontime meals. Sion knew that many from her village, as well as neighboring outliers, would attend. The need to feed them was her honor to provide. She had asked him to help. She had tasted his skill at preparing simple and delightful meals in a very artful fashion, so on this occasion he would cook, and his well instructed students would make the music at tonight's revelry.

This morning, his students were passing out steaming mugs of chicory, as well as beechnut coffee. There was also ceramic steamers full of spearmint, jasmine, and rosehip tea. The soothing drinks were welcomed by all, in the winter morning, cooler air.

Cy was putting finishing touches to vast pots of steaming mushroom soup. He was stirring a flavoring of smoked sunflower oil into it, along with chopped leeks, and purple garlic flowers, and rich cream. The soup would feed both the present and the arriving guests, as it simmered slowly through the entire day. It would serve both as breakfast repast, as well as lunch, whenever anyone got hungry.

It would sate hunger well into the evening when the night feast would be served in the darkness, lit well by the light of the flame-pouring tree.

Baskets of squash bread and sunflower seed flat wedges would be available with the soup, along with an assortment of cheeses and grapes, and bowls of winter-tart apples.

Sionee sniffed the air appreciatively. For a breakfast addition, he had also prepared battered and fried golden squash blossoms, served with cherry birch syrup and honeyed mustard seeds. There were vast basketfuls of colorful hard-boiled eggs of different variety. There were tiny brown-speckled quail eggs, blue chicken eggs, white swan eggs, as well as golden goose eggs.

Sion had just sat down to eat, when she saw Eah and his sister arrive. She was delighted that they had come so early.

"Did you call?" He asked her.

"I did." She smiled at him. She hadn't seen the room beneath the tree since the night when the two of them swam in the pool.

Sion's heart beat in ... Oh, what was this? Was it fear? Was it joy? She didn't know what it was, but somehow the day seemed brighter, yet, at his presence.

She smoothed the top of her hair. Surely she couldn't look that great, though she wished she did. It was a good thing that she had washed her hair the night before, during a quick break, and had braided it tightly so that it would still look freshly done ... for the night revelry. Surely it had to look better than it did the many times of late that he had seen her with dust in her hair, or worse ... gobs of dried clay. Not that it mattered ... not at all.

She extended her hand to Ninmah, and bid them to enjoy breakfast.

She would have liked to stay, and share a cup of chicory coffee with them, at least, but she could see Cy working hard in preparations for the night meal.

"This is great, Cy!" She kissed him on the cheek. *"Can I help you with your getting ready for tonight's feast?"*

"Go have a cup of coffee with your lover," he replied.

"I will in just a bit. However, I wish to help with the evening feast. Oh ... and he's not ... !" she informed him, hurriedly with one breath.

Since clay baking was the real purpose of tonight's celebration, Cy had told Sion of a way that he prepared pieces of wild meat or fish, while he was out on a crafting rampage. He suggested that tonight's fish be prepared the same way, in honor of the clay.

They thrust fresh-caught catfish with sprigs of sea-salted rosemary, and buried the entire fish individually inside thick layers of wet clay mud. These would be baked in a fire closer to night time, and served with the evening meal.

Some of the boys were busy digging a pit, which would be lined with moist seaweed and green, soft moss. Other boys were bringing in clams and mussels, quahogs, conch, and lobster they had caught in quantity this early morning. They would be bedded in the seaweed pit, along with scallions and groundnuts, garlic and puff-balls, arrowhead tubers and sweet potato ... all sprinkled with sea salt and pepper berry. More layers of seaweed and soft moss blanketed them securely in the pit, where they would steam slowly all day long, lending a wonderful fragrance of savory anticipation.

The girls in cook training were busy preparing a stuffing of apples and purple grape to be placed inside leaf-covered whole partridges and quail, that also would roast slowly in the embers of the fires which baked the clay-wrapped fish.

All in all, Sion felt well prepared to host a great feast.

She watched in pleasure as Ea helped the boys dig the pit and line it with seaweed. He helped Sion with interest, as she thrust vast amounts of wood through the windows of her tree ... as the fire became hotter and hotter still, throughout the day.

Once, during the day, she saw Eah and Cy casually walk back into the festivity arena from the woods, engaged in rapt conversation.

Sion frowned. The last time she had seen them together, fists were swinging and Cyex had called him something really ... not nice ... to call anyone.

People from close neighboring tribes came as Sion had expected, from short distances away, to join the festivities. Sion knew they were not used to seeing the fish heads up close, but she noted with satisfaction that it seemed as if the two strangers were but people of neighboring outliers.

Ea's eyes followed Sionee in admiration the entire day, but he wove in and out of the crowd of people, well pleased at the vast opportunity to further explore the cultures of Ki ones, and their great imaginations.

Ninmah had come eagerly this time, taking care to dress a little more lightly. Ea nodded in approval at her thigh-length golden wrap, folded and wrapped much like the simple linen ones the Ki girls wore, though her fabric was of a glimmering material. Ninmah would never be seen in anything less than bright. But her earrings and necklace were simply constructed of small, white jade, rose petals with apple green jade leaf dangles, and her hair hung unfastened down her back. Ea was unprepared to see her with one braid hanging down her cheek side with a green ribbon woven within. He'd never seen her with a braid before. It was a charming custom of most of the Ki girls.

The fragrance of the steaming food was intoxicating to the senses. Laughter, wine, and wonderful camaraderie were shared by all.

The flames inside the tree were growing, minute by minute, with the continual addition of heaps of wood stoked through the windows and the portals.

The sky was beginning to darken into the evening depths, but the fire from the tree illuminated the arena most brilliantly, as the stars began to peek out over the celebration. The long-baked food was set out, and everyone cheered, helping themselves in murmuring excitement. Everyone sat down to feast together and watch the flames.

The fire crackled, and lit the tree with translucent glory. It threw fireballs and sparks dancing into the heights as its volume increased. The flame roared within, singing a song of bellowing rage.

"Now, this is ONE FIRE!" All agreed and gazed in spellbound rapture.

Sion spoke softly to Eah with her heart, and giggled in awe. She came to sit by his side, whispering a sigh. *"This is why I built the tree ... to see this!"*

Cyex sat by her other side. "Is this the chef?" Ninmah smiled at him appreciatively. Now, this was one handsome Ki creature, so lithe and well built. "I must offer my compliments. I ate white lilies once," she exclaimed to him as she sat down by his side.

"The breakfast flowers ... did you say they were squash blossoms? They were like the lilies, except the lilies made me sick. However, my brother told me it was all the coffee and the cream that made me sick. Tonight I really liked the fish ... my goodness the way it was cooked was most amazing! Who would have thought that putting it in mud would keep natural juices within? We Annunaki like our meat and fish juicy, as well. It is why we really prefer it bloody," she said all in one breath as she inched closer to Cy.

Sion was busy whispering something with Eah. Everyone sat back in relaxation, waiting to see the tree reach its zenith of flame. As they waited, they visited while they munched on the late season apple harvests of golden apples, and popped emmer kernels sprinkled with melted butter and sea salt. There was wine aplenty and cinnamon tea for the children, who were falling asleep, one by one, as their parents visited.

Cy's boys came out and played their flutes. After a while, Cy joined them. Some dancing priestesses came out and followed the dancing flute player, who stepped in lithe motion in and out of the merry crowd.

It was well past midnight when the tree bellowed forth a weary sigh from the porthole at the top. "*I have cast forth all my waters, as tears of change have besought me,*" it seemed to say, alive and throbbing in glow. "*I AM ROCK NOW!*"

The children were fast asleep by then. The spectators fell back upon the ground looking upward.

The entire tree glowed, its color having transformed during the night from pale red to brilliant ... from pale orange to deep ... and again soft pale ... until at last it was no longer just a tree. It was a spirit that danced in the shape of a tree in an incandescence of white light ... THE SACRED TRANSMUTATION WAS COMPLETE!

Sparks fell softly, now, from off the tree and from the top. White flames shot skyward like fireworks expanding into a million stars.

Sionee stood before the tree, tears of joy pouring from her eyes. "*Bless You now my Living Tree. Deep inside you I will be ... my life ... your life ... entwined will be ... root and trunk and fruit are we ... apples on this living tree.*"

Somehow, it seemed so natural, at this point ... to use the song of the living spirit within the living body. Everyone reflected on the great GNOS song ... and how it abided on this occasion. Again, their Songkeeper had given to them!

"*It is done!*" She called forth. There was no more wood put into the ports. The tree still crackled, and moaned, and glowed through the night, slowly losing its pale white luminosity, and fading to orange, to yellow, to red, as it began its cool down. It would take several days before the heat totally abandoned its place in the tree.

Sionee went to sleep at last, wrapped within Eah's arms, as he, too, fell asleep on the soft grass at the place where hill began its mountain ascent.

When she awoke at dawn, she was in Cyex's arms. Eah was fast asleep on her other side. His sister had one leg curled over Eah's, and one leg curled over one of Cy's young flute players ... the one Ninmah had danced with at the night of spring time revelries.

Sion saw that Ninmah had a wreath of white flowers on her crown, and a smile on her face.

"Brother," she told Ea, "I must return to my quarters," she winked at him. "I forgot my pills again ... silly me!" Ea looked at her indulgently. "And, Adapa has teeth coming in, the poor wee one. I need to insure his comfort."

Sion's ears perked up. Daysong was going through the same ordeal. Last night, after the food, and a little of the fire spectacle, the older priestess had taken her back to the maiden huts to put her to bed with a hot water pouch on her cheek.

"*Who is Adapa?*" She asked Ninmah. "*Is he your son?*"

"Mine and Ea's," Ninmah replied, saying nothing else, when she saw Ea shake his head as if to hush her.

Sion was a little surprised that Eah had never told her he had a son, who was the same age as Daysong.

"*Eah,*" she addressed him. "*Daysong is learning to walk and growing so fast. Perhaps we can take the babies on a picnic so they can romp together. Ninmah, we would love you to join us.*"

Ea did not respond. "We will be off, then, Ninmah." He turned and kissed Sion on her cheek, and softly whispered in her ear. "I will see you in a day or two, darling." Then, he disappeared with Ninmah through the cedars.

Sion sat on the grass with Cyex and shared breakfast with him. Truly she was ravenous after the task she had been attending to. She giggled with Cy, and explained to the guests that still joined them, that it would take about three days for the tree to cool down before she could remove the bricks from the portal door, and go inside to examine the work of the fire.

"Oh, yes." She smiled, enjoying the rich roasted dandelion root coffee that Cy had placed in her hands, thick with cream and honey.

She enjoyed three thick apple spice muffins, fresh from the stone hearth he had fashioned at the site. They were drenched in butter, and fresh new-made purple grape jelly.

She wished that Eah had stayed for breakfast.

Chapter Thirty-nine

Everything was perfect to her most profound wishes, almost. She didn't know if ever there could be a better place than the one she was in, except than if she could repose her restless soul, ever running to escape the image of haunting eyes.

But she was learning to live with that image, like one who lives through a bad dream and is happy when morning arrives. Just how brighter could her day actually get?

The tree had held its form to life, in a birth which sprang forth to support the reality of strong thought. Its roots held up an image of breathtaking beauty.

Sion called her tree the story tree. "Why?" She was asked.

So she sang another song that had been told before, by Songkeepers who reminded the people of wisdom.

"When you look at my tree ... haya ... haya ... yaha ... haya ... aya ... ayah ... aaaaaaaa .... Remember the story, my friends. Know well the story the tree sings as it stands in the silence. Can you hear it sing to you?

"Its roots in the earth, it will stand in the wind ... in the flash of lightening, it will be strong ... In good times and bad times ... in sad times, in joy ... it will age and fade ... but stand, still beneath the sun and the moon and the stars ... while birds raise their voices with song in its heights ... and spiders spin their web from branch to branch ... and stars dance above its curves ... and rain falls to quench it's thirsy roots ... and vines grow upward ... and moss grows downward ... and apples grow on every limb to sustain life."

She climbed a ladder, and hung golden apples she had fashioned from clay on the knobby branches of her tree ... apples polished with the gold dust that Sionee had adorned herself with on the night she first had danced.

She invited many visitors to come in, and see how the fire had polished the inside of her tree in beautiful colors of molten earth, and perceive how the universe could be caught by a space, then, let go through the portal of the tapering hole at the top.

Tales of Alsionee's Song Tree spread throughout the outliers, near and far, and was whispered of over all of the Snake of the Sea. "In the northern cove of the Snake's mouth, lives the girl who dances with the fish from the stars." The story was repeated over and over at many a nightfire song.

"The girl who lives in the story tree, sings songs that are truly worth hearing. She sings of wisdoms the bad fish head do not perceive ... all this without words on her tongue. She sings in thoughts ... of what spoken words clothe truth, in lies.

"This girl is blessed, though, by who we are forgetting, for we have not heard her singing in person. We do not know if it was She Who Creates By Thinking, or what she, herself thought ... or what the fish head brought her. Is it true that this fish head is not like the ones in our Major? It is said that it was he who helped her. This one brought her clay with which she built a tree. And, this one helped her dig beneath the earth, for it is said that the tree goes up and it goes down ... and it touches both earth and sky."

By the time Sionee had pushed aside the bricks three days after the fire, someone had been busy, beneath.

Her entrance room with the cobb frog had been cut with conformity to where the upper floor shelves would rest, upwards the trees vertical height. Eah had understood her intentions. She had wanted the floor shelves to stack in the heights on the same side of the tree. They would be like half shelves, leaving the entire other half of the tree open ... up and down, so she could see from beneath the base all the way up the tree interior to the sky ... and float in the pool in the below, while gazing up to the stars at night.

Each of the shelf floors would create its own room up the tree hollow. Sion planned five major spaces, including the cooking floor, each one atop the other. Going up the tree interior and starting with the pool cavern beneath, the next level was the cooking floor. Then, a sitting floor, followed by two top on top sleeping floors. Of course, there also were the hollows created in the bulges, and sculptural designs of the tree. These could be used for other purposes, like the eye closets, the cheek nooks and the forehead round, which made the sitting room just a bit larger. There were also the root hollows and the small rooms off the amethyst room. There was actually quite a bit of space for living and storage of all kinds. This was going to be so much fun to decorate and furnish her home within a tree.

While the view going up was quite spectacular with the sky crowning the tree with cloud and star, viewing the downward portion was like being in an entire different world. Sion climbed down a carefully constructed ladder that *someone* had built of flat wood rounds, to insure safety when climbing down. The stairs spiraled from a single pole that extended down to the steamy pool of shining amethyst reflection.

Someone had already lit the torches so she could see. The entire cavern was a sanctuary of soft glowing, fire breathing, amethyst crystal points that jutted downward in various hues of stalactite purple light.

There were small, natural shelves within the amethyst walls, which Eah had smoothed and covered with layers of gleaming hematite sand. Also, sparkling linens of fresh white had been spread for reclining comfort. One merely had to climb up a rope ladder and sleep within if they desired, or just lie down and dream above the mirrored pool. Oh, my!

There was barely time to look at everything. Already Cyex had arrived with a hoard of boys to put in the floor shelves. He was busy measuring and laying out flat planks of smoothed and fragrant cedar.

Sion climbed up the stairs to welcome him. Then, she saw that Eah was smiling down at her from the sky hole at the top.

"Good morning, Daffinina!" He winked at her, as he climbed in and folded his wings.

"Alsionee!" Cyex shouted upward as Eah swung down on a rope from the top. Cy hoisted one of the gnarled silver juniper tree lengths to begin the spiral for the staircase that went upward.

As the boys began laying out planks for the three upper floors, Eah joined Cy in the building of the stairs.

~~~

That night, Sionee slept beneath and between goose-down stuffed linens on a swinging bed that hung from the ceiling above. The hammock conformed to every curve and every move of her body. The goose-down linens were puffy and soft. She slept sweetly, folded in feathery comfort, and her dreams were sweet. She slept on the lower bedchamber for now, until she collected all her things for her own bedchamber above.

Daysong slept close to the rounded wall in a small bowl-curved wicker bed. Cyex and Eah had both insisted on placing a railing on the edge of each half floor. "They can be removed as Daysong gets older," Eah had assured her.

"You may keep them up for your other children, also." Cy finished Eah's statement. She had looked at both of them, frowning. Eah and Cy, had smiled. "When you have them." They both added.

Sion had certainly ignored the comment. "*Daysong is too little to know she could fall and really, she will be walking soon. She is beginning to climb ... .*"

"Everywhere!" Eah finished her thought quickly.

"*Well, yes, Eah, as you well know. Surely, your son also climbs? Thank you both!*" Sion looked up at the two men, blinking her golden topaz-hued eyes at both of them.

~~~

As Sionee woke up, listening to Daysong's soft breathing, she thought about how Eah had not answered her. In the early morning, she could hear the wind rise up softly. It pushed wind song through the open port of the treetop. The curve had been fashioned just so, on the same principal as the curve on the lips of Cyex's globular horns. The air, blowing inward, vibrated a sighing hum of greeting.

Sion wondered if she was in a dream or something. She blinked, rubbing her sleepy eyes. She became wide awake as a melody of wind chime tinkled in the air.

Sion swung out of the hammock and lifted Daysong, still

sleeping, into her arms. Holding Daysong on her hip, Sionee scurried down the spiral ladder, thrusting open the door.

Now awake, Daysong peeled in giggles of delight as the ringing of one hundred chimes tickled her ears.

Sion stepped outside her portal door. Her heart stood still to listen. A choir of tinkling voices sang music on the wind song of morning.

They were everywhere, hanging in rhapsody with the winds every motion. On every available branch and limb, from every tree that the story tree neighbored, from the vines that spread from branch to branch between the distance of two close trees, from the short stubby limbs of her story tree ... all the way up, someone had placed wind chimes in every available space.

Holding her giggling daughter, Sionee ran from tree to tree trying to look at each one. Tinkle, tinkle, tinkle. Each chime was unique, and lent it's personality to the wind voices of Feyri. Some vocalized loudly. Some hummed softly. Some lent vibrations of scant whisper. Some teased in promise of chiming. Some rang like a bell. Some had an alto-depth akin to the stirring of a drum. Some peeled high like the shree of an eagle. And, still others clacked, while some hissed like snake song. There were the echoed whispers of a single raindrop as it fell into a deep pool, and reverberations of one hundred happy mourning doves on a spring morning. Other of the sounds pierced the morning air like a loon song. Some were as cicada, rapid chirps, and again some were soft as a butterfly-wings in flutter.

Her first thought was that Cyex had done this. His skill at the making of beautiful sounds was evident everywhere. They were done in his style. Many were thin and straight, made in a manner as he had made his clay flute, by molding them on pieces of round reed. Others were carved from cedar. And, many were shell, found in the tidal pools of low tide. These let wind whisper the sound of the sea into the chorus ... ah!

"Cy!" She sang in delight, her arms thrown up in amazement. *"You did this?"* She called. *"For me?"*

He stepped out from the cedar trees, where he had been hiding.

"Twit… twit… twit… twit… twit…." Kinga was on his shoulder, cocking his head. *"Love is crazy!"* He chirped.

Then, she saw the reflection of sun on something gold. A spark of white brightness momentarily blinded her. What was this?" Sionee's jaw dropped in wonder. Her hand flew upward to smooth her long unbraided hair which hung in ripples across her shoulders and down her back.

"Eah!" She gasped in startled sigh. Ea stepped from the cedar trees. Both of them stood side by side, well pleased with themselves.

Kinga had a long red ribbon in his beak. He flew from tree branch to tree branch, weaving the ribbon in and out, himself well pleased.

"It was both of you?" She exclaimed in wonder. As Kinga looked forlornly at her, she added, *"The three of you."* She smiled at the bird. *"But… but…!"*

"Your love boy … he instructed me … ," Ea began. Ea put his finger up to her lips to hush her, though truly her words were silent. "He showed me the flutes. When I held them together I noticed how when they touched each other their hollow chambers made a chime sound. Oh, and I can now … maybe … play you a song on the flute … not as good as he does, though." Eah grinned.

"Yes, your old lover came up with the idea for these," Cy began.

"But… he's not… ." Sionee was not sure which of the two to assure. Cyex laughed at her.

"We both made great wind sound, wouldn't you say, Alsionee Tree Song."

"Daffinina, you like the music the wind plays?" Eah beamed.

She looked up and saw above her head that many of the chimes were made out of both gold and silver, and that many were designed with straight hollow bodies, textured with a reptilian skin, with heads of snakes that had tiny, glistening ruby and emerald eyes.

She didn't know what to say … or sing … or whisper … from her heart … or what. So, she put Daysong down to toddle about, giggling in glee beneath the songs. Giggling, herself, Sionee ran to Cyex and kissed him full on the lips, long and lingering. He fell backwards. Then, she turned to Eah and kissed him thus ... and planted a kiss on Kinga's beak. *"twit ... twit ... twit ...!"*

She fixed the men breakfast, baking berry bread on her new hearth. Afterwards, she and Daysong hung crystals from the knobs of the silver juniper tree poles, as well as from the few extending branches left on them, that stretched their spindles out into the room.

During the day, the crystals caught light from the window slits she had disguised in the outer bark of the tree. As well, the light from the sun sent its ray down from the portal above. As the rays of light danced across the hollow of her tree interior, the light turned into multi-prism rainbow wisps of ballet. The light rays danced about until night time came. Then, the stars took over.

Chapter Forty

Win the negotiation? Never! He would see to it. Not ever!

His father's pride had been hurt. It was more so for Ninurta. The look his father had given him. and the words he spoke were insufferable.

Marduk had made a fool out of both of them. Afterwards, Enlil had offered to give Ninurta lessons in fighting skills. "I could teach you son. I am well skilled."

"Yes, Father. I know, as does all of Nibiru, that you learned from your father ... blah, blah, blah ... who won his supreme rank as King with a mere wrestle ... blah!"

"Father, you and I know that it was more than the actual fight that allowed Anu to win. It was the way he played the game."

Enlil had laughed, then. He said that perhaps he could persuade Enki on that one, but as Enki was Marduk's father, it wasn't likely, because ...

"I've never been more sorrowful to have such a weak son. Just look at you! You even look like a scrawny sex miscreant. I wouldn't have even threatened Marduk with the whip, if you had upped him with the punch."

"He caught me off guard, father."

"That is your weakness ... and mine as well ... as it is my misfortune to be your sire! Would that you were Enki's son, and that Mordukku was mine!"

Ninurta seethed. He was no weakling ... as his father ... and Marduk ... would soon be discovering."

"Slaves ... slaves!" He bellowed. Five naked men came immediately to his bid. These were the uncouth of Nibiru, the real weak. Ninurta felt his blood turn cold in an excitement of the power that was his for the taking.

His face remained emotionless, stony, as he walked down the

line of law breakers. Of course, these were perhaps the finest of the uncouth. He ran his hand over the bare hairy chests, as he walked past them slowly, stopping now and then, to run his fingers over a gleaming back. He motioned for the new slaves to turn around. They were well-oiled, glistening with big and beautiful muscle ... all of them. He certainly would not have anything of a puny nature doing service for him. These appeared as suitable.

"On your knees!" He ordered. One of the slaves moved just a wee bit slowly. Ninurta walked around him, thrusting him forward with his jewel-sandaled foot. The slave fell, bent over on his knees with his elbows to the ground.

Ninurta kept his stony face. With his whip he put a stripe across the well-muscled ass. Ah! He ran his hand over the stripe, soothing the glistening skin, rubbing the oil well over the swollen welt. He made a mental note of the quivering he felt on the lubricated cheeks.

"There will be a release for you, my wayward heroes, for a job well done, which I expect from each of you. If you fail, I will arrange a ship to transport you to Mars, which I can assure you, has no breath of air left. You would not live long there. I have called only the finest among you to redeem yourselves, and share, as well ... in the reward ... if you bring forth, as I instruct.

"As you know, seeing as you are all among the misfits who got caught in the kidnapping of my father during the mine issue, our workers in the mine have grown even more tired. All of you have toiled countless hours in the mines, especially those of you who have worked with Marduk, when Mars still had atmosphere. And now that so many have returned to Ki, what is here for our working heroes, but more toil and boredom?

"And yet, our successes, with the persuasion of the lu to do our work, is easing all of your work days, and you are left with more hours of leisure, except for those of you who have been called to my father ... or my own ... in personal service.

"We have succeeded in forcing a work ethic on the lu, as well as we have with you, our slaves ... my heroes." Ninurta struck his whip through the air, making a most impressive whirring sound. "We are garnering our successes!

"As you know, Mordukku, who officiates all Annunaki miners, is currently engaged elsewhere on the other side of Ki, attending to the gold in the far west holdings."

Ninurta lifted his chin in what he felt was a most authoritative manner. "While he is gone, I wish to reward his hard working heroes for their labors, as well as relieve each of you from the boredom so overwhelming among you young ones. This includes all of you, my heroes. Your success in accomplishment of this small task will negate the crimes for which you so unfairly have been charged. You will become numbered among the Annunaki ... free!

"You have all served capably with your acquisition of the lu that we brought here from the Abzu, where they were created to toil.

"But for you and for all the Annunaki males who came down to Ki and have suffered so intensely for so long a time, there has been an unease of a different nature.

"Few of our females have come down, and the suds who volunteered are do-gooders with small interest, and a few wives who serve only their lawful husbands. And, then, there are the whores who have been used so many times, they are flaccid in our reaches. There are so few."

The heroes began to nod. "How do we toilers of the mines receive the offerings of a wife? While some of the suds may be willing, there is such an undesirable availability, their servitude to the heroes are quite unrewarding. The ladies who came with us are of a spoiled nature, thinking themselves superior to a miner or a lawbreaker!"

How could he say this? It would be a great way to achieve the loyalties of all of Marduk's men, and win them to his side.

"I have come to the acquaintance of some of the lu. I have heard them say that their women and the natural Ki women, as well, are highly skilled in the arts of pleasing male properties with tight and hungry holes to fill, which, indeed, are of a more pleasant nature than are the holes of the mines ... arar.

"This matter is little spoken of by us, who are of the fine nature of Nibiru, but have any of you ever really looked at one of the naturals? Have any of you ever noticed how beautiful the Ki ones are?"

This was going well. He began to allow a smile.

"You, who were supreme in helping to persuade the lu to toil in the mines, I call you forth to another task."

They were catching on, whispering back and forth among themselves, already beginning to plan.

"Go get them boys! The females! Bring them forth, the best! We shall choose among them!"

"And, you! Did I hear your fellows call you, Ennuzzi? Come with me, Ennuzzi." He bid the slave whose lash mark curled across his buttocks like an angry snake, glistening.

He, himself, had no need for a female. They were an inferior lot, especially in the pleasures of sex. Though occasionally, they could be tolerated, if necessary, which wasn't often. He preferred other, more tight means.

Chapter Forty-one

"*I feel like when I am floating in these waters I am in the world of my ancient ancestors.*" Sionee sent Eah her thoughts of peace, as she lay back in the shimmering warm pool, and dreamily gazed at both her amethyst sky and her star sky above.

"*Right now, I believe I could be in the purple world where spirits dance on a different star. Did I really die that day when I went through that tunnel, and did I really drown? Did I dream that I built a beautiful tree home, and that I have a sweet little baby, and that you are my angel? Hey, Eah, are you spirit?*"

"Why do you ask?" He floated beside her.

"*You come from a different star. You are different from the people that I know. Your understanding of beauty is vastly above and beyond any perceptions of normal beauty. Oh! Eah, when I look up at the amethyst at night, in the light of the torches fire, when I am bathing in these clear waters, it is so awesome, I almost ... I said almost ... forget about looking up to the stars.*"

"Why not just enjoy them both, and quit trying to decide which one you like best. Each has a place of value in your life, to be cherished. The dimensions of your universe are for your many eyes to enjoy.

"Of course, I am spirit, as well are you. But then, on my world, we call it code ... but you understand ... spirit ... code ... the same thing."

"*But there is really so little that I know about you. Hey, don't splash at me. I am relaxing ... or trying to. I'm thinking.*

"*I am weary. I have been chasing Daysong all day and I am really, really tired. My legs ache from all the running, and now that she is asleep, I'm really glad that she is asleep.*

"*But you are a man, and fathers do not spend all their whole days on one project, which is the minding of their children.*

"I bet Ninmah is doing a fair amount of running about, herself. I have heard that boys are even more active than girls. It is what the mothers all tell me at nightfire."

"Don't bet on it." He said. My sister doesn't spend all day chasing my son, she is a nurse and has sciences to attend to, as well."

"Who watches him, then ... ?" Sionee was puzzled.

"Other suds who work at the science facility. Adapa is beloved by all. His older brothers adore him, and will teach him and guard him all the days of his life. Ninmah adores him. Even my wife, Damkina, loves him well.

"I have no pleasure greater than the moments I spend with him every day. It is I who tuck him into bed at night, and sing him to sleep."

"I still do not understand why you never told me about your son, who must be about the same age as Daysong. Come on, Eah, not even a mention! Because we are friends, I have been thinking I really do not know you. Oh, and I think that I love you."

Her face was red and she added quickly, *"Now, tell me a little about you and your sister's son. Is he as active as Daysong?"*

"Quite more so. Ninmah loves him as a mother, but she is not his mother."

"Oh? I thought you and Ninmah ... I think you have been a busy one, Eah. How many women have you loved?"

"Well, Daffinina, it is like this. As you know, I came from a different star. Our peoples are different. Our cultures and traditions, as well as our way of living, is not the same as how your people embrace life. Your question is a difficult one to answer, so I will just tell you.

"I have been with more ladies than I can count on all my fingers and all my toes times ten ... ten times. He tried to multiply the numbers in his head. "Then double it ... Oh, maybe triple it."

"What? Is it a mere game to you?" In the waters to her chin, she backed away.

"Daffinina, I could count every one of them, and tell you each of their names. I loved them all. I must tell you, I have lived longer than the numbers you could imagine. Remember, you asked me once how old I was."

"You said it didn't matter."

"It doesn't. I have heard the stories you people tell, and we both know that the spirit is ageless.

"Our bodies for our spirits are of durability far longer than your bodies. Perhaps if I share this with you, you might understand a little, why there have been so many women in my life."

"I don't care how many," she began.

"Of course, you do," he said.

"My age is not defined by the spins of your Gaia's sun. But according to time, in the way that you know it ... oh, let me see ... one hundred thousand ... oh, maybe one hundred thousand and nine hundred million years ... Oh, Daf ... I am really old. I am most ancient of days."

"You don't look that old. Eeeeeeeeeeeeowow! My goodness. Don't you people die? Are you all that old?"

"Oh, I am but a young one on my planet. So you can see, I really have had only a few lovers. One or two."

"I cannot conceive of this! How can someone not die? How can one's spirit grow with the experience of only one body for all those years, Eah? With a body life that long, how does your spirit ... hmm? I forgot the question ... I was trying to find the way to ask."

"This is why perhaps I did not mention my new young son."

"But he is like a mere fraction of a second, in your own life, to you?"

"Daffinina, no. He is far more than just a piece of a second. There is much about me that I haven't or could not even begin to tell you ... all about myself. Some of it is good, some of it is bad. I really hope you do not ask me about the bad. I have had a long life, Daffinina."

"I do not see anything but light when I look into your eyes."

Ea sighed. "About Ninmah, Daffinina. She has always been the most important woman in my life." Perhaps by telling her this, it would begin to better acquaint her with the Annunaki lifestyle, because it was becoming an unpleasing fact that there was more that he should tell her ... much more, and he didn't think her pure mind could understand. And, he didn't wish to burden her with it all. But how could he not tell her ... about the worst thing he had ever done in all of his aeons ... and that it concerned her?

"More about Ninmah, Daffinina. She is the mother to many of my daughters."

"Now, I get to hear about your daughters and hers?"

"On Nibiru it is a much desired thing for a brother to mate with his half-sister. She is just half-sister, Daffinina. I was only following the traditions of my people. It is said that it keeps the bloodline pure.

"I am a prince on Nibiru. It is well expected. Ninmah never bore me a son, only girls. She was going to be my wife before Damkina; and I, as I still do, loved her well.

"But on the night of our promise to marry and become partners, she had sexual intercourse with my brother. She bore him a son! I, firstborn of our King ... she bore me no sons!

"When my father found out, he was furious with her. He issued that henceforth Ninmah be wife to none, mistress to many! It was in the verdict that she be a sud, always a sud!"

Sion's mouth stretched into a straight line of perplexity. *"Eah, I am really trying not to judge about that. I told you before, when you tried to explain this marriage thing to me, that it seemed like a foolish thing. Do you love your sister?"*

"Probably more than I have ever loved any woman of Nibiru. One day, however, on the world of Ki, I saw this beautiful Daffodil growing on a hillock by the sea, whose petals were lit by a light I have never beheld before in all my aeons ... ever ... ever.

"Oh, Sion, I do not believe in comparing. I do believe that I have never, ever got the chance to really experience love before I found you. Emotion this strong is forbidden on my world."

"What! Forbidden? How can the heart be forbidden?"

"It really can't, Daffinina. In truth, I am a miscreant on my world, who does not abide with the laws of my people."

"*I do not understand your laws,*" Sionee said in wonder. "*My people have only an understanding of abiding love for each of our fellows.*"

"It is my fervent hope that it will never be different for you, Daffodil."

"*This is all more than I can think of, Eah. I do have one little question, that I think is a big question. In the vast world of your forever, it is not so important. I am still curious about Adapa. What about his mother? His real mother? Where is she? Who is she?*"

Ea was silent for more than just seconds. He was deep in thought. He avoided the answer while trying to help her understand sort of at the same time.

"On my world, all female take care of the new hatchlings. Who the mother is, is of small consequence, except for the matter of their blood bio."

"*What? Did you say hatchlings? Like they are baby birds or something?*"

"Birth, too, is different among our peoples, Daffinina. Babies are hatched, so to speak."

"*I do not get it.*"

"It is painful to have a child, Daffinina. You saw what happened to your friend, Coelle. See, I remember her name. Female of all species suffer travail in the birth. We have provisions of medicine to make it easier. When a couple conceive, the baby is removed from the mother's womb when it is but a germ.

"The beginning life seed is placed in an incubator that comes complete with a beating rhythm that simulates the mother's heartbeat, as it provides ultimate safety for superior growth of the child. Sometimes ... and even often ... our females also conceive without the womb ... the same incubation process. We get to watch our babies grow, as they grow inside sort of a window box.

"Their mothers suffer no pain, no risk of danger to themselves or the child. Also, nutrients may be fed to ensure that the child has better opportunity for an advanced bio body."

"*Eah, Eah! Stop ... stop! You cannot be serious! This makes me ill!.*"

I cannot conceive."

Before it was too late, if it wasn't already, before he could even to begin to hope for a more serious relationship with this girl, he would have to help her understand that ... Oh, but she could.

Chapter Forty-two

"The colors are very beautiful!" Taya and Sionee sat in the sunny kitchen level of the freshly-fired new home. They were tearing strips from pieces of Daysong's swaddling linens. Even though Sion had shared many, and used many, there was still many.

"Why do they make them in so many colors? Like flowers in a meadow, or colors of a rainbow?" Taya asked.

The fish heads never do anything in ordinary ways, Taya. We enjoy our linens fresh and white. They are so satisfying to wash. The white linens smell so fresh when I drape them over the lavender bushes to dry. I think white smells the best. I don't have much call to mess with all these colorful ones, anymore. Daysong is so growing, I couldn't keep her swaddled now, if I tried.

I have enjoyed these colorful pieces, though. Eah brought me so many. I see these colorful swaddlings drying over many a bush, now, and I think they look cheery.

"I only know one fish head man, Tay ... and his sister. I'm not real acquainted with her. I think Eah is Fey. I haven't quite understood exactly, yet.

"This ribbon he gave you is so pretty, you can see through it!" Taya giggled. "Are you sleeping with him, or what?"

"Both Eah and Cy hung the windchimes with ribbon, and they gave a piece to Kinga, Taya. It was Kinga, my bird friend, who gave me this ribbon. Is this what everyone is saying? That I am sleeping with Eah?"

"Why not Sion? I would, if I were you. He is quite taken with you. Everyone knows that he is in love with you. Who do you like best, Eah or Cy? Both are handsome, are they not? Eah is a bit older. Do you like older men, Sion? You did say he is really but a man. I would win either of their affections for myself. I have a boyfriend, already. One!" She laughed and winked at her sputtering and blushing friend.

"I *haven't.*" Sion answered her question. "*We are friends ... all of us. I didn't realize as such, until Eah and Cyex worked together to make for me the beautiful gift of chimes!*"

It was well into midmorning. The sun shone its morning song on the tree, and the first of the crystals were beginning their rainbow dance across the walls of the tree rooms.

Sion took several lengths of linen and tied them together in various random color strips. She made each knot tight and small, double-tying them for strength. Taya did the same.

"*Could you hand me the ribbon, Taya?*" Sionee tied the multicolor strands to the hand rail of the topmost level that Ea and Cyex had built for Daysong's protection. Taya was helping her fashion beautiful ropes of the colored linen, with the pretty red ribbon woven through the braids.

"I can't wait to see them hanging, Sion."

"*Thank you for helping me. It makes it so much fun!*"

Taya nodded, concentrating on twirling the thick lengths into a single braid.

Daysong cooed and giggled as she played at their side. She got herself all tangled up in the colorful strands of strips. Sionee undid her, and sat her in a swing that Cyex had made for her. The swing hung off the upper curve of the half ceiling. A small tray had been tied across her lap, both to hold toys and goodies, as well as keep her from sliding out.

Sionee went downstairs and brought back a handful of honey-crisped popped emmer kernels of wheaten berry, and placed them on the tray for Daysong to entertain herself with, while the ropes were being woven.

"*Tight ... Taya ... tight!*" Sion reminded her. "*They must be strong.*"

"Sionee, I met a fish head. He is my boyfriend."

"*Taya! You have a fish head boyfriend? I do not. He is not my boyfriend.*"

"Oh, come off it, Sion. Of course, he is."

"*Is not!*" Sion shook her head, frowning. "*Hand me that green piece over there.*" She motioned. "*Now, tell me more about your boyfriend. What is his name?*"

"The fish heads have strange names, Sionee. I can hardly pronounce it right. I call him Mars for short. It is easier to say than his given name."

"*Mars?*"

"He says that he lived there once, and that I can call him Mars. It is almost the same, Sion. What do you think of this one? Is it good?" She held the rope up.

"*It is beautiful, Taya. What is this Mars like? Does he please you?*"

"He is kind and thoughtful of me when he and I share nights."

"*You do?*" Sionee asked, astounded. "*What is it like with a fish head?*"

"Sion, it is as you have said over and over. He is just a man, but a highly apt man ... highly!" Taya giggled. "Get it?"

By evening Sion and Taya had the ropes they made hanging down from the safety edge railing. It would be a faster way down than climbing the stairs.

Sion grabbed hold of one rope and swung out, sliding carefully down the knotted braid, laughing gleefully as she landed at first level. She had apple bread with plum and hickory nuts baking inside the frog, and it smelled so good, she could hardly wait to dig in.

"*Come on.*" She motioned upward to Taya. "*It's done! I'll put a vessel of hot water on for spearmint tea.*"

Taya tied a braid. It seemed strong, so she swung out, giggling and then, joined Sion. "It was a great idea."

"*It was fun, huh?*" Sionee joined her in giggles, as did Daysong. The little girl had wet crumbs in her hair, and all over her face and belly. After the bread and tea, the girls and the baby went down the ladder to the hot pool.

After the day with their heads bent in braiding ropes, the hot water felt wonderful. Daysong floated in her tiny little canoe, while Sion and Taya lay back in the water, floating on their backs. The beauty of the amethyst reflecting the flickering light of torches, was something Sion was sure would never cease to amaze her. Taya was thrilled when she looked up into the curved portal at the very top ... and saw the stars twinkle.

Chapter Forty-three

When Sionee whistled for her unicorn, Vastari came. The beautiful white mare brought a friend with her, who followed, responding to Cyex's whistle.

The stallion was beautiful. He came to Cy and accepted the reward of the apple he offered in greeting. "Nice boy, Lightning." He stroked the long nose and patted his unicorn in affection.

Kinga came also, perched on the unicorn's horn. *"Twit ... twit ... twit ... twit ... twit .... What a couple of grand misfits!"* The bird cocked his head teasing, *"Not you my baby girl, sweet."* He lovingly twitted to Daysong.

Cyex smiled and stroked the top of Kinga's tiny head with his little finger. "He only calls names when he is attempting, quite poorly, to be friends," he explained. "Kinga, my friend, would you care to join us?"

"It depends ... depends," Kinga chortled. *"Here ...there ... I go wherever I please ... not here ... but there ... not there ... but here. As I please I shall go ... Maybe I shall ride on the horn of the unicorn for a time."*

"Yes, Kinga." Sion nodded to him twitting. *"We are going to go get moss. You can help mind Daysong."*

"To get moss? Get it where? It, as I, is here ... there ... and everywhere. What moss can be finer than that which grows right beneath both your feet already. Why must you go somewhere else to find it?"

Cyex ignored the bird. "I know where there is a lovely patch of moss. It is so green it is the color of the peridot beads you have strung over your windows in the uppermost room. It will match, quite enticingly, the carpet of moss which you are planning. Do you wish me to take the baby?"

"She would love it!" Sionee handed her daughter to Cy, who always seemed to know how to get the little girl to behave.

"Nay ... Nay." Daysong giggled, imitating the sound of the unicorn

369

as her little hand patted the stallion's nose as she had seen Cyex do. *"Bye, bye!"* She giggled as she knocked Kinga from Lightning's horn.

"Twit! I think you mean 'hello' my sweeting. Can you say 'hi'? Come on wee one ... twit ... twit ... twit ... twit ... twit ... hi!"

Cyex and Sionee took a scenic route, following one of the many little creeks that made journey to the sea.

"I believe that there is a fine pool at the moss place," Cy assured Sion as they rode their way up into the lava strewn hills.

They stopped at mid-meal and rested at a place, where the stream separated into two fingers of water on two separate courses, downward.

~~~

Sionee was busy examining the small rounded pebbles of lava that had been polished on their turbulent course to the sea. *"I like the little round ones,"* she explained to him in thought words as she lay on her belly in front of the stream. He was engaged in fixing a meal.

"Look at this! I have found a perfect little red one, and a white one, and a black one, too! Something is really smelling good, Cy."

"It will be just a bit yet, Sionee. Remember, we need to get the rocks you collect home. I know you well girl, dragging all manner of things home to make your house all pretty! Save some room for the moss!"

"These will fit in my pocket. I just need a few." Laying on her tummy and peering through the crystal clear waters, the colors of the stones were magnificent.

Daysong splashed her palm flat over the surface of the stream, sending water into her mother's eyes. Sion splashed her back, drenching the little girl's face as she giggled.

"Look Day Day ... at the spider, see! She has made a web. See how it glistens with the little drops of water on it?" The two of them watched the spider hanging before their eyes on a single thread. It began to scurry back up the gossamer invisible thread. Sionee held the tiny, impatient little hand of her little girl to keep her from reaching out

and breaking the web.

"Spider spinner ... you are the winner ... **THIS MY MOTHER TAUGHT ME HOW TO SING ... THIS YOUR MOTHER TEACHES YOU HOW TO SING ...** " Sionee crooned to her baby, cradling the squirming soft cheek next to her own, and marveling at how the sun made Daysong's downy curls the color of its ray.

She kissed Daysong on the top of her flaxen head and sang to her the song of the bubbling stream. She held the stones out in the palm of her hand. *"See how they are round, Day? The water spins each one ... around and around they tumble ... the sand and the other stones help them become smooth. Their journey to the sea polishes the imperfections off of them, and they become well rounded."*

Daysong tried to catch a golden sun ray, but couldn't seem to get hold of it. Her mother sang her the song of the sun ray.

"It's ready!" Cyex called. He had baked three pink trout on a hot stone, sprinkling them with sea salt, fine crushed juniper berry, and sorrel.

"Tonight we will have a great meal," he promised his two girls.

"It could never get better than this," Sionee told him, eagerly taking a soft and steaming morsel of savory fish. She chunked up a piece for Daysong to pick at. *"I love the lemony flavor the sorrel gives."*

Cyex handed her a perfect wild apple. After she ate the fish and finished off Daysong's leftovers, Sionee took a bite of the sweet, crisp apple. It snapped with freshness, and juice ran down her chin.

"Sionee, I suggest that when we get to the moss place, we get our beds arranged, and have our night meal. I think we should gather the moss in the morning before we leave, roll it, and get it home so you can lay it down fresh.

~~~

The happy trio rode for a little longer and came at last to the place where cedar trees split the lava flats into many pieces. Somewhere in the middle of the disarrayed stones, beneath the shade of the cedar there was a large flat, entirely covered in a vast mass of beautiful, soft green moss that bore no stones.

"We'll make our beds on the soft moss and try your carpet out," he grinned at her. "While you lay out the linens, I'll get started with dinner. I'll build a fire on these flat stones. I can bake here, and use this piece as a fine hearth."

Cyex found hawk eggs in an overhead crevice. The next task was a bit more detailed. He had noticed some katniss with roots poking out of a chunked lava flow at the nearby stream side. He found a piece of smooth lava that had a bowl-shaped dip in it. He pounded the root with another stone and put it in the dip and poured water into it. "This will take a bit, Sionee. I assure you, the cakes will be worth the wait. This flour is tasty and light as a feather."

After he poured the water in, he watched a white starch begin to separate from the bulb, and settle on the stone bowl bottom. He poured the water off and gathered the wet powdery flour, and repeated the process over and over until he had enough. He spread the mass out to dry, making a fine white flour. Truly it did take a lot of time and patience.

He stirred the flour into a quantity of sweet, mush-ripened apple, a bit of honey and some sunflower oil. Next he broke two of the eggs, frothed them into a fluffiness and added them to the mixture. Lastly he sprinkled a bit of cinnamon and a pinch of sea salt.

After he baked the flat-cakes on a hot stone, he wrapped the thin and fragrant cake in a roll around fresh steamed spears of sparrow grass drizzled in honey. As a final touch, he served the crepe with hot thick raspberry syrup. They were so good, even Daysong liked them, holding her red sticky fingers up for more. Cy proudly served her, with a smile on his face.

After the delightful meal, Sionee let Daysong play in the shallow edge of the warm hot pool that made its depth in the craggy moss-strewn flat. After her bath, Sionee wrapped Daysong in soft linen where she had made her daughter a nice warm bed. Cyex played his flute for the baby; Daysong fell fast asleep after a very exciting day in her young life.

The fire flickered gently, and Sion and Cy roasted hazelnuts sprinkled with sea salt over the coals. Sion cozied up in a comfortable position, reclining against him as she lay between his legs. Her head rested as if on a pillow, in position against his stomach. The two munched the hazelnuts in content, watching the sparks crackle off the burning log and rise to the air.

He pulled out his flute and played her a song. Her eyelids began to droop. Cyex was disappointed. They hadn't made it to the pool yet ... but this wasn't too bad ... nice and cozy.

"My mamun said that when you find a man who makes you want to become one in his arms ... ." She turned her head and looked into his eyes.

"Sion, what do you want?"

"I could be part of your arms." She spoke in her quiet way. *"You and I work well together."*

What did your mamun say happens when you find a man who makes you want to become one in the heart with?"

She sighed softly in his arms, not answering him in thought. She was already fast asleep, lulled by his song.

~~~

An owl pierced the night sky with a screeching hoot. His sharp nocturnal eye had spotted a fat mouse, a big one... a rat perhaps ... and he was hungry. He swooped low to pursue his target. Cyex felt the wind of his wings rush over both of them.

"Sionee girl, wake up! wake up! Are you dreaming?" She still slept between his knees as she lay back against his chest. He had breathed with her for hours, relishing her warm softness pressed against his body, as he reclined comfortably against the curve of a cedar tree.

She was trembling and moaning softly. He put his palm on the crown of her forehead, his fingers in her hair. He noticed that she was damp with sweat.

"Sionee!"

Sion sat up dazed, rubbing her eyes. He put his hand on her

heart and felt its motion, beating fast.

"Are you ill? You are sweating."

After she became orientated, she realized that she was quite damp with sweat.

"I'm shivering; I don't think I'm cold."

He put a linen blanket across her shoulders. Was that a tear he saw gleaming in her eye? "Sionee. It's okay, darling." He held her in his arms while she sobbed. He stroked her hair. "Let me build this fire up."

The firewood had been stacked close by. He reached over and thrust a few pieces into the still glowing embers. After a few minutes, the fire sprang to life.

He dried Sionee's tears with his fingers, making soft, soothing sounds. "Why do you cry?" He asked, hoping she would answer. Sionee seldom gave his questions answer.

"It was the owl eyes!" She answered at last, with sorrowful eyes.

"It was only an owl, sweetheart, only an owl hunting for his supper."

"No ... No! It was my dream owl."

"You had a dream? The owl screech must have frightened you."

"No! It was not that owl." Sionee looked up into the sky where she could see an owl riding an air current with a mouse in his talons. *"The dream I have ... it makes me afraid."*

"It was only a dream, Sion ... hush ... hush, darling. Everything is okay."

"Then, why do I keep dreaming it? Over and over again ... it keeps coming."

"Tell me about the dream, darling."

Sionee's sweet face was troubled. Her eyebrows curved upward in a wrinkle of dismay. *"I don't know,"* she insisted. *"I never remember anything. I have the dream often. Oh, maybe a little less lately ... It still comes. All I ever remember is those owl eyes ... and they are the wrong color of orange, Cy. They stare at me!"*

"It probably has something to do with that damned tunnel with the strange wind that we both got sucked up in. I remember the twirling colors when I first stepped in. The remembrance of it would bring anyone nightmares." Damn him. He would have to tell Ea that his damned tunnel still frightened Sionee.

"I thought maybe so at first, but they weren't the same exactly. Eah explained to me that the tunnel is a principal of an energy vibration moving, like an air current moves wind."

"What the hell?" Cyex frowned.

"Oh, they make natural things so difficult. It is their way. The tunnel is just a means of transportation, of which they have many. It seems a little much to me. We would just hike or ride around the mountain on our unicorns, perhaps take a canoe across the bend. You have seen their complicated devises ... like wings. I am certain it is not the tunnel that I am dreaming of. I really cannot decide about my dream. All I ever remember is the way the eyes glow at me. They are an orange that is not an orange ... like a brilliant fire that is not a fire."

"Oh, surely it is but a silly dream. We all have them. But you know what they say about dreams. What is in your heart, Sion, to the extent that the threat comes out in a dream? This is what I am wondering about."

"I, too, have wondered, each time I see the eyes again. I have tried to make them go away. It's been better since Daysong came into my life, and made me feel happiness with her." Sionee touched her AH-DAWN. *"Before she came, I thought I had a hole in here. I think it is still in there, though. This is why I still see the eyes."*

"But Sion, you have the most whole heart of anyone I know."

"Everyone thinks that I do. You asked me once why I made the vow to speak no words. You've wondered why I speak only in the way our peoples spoke anciently."

"You said you would tell me sometime."

"That was a mere excuse. I didn't think I could explain to anyone."

"You have your way, Sion, of making everyone hear you."

"I made the vow that I would not voice in words the song of a heart that was not whole."

"Your heart is a far way from being not whole."

"It only appears that way, Cyex. The words expressed by voice of

tongue are only an impure and muddled voice seeking to express the heart. Tongue words are only a veil to a lesser communication that is easier to express and likewise easier to twist. I don't want anyone getting any wrong songs from me."

Cyex was quiet in thought.

"So I vowed that until my heart was whole again I would speak no words with my tongue. Do you see?"

"Barely! But why have you not told me this before?"

"I've told no one, Cy. I thought that if no one saw the arrow fly through the air ... me especially ... there must not be an arrow. And if there was no arrow, it was all in my foolish fears ... fears that I didn't want chasing me ... to bite me in the-you-know where."

"Makes no sense to me." He said.

"And ... ," she said softly, her eyes frowning in the night. "If I cannot speak with a tongue that is not whole, how can I give a man only a piece of my whole, unbroken heart?"

"Sionee, darling, perhaps the love which I feel for you in my AH-DAWN could be enough to ease your fear. I love you!"

"I feel your love, and it is a comfort. I need you to know I cannot give to any man what is not complete until my tongue can speak words of a whole heart again. But we can be friends, Cyex. You are truly my very best friend!"

Cy sighed, pulling out his flute again. He played her a soothing melody that made her close her eyes in peace and sleep, soft within his arms.

The sound of his flute song echoed in the stillness of the trees for quite some time after she slept. The notes took on the profound beauty of a sad song.

Oh, he wished that her AHDAWN spoke to her of love for him.

Chapter Forty-four

The night when Sion and Cyex returned home with bundles of rolled up moss layers wrapped in wet linens, Taya stopped by the story tree to see Sion's treasures.

She had been a tremendous help all summer. Taya had assisted with the clay, mixing it and forming walls as well, learning from Sionee the art of molding with her hands. She also minded Daysong frequently, while Sionee finished up. The two of them had become the best of sister-friends.

Sion lifted thick lengths of soft, verdant moss in her hands, pressing its sweetness to her nose with pleasure. "*It smells green,*" she sighed, holding it out to Taya to sniff.

"It tickles my nose!" Taya giggled. "Sionee, who is going to join you in this bower you are doing up?" She asked, smiling with mischief. "When you and Cyex said you were going to fetch moss, I thought you were crazy!"

She looked about the tree interior appreciatively. That's what she loved about Sion. She had a way of taking silly ideas and making great beauty. Who but Sionee of Tree Song would have ever thought? "Are you really going to plant it?"

"Uh, huh," Sionee sighed. "*I intend to cover the entire upper floor with this sweet carpet of soft moss. That's why I brought a lot home. It will be soft and cushy when I step out of bed with my bare toes.*

"*Why don't you join me in the morning? We will have a great time! Eah said he would mind Daysong for me all day long. I think a man should spend time with his babies, don't you think, Taya? He said he would pick her up when he comes to deliver fresh sand and mud to lay on the floor, before I spread the moss.*

"*You know, they have wings of sorts ... several kinds ... and tools as, well ... that do things faster than our hands can work. I have already put the tiles, that I fired with my tree, down on the floor. They will give* the wood durability, for when I water the moss. Ea offered to bring me ground to plant my moss in. He said he could arrange for the soil to be dumped in through the portal at the top. We could lay the soil out, roll out the clay, and have it down in little time."

"Geesh, Sion. I think the fish head are real smart."

"*I don't think they are smarter than us at all, Taya. They make everything difficult as they seek ease. They try to do physical labor with silly contraptions of things I cannot imagine. This really should be tasks for the hands to do, hands that serve AHDAWN. It is really important to them to save time. But for what I do not know. They live forever.*

"*Originally, I figured it would take several bags of soil hoisted up. If he wants to dump mud down my hole, that's real nice of him to want to help me. I'll get this planted without that task.*"

"Sion, what do you give him in return for the help he gives you?"

"*Not that!*" Sion answered quickly. "*It seems to please him to help me. It seems to please me to let him. I don't know what I give him. Once I gave him some stones I found in a hot stream bed. I gave him some of my little children animals ... horses and a dove to send to his mother. But that is all I have ever given him, except for a smile and ... .*" Sion put her fingers to her lips, remembering a kiss ... two kisses. She decided not to tell just yet.

"*Now, the moss. We will do it the simple way, with our hands. We will put it in baskets, fasten those extra ropes we made on the baskets, and hoist them up see? Easy!*" Sion yawned widely.

"*I think I need to get Daysong to bed, Tay ... and myself, too. I will look forward to seeing you in the morning!*"

~~~

The next morning, Sion and Daysong arrived home early from their morning festivity of greeting the sun and singing with the birds.

"*You are a little bird, yourself, my wee one. I would say that already you can perfectly imitate the song of any bird. No one would know the difference, my little daughter.*"

Kinga loved the little girl. Every morning he greeted them at the tree, just as Sion and Daysong greeted the sun. Daysong was especially keen in Kingfisher language. The two of them spoke together every morning. Daysong twitted and giggled at the same time Kinga and the chorus of a hundred morning birds sang their song with her, in the yellow cedar boughs.

Daysong, though not quite one year old, could also speak with the sea, making sound of wind and wave. She communed with the rain, and with the flowers, too.

Upon arriving home, Sionee put Daysong in her swinging chair. *"We should make morning meal for Taya and your father. They will be arriving soon."* Sionee put quail eggs on to boil, and water to heat on a special place she designed on her frog's body. There was fresh and fragrant rose petals for a fine tea. She made cakes with acorn flour and soft banana, which were good and ripe this time of year. She stirred cinnamon and damask spice into the bread, along with chopped pecan.

Taya arrived just as she was getting the cakes out of the frog. She was bright and cheery and all full of sunshine.

"Sionee, when I build my house, will you help me? I want a frog inside of it, too. Marisol says that I may leave the maiden huts soon." She giggled. "Do you think she knows that I am no longer a maiden?"

"Taya, doing that is not really what makes a maiden ... or not. It is the things that we are understanding of. Marisol releases her charges when she believes they have wisdom. I left the maiden huts with skills she deemed necessary. However, I know absolutely nothing of how ... to say ... Taya how is it that two who are friends, go from the place where they are friends ... I mean here you are with a person you like and he kisses you. How does that lead to ... ah ... ?"

Taya giggled. "Who might that be? Which one of them did you kiss? You will find that it is easy, Sionee. When he kisses you, kiss him back long and slow ... close your eyes. Kisses are grand, Sion. Just kiss him until you feel like you are about to drown." Taya pushed her lips out in an exaggerated pouf, closing her eyes dreamily. "Like this Sion! Make the kisses go everywhere not just the lips. Then, just relax and let yourself drown in the waters ... and become wave, Sionee! Go with the flow. This rose tea is delicious, like my lovers tongue. Is this why your cheeks are suddenly so red? I'll have another cup please."

The imagery Taya created, made Sion almost drop her cup, when she heard Eah arrive to pick up Daysong. There was a loud thud on the top shelf floor.

"Eah," Sion giggled. *"Can't you just use the front portal door? See?"* She gestured to Taya. *"These are the wings I was telling you about. Don't track the mud, Eah. I don't need it down here."*

Ea swung down from the upper level on one of Sionee's braided ropes and landed precisely on the extra seat beside them.

"Daysong and I are going flying today." He told Sion and Taya.

"Oh, she'll really think she is a bird now." Sionee laughed. *"Make sure she gets the sounds right! She is learning their language quite well, Eah. Have a piece of banana bread."*

"This is great, Daffinina. Oh, Ninmah would love this!" He caught the butter dripping down his chin with the tip of his tongue.

Sion and Taya giggled until they nearly fell from their chairs. It was only because he looked so funny with his tongue stuck out all buttery, and looking up at the girls with eyes as green in the morning sunlight as the moss they were about to lay down.

"He has eyes like my Mars." Taya whispered to Sion.

Ea looked at them both, puzzled as to what they were laughing at.

"Have her home by nightfall, Eah, after supper preferably. We are going to have a great day! You, too."

~~~

Sion and Taya first spread the sand over the tiles, Then, raked the mud over the sand with their hands and feet. They spread it smoothly over the entire floor and pressed it down slightly. Sion misted it until it was damp.

"It reminds me of the clay!" Taya exclaimed.

"They are all Gaia's sweet earth in her many forms. Eah retrieved it from beneath a big cedar tree deep in the forest. It is a rich and fertile

soil, and will keep the moss healthy. I will need to mist it regularly. Since my bed will not be touching the floor, there will be no problem."

The hues of the moss featured many variations of green, including pale hints of feathery plum which added a subtle dimension of soft beauty to the overall effect.

"We need to make sure and get the roots pressed in well," Sionee admonished, as the girls laid out the moss in lush carpeted glory. Giggling in jubilation, they rolled over and over the spread moss, pressing it down firmly so that the roots could take hold in the thin layer of rich soil.

It looked like it had been growing inside the tree for all time. The verdant hue matched the strands of peridot beads she had hanging over the window slits.

"I can't wait to show Eah!"

"Why do you want him to see your chamber?" Taya rolled her eyes.

"Because it is going to be so beautiful. He has an eye for what is beautiful." Grinning despite herself, Sionee stuck her tongue out at Taya.

Taya giggled. "Sure Sion."

The two girls decided to take a break. It was time for noon meal, and they were hungry. They enjoyed a light lunch of crusty buttered bread, topped with sprigs of fresh watercress and small wedges of soft gazelle cheese.

After lunch, they again climbed the spiral stairs, up past the sitting room and past Daysong's bedroom, then on up to Sion's bower. Now it was time to do the fun part, one Sion had been dreaming of.

Loosely, they wrapped curling tendrils of wild white grapevines around leftover braid ropes that had been woven in hues of blue. They managed, with a little difficulty, to hang Sionee's cozy feather bed. Supported and framed within intricate swirls of vine and curling tendril, the bed swung freely from the tapered curve ceiling above the floor.

Sion had traded for a beautiful goose down, sumptuous, soft linen coverlet. It was heaped high with an airy fluff, light as a breath of fresh clean breeze. It was embroidered with white on white wild rose design. The only color was found on the delicate green, heart-shaped leaves which twined about the corners of the spread.

After the girls fluffed the coverlet and topped it with big downy pillows, the bed appeared as a white petal hanging from the vines of the wild-forest.

Sion gathered a few stray tendrils from leftover vines, and she and Taya wove a few small bird-nests. Inside each nest, they placed three tiny clay, blue robin eggs. They fastened the nests in the boughs of her bed bower to make it appear charmingly as if nature had produced this beauty.

Throughout the afternoon, the girls worked with bare feet on the soft moss, carefully arranging the final touches. Eah had given her the idea with the real dried starfish in his own private little nook.

As she had been building her tree, Sionee had also made a sky full of soft puffy stars with bits and pieces of leftover clay, all in various sizes. She had left them hollow so she could put tiny stones and beans in the inside to make them rattle. They tied the white pearly hand polished stars with thin strings of golden ribbon, and hung the stars from the ceiling curve in random lengths. The girls giggled in delight and almost forgot to get their work done as they danced about the room, hitting the star rattles with a soft stick and making each star rattle with star song.

Sionee had also made a crescent moon orb, which she left hollow. They placed the moon among the stars, and placed a shell candle inside. When lit in the night, it would glow and flicker amongst the stars that hung down above the rose bower among the trees.

But they weren't done yet. They fastened small limbs of the silver juniper trees along the wall and edge railing, some from the grapevines as well, to increase the wild-woods effect.

In the nook shelves, which Sion had designed in the adobe walls, Sion placed five tiny white horses, like the ones she made for Daysong, and for Eah's mother. They seemed to dance in a row upon her shelf. Then, she arranged pretty rocks she'd found on many of her woodland and seaside adventures on her shelves, along with pretty shells, pieces of coral and other oddments.

There was a special pot she had made, and saved for her wild bower sleeping sanctuary. It was perfectly round, and pearly polished with flecks of golden mica, glimmering ... here and there. A crescent moon, with a beautiful sleeping woman's face, made a curved design in the shapely round of the exquisitely powerful vessel. "She Who Creates By Thinking." Sionee kissed the lips on her beautiful pot, and placed it where it took command in full view of what it was an honor to the greatest mother of them all.

When the girls completed their task in mid-afternoon, they stood in their bare feet on the soft moss of an enchanted Fey forest of star strewn beauty.

"Let's go make some apple pies now," the two girls agreed.

~~~

"I'd really like to bake Eah a pie and surprise him with it tonight when he brings Daysong home. I should make Cyex one, too, considering all the help he has been with the moss and all."

"You better, or he will think you like Eah better. Do you?" When Sionee scowled impatiently, Taya continued. "Since we are going to be making pies ... there is this place in the wildwoods that I found some apple trees of a different variety. I've been eager to try them in a pie. It's not very far away, Sion. We'd have time. I'd like to make a pie for Mars. Do you think he'd like it?"

"Of course, he'd like it. Why do you think I want to make pies this afternoon? You make such good pies. But we better not dawdle!" Sion smiled at her friend.

"How about you make the crust while I cut up the apples?" Sion suggested as the two hurried out the door.

With linen bags in hand, the two girls disappeared into the forest. No one saw them leave, or noticed anything amiss about the giggling girls as they left on their adventure into the wilds.

One of the girls, however, was never seen again. Not on the cove in the Northern regions of the Snake at least.

Chapter Forty-five

Oh, ho! So it wasn't the she donkey with the big golden eyes after all. She was an animal, however, of a different nature, and precisely the kind he was looking for!

Marduk had been trysting with a Ki girl, and she had big golden eyes with long lashes ... ah.

Ninurta wondered if it was really true that the Ki girls were tight and willing. This one he would like to try. Of course, he'd have to keep his participation a secret from dear old dad. Enlil would never approve ... and Marduk?

Ninurta's grin widened. Indeed. Of course, Marduk would find out, but by then it would be too late.

Surely an ample reward must be given to the heroes who brought him this juicy bit of information. Perhaps he would let his hero slaves try the girl out, also, after he was through with her, of course.

The heroes had found out a small secret about cousin Mordukku ... a dirty little secret forbidden in the Halls of Titain, something that should not be done between one world and the next. One of them had taken visuals of Marduk with the Ki girl in action, and the place of their tryst as well, and the hero was eager to show the place to his Lord Ninurta.

"You said to find the finest, my Lord. I am proud to say that we have accomplished your request. You will see that of the many girls we have already placed in the pen, the ones we plan to retrieve from the North will be the finest.

"We have exceeded the number you requested. We captured extra because some of the heroes have said they want two or three. Some of our greedy members think four or five would be fine."

"I wish to escort you," Ninurta replied. "because I think tonight will promise to be most fine! Job well done! After it is done I shall

385

declare all of you free men! You will choose, as is the right of all hard working Annunaki male, a female or two or three," Ninurta grinned, "to have sex with. Let it be known, and spread the word, for all Annunaki heroes to come tonight to the pen where we are holding the Ki women. Ea was not the only Annunaki who had skills in forsaking law.

~~~

"I told Mars that I would make him a pie from these apples." Taya's bright eyes peered up into the tree where Sionee was already climbing.

Sionee thrust her head through the leafy fruit-laden branches and sent her thought words down the tree to Taya. "*We may as well pick a few extra while we are here. These are great apples, Taya.*"

"I think we are very blessed to have so many different kinds of apple growing on our Snake. I love them all, the sweet ones to eat around the fire, as well as the ones like these that bake so tasty. Geeeesh, Sionee, don't you just love apples?"

"*Who does not? Of all foods, apples are the best. Hey, hold that bag open will you? I want to see if I can aim from up here.*"

Sitting on the crotch of a broad limb, Sionee put a long stem between her toes, and dangled a red apple with yellow stripes in her toe grasp.

Taya looked up and saw a bare foot thrusting through the leafy branches, and giggled when Sionee wiggled the apple within her toes clutch. Both girls exclaimed in glee and more giggles, when the apple dropped perfectly into the sack.

"Sionee what are you going to wear to Yule this year? It is coming soon ... have you thought?"

"*Ah, little else, likely, except for my two feathers and a bit of gold dust, of course.*" Sionee put another apple between her toes and thrust her arching foot downward. She couldn't see Taya or the bag, either ... and Taya did not reply.

"*Can you reach it, Tay?*"

Taya did not answer, so Sionee watched the apple roll to the ground as she scrambled higher, intent on her task. Working in silence, she dropped several more. The apples were going to be cut up anyway, when they returned. A little bruise wouldn't hurt a thing.

Where was Tay? The apples were stacking up. *"Taaaaaaay."* She called in bird voice, looking down. Then, she saw the linen bag spilled with fallen apples scattered across the deep forest floor.

"Tay! Wha ... hoo ... hoo ... hoo ... hoo ... hoooo ... wha ... hoo ... hoo ... ." Sion made the call of a mourning dove. It was the sound the priestesses in training were taught to call each other with when they were out among the thick trees of the wild-forest. It helped in keeping track of each other.

In the far distance, very faintly, she heard a dove call out. Sionee frowned. The way distance ... where was Tay?

She dropped her apple and scrambled down the tree. Before she reached the ground, two hands reached up and grabbed her by her bare feet, and roughly pulled her to the ground. Sion tumbled to the leaf strewn ground, her thigh stinging in tremendous pain as it scraped on tiny limbs sticking out on the tree bark.

"Eeeeeeeeeeow!" She used voice to cry out in pain, her eyes looking about in wild panic, her heart rushing in fear. She tried to turn around about and see her captor, but suddenly a bag was thrown over her head, enclosing her in a world of darkness. She frantically tried to pull the bag off, but two strong arms held her tight.

She screamed! Then, she heard a sick laughter and a nonsensical gibberish of words. There was more than one. She knew of no one who could be so unkind.

She was pushed forward in a rough thrust. She cried out as her cut and scraped thigh nearly overwhelmed her in pain. She kicked at the evil one who held her firmly, and heard him call out as she thrust her knee up with as much force as she could muster.

She heard a shrill screech. "She's a wild one, this one. She got my gis." She could feel her assailant bending over, moaning in pain. Sion turned to blindly flee. She felt other arms enclose her in a thrusting embrace and pulling her forward.

"I'm sure she'll get more gis before we are through with her!" She could hear much laughter about her. It was only when she felt herself thrust through a doorway of sorts, and felt cold metal beneath her bare toes, that she perceived her connection to Gaia's sweet earth was broken.

She felt herself covered with straps of sort. But she wasn't alone. She heard a muffled whimper at her side. Then, she felt the warmth of another body beside her, also wrapped in a bag.

"Tay!" She screeched out. This was absolutely not a time for silent word. Sionee heard nothing but men laughing, like a bunch of hyenas, and moaning gasps. Surely, that was Taya!

Then, the bag was removed and for an instant she saw Taya lying beside her, limp and unresponsive. She had blood running in a stream down her forehead. Sion could see nothing but blackness again as a linen strip was tied over her eyes, and a gag was roughly stuffed in her mouth.

The room moved. She could feel it rise. She knew that she had finally met some of the fish headed ones that Benan had spoken of, the bad ones. Eah had even warned her that some of his people were not nice. "Most of them," he had said. But there was nothing ever that had prepared her to experience so much evil.

It was her guess that she was in one of those flying ships that Eah had told her about. He said that he flew over mountains and seas in them. She felt hands upon her. She wiggled and kicked with every fiber of her bodies energy and spirit. A hand thrust up into her linen, and grabbed hold of her breast, pinching her on the nipple. She squirmed. The hand became fist and punched her hard on her chin. Sion felt herself sink into momentary oblivion as the hand invaded her body in the place between her legs.

~~~

"Where did you take my friend?" Sionee screeched, at first in thought.

"Where did you take my friend?" Beings of such an evil nature could not hear her, so she screamed loudly in words. While she twisted in an effort to free herself, the blindfold slid off her eyes.

Someone ... someone really ugly ... took her wrap off. She could see now, leering blue, bloodless-looking eyes. Every eye in the whole ugly room ... on all the ugly faces ... were blue. Their hair was as white as sun bleached wool. Of course, these were the fish head, the bad ones. The whole flying vessel was full of them! Where were they going?

"I want this one for my own," the ugliest among them, the one who was still holding her, spoke with an eager voice. He kissed her with fish lips, wet on her mouth, covering her with slime. Sionee tried to brush it away. It was cold. Not only was his face ugly, because of the evil that he stunk of ... this was no man!

Sion did not know, nor had she ever experienced such vile evil. The concept was barely possible, but she was looking at IT in the face. Evil had been spoken of in priestess training. There were a few aberrant spirits who followed the rule of one, explicitly in service to one's self, rather than service to others.

Sion's stomach twisted and turned inside of her as she felt the ship going downward. They didn't seem to have gone real far away. For a moment she felt a small stab of hope. She held inside herself the bile that threatened to rise in her throat. When they stopped, the ugly fish head pulled her down what felt to her like a ramp. It was dark by now, and Sion saw little, but she could smell the sweet earth again ... a forest ... the coolness of night. Sion felt grass beneath her feet, and fallen soft leaf beneath her toes. The strong arms of the ugly fish head thrust her forward, and pushed her into something like one of the pens where tame gazelle were milked, back home. It was round. Now she could see because there were artificial lights above it. Sionee felt less than human, but no ... it was these creatures that were less than human. They were monsters! In the cage, she was not alone. There were so many girls inside, Sion could hardly breathe.

She suddenly remembered the little button thing Eah had given her, that he made her promise to keep with her at all times to call him if she needed him. She had never used it before ... thought it was foolish. Actually, she was afraid to push the button of the damned thing. Suddenly, that fear seemed so tiny, compared to the real fear she was experiencing right now.

She managed to get her hand into her shift pocket. She had tied the device to a small gold ribbon, strung around a wooden button she always fastened the thing to. She had sewn a wooden button inside each of her shifts. It had pleased Eah. But a lot of good it had done her. She fumbled in the corners of an empty pocket. A tear fell from her eye. It had been torn when she had slid down the tree, and she had been grasped in rough hands.

"Let me look at you, my sweet." The monster ran his finger across her cheek and stopped at the swollen and bloodstained jaw-line, where he had hit her.

"We must take care," he hollered at the other men. "We are marring the beauty we wish to ravish. Choose now! Not more than three each, my fellow heroes, unless we have others left. But back off! All of you. This one is mine! Mine boys! Mine, until I tire of her, of course. When I am through with her, any of you may have her. She will be well stretched out by then. As for the other one, if she lives ... I told you not to tie her so tightly. I really wanted her. She was Mar-duk's girlfriend. Whoever takes her better run! Because I can assure you, Marduk will find you. So, if I were any of you, I'd leave her sorry ass here to die!"

~~~

Sion watched, horrified as clumsy fish head brutes came into the pen and grabbed the girls ... one, two and three ... as they wished, and hauled them off, screaming. She saw a brute stop before Taya, and put his palm beneath her chin, looking into her eyes. He spoke softly to her, and lifted her up. He threw her gently over his shoulder and made haste to a flying vehicle which seemed to be a bit smaller than the one she had just gotten off. Sionee watched the ship rise to the sky and disappear.

Sion was alone in the pen, now, with the ugly fish head. The foul fish drew her out onto the soft grass. "Come, my white dove. Oh, don't be afraid, darling. All you need to do is cooperate with me. I need you to make me big."

He had a stick in his hand. Sionee closed her eyes. Hypori had told her of the stick. She would never see Daysong again ... Or Eah ... or Cyex ... or Marisol ... or any of the ones she loved ... and Taya where was Taya?

Where would she, Sionee Song Tree, go when her body disintegrated into permanent thin air? Would her body, when it was poofed into ... who knows where, still retain the invisible spirit? After all, Benan had said that the stick made the body disappear into the air ... how would that all work?

Instead of making her disappear, the stick lashed across her scraped thigh. She saw blood pour forth. But no matter what he did, she couldn't make him big, as he had demanded. She would not even try. She would not touch the foul thing.

Naked and bloody, her raw thigh felt the horrible sting of the lash strike again. Then, the pain hit higher, across her back, across her buttocks.

But she wouldn't feel it. No! Not she ... who was her wholeness.

Sionee became a bird and flew to a branch in the tree high above her body.

"Twit ... twit ... twit ... twit ... twit ... !" She trilled in rapid succession.

Chapter Forty-six

"Come on now, my little man. You know her voice is more beautiful than yours. She is more beautiful to look at, as well. But you are a handsome lad, and I love you well."

"Again, my little birdy." Ea motioned in applause as Daysong chirped like a yellow canary in the morning.

Adapa screamed, rubbing his little eyes. He was tired of this little game. Ea decided it was well past time to return his little bird to her nest in the tree, where her mother bird awaited. It was almost dark, and both children had been fed as Daffinina had specified.

Ti Ti, who had been toddling on her little legs for two months now, was standing at the base of one of the giant stone serpents. Her verdant eyes were studying skyward.

"*Twit ... twit ... twit ... twit ... .*" She sang eagerly, giggling as she reached upward with her little hand. Ea shooed away a tiny blue bird that came to rest on his daughter's hand. Ti Ti began to cry big tears. Ea looked into big, sorrowful eyes. Something was not right.

~~~

"Father, father! I've been looking for you! They said you were out here!" A younger version of Ea approached in great haste.

"I've been busy all day, Mordukku, with the babies. Aren't they cute, my son?"

"Father."

Ea glanced up and quickly sent for the suds to come attend to the children. The look in his son's eyes made the beat of his heart speed up erratically.

"Son, son. Sit down ... sit down. Is all well? I'd say not. You look terrible."

"Dad! There is this girl I met in the forest. She is a Ki girl, father. I know it is forbidden ... I love her."

Ea bid the suds to take the babies back into the facility and care

393

for them. Adapa had a louder scream even than Ti Ti. He was well spoiled and wasn't happy at having to share his attentions with another baby all day long.

Ea grinned at his son, hoping to soothe him. "So what's with the panic, Mordukku? Did Enlil find out that you have disregarded the Titain Law? You have slept with her, I hope?"

"Many times father. I have been away for a few days, and we promised to meet this evening. I've been waiting, but she didn't come!"

"Well, get back there son! It's early yet. I'm sure she will be there soon."

"No, Father. She should have been there by now. She is very eager, my Tay."

"Tay? Did you say Tay?" Ea sat upright. "Taya?"

"Yes, that's my girl. She lives in the community on the other side of the mountain ... and I found this. He held up a gold ribbon. It was lying next to a spilled linen of bruised apples. Something is wrong, father."

"Take me." Ea shouted in panic, his face white, his heart pounding. The two of them put on their wings and flew to the place in the forest on the other side of the mountain.

"Why would my Tay drop her apples?" Marduk lamented.

Ea felt his fears come alive, when the two of them landed. A quick glance about showed him two sets of bare female footprints leading to an apple tree.

His eyes grew wide when he saw Annunaki sandal prints covering the slight girl prints at the tree base.

"Aaaaaugh." Ea roared in anger and fear. "I, too, know a maiden," he confessed, "who is a friend of your Taya. I am knowing that she spent the day with my Daffinina. I breakfasted with them both this morning. I told them I would mind the girl child this day. Then, I was off, to leave the girls to have a great day!"

Ea flit his hand at the little bird that kept chortling in his ear, annoyingly. "Go away little bird. Silence!"

He began to wail when he noticed that the bark on the apple tree by the fallen linen bag had a great smear of blood on its bark. He ran his fingers over the scuff of disturbed bark. "It is blood!"

Marduk was on the ground examining the prints of the sandals. Ea caught a bare glimpse of something metallic lying in the grass. The last rays of the dying sun had lit the clue with grim illumination.

Of course, the gold ribbon in his hand. He stooped and picked up a large wooden button with jagged pieces of thin frayed gold ribbon still stuck to it, as if it had been torn in a violent motion. At its side, the metallic calling device he had given Daffinina lay broken.

Ea's wail shook the apples from the tree top. They fell down on his bowed head, splattering.

"Father!" Marduk stood up. "It's Ninurta. I recognize the print. I have angered him, father."

It was then that the twittering little bird flew closer to Ea, swooping down to the figure bent in sorrow. The bird fluttered his wings in rapid motion, keeping at eye level and looking Ea directly in the eye.

A blue haze caught his attention, as the very last vestige of light sank into the sea, and Ea saw blue feathers. It was the same bird he had shooed from his daughter's hand before Marduk had come.

Ea remembered that his Daffinina talked with birds all the time. This one seemed to have something to say to him.

"Follow me!" Kinga trilled. *"I will take you where she is!"*

~~~

"What do you think I have been trying to tell you?" Kinga's tiny voice was raucous in breathless panic. Ea and Marduk joined him with their wings, and the three flew high over mountain ranges and into the wild lands of tree.

"I decided long ago on the admonitions of my master, Cyex, that the girl needed someone to watch over her. If it was me, who had a form with two legs, and two arms, and the proper appendage, I can assure you this would never have happened.

"As it is, I vowed to serve this girl all the days of my life, and the

little sunshine child, as well. They are of an innocent sweetness that I have come to adore. Twit ... twit .... And, you, numb nuts! You are not worthy of either of them. Alas! But they love you, and only you can save them ... who else?

"*I usually do not fly over the mountains, but with her first cry, I was there. I saw them take her, and I can assure you we must hurry!*"

"You have wisdom, raucous twit! I, indeed, am not worthy of her love. I swear to you, when we find her, I will bring her home!"

~~~

None too soon, they came at last to a small clearing within the forest of trees. Ea frowned. It seemed there was a holding pen down there.

Kinga lit in the treetops of a scraggly tree, and Ea and Marduk took caution and landed also, like birds themselves, in the branches and peered down.

With one swift jump, Marduk leaped to the ground while Ea slid down the trunk. The whole tree trembled when Marduk slammed Ninurta's hard head violently against the trunk. Ea finished his downward flight with a leap, himself.

Marduk had grabbed Ninurta by the hair of his head, when he saw his scrawny cousin straddled over a girl's inert body.

Ea saw only that it was his Daffinina. While his son attended to Enlil's foul spawn, Ea knelt in shock at Sion's side. She had one wrist tied to a tree trunk, and one ankle bound to a tree at its side.

He placed his ear against her chest. He could hear her heart beating in faint rhythm. She still had pulse.

He called her name, but there was no response. Quickly he untied her wrist and her ankle. They were bleeding where she had been bound. The scraped thigh caught his attention immediately. It was bloody, still bleeding, and he could see that there was dirt and debris caught within the abrasion. A bump on her forehead had him concerned. He would need to check her out for cracks in her skull. He turned her on her side and saw the raised, bloody welts of several whip lashes. Ea threw up.

As he wiped his mouth, a blue feather wafted gently from the tree heights. It lit on Daffinina's broken body. *"Twit ... twit ... twit ... twit ... twit ... !"* Kinga was perched on his shoulder and was peering at Sion, anxiously. Both Ea and Kinga looked upward.

"It is one of my kind." Kinga twitted. Ea and Kinga both sought the source of the feather. It seemed to have come from nowhere.

Ninurta's squalid rasp brought the attention back to the source of Daffinina's trouble. "No, Marduk. No!" Ninurta was squirming now, trying to break free of the rope that Marduk had used to tie him to the tree trunk.

"Enough is enough! Let's call it even, cousin. I owed you this one. You degraded me in front of my father."

"I am going to degrade you some more, you worthless worm ... I intend to cut you down to the size you really are. I will make you even less, YET!" Marduk pulled his knife from his loin pocket and flashed it's blade before Ninurta's panicked eyes.

"Where is my girl?" He had Ninurta by the balls, twisting.

"Shhhheeeeese gone. Probably dead by now! I 'banged' her up thoroughly, but she was worthless to me."

"Where is she?"

"I let one of my heroes take her. He was a big, big one, cousin. He will serve her well, if she lives to fuck again."

"Your heroes, did you say?"

Despite his pain and because of it Ninurta broke into giggles. Marduk might have him by the balls, but in a way, he had already won a victory here. He smirked as he thought *who had who by the balls?*

"Oh, yes! I must tell you I gathered fifty of your finest! I had command while you were away, dear cousin. You never are around. So I took command of the mines. I offered our boys the reward of women for their labors."

"Ki women?" Ea lifted his head from Daffinina's wretched form, and went to stand at his son's side.

"Uncle, uncle, of course they were Ki women. Where else would we have gotten them? We were successful. Each of the miners had their choice ... one, two, three ... each. However they desired. I chose this one, but neither could SHE give me any satisfaction. She, too, is worthless!"

Ea nodded to Marduk. His apt son flashed the knife again. His hand moved upward Ninurta's wrinkled balls and grasped Ninurta's puny gis ... and stretched it tightly. He cut it off at the balls, with one swift motion.

With a quiet smile, Ea sent approval Marduk's way, as he watched the tiny worm thing sail through the air above his head to land in the darkness of the trees beyond ... somewhere into the wild forest.

Ninurta screamed in shocked dismay.

"Untie him son," Ea spoke at last.

"I would advise you to go find your thing and find it fast," Ea admonished Ninurta. You might be able to persuade Ninmah to sew it back on for you. I would hurry if I were you. It will die soon ... and then ... no one can fix it. That is if you can find it at all. It is dark out there.

"What is that I hear? Is it an owl hunting for a tiny little mouse ... or ... a worm perhaps ... to feed its hungry little owlet's mouths? They hunt in the night with radar eyes!

"Alas! Too, when it is dark, the boars come out rooting into the ground for ... grub worms!

"Or, perhaps some other of the thousand creatures of the night who come forth to feast on the blood-scented fragrance of even the smallest of morsels ... may fill their hungry desires.

Hurry, now! Perhaps already they have taken a puny bite ... of nasty."

Chapter Forty-seven

Thanking the bird who helped her fly away, Sionee Tree Song bid it adieu. She walked now, in a gold-hued world.

It was not the purple horizon that she crossed, though she knew that if she kept walking, that line would soon be reached. For now, she was content not to cross. It was not her body that was ailing, despite a scrape that was painful, indeed, along with several welts that stung in a most excruciating way. Also, there was the bump on her forehead. But that part of her was now in repose. Rather, it was her spirit that she sought to ease.

Golden seas broke waves on the golden sands of dream. The deep waters were brilliant in the sun's illuminating glow.

Barefoot and naked, she arose from the waters, where she had decided to walk in the foam. She dripped pure waters from off her body of light.

She was in the world only known when one closes one's outer eyes, and goes deep within.

White cranes flew above her head, bidding her welcome to the threshold of the lights horizon. On glistening golden sand, she followed the beach inward to the mountain. Inside, it was said that there was knowledge. A doorway marked the entrance, therein. It was barred shut with rusty golden bars across a dark oaken door.

She went to the door and knocked upon it. It took forever. So, she knocked again. Finally the door opened. There was an old woman who stood at the entrance, surrounded by sleek-haired cats with green slanted eyes.

The woman was dressed in a white robe. Her silver braids formed a crown across the top of her head, from ear to ear, with little curling wisps framing her face. There was a white flower behind each ear. She was beautiful, and her body of light was so old that it could not be known what her age was in the scope of eternities.

Sion spoke the words of the spirit in the voice of the spirit which knew no boundaries of words. *"MAY I ENTER?"*

"There is wisdom, you seek?" The woman asked, guarding the door protectively.

"IT IS A MATTER OF WHOLENESS TO MY SOUL!"

"You are aware, my golden daughter, that sometimes wisdom has the fangs of a viper. This is why wisdom is guarded here, deep inside. If you dare to enter, you must know of the risks. Are you strong enough to gain the truth?"

"I AM WEAK. THERE IS A HOLE IN MY HEART THAT MAKES ME PUNY. I HAVE LIVED LONG IN IGNORANCE ... BOTH HAPPY AND SAD. I COME TO BECOME WHOLE!"

"Do you believe that you have come to the right place to find which piece of your heart is missing?"

"I DO! WILL YOU LET ME IN THAT I MAY RECOVER IT?"

The old woman smiled softly, stepping aside. "Come in, child. May you find your wholeness here."

Sion entered a large cavern inside the mountain. The room had a great sense of peace. It was lit within, softly, soothing the darkness into a symposium of flickering torches that silhouetted every shadow with illumination.

"You may wander the cave at your will, child. I will leave you now ... within yourself ... for only you may find the way. Go DEEP INSIDE! You will come to what it is that you seek."

The woman turned and seemed to disappear. Sion was alone in the spacious hall. There were shelves everywhere ... each shelf stacked high with tablets that reminded her of the tablets that she had seen on Eah's desk. They were beautifully bound, gold leaves that were scribed in wondrous designs. The volumes had illustrations, also, some stylized, and still others that were beautifully colored in exact replication.

Which one had her answers within? She wandered about the cavern going down tunnels that led to different books. There were more books than she could count, as many as stars in the sky.

The smell of the book trove reminded her of her amethyst chamber beneath her tree. It, too, had halls formed by the tree roots she had made ... and that Eah had built to extend deep into the earth beneath her tree. But the halls were empty in the story tree. Perhaps this might be a good way to fill those spaces. She could make books of the stories she told as Songkeeper. Would not that be a grand way to keep the song? Surely she could illustrate images and touch them with color. Perhaps Eah could teach her how to scribe.

But, oh! For now, she must continue her search for the missing piece of her heart. In which room would she find her AHDAWN? She stepped across a narrow bridge that crossed a small underground stream. There was a door on the other side. It was closed, with golden bars across the door. She removed the bars and found that it opened easily when she turned the knob.

Inside, there was another treasure trove of books. There was a table herein, of solid and smoothed golden oak, with heavy and solid chairs. She climbed a ladder and reached for a book that she could see on the top shelf. She knew it was hers because it glowed for her with a golden light.

She pulled it down and sat at the table to open it up. It was the Book of Alsionee Tree Song. She held it reverently for a moment, relishing the beauty of its promise in her hands. She polished the golden cover with the burnishing of her fingertips, making it gleam in mute beauty.

The book opened for her, on its own accord, revealing pictures and thoughts which she read by just touching the book with her hand.

The pages turned and turned, then suddenly stopped at a place that made her catch her breath. It was a chapter about the spring time when she and Coelle went to bathe at the hot-pool in the stream. They were preparing for the Spring Rite. They were sixteen sun spins.

Inside her head the images danced. She breathed the happenings once more. Sionee laughed. Then, smiled. She and Coelle were having such a great time! Oh! It was good to see Coelle ... again .... to see her smile in the way she had of brightening any day.

"Oh, sister," Sionee laughed. "Do you think we will participate in the rite this spring time?"

"If Cyex is there! I would like to," Coelle giggled. "as long as it is okay with you. I know you love him, yourself."

"I did when I was a child," Sionee replied in truth. She was using words at this time, as there were yet no word-veils in her heart.

"But we are children no more. If it suits you and Cyex, I am happy for you. He isn't mine."

Sion wasn't exactly happy about it. She had thought that she, herself, might ... but Coelle's smile was so bright, mayhaps she could catch Cyex some other time. If it pleased Coelle, it would please her ... somewhat.

"He will be playing his flute, so surely he will be there, waiting for a maiden to choose him." Sion took Coelle's small hand in her own, and they sat in the waters up to their chins.

"Do you think Cyex likes me?" Coelle asked.

"Of course, he likes you." She assured her friend. But Sion had notions about Cy, herself. It had been some time, though, since last they had been together as children. But she had been thinking of him a lot lately. She had sort of hoped ...

"Sometimes I think he still believes I am just a child," Coelle reasoned. "I am not. Maybe I will show him that I am not a child. Sionee, have you ever done it?"

"Done what?" Sion asked in innocence.

Coelle splashed her playfully in the eyes. "Have sex! You know what I am talking about."

"My mother had so much sex in her life, I think sex is something not everyone understands. I'm sure it may feel great, but I want to make sure that I am totally in love. That is the real matter of the expression."

"Well, I am totally in love with Cyex, Sion. Perhaps a girl needs a little practice now and then, do you suppose? Then, when you find someone special, you will be well skilled to please him. I would really like to impress Cyex with remarkable love skills. I wish I wasn't a maiden anymore, Sion, so I would know exactly what to do! I am tired of being a maiden."

Sionee giggled and splashed Coelle back in the eyes. Then, she held a yellow rose up to her friend and pressed its softness to her nose.

"For you, sister ... maiden or no ... you will always be my closest friend ... forever."

The two girls tore the petals off the rose, and off several others of the roses they had picked along the way to the pool. They strew the petals over the waters and watched them float softly on the slight current beneath the still waters.

"What's this, Coelle?" Sion sat upright in attention. "What do I hear?"

"I think it is a canoe. Someone is coming, sister."

"Duck, Coelle ... duck down. It is not one of our boats. Who is it?"

But Coelle didn't duck. She pulled Sion up out of the water. "You can't stay down there forever," she urged Sion. "It is a stranger. I don't recognize him from our outlier, or from any of the rentals at the harbor."

Both girls had big eyes as they watched in fascination. They were unable to do anything, but gape. They were quiet, their mouths open in astonishment. Whoever he was, he was beautiful.

Coelle nudged her, gently whispering. "I think it is a fish head canoe, Sion."

"Is that what they look like? He looks like us, but he has lighter hair, and he is very tall, and... Oh!"

"I find him totally fetching!" Coelle giggled. What do you think?"

Sion was spellbound as the canoe came off the quiet little river and down the stream into the little pool, where she and Coelle were bathing. She gazed eye to eye into the face of the intruder.

She looked into the silver burn of the stranger's almost green eyes. They glinted with a fire so hot they seemed to emit a flash of light that exploded deep within her.

Never in her life had she seen so much beauty in anyone. Holding the book tight in her hands, Sionee gazed at the picture and gasped. It was Eah!

~~~

Sionee turned to the next page. The old woman had said that wisdom was not always pretty. But Eah was pretty breathtaking. His smile was friendly, as he stopped his canoe to speak with the girls.

"Of all Ki's treasures ... On this journey ... I have found the most beautiful of all gems ... far surpassing mere gold and sapphires, which my people seek. Hello girls! I have been out this day vastly enjoying the beauty of the waters. And, lo, here I find two of the most beautiful, lovely fishes I have ever seen. Perhaps you are maids from the deep ocean, swum from the sea with bejeweled eyes?"

"Oh, no," Coelle began. "We are but Gaia's daughters, and we have never seen your kind before, though our stories speak of you. Where did you come from?"

"The stars," Eah smiled. "Though, none brighter than the four stars I see shining into my soul, right now. I haven't seen many earthen females as enticing as you. Let me look!"

"Coelle rose proudly, out of the waters, and pulled at Sionee, who soon joined her. Sionee felt shy, and her knees felt wobbly.

She loved this star man ... of that she was certain. She loved him at first sight, though surely she had known him in spirit before, because ... why did she love him? Was it merely because he was so beautiful?

Coelle picked up a yellow rose that still had petals on it, and gave it to the strange Eah. She giggled and batted her big golden eyes at him.

Sion picked up an apple from a pile the two girls had placed at the poolside to eat while they were bathing. "We have apples," She shyly held one out to him.

It was big and beautiful and shiny and sweet. Eah took out a small knife from his waist robe. Every muscle of his well-built body gleamed in the sun on skin paler than either of the girls had ever seen before.

He cut the apple in three wedges and gave each of the girls a piece. Then, he took off his waist linen and joined them. They all bathed in the pool of gentle warm waters and ...

Chapter Forty-eight

Sion awoke when she heard Eah call her. She was lying down, and aware that she hurt everywhere. She had come back from the world of dreams, suddenly ... too fast ... leaving the book open and spread across the oaken table.

But she had seen inside the piece of her heart. She grabbed it tight to put it back before it slipped away.

Eah held something in front of her face, moving it back and forth before her eyes. He spoke gently. At first, she smiled up into his beloved eyes, Then, the thing he was holding caught her attention. She followed its motion. But what was this thing that Eah kept waving before her eyes?

It was a stone. The stone was round and white, polished as if it had tumbled for aeons in tumultuous waters. Its glassy shine first drew her stare. Then, she noticed that within the white stone, an agate with crystal striations, there was a big splotch of perfect roundness. The splotch was orange ... too bright ... almost florescent ... and made it appear as an eye of the wrong color. Whatever it looked like, the stone resembled the eye of an owl, an eye of the wrong color. Profusely, it caught a life-giving light in the reflection of a torch that was lit by her side. The orange light turned purple and leapt at her, pierced her through and through.

"No, Eah! NO!" The sound of her voice so startled him that he dropped the stone on her chest as he bent over her. She took the stone within her hand to examine it.

It wasn't just that her voice was loud, it was that she spoke in WORDS. Ea smiled. Her voice was as sweet as a chorus of a tree-full of yellow canaries. The sound of his name echoed like a real live word!

"Oh, Daffinina!" He embraced her. "I thought that I had lost you!" He smiled into her eyes, and stopped short of kissing her full on the top of her head, all the way down to her lips.

It was because he didn't know this Daffinina. Her eyes sparked with the fury of a raging fire, sending molten explosions of lethal flame from the topaz brilliance of her eyes, that shuddered in gases of hot blue ... smoking purple ... and deadly black.

"You never had me!" She shouted at him.

He stepped backward. He had come to understand the waves of thought that emerged from her pure heart. But her voice-words were ice ... and most terribly chilling!

Daffinina held the crystal eye rock in her fingers, spinning it around and around in examination.

It was now clear; he knew ... that she knew ... at least part of it.

"Now, Daffinina, give me some good ... please. I did have you once ... and quite willingly, as I recall."

"I was barely more than a child!"

"On my world, you were ... and are ... anything but a child. You were loving, happy, and beautiful! You were warm in my arms. You giggled, and hey! Did you know that giggles are lovelier than bells when they ring? Ding dong!" He tried to smile at her. "I love giggles, Daffinina. I love you! I always have and I always will ... in all my sars of eternity!"

"You lie," she screeched, "about everything! Do not touch me!" She turned away, sharply.

"Ooweeeee!" She winced in pain.

"Does your leg hurt, Daffinina?" It is in terrible shape. I can heal that, too, with this..." From his pocket pouch, he retrieved a second stone, a clear crystal. "Come, darling, lay back down!"

"Not for you ... Ever! You are a liar!" She grasped the owl eye stone he had dropped on her chest tightly. Her fingers enclosed it in a wrap. She jerked the second crystal from Eah's hand, and swung her arm backwards. In one thrust, her palm opened and shot forward. She threw both stones as far as she could ... out into the blackness of the trees.

On that reflex, as her hand let go of the stones, her now flat palm slapped Eah hard on the cheek.

Two cries of pain resounded. Ea's cry was almost quiet. He knew he deserved it. But from the trees in the distance where the stones landed, a loud screech of pain echoed through the night.

Sionee's hand still smarted and she jumped, herself startled.

Ea smiled, cupping his cheek in the palm of his hand. "Good throw, Daffinina. It's only Ninurta, my nephew. He is out in the trees looking for something he lost.

A loud volley of curses resounded, muffled in the deep forest.

"I wish I had thrown and aimed for your head!" Daffinina did not think it was funny. None of it, none at all.

"The owl eyes, Eah. I have been tormented by the unnatural owl eyes that have been haunting my dreams ... and turning my AH-DAWN impure. While all this time, it was only a stone ... and YOU!" She glared at him.

"I don't know what makes me the angriest, even now ... the owl eyes ... or that you have kept something from me ... and would still take more."

"I was only trying to help you, my Daffinina."

"Shut up!" She shouted. "You are a cold-hearted, reptilian fish head nin-com-poop! You lied to me, even as you stole from me!"

Ea waited for a further volley of accusations, which he deserved. They came. He decided that he liked her no-word policy better.

"It was not your right!" Now tears were coming from her big amber eyes of molten fire. They rolled like rivers down her cheeks ... big golden drops. He reached out to dry them.

She slapped his hand away. "You took my memory! With the image of the owl eye, you took my experience from my soul. You took my choice ... and terrorized me with a false image in exchange. I have been so haunted!"

"I had no intention to frighten you so, Daffinina. It is a way my people have of taking things that hurt ... or disturb ... away, so that the emotion of suffering is not experienced. I didn't want you to carry the pain of what my evil nephew did to you!"

"What about what you did! Was that not evil? I thought you

were different than the others! Do you actually think you can just erase your ill doings by just taking it away? Come on, Eah. How is it done? Why?"

"We call it hypnosis, Daffinina. It is a scientific process that helps one forget one's pains and troubles."

"It is a shame that I threw the foul stone away!" She cried. "Mayhaps I would beg you to take away my pain at knowing you!"

This was getting alarming. Ea tried to soothe her by reaching out to lay his hand on her shoulder. She thrust it off like it was a louse ... and backed away.

"It was not your right to take from me the memories that I make in my soul. You robbed me! But some of them I have recovered, and I see that they are all dirty, now. What could have been beautiful is now of disgust."

What could he say? He knew she was right. He knew that if she found out, she would never understand about ... nor, could she ever forgive him. It was unforgivable. Then, it got worse, as something else dawned in her head.

Suddenly, Daffinina was quiet. Too quiet ... much too quiet ... except for a deep inward suck of her breath.

Pallor again stole the color from her cheeks. Her eyes became much too big, then bigger ...

"Where is my baby?" She screeched.

"She is being cared for at the facility," he assured her.

"A facility? Is that your fancy name for it?"

"You've seen it Daffinina. It is lovely. There are places where it is truly a home environment."

"My name is Alsionee Tree Song! I want my baby back. I want both of my babies back!"

His eyes widened. Oh, oh. She DID know.

"It is Adapa isn't it?"

Ea was quiet.

"You took him from me! Like you told me your people did on your star! When he was just a germ, you got him out of my womb... when he was but a sprouting seed. You planted him in your evil box made out of glass, and you watched him grow."

Tears poured from her eyes. "You saw him as his legs grew strong ... as his hands made tiny fingers ... as his heart beat ... each day without a mothers heartbeat to soothe him ... only a farce of a simulation.

"I had NOTHING ... nothing but owl eyes ... to make my soul tremble in fear!"

Tears overcame her as she began to feel faint in the pain of her broken and bleeding body and soul. He had come to know how to read the soul inside of her. He could feel her thought words that still came forth un-tongued.

Her pain stung his soul. He felt her meltdown of misery. It was a virtual volcano of burning sorrow ... deep in the depths of her hidden soul. No wonder emotion had been forbid on the Perfect World. Never in all his eternities had he felt or experienced such agony. Maybe the Annunaki had it right to forbid feelings. It hurt so badly.

"Oh, Daffina," he crooned sorrowfully. "Daffinina, I love you so much, my sweet, sweet, girl. I cannot begin to express restitution for what I have done to you. I didn't mean to hurt you so badly, deep within your soul ... as well as in your body!

"Let me help you, darling. You must be attended to." He reached out for her again.

In deep pain, both physical and emotional, she got up and fled. She didn't want to be anywhere near the foul fish-headed liar and thief. Where she was going, she did not know. Surely, she would be able to find her way home.

What she would do, she could not imagine, only that she must get away from him ... from them. But she could not think very well. Her head buzzed emptily as her thoughts were growing dim. She struggled to recover her thinking ability.

The forest reached out to her ... SANCTUARY. She went in a different direction than the sound she had heard when she threw the evil owl eye away. She was glad that it was gone. By tossing it away, she truly felt free of fear.

She ran into the dark woods, where he couldn't find her, where no one could find her. She only needed to rest for a bit ... and lay down until her head quit throbbing. She felt the trees enclose her safely in their arms.

She kept running, though every step made her cuts and bruises livid with pain.

Her only present thought was confusion as to why her world seemed to be veiled within a fabric of dark shadow.

After a time, she bumped into a big tree and felt her head bang sharply. She did not recall that already she had bumped her head earlier. Why was her sight fading into a blackness darker than night?

She put her hand on her forehead and felt the blood of two split goose-bumps.

The tree spoke to her, "*I am sorry darling. Let me hold you for a while. You will be safe. I will hold you in my arms on this long, dark night.*"

She scrambled up its large trunk. Its arms bid her with comfort. She lay down, curled and comfortable in its ancient crotch, where two large branches spread in opposite directions. Her body fit perfectly in the dip between the branches. She felt as if she was laying in the arms of her ancient yellow cedar back home. "Mamun!" She cried. But Mamun did not hear.

With tears running down her bloody cheeks, Alsionee Tree Song sank into a world of nothing ... where it was so dark ... and it was nothing ... nothing at all.

Chapter Forty-nine

The first ray of morning light began to softly diffuse the blackness of the night. Sionee Song Tree heard birds waking up in the branches of the trees above her head.

"I AM THE LIGHT OF THE PERFECT DAY. IN ME IS THE LIGHT THAT DOES NOT FAIL." Partway, she opened one eye. Where was she? How did she get here? She had dreamed that a tree held her in its arms all night long. It was true! She had slept very comfortably.

As she lay in its midst, she looked upward and saw that she was beneath the canopy of a gnarly network of leafy branches. The sun was shining through translucent green leaves, tinting the bower above her head with a transcendent green light. Through the green depth of the forest ceiling, the glimmer of new day enshrouded her in peaceful sanctity.

Surely she was in a holy place. The early morning pulsed with the music of the spheres. Strangely, she nestled within the tree's arms and quietly listened to the song of the morning birds.

Deep within the forest, the joyfully raucous cry of a raven announced this day was at its beginning. Who had covered her, with something so soft? It tickled her nose. It was a blanket of tiny white feathers. Oh! It was so nice. Soon her eyelids began to drift to sleep again.

"That is it, darling. Rest my child ... rest."

Sionee's eyes flew open. She raised herself, propped up on one elbow, and peered about. Who was speaking with her?

The sun, now having taken its full position in the sky, lit the bower in emerald glory. It was no longer a world of shadow.

An owl hooted, but she was not afraid. It was just an owl, making noises as it settled down for a day of rest. She hooted back. *"I AM NO LONGER AFRAID OF YOU."*

"So, you are awake!" She heard again, someone speaking. Two

bright eyes peered down at her from a limb that spread its branches above her head. It was a dove, a beautiful white mourning dove. *"Oo ... whoo ... hoo ... Oo ... whoo ... hoo ... Oo ... whoo ... hoo ... whoo ... hoo ... whooooo."*

"**THIS MY MOTHER TAUGHT ME HOW TO SING ...** " Sionee began. "She used to tell me that your song meant, 'Sionee is a pretty little girl.' "

"So, you are." The soft eyes of the dove seemed to twinkle.

"I was, before I was broken." Sion sat up stiffly, cautious so as not to make her cuts bleed again. She put her hand up to her forehead. She remembered vaguely that she had bumped into this tree last night ... really, really hard. The bump was not there, and there was no pain. She held her wrist before her eyes. There was no blood! Sionee turned her thigh at an angle and peered over her shoulder, running her fingers over smooth, flawless, sun-colored flesh. Not a speck of blood.

"You are broken, did I hear you say? I see only a girl who appears quite whole to me."

"Heeeeeey?" Sionee exclaimed out loud. "How is it so?"

She looked suspiciously at the little white bird. She blinked her eyes to see a peculiar light begin to swirl around the dove. It was a very white light, and it seemed to be fading the bird into its brilliant vortex.

The light reversed and twirled outward. It was a beautiful woman dressed in a white robe of tiny white feathers, who now sat on the tree limb beside her.

Sionee gasped in awe. In this life, she had never seen a woman with such radiant beauty. On the top of her head, she wore a crown of sunlit braids. Otherwise, the rest of her hair fell in a flowing stream of gold, down her back and across her shoulders, free and long. It almost reached her ankles. Surely her hair was made of pieces from the ray of sun. Her skin was the white of the moon when it graced the night sky with a fullness of light. It glowed with a pearly softness. Her cheeks had hue as a wild pink rose and her lips, the bud.

Her skin was as smooth and unwrinkled as the newly formed skin of a baby, but her eyes were as old as ancient song.

Sion noticed beads of light entwined in the crown of her braids. When the lady turned her head, Sionee saw that the beads were multifaceted stars.

When Sionee's eyes met those of the lady in fullness, she found she was gazing into the infinite sea of stars within the Sapphire Blue ... and that there were too many stars to count. The secrets of the universe laid within those stars, in fathoms of deep wisdom.

"Who are you?" Sionee asked. "Where did you come from, and how did you find me here?"

"It was not easy, my sweet girl, but learned I well the secrets of my Feyries... your people, my child. Yet, that was a purer time that only few of your number remember. Your people taught me the ways of the wildwoods, and the ways of the ocean waters of earthen depths. They taught me the voice of the wind, the spirit of the mountain, the songs of the sun and the moon, as well as the earth and stars ... as they see them with their eyes. I received GNOS of the earthen shores when I heard them sing. I taught them the voice of the universe and the magic it holds within its mystery. I gave them GNOS of the Sapphire Blue from whence come I.

"Thus it is that I know everything, my child ... of Heaven and Earth ... and the stars ... within and without. On your world, and mine, I am called Wisdom. Your people call me their Queen ... or once they did.

"Who are you?" Sionee persisted.

"I am that I am," she replied softly. "A little bird came to me, and whispered to me of where it was that you were hiding. Oh, he was a funny little man ... he knew exactly where you were. Oh, you know him, darling. His raimant was a shimmering blue, and he wore the cutest little crown on the top of his head. He made a pass at me!" The white woman softly rumbled in mirth.

"I became dove and flew with him. Oh, my!" Her smile was wistful and far away.

"Kinga? Kinga is here? Where is Kinga?" Sionee looked about her, but could not see him.

"Your Kinga had a very long night! He followed you in vast distance. He and I got along so finely we ... well ... ." She smiled a mist-like smile. "He said that you were a dim-witted little thing, yet the wisest of all earth creatures that he knew ... all at the same time!" The white lady laughed. "How is this so?" Not waiting for an answer, she went on.

"My little King flew back to your home by the sea to your beautiful story tree, and I am most impressed, Miss Tree Song.

Kinga said that a "Cyex" must be informed that you are okay. Oh, and not to worry, my darling. Cyex is caring for your lovely daughter. Little Day is in good hands."

"I must return," Sionee sputtered. She missed Daysong, and needed to see her smile ... and Cyex.

"By and by, my little one... you shall return." The white lady stroked Sionee's smooth forehead softly with love. Sion felt warmth infuse her entire soul with love's powerful energy.

"Let me braid your hair, my darling. Then, we shall feast."

~~~

The beautiful lady brushed Sionee's coppery-dark hair with an ivory comb. Deftly, she wove long braids that hung in glistening strands from all the places on Sion's head.

From inside her feathered robe, she retrieved a handful of tiny topaz beads that were shaped like stars.

Some were of golden topaz, and some were of blue. The lady wove the jeweled beads into Sionee's braids ... here ... there ... and everywhere ... and filled her head with the glory of the stars.

Sion sat patiently, beguiled by the woman's voice as she sang while she braided. She sang of quiet rain and of glistening morning dew. She sang of the west wind and of the east. She sang of the cold north wind and of the gentle south. She sang of fire flame and the silver moon. and of the green grass, beneath bare toes. She sang of the sweet brown earth, the pale blue sky of white clouds and all the stars of the heavens. She sang of deep peace.

At last, she made the final braid, and turned Sion's head from left to right, smiling at her handiwork.

"Indeed! It is beautiful my daughter. The jewels catch the morning light as you move your head. You must wear your hair thus from now on, my dear for it is covenant that you have been chosen as blessed of the blest. You may look now and see."

She handed Sionee a small white clamshell. Sion opened it up and inside the shell there was a silvered mirror. Sion touched her hair in wonder. It was beautiful. It was shining ... it was awesome! It was ... she was ... well, surely she looked as if she was star herself shining from the depths of the high universe above in radiant glory!

"Are you She Who Creates By Thinking?" She asked.

"I am who I am, and I am ALL that I am ... I am She who is, and is I who is I ... ," The lady answered, giggling. "Why is it you mortals try to name me in different names when I am only all that is? As you, too, are only that which is all.

"Now my daughter, I have for you a riddle. Before we feast I shall inquire of you: How many stars are shining in your hair? If you may tell me, I shall give you a prize."

"A what? What for?" I didn't count them."

"Silly girl!" She smiled indulgently. "Did you not see that there is one star shining in your hair that is of a different color than the rest?"

"Oh? I thought they were all blue and golden topaz." Curious, Sionee held the mirror to her eyes to find the star of a different color.

"I cannot see it!" She exclaimed, turning her head in all directions while lifting her braids for further examination. So what color is it? They all look the same to me!"

"Try looking at the back of your head, darling." The lady tinkled a bell like laughter in gleeful merriment.

"What? You don't say! You do not have eyes in the back of your head? Well, darling, where are they then?" Her giggles peeled out and sent forth sparks of light dancing from treetop to treetop.

"Come," she tossed her shimmering golden head and slid down the tree.

"Let us feast now, my silly child."

~~~

"PERFECT LOVE AND PERFECT TRUST MY DAUGHTER ... ARISE AND COME WITH ME. No one knows if, and no one knows what, and no one knows why ... and does it really matter, my darling?" She asked, dining on an over-ripe persimmon she pulled from a crane-skin bag. She pulled out another one and gave it to Sionee.

Sionee frowned. "I am hungry. What else do you have to eat?"

"Oh, I have an entire bagful," the lady replied, pulling out several more persimmons, "of food for thought! Eat child and be full!"

"What does matter, Mother?" Sionee asked. Surely, she was someone's mother, or something's mother.

"Your heart matters." The white lady lay her hand on Sionee's AHDAWN. "FOR IF THAT WHICH YOU SEEK YOU FIND NOT WITHIN YOUR HEART YOU WILL NEVER FIND IT WITHOUT. You know this. Did you forget to remember daughter?"

"I always listen to hear what my heart is saying."

"Oh, child, sometimes it is a quiet, quiet voice. All hearts need remembering now and then, even the Feyri Queen. I, too, once forgot that I had wings to fly. A lovely little lady gave me a reminder. Did you forget that you, too, must remember your heart's voice? What found you in the volume you beheld in Tua?"

"I ... I ... ."

"Did it sing to you of a whole heart ... ? Of a pure heart ... ? Of peace, beauty, joy, light, and most importantly of love ... ? Did you hear GNOS?"

"I ... I ... ."

"Within the halls of Tua you sought to find ... and there you thought you held in your hand the missing heart piece. I will tell you this ... listen, listen. You fought so hard to make sure that you put the missing piece back in!

"Nothing will putrefy a heart like the broken piece you placed within. Love cannot be denied, my dear."

"But he ... he ... ."

"Nothing of judgment or anger will ever heal a whole heart. LOVE IS THE LAW, the one thing your heart should hold and cherish, my darling. It is the heart's law, the only law a heart understands."

Sionee frowned, what had that slimy fish head said a law was?

"He said it was a power, Alsionee Tree Song. The power of love frees your soul. You have sought a pure heart, my dear. Tell me now that your seeking was sincere!

"Go to him my child. There you will find your prize."

Chapter Fifty

Sionee Tree Song climbed the slippery wild white grape vine, holding fast to the thick tendrils and the leafy nodules that sprang from the ancient stem.

The moon was fixing to be full soon, as was Yule night. It was still in its wax, and lent a bit of light to a girl whose heart pulsed within her like the music which sang within the spheres.

She was not afraid ... not afraid ... not. Oh, maybe a little. It was quite unrelated to her past fear, yet it had already pierced her with an arrow of sorts.

She swung into the cavern entrance, drenched with mist from the moon-silvery water. Her senses were quickened with the satiation of epiphany.

The key had been lost, along with that nuisance push button thing, when the evil fish headed ones had overtaken her.

But Eah was not of their kind. He was good. And, she knew where to find him.

She was not afraid. Oh, she was not afraid ... well mayhaps a little. The cave was dark within, but she knew exactly where it was ... how many steps to take ... and in which direction from the entrance. For safety measures, she lit a torch. She didn't need a fresh bump on her forehead to decorate her coming Yule regalia.

Sionee sighed took a deep breath "Heeeeeeeeerrre goes."

I go to the night as a lover in waiting ... I hold to my heart that which spills its fullness as a spring that seeks to reunite with the sea ... Yet, quiet still ... the essence flows from the moon to my veins ... my hunger yet waiting ... to be sweetened with one last need.

She spoke the words inside her head by the way she had grown accustomed. She chanted them with closed eyes as she gave herself to the mystery of the depths. The thick glass tunnel reached for her and pulled her in ... to swallow her whole.

421

He had explained to her that it was a way to get through the mountain ... easily and swiftly, without having to go above or around ... just straight on, into the sea depths. She knew that it was a secret way he had of getting to his sacred place, that was as dear to him, as her story tree was dear to her.

It was likely he was somewhat upset right now. He said that watching the fish calmed him down ... that he loved to sleep there. Sion had no doubt that he would be there.

He had explained that the tunnel was perfectly safe, yet quite unsettling if its scientific properties were not understood. Both she and Daysong had traveled thus, before. But this time she knew a little more about it, like where it would end, and that when she got there, she would need to swim like a fish on the sea floor. She would need to find the door before she ran out of breath.

He said that he would not lock it in case she ever came this way again. She had found his secret ... as Cyex had, as well. He had said she could come this way anytime. She had assured him it was not likely.

"Just know it is easily opened, darling. I keep it well oiled. Just in case."

She needed to tell him something ...

~~~

The tunnel finally spat her into the waters, turvy-topsy beneath the sea. She was not afraid ... not at all. It was peaceful in the depths of the vast undersea garden. It was quiet ... so quiet.

She swam promptly to the glimmer of the portal door. She was guided by the blue light that illuminated the waters, the light he had put there so he could watch the fish.

Sionee turned the wheel of the door firmly. It wasn't exactly easy. She was feeling the pain of holding her breath, and the wheel gave. She hoped that with its turn, the shrieking alarm thing would not go off. It would sort of spoil things.

A current of water pushed her inside when she got the door opened. Quickly, she swung the door back in place. She slipped on the wet stone floor.

She must be quiet as possible. *"Can you surprise him?"* She asked herself? Would she? No sense guessing. She was here, now ... whatever the consequences.

She was drenched in heavy ocean waters. She slipped out of her wet linens and shook out her sleek tight braids. Cautiously, she peered into the softly lit room of stars.

It was likely that he would be sleeping. She tiptoed into the room. It was well past the midnight hour. It had taken her much time to gather her courage to come.

The sanctuary was lit only by the soft cobalt light that shone from the outside in.

He was asleep on the floor, lulled no doubt by the graceful motion of the fish. He slept on a bed of plush lamb fleece with thick goose down pillows that were soft beneath his head. His arm cradled another pillow, holding it close.

Sionee lay down at his side. She could feel his every breath. He was so nice and warm.

As she lay beside him, she was struck with the peace of watching the life of the sea on the other side of the big window. A big golden fish swam in graceful motion exactly as he had described to her. They did not care if it was past midnight. They were oblivious to whether it was night or day.

She molded her body into the curve of his, and felt his heartbeat in rhythm with her own. She looked to the starfish which he had placed dangling from the ceiling. In the far reaches of the room, it was darker where little of the blue light penetrated from the other side of the window. The corners of the room glowed with bits of fluorescent coral he had placed in his undersea universe.

His quiet breathing lulled her like a lullaby. The grace of the fish silently sang her the song of the sea. She counted them as they swam by. Her eyelids drooped and dreamily she fell deeply asleep, warm beneath Eah's soft fleece. She was at his side.

~~~

Ea did not know how possibly he had slept through the night ...

and a good sleep it was. He was worried about Daffinina. He was torn with the knowledge that he had really hurt her.

It had been her choice to flee. She had made it clear that it was not his right to interfere, and of course, he did know this. It was the Law of Titain. Again, the breaking of laws always had consequence. He understood that he had messed things up bad. Surely, she hated him now. What he had done was deplorable in the perceptions of the innocents.

On the other hand, could he have stopped her, prevented her from injuring herself, endangering herself? He should have. She had been in a most distressful state of mind. Would she return before an infection set in, or the bump on her head burst inside her brain? When she did ... if she did, he would just have to let her go. Surely she was lost to him.

He hadn't slept at all the night before, and tonight sleep hadn't come easy, following a worrisome day that he had spent calling himself every conceivable foul name he could think of.

To make matters worse, Marduk was searching, still, for his girl. He had said that some of the men told him that the hero who took Taya had taken a flying vehicle, while the girl was still slung across his shoulder, alive and kicking. Marduk had left in attempt to find her.

Watching the fish swim ... to and fro ... somehow ... Ea finally had sunk into the temporary respite that sleep made possible. As his eyelids closed, he thought of how the fish served as a hypnotizing focus like the crystal agate.

Damn! Damn him for what he did to Daffinina. He had stolen her free will and her baby!

Of course, she was angry, and well she should be. Ea's fitful sleep was eased by a dream. He dreamed that Daffinina was lying soft and warm beside him as he slept. He felt a strange sense of euphoria and slept comfortably, in peace for the rest of the night.

Ea moved beneath the cozy covers. How was it that he could sleep so deeply given the circumstances? His Daffinina ... he prayed that she was safe.

"I deserve her hate." Ea cursed himself as he slept. "I didn't know then, how it was to love someone so much. I didn't understand that anyone could rock my world of infinity with one small smile ... ah! But that she hate me forever, even THAT I might abide, if I must. If only she is safe this night, my Daffinina.

~~~

A gentle sigh whispered through the silence of his sleep. He woke in the darkness before the dawn. He found her lying beside his bed.

Surely, he was still dreaming! All night long he had dreamed of her. He did not wish to wake up, because she would be gone again. Now, he could have her only in his dreams.

Though his dream was lit only by a faint hint of light, he could see by the blue glimmer on her hair that she wore topaz jewels, like the ones his mother always wore in her hair. Indeed! Only in a dream ... for his Daffinina hated him, now. He had done something so ill, that she could never forgive him. He would never be close to her again ... only in his dreams!

Ea caught his breath as he beheld her dream-beauty lying naked beside him. He reached out to touch her cheek. In his dream, how could it be possible that her skin was so soft and warm? Oh, and flushed in sweet sleep? How could this dream fragrance of honey locus, mixed with the tang of sea salt, be so real?

He was so lonely! It wasn't that he was alone. It's just that never, in all his aeons of time, had he ever been touched with such strong emotion. Glad he was, that he had at least experienced her for even a brief moment of his ancient of days, and been given the priceless joy of knowing her. Eternity seemed so blank without her presence!

Indeed, his spirit was dimmed with loneliness for her. Ninmah made him laugh. But, he never had felt for anyone what he felt for one small girl of the earthen shores. He'd never even shared with his half-sister his sacred hide-out beneath the sea. He would show Daffinina his sanctuary anytime if she was still interested. But no, he had frightened her so badly, she certainly would not come this way again. Oh, blessed, blessed dream where she abided with him as real.

Sionee felt his hand on her cheeks, and opened her eyes.

"GNOS!" He whispered, gently. She had given it to him ... Song ... As he looked at her, his eyes were the limpid softness of the silver moon. He bid her dream image... "Songkeeper, I see you."

~~~

She shivered. Her soul sprang rhyme. She quivered when his fingers rested on the side of her face. She trembled on fire as she felt her spirit dancing with his in the music of the early morning.

"I am here, Eah, to tell you something. I love you!" As her eyes melted into his, the gold of her orbs made the stars in the heavens pale in glory. Her liquid light of love infused his small soul.

It was then, that he knew that her love had awakened him, and that she was no dream-wraith. She was really here ... naked inside his bed. He softly said, "Come take me."

With a whispering cry, he drew her atop of him. Heartbeat to heartbeat she trembled in rapture, melting into his breath. She touched the tide of his tears with the tip of her tongue. His waters flowed into her ocean within.

She kissed him with open, wet mouth kisses all over his tear-streaked cheeks. She sank beneath his waters ... DEEP. She drowned in the fathoms of his sea.

He tasted his salt on her tongue. The breath they both drew as they came up for air ... gasping ... was only one breath!

They lay together ... quiet and still ... their bodies pressed together, as one. In graceful repose, on top of his, her body rose gently with the rhythm of his pulsing heart. Her own heart pulsed in motion with his, until there was only one heartbeat throbbing in synchronistic motion.

Together, their souls flowed in ebb and tide, and deep-thrummed to the endless call of eternity's moon.

They lay thus, in languid peace and listened contently to the beat of their shared heart.

For the first time in all his millions of years, as an Annunaki blood body, Eah felt the true code of his Pleiadian heritage.

His heart became the solid, priceless treasure of authentic gold, emotion! At last he could write mother that he understood what it was that she had been trying to get him to see. There was no teacher better than experience itself.

How long the two of them lay together in silent adoration of their common breath was of no measure. There was only the song that filled the chamber beneath the sea with symphonic rhapsody.

The pulse of the universe began to throb like fire! His spirit leapt to life, as part of his body responded to the voice of the sea calling him.

Her spirit overflowed her cup of AHDAWN! It spilled its flow over her thirsty body. Together their bodies moved in unison of rapture. Light waves of the soul sang their bodies whole in the vibrancy of rapt ballet ... increasing their fluid emotions in graceful motion.

Their tongues tasted and devoured the insatiable sweetness of their love. Together, their tongues danced the snake dance they had begun one year ago on Yule nightfire. Up their spines, great energy flowed, and dissolved both of them into the dazzling darkness of infinite bliss.

He spun her around and lay her back upon the pillows. Her star-studded braids spilled their splendor upon his bed. He hungered for her. He would taste of her sweetness ... every part of her beautiful body.

~~~

The sea escaped its confining boundary. The waters began their rise when the moon whispered "Come unto me!" The luminary demanded now, with increasing urgency.

"I am the moon on the waters of the crystal blue sea, and I call to your soul ... Arise and come unto me."

The depths began to respond to ripples that rolled undulating in a motion that sought to heed the song of the moon.

Small thralls of water mounded and began an ever increasing dance of rhythm, rhythm, rhythm ... seeking union with the voice of the moon, whose call bid her from pearly heights.

The watery hillocks mounded in crescents of rolling motion, the surge reached higher and higher in a vain attempt to reach the moon. The waves of big water circled within, and spun round ... and round ... the current rolled toward the shore ... seeking now, the sands on the shore edge.

The moon smiled down on the moving waters. The Goddess ... the sea in all her glory ... responded to the silvery voice rising ... again, rising ... rising ... rolling on and on in endless pull of gravity.

The waves rolled in closer and closer to the shoreline ... one wave after another ... just beyond lulls of surging motion ... one by one ... by one by one ... the waves rolled in. They crescendoed ... one by one into a tumultuous crash of white foam ... and salty sea ... as the waters broke upon the sands.

Their motions sated, the sea wave completed the cycle of ebb and flow, returning once again to the deep ... which was its original home.

Taya had said, "Become a wave." Sionee breathed her own breath at last ... *when she remembered to breathe again.*

"Now, that was one big wave, Eah. You are the waters of my soul!
~~~

"We have already created a life together, Eah ... You and I." She spoke at last.

Ea sat upright. "You have long been patient, my Daffinina. Let us go my darling ... and introduce our son to his mother."

Adapa. She would call him Naaman, beloved. Sionee caught her breath. She caught her breath ...

Chapter Fifty-one

Cyex waited, even though Kinga had told him that Alsionee was okay. "*She needs attending to,*" the kingfisher twitted.

"Is she hurt?"

"*Well, my master. She was! I know so little ... only that I saw her in the care of a most magnificent little number.*"

"What are you saying?"

"*Twit ... twit ... twit ... twit ... twit .... She is being cared for, Master Cyex. She will return home to you and Miss Daysong promptly ... when she is healed ... I assure you.*"

Cy had no idea how seriously she had been hurt, inadvertently the bird had answered his question. If she needed healing, she must have been hurt.

When Kinga came to him earlier in the morning to inform him about Sionee's abrupt departure, albeit minus infinite details of how and why, Cy pressed him for more information, which the bird seemed reluctant to give.

"I must go to her, Kinga! Surely you know that! Do you know where she is? Oh, surely, you do!" He begged. When Kinga twitted bird language, Cy tried a more authoritative approach. "Tell me, Kinga!" He shouted with enough force that Kinga's blue feathers ruffled.

"*As you wish ... it has to do with a fish!*" Then, the bird flew off, leaving him alone to worry.

~~~

Ninmah found Cy dancing atop a hill in the wildwood forest. She spotted him from the air. She was out flying with Ea's Ti Titum, who had been annoyingly cross all day because she missed her mother. She had fitted the baby girl with a pair of small wings and was attempting to show her how they worked. The girl was not as adept at flying as was Adapa.

She hovered, unseen above the one they called Cyex. He danced

429

like a young sapling tree in the breeze at the edge of the purple mist between the folds of dimension. He bent with the breeze in a mournful dance. Lithe and beautiful, he was. Poor little man. This one could be Lord of her dance, anytime. He needed cheering up.

Downward she descended, carrying Ti Ti in her arms. He looked up from his dance in surprise. Ninmah put the child down. The little girl scampered on her tiny toddler legs to catch a butterfly that was gathering nectar from a ripe laden bough of apples that hung low to the hilltop flat.

Ninmah stood before Cyex, her hands on either side of her short linen shift, lifting it up to cheer him with the pleasure of her glory.

He gasped and stepped back in total shock. He turned his head away quickly, putting his hand before his eyes.

"Do I not please you? I am fine. I will heal your troubled heart."

"Oh... ah... Ninmah. It is not that. You are most beautiful, I must say. It is not that I am without temptation to accept your kind offer, but right now I have issues."

"I will issue you in a most pleasing manner." She smiled at him, sweetly. "Come to me, now. Hurry we must before the child grows weary of her butterfly!"

"Sweet Ninmah, you are beautiful and have pleased my eye, It ... my rising does not work efficiently while I am at worry."

"It is about the girl who sings with no words, is it not? She is well beautiful. I will agree, though quite young. She is why I have sought you, my friend, and Ea's friend."

"You came looking for me?"

"Indeed. Since this girl has been missing, this child has been a-whine for her mother. I have heard that you have a charm with all the girls. Cyex, would you mind the child for me and for your Daff ... A ... Sion ... ee, I believe you call her? I have another young one who is most demanding of my attentions. I must say, he is not as well-mannered as this little one, even when she misses her mother so."

"What about her father?" Cy asked. "Where is he?"

"He is beside himself. He says it is his fault that this whole thing happened."

"Has he searched for her?"

"No. She asked him ... Oh, she told him not to."

Something was not right here. What had happened?

~~~

Daysong was happy to be with her Fa-Cy, who she loved so much. Fa-Cy played her songs on his flute. Her mother called him Cy, but sometimes she confused his name with the name of the other man she liked ... her fa fa. It was easier to say, so she called him Fa-Cy when she wanted him to hold her in his arms as he played his music. When everyone else was too busy to play with her, she could always count on either of her men.

~~~

After two nights gone ... in the morning ... bright as sunshine, Sionee came home at last, bounding into the tree, and holding her arms out for Daysong.

"Mam maman!" The little girl called in glee, running full of giggles to her mother. "Mammaman."

Holding Daysong in her arms against her heart, Sionee cried in joy. She managed a smile for Cy, who stood eagerly, close by.

"Sionee, I have been so worried! We all have ... the entire outlier and beyond. We have so hoped for you to be well and able to attend Yule fire with us." He stood back to look at her.

She seemed fine ... and beautiful. Her hair was a-glimmer in tiny stars and many braids. Cy caught his breath. He had never seen her look so beautiful. Something in her eyes made his heart want to stop beating.

She had chosen, then. Sionee Song Tree had been *with* him.

He turned, putting his hands up ... his palms flat. "It's okay, Sion. I can at least breathe now that I see you are safe. You don't owe me any explanations." He began to gather his things to leave. Cy stopped when she spoke ... in REAL words.

"Cy, please. There is something I must tell you."

She had said that when she found the words of her whole heart again, her vow of no words would be removed. Now that she was talking, he didn't want to hear her say what was so obvious. She was as shimmering, surely as anyone could get.

Daysong pulled on Sionee's hand. "Mamman ... Daaaaaaay Day."

"Cy." Sion tried to tell him, but Daysong was eager and impatient for exclusive attention. The little girl started to cry, wanting to play. Sionee tried to continue her conversation with Cy.

"Taya and I were stolen by some bad fish heads when we went to get apples in the wild forest. They did bad things to us! No, Cy, not that ... but there were other girls they did it to. There was this one ... he tried. He hit me! I banged my head and blood was dripping ... I felt so dizzy. I can't tell you everything, Cy ... not here in front of Daysong while she's pulling at me. For now, my only wish is to hold her. I thought I would never see her again!"

"I am glad you weren't hurt too badly, Sionee."

"I was hurt, Cy. I will tell you all of it! So much has happened. There is something specifically that I really need to tell you, though."

Cy turned. Again, she had not said thank you for taking care of Daysong. But then, that's what friends were for. "Sure, Sionee, later." It didn't appear as if she had suffered in the least. What had happened, he couldn't guess, except that somehow in all of this she had been with Ea ... really been with him! It was so visible in her eyes and in her thoughts which still spoke truer than words. He didn't need her mere tongue words to hear her say, "*You are my best friend, Cy... always ... Just friends.*"

He waited for a moment. Maybe if he physically heard the words he could begin to put wholeness into his own empty life without her, since she had chosen Ea.

She was silent, though. Seeing as she had gotten her tongue back, he had a stupid desire to hear her voice one more time before he left.

"What was it you said you really needed to tell me?" His voice was abrupt.

"You are no longer my friend!"

It was even worse than he had thought. Not even her friend?

~~~

He couldn't have possibly heard her wrong. She had said it loud and clear with ... like ... words. He frowned. Suddenly he wanted to be her friend, more than anything he'd ever wanted ... at least her friend.

Her heart broke when she saw the pain in his eyes. She giggled in merriment.

Oh! So, she thought it funny? Looking at her suddenly with comprehension, he wanted to take her over his knee and spank her on her bare... "Not your best friend?" He asked her again.

"Well, Yes and no. More importantly, you are you, Cy ... hey! You are squeezing me! You are squeezing both of us!" Sionee put the protesting little girl down and motioned for her to go play.

Cy was kissing her full on the lips and it was ... he was ... his lips were as good as she had dreamed about ever since she was ten years old, when they had first kissed.

His hands slid up her shift. She managed to pull away, breathless.

"We should take Daysong out, Cy, on a picnic, perhaps overnight. She would enjoy it, and us too."

"Sionee darling, is this a promise? Or is it a by and by ... because my by has just gone high!"

Sionee giggled as she found dry bread in her eating nook. "Could you go fetch the cheese in the cold storage? Oh ... ." She bent to get puffed millet for Daysong to munch on. She stood up and put the millet in a small pouch. "What I was trying to tell you ... is that ... I love you!"

Sion threw both her arms around Cy and gave him a wet one on the cheek.

"Wuv." Daysong hugged Cy's knee, wanting to be picked up. "Wuv Fa-Cy."

Sionee fell to the floor, giggling and happy. Cy fell beside her. Daysong scampered over both of them in glee, happy that they both wanted to play unicorns with her. She climbed on each of them. She jumped on Sionee's belly, and then on Cy's back. He rolled on top of Sion. In delight, Daysong sat astraddle them both. Her tiny legs dangled down into her mother's face.

Cy moved a tiny bare foot off of Sionee's lips, kissing the tiny baby toes. He smothered Sion with kisses. His lips had a pulse of their own as he put kisses all over her face, from her brow to her eyelids, and to her cheeks. He made a wet path down to the pulse at the base of her throat. He rubbed his nose in the soft hollow of her ear. Playfully, he stuck his tongue within its cup, as he had done when they were ten.

She smelled like cedar berries. He wanted to taste all of her ... every blessed part of her. He kissed her chin with his open lips, relishing the soft triangular cup with his tongue.

Again, his tongue swept her soft mouth, opening it with the urgency of his tongue. Sion opened her lips to let him in.

"Fa-Cy ... Mamman," Daysong giggled, digging her foot into the nonexistent seam where both their bodies pressed against the others every curve ... undistinguishable from being anything other than one body.

Sionee giggled and squirmed out from beneath Cyex when she felt a tapping on her thigh.

"Hey, I was getting to like this!" He protested.

"Later." She promised. "I will show you what I mean, when I say I love you. But for now, you and I have a very rambunctious and impatient one year old to take care of. Remember?

~~~

"If we let her chase butterflies and scramble after lizards, and talk to all the song birds, she will be ready for a nap in no time. However, if we keep her too busy on our adventure to nap, she will go to sleep early tonight. So let's go wear her out, Cy!"

Sion grabbed a blanket, or two, or three, for them to sleep with. She put the bread and cheese in a pouch along with the millet puffs.

"Maybe I can catch us a fish or two at evening meal. Say, Sionee, where are we going?"

"Wherever it takes us," she replied.

He put Daysong on his shoulder. One little leg dangled down from each side of his neck. The three left for another adventure.

~~~

Back to the moss they rode, on Vastari and Lightening. "We have unfinished business there." Cy told Sion. "I have longed to lay you back on that moss!"

He pulled out his flute as he rode astride Lightening, and played Sionee a love song that made her want to hurry and get there ... and for night time to fall ... and for sweet Daysong to be fast asleep.

During the day, Sion was hardly silent, as if she was making up for her lack of REAL words this past year.

"I told you I could remember you chatting like a magpie when we were young," Cy said at last.

She told him about the evil fish heads, and how they had hurt her, and how the worst hurt was the fear, and the hate they led her to suffer.

"They are real, Sionee. More and more they are coming to our Gaia. Poor Taya, she was such a bright and cheerful little one."

"She was my best friend, except for Coelle ... and you!" She giggled at him on that one.

"I thought I'd lost you, Sionee."

"While Coelle is but a dimension away, Cy, Taya is much further. She still lives ... in a land across the seas. She isn't dead. As one of the brutes carried her away, I caught the life-spark still inside her. The mean one, who hurt me, told the others that anyone could take her.

The big one, that took her, swung her over his shoulder. As he walked before me, I saw sorrow in his eyes. When I looked, I saw that the big one had a good heart. Some of them do, Eah ... for instance.

As I began to fade from loss of blood and pain, I saw visions before my eyes. I saw Taya alive on Gaia. Eventually she will find her love with this man, and be happy. When he took her he knew that it was the only way to save her."

"Are you certain?" Cy asked doubtfully. "How could that be?"

"You do not believe me, Cy? I saw for myself that our Taya will be a Queen on green shores, somewhere. She will be happy there.

"While I was out walking between the worlds, I saw many things. I learned to read books."

"You what?"

"Books ... I went to the halls of Tua."

"What?"

"I did! When I came back I was reminded that this dimension, itself, is sort of a dream. I was in the depths of hell's hate because of something I saw there. Then, she came!"

"Who came?"

"She Who Creates By Thinking. I believe it was She. She healed me, Cy. She restored the missing piece of my heart. She restored my life ... and my AHDAWN."

She showed me that the power of love frees your soul to a better life. Perfect Love and Perfect Trust ... She instructed me. I learned that Love is the Law ... the only true law."

"But you already knew about the one, Sionee."

"I needed reminding. I am afraid that our paradise world of people, who have no perception other than the mantra of one, will change with the coming times. The fish head laws are being thrust into our lives with a force that we do not understand. I perceive that their laws are about power and control.

I am to teach our people to remember the power of good, and the only true law ... which is to love each other. Our people have lived in this way since ancient times ... that ALL LIGHT FROM THE SUN IS ONE! This includes the fish heads. Some of them understand this, like Eah!"

~~~

Daysong slept content and cozy beneath the stars, wrapped snuggly in soft linen and resting on the soft mattress of moss. It was dark at last, and Cy put more wood on the fire. The soft flickering warmth cast its light in a glowing circle of intimacy.

"Did I hear you, then, when you said, 'I love you'?" Or, am I just ONE of those lights from the sun?"

"Cy. You ARE the light of my sun!" She pulled the linen wrap from off her body.

He had seen her without her clothes before, naked ... but at this moment she was HIS naked. He reached out to touch her moon-glow skin, but she raced away from him, laughing.

She dove into the deep pool that kept the moss so lovely and green at their overnight bower. He could see nothing but the concentric ripples of expanding motion where she had parted the waters. He wondered if he could jump into the exact center of that spiraling whirl.

The waters mirrored the moons silvery reflection, and made ripples when he took her into his arms and kissed her. Their lips locked together in trembling passion.

He swung her around and straddled her on his thigh. Both of her legs wrapped around him. Fused at the lips, his tongue sought her taste.

Their mouths wrenched apart, breathless and needing to breathe. "Sionee ... Sionee ... ! Stop! I want more ... slowly. I want to honor your body ... every inch of you ... before I enter the temple door.

"I want for you to meet me on the soft moss by the fire," She whispered.

"I want to see you in the moonlight." Cy spoke with husky softness, trembling, "As the moss knows your nakedness, so shall I."

Cyex put more wood on the fire, enough to last for quite some time. They lay entwined, cradled on the soft sweet moss. He could smell the cedar berry fragrance of her star-strewn hair as it spilled over the moss. The beads glimmered in the soft light of the moon. Cy knew that he held the greatest of all stars on this night.

~~~

The earth rumbled within the valley deep inside the moon mountain of the Goddess.

"Come in ... come in!" She ... Goddess ... bid the dweller at her door. "Bring your flute and we shall make song.

"The portal is open for you. Sweetly, I shall swallow you in the

chambers of my secret."

Eager, he was ... to enter and pay homage to her. He thrust into her dark softness. The halls closed in, and in the great room, he could feel the echoes of her heart beating the pulse of a drum song to his soul.

As the hollows trembled in the cadence of her rhythm, he danced in the chamber to her song. He remembered that it was not a flute with which he played homage. It was his instrument of sex. His hard shaft plundered her depths as she bid him ... Yes ... Oh, yes! At last, the volcanic lava burst forth expanding and spilling inside her.

~~~

When the tremors abated, the two of them lay before the fire. They were glowing with soft light, happy and warm, and weary. Sionee broke the silence at last.

"Cy, my love. The earth shook for me on this evening. It opened up, and I found myself melting into a wave of liquid fire.

"Taya told me to become wave. That was one really big wave! You are my earth, Cy!"

Chapter Fifty-two

When dawn's first light was yet to be hinted at, the two awoke after only a few short hours of sleep. They felt more awake than if they had slept for hours. After making love again, they agreed to rise, and depart for home in the early hours. There was much for both of them to do to get ready for this very important night.

Side by side they rode on their two unicorns. Day Song was still sleeping, wedged in Cyex's arms. The two, enraptured in a state of awe, conferred quietly.

"Earth and fire. So I am your earth and fire. But do I not complete you?"

Sionee sighed. "Oh, Cyex, you know that you complete my soul so perfectly. And you know also ...

"He is my water, and he is my air. I breathe love for him like I breathe the very air which sustains me." Sion spoke in a whisper.

"I make you tremble with molten liquid light of love, and your heart lives in my heart, as my heart lives in your heart. I am the ground of your being. Hummmmmmm. Oh, Sionee, I like being your earth and your fire. I will be anything for you, and everything."

"You are my water and my air, as you fill my soul and make my *AHDAWN* whole!"

"Glad I am, darling; he, too, is your fire and your earth." Then, he silenced her with a deep kiss. Day Song's giggles, as she awoke, brought them back from where the kiss had taken them.

"Ga, Ga, Keeeeeen ga!" The little girl thrust her little hand out from where she sat, folded in the safety of Cy's lap. Kinga joined them, lighting upon her tiny finger. The little family rode home. It was the dawn of Yule morning.

~~~

Near the tree, Cyex bid Sionee and Daysong goodbye for the time. He needed to attend to his boys' instructions for the music at nightfire. Sionee and Daysong reached the ancient cedar just a wee bit later than usual, as morning goes ... but by only minutes, because the sun was still early in its place in the sea.

"Say to yourself, Daysong ... sing it to the sun, every morning of your life ... I AM THE PERFECT DAY AND IN ME DWELLS THE LIGHT THAT DOES NOT FAIL." Sionee's birdsong chanted from the crotch of the ancient cedar. Daysong joined her in the baby form of natural straight song. Kinga contributed his twits to the morning sun song. The chorus sparkled in the magic of dawns early light.

"Daysong, my darling, remember the story I have told you, that the light that lives inside you is your spirit which shines just as the sun shines. This is what our song is all about." Daysong clapped her hands.

"Kinga, my friend. I am so happy that you joined us this morning. I am remembering one year's time ago from today. It was then that I became acquainted with you. You dropped a gift for me."

Kinga smiled. *"I lent my feather to a beautiful girl,"* he twitted. Then, he dropped a tiny feather into Daysong's hand. The baby picked it up reverently in her tiny fingers. "Ooooooooooo," she sighed.

"Kinga, I have a favor to ask you."

"Of course, you do, my lady. I already heard it in your heart. I am well acquainted with the silent words that have their rising in the heart home. Though when you speak your huu-man words, it is a form of music alike." He gave her another feather, one of his most exquisite tail feathers of azuline blue.

"Thank you, thank you, my handsome king. In my heart, did you hear the rest?

"You may explain."

"I haven't exactly had time to prepare my regalia for the night. I've been so ... ah ... preoccupied. However I must have the costume that I see in my heart's eye."

"Oh, yes, darling," Kinga laughed. *"It is an idea of magnificence, and truly you must have your robe. Oh, I suppose I might be able to help."*

Sionee smiled. "Where are you going now?" She asked in delight.

"I have a lot of my friends I must see this day." He twitted. *"For you, my darling dunderhead, I would do anything."*

With a smile, Sion watched him fly high and disappear into the morning light. Then, she turned her attentions to her daughter who was trying to talk to a little spider that dangled from a silken thread that extended from an upper branch of the cedar. The spider stared directly into Daysong's eyes.

"Spideeee!" Daysong greeted, reaching out her hand to touch.

"Hush, darling," Sionee instructed. "We will frighten her! Come on sweetie. Spider ... Remember daughter, as I have told you. We must talk spider to her. It is the only language she understands." As Daysong cooed to the spider, Sionee also had a little chat with her little friend. There was a favor she wanted to ask.

~~~

Somewhere midpoint the lands east of the sun and the lands west of the moon, surrounded by the waters of Seamother's great depths, the priestesses gathered in a circle. It was early evening, almost time for the nightfire songs.

Marisol of the Sparkling Shell walked around the circle center with a basket of herbs. "Thank you for the gatherings!" She spoke fondly to the girls. "The herbs you have brought forth will rise to the Mothers on this night in fragrant offering. She Who Creates By Thinking will be pleased with the gifts of your heart." She held a sage wand to her nose. Her eyes closed in pleasure at the breath. Deep contentment made her wisdom-aged face beautiful.

Many of the girls pulled from the basket a dried button of exquisite mushroom, and popped the fragment into their mouths in joyful anticipation. Marisol winked at Sionee. "I know darling, but not everyone can do it! Some of us need a little assistance to help us get into that vast world you so naturally have entrance to." She popped a mushroom into her mouth and chewed it. "Goddesses!" She called out. "Welcome us into your domain this evening.

"But you know, Sionee; the fumes of the incense from this button will take a person such as yourself even further in."

"I found out last year." Sionee waved her hand. She pulled out

441

wands of incense, to light at the first call.

"The regalia award will be given at the evenings end!" Marisol's eyes swept over the wonderful array of colorful and creative costumes. Then, she winked again at the girl who wore only two feathers and a universe of stars in her hair. "Some of you like to surprise us all!

"Alsionee, dear, we have all agreed on this. Traditionally, a new girl tells the story on this night, but last year your story was interrupted. We are really anticipating your wonderful straight song stories told in words. You really do have a lovely way of using the voice of spirit, either way. Will you honor us?"

"Thank you, Marisol. I will be honored to be Her mouthpiece. This year, my heart is whole! Who will be leading the dance?"

"Of course, Sion, you know well that honor is given to the storyteller. So, I guess it's you! It is consensual between us all. It is you! Oh, Blessed Be, my child!"

Sionee was pleased that she had thought about the story just a bit so she could tell it if asked ... and the costume too! Her head began to dance in further ideas to present this evening at GNOS.

One of the young priestesses offered to take Daysong from Alsionee's arms. "Thank you, but Daysong will dance with me around the snake spiral. But afterward she may join the other babies around the fire. If you will help me with her at that time, I will bless you for your assistance."

The priestess smiled in honor. "Of course, she may sleep with the other babies on this night after the celebration." The young priestess giggled. Of course!

"Will the fish head be observing?" The girl asked, smoothing the butterfly-wing short tunic she wore.

"Oh, we shall watch for him," Sionee replied shyly, all of a sudden tingling in anticipation. "We shall see. His name is Eah, you know. Eeee aaah. I know it is a little different to sound, but remember his name consists mostly of the straight song sounds, and it is easy. I think it is a beautiful name. Eeeeeee-aaah." Sionee closed her eyes, smiling a little smile to herself.

The soft sounds of flutes rising in song brought Sionee back into the present moment. Sionee looked to the arena center and saw that the instrument players were arriving. Her heart was happy when she saw that Cyex was with his boys, instructing them on the songs. From across the circle, he winked at her, lifted the flute to his lips and she heard that the song he was warming up with was the song he had made up especially for her.

~~~

The dance of life begins there, in the heart, in *AHDAWN*, which really is the home of the spirit. One hears its voice there, in the quiet. There it is that the steps first form.

The spirit of snake called to Sion, reminding her of who snake is. The snake is the physical robe of the spirit. This is why Sionee preferred to begin her dance in nakedness, because the pure spirit, in being a voluminous spark of light on a finer dimension than is Gaia's earth, stands resplendent in its utter purity.

Sionee stood utterly resplendent in the utter purity of her body, to dance the serpent dance with the other Children of the Snake of the Sea. The crowd gasped, as a shining Alsionee Tree Song, wearing only two feathers, one blue, one white, led the dance.

"*Breath, Breath ... Oh, almighty Breath, I Breathe.*" Sionee told her spirit. The pillar that linked the earth to sky began to rise.

The sage and rue wands were fragrant as the priestesses carried them around the circle, offering sacred smoke to cleanse and purify the space which was holy. Other priestesses offered skullcap and jasmine so that heart homes would open freely this night, and henbane to welcome the spirits from other worlds to join them. Lavender, sweet cedar, sandalwood and other herbs invited the holy Mothers from all the dimensions to join the circle, as well.

A smoky pungence wafted to Sionee's nose and she smiled softly. Perfect peace profound.

Ka-tak ... ka-tak ... ka-took ... the drum sounded deep ... Mother's heartbeat kept time with the rhythm of life.

Sionee tossed her long star-strewn braids and surrendered her inhibitions. She welcomed other dancers to join her in the dance. She raised her arms, her palms thrust upwards, and bid them come. And, come they did ... a long line of colorful dancers, each with their hands holding on to the waist of the dancer in front.

The sounds of the night made melody with the wind of the flute. The song of loon, the song of owl, the song of cranes in the marshes joined the song of the cicada, and the chorus of cricket, and the eerily distant rumbling song of the mammoth calling to its mate. The night breathed its living pulse, flickering like a heartbeat, in tune with the light of the central fire. Breath, Breath ... Oh, the Breath. The heartbeat of the Mother began its dance with the drum. Katak ... katak ... katak ....

Daysong was happily supported between Sion and Cyex. She giggled softly.

"No giggling, Day Day. This is a sacred moment. Go within my sweeting."

"Perhaps she is within her sweetness," Eah spoke softly, suddenly entering the circle from the outskirts of the meadow. The dancers, as well as the viewers, murmured in eagerness. He had come!

Cyex greeted him warmly, and put Daysong in his big hands. Ea had tears of joy in his eyes as Daysong squealed at him, happily.

Cy whispered, "Sion loves us both." Ea nodded and tried to stand behind Cyex in the circle, placing his hands on Cyex's waist. Cy stepped behind and placed his hands on Ea's waist.

"There is no end to this circle, my friend ... no first, second, or third. Only one. We are all one!"

Sionee began the lead in to the dance with a straight song, to keep the beauty of the tradition familiar to all the people. The straight song had a magic of its own. It could be heard only by those with ears to hear, the sound of birdsong turning into windsong on the waters of the spirit, and the wind on those waters turning into the silence of the stars in the dark sea of the deep blue abyss.

It was time to make a call to the light for which the tribe had named themselves, and for which this dance honored. Ea closed his eyes, himself having found at last perfect peace profound. His footsteps joined the rhythm of the music and the song.

~~~

"OH WINGED SERPENT DANCE WITHIN ... WITHOUT BEGINNING ... WITHOUT END ... SPIRAL ... SPIRAL ... ROUND AND ROUND ... THE ROOT ... THE TRUNK ... THE BARK IS FOUND ... RISING ... RISING ... HIGHER ... HIGHER ... UNTIL THE SPIRIT DOTH ACQUIRE ... BRANCH AND LEAF AND FRUIT ALL BE ... THERE UPON THE WISDOM TREE."

"Eat, my friends, feast of the fruits that fill your souls! Let us dance this song. The dancers began their dance of the snake, spiraling the pattern, in and out. Colors and rhythms and firelight-reflections lit the dancers with a thousand stars, the constellation being the stars in Sionee's hair as she led the dance. While they danced, the priestesses waved in and out of the spiral and the crowd, handing out apples ... for all to taste of the sweetness.

These were the special Yule apples, the best of the best, picked particularly for this occasion, and allowed to age so the sweetness and the succulence melted into sublimity inside the mouth.

The dance ended at last at the arena edge, when the circle was wide. All the dancers sat to watch. All eyes were now on the lone dancer in the center.

Alsionee swayed sensuously, her eyes closed in pleasure as she bit into her apple. Juice ran down her chin as she hummed sweetly. In a graceful motion, she rubbed her juicy, dripping apple over her entire body.

She moved to the rhythm of the delicious pulses rising within her. The stickiness of her naked body caught the reflection of the flame. A second dimension of light and shadow danced across her form. The crowd swayed in awesome rapture at the radiance of the woman clothed in light.

Her bare feet moved to dance her story. The observers whispered in hushed awe, long afterwards, about the rest of her performance.

Sionee's skill as storyteller entranced the entire gathering.

Beneath the full moon, Sion almost faded into the light of the flickering fire. She danced in and out among the crowd, and within the circle center. Twirling scarves, spun of a fiber so fine that it appeared as if they were living streams of light, swirled over her entire body. She made the scarves dance with her, twining around her ankles, teasing the length of her glistening skin.

The air was deep in the fragrance of charred herb and cedar wood. The rhythm of the dance, along with the breaths of the crowd, made the air vibrate in rich waves of scent and sound. Floating on the heavy air, Sionee's scarves drifted to the ground, gentle like the feathers of a bird wing, when she stopped her dance and raised her arms to the sky.

In response to her call, tiny spiders began a gossamer dance of almost invisible splendor around Sionee's naked body, making their way downward from a high overhead tree branch on long, silken threads. The spiders wove a web around Sion. She held her arms out in welcome, standing still while the spiders created a pattern of intricate and delicate beauty around her form.

When they had completed their artistry, the spiders crawled up their invisible threads back into the trees. Their silken strands of shining design caught a pattern of reflection which glistened upon her beautiful body as tiny filaments of light.

Suddenly, the stars that glimmered in the sky were crossed with the silhouettes of a thousand tiny birds fluttering their wings over Sionee's web-shrouded body. Their voices filled the air with the music of their presence. Sion's song became another note of the bird's song. Though spoken in the language of birds, her words were distinct.

"Thank you, my friends, for your gift. Now!" A thousand and more tiny feathers in every shade of blue fluttered down from the sky.

The heat from the fire added a heaviness of warmth to the air, causing the feathers to float and twirl as they danced in graceful rhythm, to land gently on the soft and sticky silk of Sionee's web.

Sionee stood cloaked in ethereal glory, flickering in the fire light like living blue flame. She wrapped the robe around the curves of her body. Her motions were graceful as she danced her song.

Only those who could see the world within themselves by closing their eyes, could see her at this point. She was invisible to the ordinary eye, blending deep into the depths of the night. The vibrations of her movement sent an occasional fallen feather, still alight and wafting, gently in a spinning to the ground. It was the only indication that she was there.

Chapter Fifty-three

"It is an illusion my friends." Alsionee Tree Song sang in words. The crowd bent to find her, their eyes following the source of her sound. Suddenly she reappeared, and they could see her dancing. Then, they could not find her again. Only the breeze of her gentle movements gave any clue as to where she was.

Closing their eyes, they thought they could see her again. But then, she disappeared once more. In and out of the vibrations of sound she spun as she danced. Then as suddenly as she began, she stopped dancing, and appeared wrapped in her blue robe, and visible in all her entirety.

"What is the light from the sun?" She inquired. "Is it heat? Is it warmth? Is it fire? Is it flame? Is it orange? Is it blue? Or, is it yellow? Does it dance, or does it flicker? Can you hear it singing, or does it roar? Is it real? To see with one's eyes? If one wishes, they may touch it? What might you say exactly that the light from the sun is?" Everyone pondered.

"It is one!" She chanted. "ALL LIGHT FROM THE SUN IS ONE! It comes and it goes, in one eternal spin," Sion continued. "It always returns. As it does on this Yule night with the dance of the orbs." She continued her story in full visibility, and the crowd stilled their astonished murmurs to listen.

"On this big circle we call Gaia, our earth, there are many lands where people are singing at nightfire this evening. Listen ... listen my friends ... while I sing to you the GNOS.

"In other lands the light from the sun differs in how it touches this earth. When the sun is farthest away from the spiral of this world's spin, it is cold, far colder than what we perceive as cold on our mild winter mornings.

"We are truly blessed, my friends. We live on the ever-summer land at the Snake of the Sea's mouth in the north. Here, our home is heated by the fires which smolder beneath us in the bowels of

449

Gaia, warming the waters of the sea around us, and the waters of the pools we bathe in. The roots of the trees, which feed our hungry bodies with sweet apples, ever replenish us, in both body and spirit. Here at our cove, Oh, Blessed Be, our land is rich in sunlight and apples and all manner of blessings.

"Three times three we are blessed here at our dwelling by the sea. We live in abundance and the plenty furnished by the earth and the seas around us. We have plenty, too, of time to contemplate on peace. It is not necessary for us to fill our lives with the endless quest for food. In some lands, and even on places in parts of our home, it is necessary for some people to work hard for the food of their body, leaving little time to fill the appetites of a healthy soul. Let us all sing now, a song of blessing and thankfulness to our beloved outlier by the sea."

While they were singing, Sionee's eyes spoke to the people with love for all. As she was contemplating on each dear face in the midst of the crowd, her eyes came to rest on a face she had only recently become acquainted with. It was the beautiful woman from the stars, who had no name. The wise woman's eye caught hers, and she smiled at Sion in approval. Sionee felt herself grow in the light of the love the woman directed toward her, as a rose surely must feel when she is smiled upon by a human being. At the white woman's side, Eah stood with his arm around his mother's lithe waist.

"This isn't the story as I recall." A voice called out from the crowd. A woman stepped forth and stood across the fire from Sionee.

"Listen." Sionee replied in words. "I have not finished yet."

"Please don't!" The woman spat back. Alita had taken off her shift to stand naked by the fire. Her breasts were as large as melons drooping from the vine. They swung up and down as she moved.

"If you really want the story, friends," Alita called out, "let me make it easier to hear. I won't fade away like thin air. My words will be heard by all!"

Murmurs rose like a groan from the crowd. Alita stood in proud defiance. Sionee went to Alita's side and extended her hand. Alita slapped it hard.

Marisol stepped forth from the crowd, angry. "You big mouth

with no brain, you are disturbing the story! Hush. We want to hear."

"Hear what, a bunch of bull crap?" Alita eyed Sionee hotly.

The wise-woman from the stars made her way to the center. She put her arm around Alita, and led her back into the crowd, whispering softly into her ear.

Meeting both Cy and Eah's eyes in frustration, Sionee gratefully continued the story. "As the spheres turn, the seasons change. The light is abundant, then it rests for a time. We welcome the return of the Sun's light on this night.

"Season to season nothing is ever the same. Sometimes little rain makes the forest dry, and we must compensate by doing a rain dance. Sometimes birds will eat the young fruits of the apples and we must seek our plenty in other abundant fruits such as nutmeats and damask. Sometimes, oh, friends ... ." She begged them to hear. Then, she faded into invisibility, again.

As if out of nowhere she reappeared. "As I was saying, it is an Illusion, my beloved family. It is an illusion. Our life on this planet ... The GNOS ... can all be defined quite simply in a few words. Our real life is on our spiritual home. The best things in our life are not seen, just felt with the spirit which lives in us all.

"This is what I hope you all learned from the time I sang only the straight songs ... I also showed you a straight sight! You see, the most beautiful of all sight ... and all songs ... are not heard, but felt, within the heart, in AHDAWN. AHDAWN ... my friends ... is the only truth that there is. It is our ever-abiding home."

~~~

The woman, whose name was Wisdom, entered the circle again, bringing Eah to stand at her side. An audible hush stilled the crowd. "Hello, my children," she sang out. Her voice echoed like the vibration of bells.

"Indeed, I am Sky Mother. Some of you call us the fish, for our abode is among those who swim in the Sapphire Blue Sea of Stars." Her hand extended upward to point to the stars.

"Where I live, they call me Sofeya, which means WISDOM in the language of my people. It is not the name which is important. IT IS WHO I AM. I danced around your fires aeons ago, and I got this young man from your seed, mixed with my seed." Proudly she put her arm around Ea. The crowd gasped. They knew the story ... but only whispers were ever known of the possibility of the beautiful woman from the stars. The story their forefathers and mothers had spoken of ... never told of her having a baby from the seed of both worlds.

"I have come forth to tell you something of great importance." The crowd was spellbound and silent. "Sionee, daughter, tell them of your dear Taya and what happened to her, and where she is now. It weighs heavy in their minds."

Sion looked from Eah to Sofeya. There was a resemblance, of course. Sionee repeated her story to her curious audience. "So, my family, on this night I begin to teach you the art of invisibility, and more! We must take caution, and remain unseen by the fish heads that aren't as kind as are our friends, here."

She nodded at Eah, and Sofeya, and Ninmah who watched from the sides, holding a wee boy no one had ever seen before. Sion proclaimed to all: "This is my son ... and Eah's ... together. His name is Naaman, beloved."

~~~

"It is as I said. It is an illusion. If I think invisible in my AHDAWN, my body is capable of changing the appearance of its matter, right before your eyes, and responding to the direction of my spirit. The feathered robe I wear is only a symbol of the spirit which can do anything! The spirit manipulates whatever it wants. I will teach you how."

Sofeya put her hands on both sides of Sionee's arms and twirled her around. The firelight touched each star in Sion's long braids, and made them twinkle. "Twinkle, twinkle, little stars, how I wonder who you are ... up above in the sky so high..." Sofeya sang in admiration.

"My children, it is likely that you will not see me again. I come seldom from my home on high. I have created a new race of children on this terra by mixing my seed with your seed.

"You, my children ... YOU are the chosen and blessed people that I believe can do my Work of Wisdom." She took Daysong from the arms of the young priestess who was watching her. She held the baby up high in the air beneath the light of the stars, and above the fire of the earth. She spun Daysong around until the child giggled in joy. Then she took Naaman and spun him around, until he cried. "These are the children of great light. They have been born to span the distance between your world and my world.

"I am here to remind you, that you are the bridge builders. You are the Tribe of Sofeya. You are my Fairlings, my darlings, my Fey! Listen to Alsionee Tree Song's words. She will teach you the invisible arts ... and many more. You must take care to protect yourselves from the ones from the stars who are not advanced toward goodness. You must learn about evil, yet always do good.

"Listen to the dance of the spider, as she draws from within, the magic of her life. Listen to your Alsionee Tree Song. She placed a wreath of white roses trailing with curls of sparkling white ribbon on the crown of Sionee's head. "She is your Feyri Queen now. Hear always her song."

"Her song?" Alita shouted. "I don't want her song. I want to go to the fish-headed ones. They are the wise ones, who really know how to live. Evil, bah! I do not wish to have anything to do with you simple minded idiots." She spat.

"Very well, my child." Sofeya spoke with patience. "Come with me." She extended her hand to Alita. "They will welcome you, where you are going child." Her eyes fell upon the big breast, naked and shining in the firelight. She would serve well in the mines. It was a certain thing that it wouldn't be for gold digging.

"As Feyries, my Fairlings, you must learn that when you wish for something, you get exactly what you wish for. It is the way of the Fey. Use this wisdom wisely, my children." She took Alita by the hand, whispered words of farewell to Sionee and with a wink to Ea, she left.

"We will meet again, my daughter. You will take Alita's child to raise with Daysong, in the Story Tree. Rid her of her mother's junk. Oh, and, thank you darling, for the white horses and the beautiful little white dove. I needed your gift to remind even I, of Wisdom ... that I can fly!"

It would be a long time, before Sion of Song Tree saw her again.

~~~

It was well past midnight when Alsionee Tree Song, Queen of the Feyries, bid two men into her chamber ... both at the same time. Having danced the whole night long, she whispered at last, "Let us go to the pool."

It was no uncommon thing to leave the ceremony and celebrate it privately with the blessings of love. Indeed, there was something quite magical in completing the act of love on the longest night of the spin around the sun, though this act was more of tradition on the springtime's beginning.

"There is something quite enticing about a girl who is covered with the soil of the earth," Eah replied, remembering the year before, when he and his Daffinina had danced like snakes on the ground, and how the sand had stuck to every part of their bodies.

"That is a consideration." Sion laughed, "Since I am sticky with the apple juice and the web, I do think I will keep both of you stuck to me. I need the two of you to help me get the web off without tearing it terribly, I'd like to sew it onto something a little more permanent, like some of that fabric Ninmah was wearing that looked like air." She grinned as the two men looked at each other with raised eyebrows. Both of them?

"You can each help me scrub in the pool, one on each side." The raised eye brows curved into smiles.

~~~

Inside the cooking nook of the tree, Sionee snuck up the ladder to her sleeping chamber to light the stars and the moon in her ceiling bower. She instructed both men to go down and set fire to the torches in the deep dark cavern of the amethyst pool.

"I will be down in just a minute or two," she called to them from above. From below, the two men both heard her, and knew she was getting her lovely swing bed ready for someone ... or some two ... or ... ah ... some three?

Ea and Cyex looked at each other uneasily. Each had hoped that it would be he Alsionee would choose to take home from nightfire. This wasn't quite what they had been expecting.

"We are two who are both thirsty and wish to drink." The man from the stars spoke at last.

"Is her vessel full enough?" Cyex's voice was hushed as breath itself.

"Her waters are infinite," Ea spoke.

"And, true, her cup runneth over." Cyex finished.

"Let us both drink, my friend. Let us both be filled with living water."

Alsionee Tree Song came down the spiral steps to the purple light of the amethyst cavern, which flickered in the fire of the torches' flames.

They drank, and ... then, broke bread.

**Say, then, from the heart that
You are the Perfect Day and
In you dwells the
Light that does not fail.**

~ The Gospel of Truth
Nag Hammadi Library

If you loved "Transmutation of the Fey" don't miss the continuing saga.

The Dawning of Eve
Donna Daywoman Thompson
Arriving from Four Directions Marketing & Media
Summer 2014

The story continues ...

My name is Daysong. I thought I would make this clear, though Mother tells me that it is not my name that is important. It is who I am. What I am is what this story is all about ... Day! I am Day.

This is my story, {my-stery} ... not his story, {history}. Mysteries are seldom known ... and seldom understood, for to uncover them, one has to see with different eyes than the ones that are used to view history. It is why my mother always begins her stories with those of you who have eyes, use them to hear. Those of you, who have ears, see. Those who do, know of what I am saying. Is this so much of a mystery?

I would not be who I am without the triumphs and the struggles of many whose true stories I must tell. My story is the real one, not the story of fools who do discredit to the spider and spin myths and legends with every inconceivable color of thread except for the one the spider uses.

I am because of who they are. I am proud to share who I am, why I am, and how I ... and my people really came to be.

I have studied in priestess institutions all my life, mostly under the instruction of the Feyri Star. She is my mother, Alsionee Tree Song, who taught me how to scribe. My stories have taken the form of written words, as many of her stories have done. For this is what she came to do.

So many people have sought her stories that she put herself under tutelage of my father, Ea, the beloved fisher head. He taught her to scribe, and record great truths.

Her words are written with the hand of Gaia, which makes Father smile at her fondly, for He has said, "The earth is sweet, so sweet."

I, however, am skilled with both hands, as each of my hands come from separate clans. This brings up another point, of which I have been contemplating on a good bit of time, and it is this thought you must keep in your mind's eye when you render my words ...

Other Books from Four Directions Marketing & Media

Where Are My Fairy Friends?
What Will You Eat?
Pioneer Cookbook

About The Author

In an oxbow of the Snake River in Idaho's Magic Valley, Donna Daywoman Thompson lives in a quaint small home surrounded by gardens and solitude. She lovingly calls her home Meadowstar. She enjoys life with her husband, Robert Steven (Steve) Thompson, four cats, and the fairies who live in the big tree outside her studio.

When she's not writing, she pursues her garden, her paintings, her sculptures, and other creative arts. Donna is an artist, knowing that all forms of creation are an expression of the spirit.

For more about Donna Daywoman Thompson visit her on Facebook:

www.facebook.com/DonnaDaywomanThompson

She may also be reached through her blog at:

www.DonnaDaywoman.com/blog

Or write her at:

Donna Daywoman Thompson
P. O. Box 362
Heyburn, Idaho 83336

www.ingramcontent.com/pod-product-compliance
Lightning Source LLC
Chambersburg PA
CBHW020246030726
47499CB00001B/79